TIME to RISE

TIME to RISE

HELÉNE HOLMSTRÖM
TRANSLATED BY MARLAINE DELARGY

Translated from Swedish by Marlaine Delargy. First published in Sweden as Eld, snö och stjärnor in 2021 by Lovereads / Forum

Published by Amazon Crossing, Seattle

www.apub.com

ISBN-13: 9781662511530 (paperback)
ISBN-13: 9781662511547 (digital)

Cover design and illustration by Elizabeth Turner Stokes

Printed in the United States of America

TIME to RISE

1

Nora's best friend had the worst poker face in Småland. Which was why Nora was worried when Bea looked her straight in the eye without so much as a twitch at the corner of her mouth after Nora asked her to repeat what she had just said.

"It's true." Bea was clearly excited.

"But . . . hold on a minute." Nora wiped her floury hands on a red-and-white-checked dishcloth and took a deep breath. "You're telling me a TV team is coming here? To *my* patisserie?" She gazed at her friend skeptically before realizing that this wasn't a cruel joke.

Bea's expression grew serious. She leaned against the baking table behind her, put her hands on her hips, and looked Nora in the eye. "You know that Nymans needs some fresh energy—to help you get out of this mess." She waved a hand around as if to underscore her point. "And they want to meet with you to go over the logistics." Bea shrugged, as if this were the most normal thing in the world. Brushing over the fact that she had applied for Nora to take part in a national TV show—without her friend's knowledge.

Nora loathed *Let's Get Baking*. Though she'd never actually watched it, the trailer was enough for her: an egocentric celebrity baker traveled around the country to shake up struggling bakeries and specialist cake shops known as patisseries. But Nymans—the oldest and most renowned patisserie in Västervik—didn't need shaking up. Nora's establishment was a classic. A landmark. An institution. Way too good for some dumb reality show.

"I just don't understand why Henrik Eklund would want anything to do with Nymans. Our customers like the place the way it is, and so do I. It hasn't changed since Grandma took over, and that's how it's going to stay." She looked defiantly at Bea.

"Your grandma took over in the sixties. Don't you think it might be time for a change?"

Nora shook her head, though the same thought had occurred to her on more than one occasion. She was losing customers and knew she ought to do something, but she never had the time or the money for a radical makeover. "Mom and Dad did some renovations in the nineties—you have no idea how upset some of our customers were!"

Bea sighed. "I just think Nymans needs a boost. But it also deserves more attention, which the *Let's Get Baking* Christmas special would provide." She reached out and touched Nora's arm. "It might mean you'd be able to afford to take on another patissier, or someone to work full-time in the café. You've been running everything on your own for years. How long do you think you can carry on like this?"

"You know how much I hate shows like that. What does a big-shot celebrity baker know about running a patisserie in our little town?" Nora turned around and went over to the enormous baking table, picked up a tray of loaves that had finished proofing, and carried it over to the huge oven, a recent investment that had almost brought the business to its knees. The next major project was to sort out the ventilation system. It hadn't been touched for decades, and when the oven had been blasting away for a long time, the heat became almost suffocating, and the only thing that helped was to have all the windows wide open.

"Have you even seen the show?" Bea asked.

Nora opened the oven and slid in the tray. She remained silent as she thought about the trailers she had seen, where those poor bakers were routinely ridiculed by *celebrity baker* Henrik Eklund.

"The Christmas special pulls in almost a million viewers," Bea went on when Nora didn't respond. "You must have heard what a boost the featured bakeries have had?" She followed Nora over to the freshly baked rolls waiting on trays farther along the table. Nora picked up a bread knife and sharpened it, then sliced through the crust on the first roll.

Bea meant well, she knew. Her beloved patisserie was on the verge of bankruptcy. But secretly applying to the show on Nora's behalf was a step too far. Bea was well aware that Nora would never let someone else dictate how to run her business.

Bea came and stood beside her. "You can't turn down the meeting."

"I know it's a good opportunity, but that's exactly what I'm going to do." Nora headed for the cool room, opened the door and held it ajar with her foot, leaned forward and grabbed a carton of butter and a pack of sliced cheese. She returned to the table and picked up a butter knife.

"I mean, it might be difficult to turn down the meeting, because it's today."

"Today?"

Bea's smile was more than a little strained. "Yes, they're coming here today. I waited until the last minute to tell you because I didn't want you to back out."

"I'll have to postpone."

"But you've got a meeting with the bank this afternoon," Bea pointed out.

"And?" Nora looked up at her friend.

"And didn't you say you'd reached your overdraft limit? I should think the bank will want to discuss that."

"In which case I'll tell them the truth—it's been a difficult fall. The new Espresso House down the street has taken some of my customers, and so did that hip bakery that opened last year. But I have my regulars, and they're a loyal bunch."

"It hasn't only been a difficult fall, Nora. It's been a difficult five years."

Bea laid cheese on the buttered rolls, and then Nora added two cucumber slices and put the halves together. Bea arranged the rolls on plastic trays.

"Why don't you just meet the production company anyway? There's no guarantee that Nymans will be chosen, but at least you'll have tried."

Nora didn't say a word.

"Please, Nora. This could be your salvation. The patisserie's salvation." Bea gave her a quick hug. "Call me after the meeting. I have to go, but I'll forward you the email about the meeting. They'll be here at eleven."

Nora suppressed a worried sigh. The fact that her best friend was a police officer and therefore risked her life as part of her job was almost more than she could bear. She scattered a handful of flour across the table as Bea turned and left.

Nora went back to the cool room to fetch a piece of the cold-proofed dough made from the century-old sourdough starter that her mother, grandmother, and great-grandmother had nurtured and cared for all these years. It was one of Nymans' claims to fame. She dumped the dough out on the table, sending the flour swirling. She ran her floury hands through her hair with a sigh, and glanced up at the clock: five to five. Time to open up.

She employed a full-time baker, but this was Renée's day off, which meant that Nora arrived at four, worked in the patisserie until five, then opened the café. She did some baking and prepped for the day while serving customers until eight, when one of the part-time workers arrived. After that Nora concentrated on making cakes and tarts until midday, when she took a break for lunch. At three she took over in the café until closing time. She knew this approach was unsustainable. She needed two people to work in the café, plus another full-time baker if she was going to stay open for as long as she wanted to, while maintaining the high quality of everything she made.

It hadn't always been like this. She hadn't had to cut down on staff until a couple of years ago, but since then the pressure had been relentless. She sometimes wondered why she bothered, given that some of her customers had deserted her anyway.

Soon the construction workers would be in for breakfast. She hurried into the café with the rolls, switched on the cash register, unlocked the door, and put out the sign: COFFEE & CHEESE ROLL 25 KRONOR. She hadn't changed the price since her grandmother's day, and Nora liked that. It was still dark outside, and the slight chill of early winter made the morning air feel damp. She shivered. Tiny crystal-like snowflakes drifted down and landed on her bare arms.

She went back into the bakery and carried on kneading the sourdough. She would hear the bell ring if anyone came into the café. She shaped the dough into three loaves, took the tray of baked loaves out of the oven, and slid the new ones in. She couldn't help thinking about what Bea had said. Was this her only choice? Was she going to have to sell out by providing prime-time entertainment in order to save the shop? Bea was right when she said that Nora couldn't go on like this for much longer.

She took her phone out of her apron pocket and searched for clips from *Let's Get Baking*. What a stupid name for a show. It aired in the fall, and this year's season had just wrapped up. Each episode followed a baker guided by Henrik. Each year there was a Christmas special made up of four episodes in which the viewer saw Henrik making over one business in the run-up to Christmas.

She chose a clip that began with Henrik Eklund frowning as he explained to a bakery owner how you can tell when your dough has finished proofing and is sufficiently elastic. As if a baker wouldn't know that! However, the poor baker in the clip nodded, eyebrows raised just a fraction, as if this were all new to him. She realized that everything was controlled by a director, of course. This was exactly what Nora didn't want to do: play dumb on TV. In fact, she didn't want to be on TV at all.

Then she searched for *Let's Get Baking—Christmas Special*. Instead she found *Christmas with the Eklunds*. The famous family, headed by

Henrik's father, Hasse Eklund, was celebrating Christmas at a magnificent mansion. Viewers were able to watch the family's Christmas preparations. Henrik, his father, and his brother baked wort bread and saffron-flavored Lucia buns while reminiscing about times gone by. "I never have such good conversations as when I'm kneading dough," Henrik said as he worked on a golden-yellow dough. Then he made Christmas candy and his stepmother, Anita, prepared the ham, while children—presumably his nephews and nieces—ran around the house. One scene showed Henrik and Anita bickering about the best glaze for the ham over a bottle of ruby-red wine. Two laughing children hurtled into the kitchen, and Henrik gave them a big hug and ruffled one tot's hair. His sister appeared and took the red-cheeked little boy. Then the whole family gathered in front of the fire next to a table groaning with Christmas treats. A tall Christmas tree adorned with fairy lights towered by the window, a huge pile of presents beneath it. Red baubles shimmered in the glow of the fire.

Nora felt a stab in her heart. Christmas had always been her favorite holiday. She and her family had also enjoyed their well-established traditions, but now there was only Nora left. Her loneliness became more acute during the festive season, but she had continued to celebrate just as she had when her parents were alive. It was hard to believe that it had been eight years since her mom passed. And her dad had been gone for seventeen years. An eternity.

At the end of the trailer, there was an extra unedited scene where the family was sharing a box of Aladdin chocolates. Everyone laughed when Henrik's stepmother said that it was okay to take from the bottom layer. She felt another pang of envy. Henrik Eklund had everything. Absolutely everything. A career as a baker, a big, wonderful family. Success. No financial worries.

She opened the email that Bea had forwarded. It was from the producer, explaining that they wanted to take a look around the patisserie and discuss the logistics. The producer emphasized how important it was for Henrik to meet the person he would be working with, the underlying message being how kind it was of the celebrity baker to take the time to engage with non-TV personalities.

The bell interrupted her train of thought, and she put down her phone in order to greet the first customer of the day. Ingemar Larsson, his copy of that morning's *Dagens Nyheter* tucked under his arm, had been a regular since Grandma's day.

"Morning, Nora. Coffee and a cheese roll, please."

"You're up early, Ingemar."

"Yes—I woke at four o'clock and couldn't get back to sleep."

Nora picked out a roll with extra butter, made especially for Ingemar.

He took out his wallet and peered inside. "Sorry—can you put it on my tab?"

"No problem." She wrote *twenty-five kronor* on the pad under Ingemar's name. She was grateful for her regulars like Ingemar, but she needed more customers buying her more expensive items if the business was going to survive. Her café customers were drifting away to other establishments, and people had opted for the convenience of buying their cakes for graduations and birthday celebrations at the supermarket. All of which was a big blow to Nymans' bottom line.

Two construction workers arrived and ordered cheese rolls and coffees. As they walked away with their trays, there was a tap on the glass door. She glanced over and saw Jonathan from the wholesaler's. Or the Veg Guy, as she and her friends called him. She gave him a nod, then went into the bakery to open the back door for him.

She popped into the bathroom for a quick glance in the mirror, adjusted her ponytail, and pinched her cheeks to give them a little color. Why hadn't she put on any makeup today? Even though she wasn't interested, she didn't want to look like a wreck.

Jonathan ran a wholesale business with his father, and they took turns delivering the produce. Nora hadn't expected to see him today; he'd brought the last consignment. Maybe he was making an extra visit to see her? It had been a couple of months since they'd gone home together after an evening at Harry's. He'd texted her a few times afterward, but Nora had responded evasively.

She opened the door and smiled at him, then helped him to carry in the order—boxes of tomatoes, lettuce, cucumber, and bell peppers; crates of milk, yeast, butter, whipping cream, and cheese.

"Thanks," she said as she placed the last crate of sour cream and yogurt on the table. Jonathan stood there shifting from one foot to the other; he looked as if he were searching for something to say. She hoped he wasn't going to ask if they could see each other again—hooking up with a guy more than once wasn't really her thing.

She was about to say goodbye when he cleared his throat. "It's . . . I take care of the company finances, and I just wanted to mention that our last two invoices haven't been paid."

Nora felt the blood rush to her cheeks.

Jonathan cleared his throat once again. "I think you've had a reminder?"

"Oh—yes. Of course." Nora hesitated for a few seconds. "Yes. I apologize—I'll make sure it's dealt with. Obviously."

Jonathan gave a brief nod and began to back away. "Listen, if you feel like meeting up sometime . . ."

"I'll be in touch, thanks." She closed the door behind him. Jesus, she definitely couldn't see him again.

She took her phone out of her apron pocket and hurried back into the café. No new customers. She logged on to her bank account; she was absolutely certain she'd paid those invoices.

She was thirteen kronor in the red. The payments had been rejected.

Just then her phone pinged with a message from Bea.

I saw the Veg Guy delivering to Espresso House as I was leaving—did he stop by your place too?

Yep. And he reminded me that I owe him money—apparently the payments didn't go through. It's a good thing I haven't slept with him for a while—I would have felt like I was selling myself. A fuck for two boxes of cucumbers and a crate of milk!

LOL, Bea replied.

And I'm in tears. Nora felt as if she was actually on the verge of crying.

Let's Get Baking could save you.

Nora took a deep breath. Not being able to pay her suppliers was serious. Bea was absolutely right when she said that something had to be done.

She ended the conversation and returned to the web browser, where Henrik Eklund's smiling face appeared at the end of the trailer. She saw nothing but scorn in that smile.

2

Henrik Eklund made his way toward the sign protruding between the wooden buildings. Nymans, it said in ornate bright-red writing above the usual patisserie pretzel. He couldn't stop thinking about the email from his father that he had just read. Every year they recorded *Christmas with the Eklunds* a week after the recording of the *Let's Get Baking* Christmas special was finished. However, for some reason his father had persuaded the production company to bring the family show forward, and now it clashed with the special. Hasse was well aware of the schedule for *Let's Get Baking*, but he was apparently working on some other project that couldn't be moved.

Presumably someone new at the production company had approved the change of plan without realizing that there was an issue. Maybe the situation could be resolved, but the TV company wouldn't be happy. Don, the young new executive producer for TV24 and the show, had produced a much-hyped docusoap for a sister channel, in which sporty singles traveled to a sunny Caribbean island to take part in a series of challenges during the day and date one another in the evenings. He had mentioned over lunch a couple of months ago that he was already stressed by the tight schedule. He had also underlined the importance of the Christmas special's viewing figures, and suggested that they needed to work on bringing more "reality" into the show. Which meant they needed all the recording time they could get. *Genuine* emotions. Their previous executive producer had always insisted that *Let's Get Baking* wasn't a reality show, but Don had complained that too little happened. As far as Henrik knew, the viewing figures had been solid that fall, but the competition was getting fierce because of all the streaming services, and according to the rumors TV24 had had a tough year.

Hopefully this would be a straightforward project. Maybe they could find a way to work more efficiently, which would give him time to fit in *Christmas with the Eklunds*.

He walked into the café and was met by the usual aromas of a Swedish patisserie: cinnamon buns, coffee, and freshly baked bread.

Västervik's oldest patisserie was exactly what he had expected, with its terra-cotta-color tile floor, dirty-yellow walls, and tall glass displays overfilled with an assortment of classic cinnamon buns, Danish pastries, macarons, and other small cakes and cookies. There were simple cheese rolls with thinly sliced cucumber, a few cheese and ham baguettes, and plastic boxes of pasta salad. It was clear that everything had been made with care, and in spite of the faded decor, he could sense that the place had once been something special. *Let's Get Baking* worked only with bakeries that had potential, and Nymans definitely fit the criteria: things didn't appear to be going too well now, but it had an impressive history. The fact that it was in Västervik was a bonus too; he knew that the production company was planning to include snippets of the local setting throughout the show. Though there wouldn't be much snow, the deep-blue winter sea, rugged rocks, and fishing boats bobbing up and down beside isolated jetties would be perfect. Plus there was a very good hotel in town. Henrik had stayed in plenty of mediocre hotels in various small towns up and down the country, and he liked the prospect of more comfortable accommodations.

Elnaz, the show's features producer over the last few seasons, was sitting at one of the tables opposite a woman who was presumably the patisserie's owner. She didn't smile or give any indication that she recognized him—definitely not the reaction he'd expected. The participants were usually very pleasant, even starstruck, but this woman was distinctly unwelcoming. The assistant behind the counter, a young guy with dark hair hanging over his forehead and lively brown eyes, nodded and greeted him cheerfully. Henrik returned the greeting, then walked over to Elnaz and her glum companion.

As he approached the table, she glanced up at him. She didn't exactly make a sparkling first impression. She might need to work on that. On the other hand, a moody owner, a woman in her thirties, would make good TV. Something different from the sweet, obliging small-town girl people would expect. No doubt this suited the production team very well. Henrik knew from that initial exchange of glances that he and the patisserie owner were on a collision course. TV24 would love it.

At first Henrik had refused to adopt the belligerent style that other chefs and TV personalities went for. Being angry only suited men who were dealing with meat, saws, and axes. When you were explaining to someone how an Italian meringue should be piped on top of a lemon mousse, rage was inappropriate. Worse even than trying to make buttercream with ice-cold egg yolks and the butter at room temperature. But somehow he had slipped into this more callous persona, and the viewers seemed to like the contrast between that and the sweet, creamy fluffiness of baking. He tried to be honest and direct rather than outright unpleasant. Honest even though no one had asked him to be, his sister had once said. And it was true that he could be pretty . . . harsh.

His father thought it was all ridiculous. He believed that the most important thing was to be pleasant on camera so that the audience would love you. And it had worked for Hasse. The entire population of Sweden adored Hasse Eklund, the lovable twinkly-eyed baker who created the most fantastic bread and cakes. He had captured the public's imagination as the poster boy for the family business in the seventies, and shortly after that he had been given his own TV show where he baked classic Swedish bread and pastries. He'd gone on to become a real star.

"Hi," Henrik said. The owner gave him a brief nod, while Elnaz broke into a big smile and got to her feet. Only then did the owner stand up. She was wearing loose-fitting blue jeans, a stained apron over a gray T-shirt, and a pair of worn Nike sneakers. Her pale-blonde hair was tied back in a high ponytail.

"Perfect timing—we're just about done here," Elnaz said.

Henrik held out his hand. "Henrik Eklund."

She forced a smile, then shook his hand firmly. "Nora Jansson."

Elnaz looked from one to the other. "I have to go—we're checking out suitable locations in the area, but it's probably best if the two of you get acquainted on your own." She turned to Nora. "I'll be in touch." She pulled on a quilted jacket and headed for the door in her sturdy Doc Martens.

"There's coffee over there, if you want some," Nora said, looking over at the coffeepot. After a few seconds he realized the comment was aimed at him.

"Are you talking to me?"

"Yes." She rolled her eyes. "Do you want something to eat?"

"A cinnamon bun would be good." He always chose the same thing when he visited a patisserie. It was a classic and told him a great deal about the soul of the establishment. For one thing, the cinnamon bun was the pride and joy of his own family business. Originally made by Henrik's paternal grandfather, it was the product that had made the company's name. For another, it was something that every patisserie made. Even if they were in financial trouble, they could always bake a decent cinnamon bun.

Nora nodded. "Hassan, could you please bring our guest a cinnamon bun?"

"No problem!" The guy behind the counter smiled cheerfully and picked up a pair of silver tongs. Pearl sugar rained down on the glass shelf with a pattering sound as he selected a bun.

"What kind of coffee do you have?" Henrik asked.

"Filter and latte," Nora replied. "We can do a cappuccino too."

"I mean, what kind of beans do you go for?"

"We use Gevalia medium roast, but Espresso House across the street has different kinds, Golden Estate Fantastic and Very Good Arabica and Limited Edition Extended Wholesome Dark Brew, maybe Royal Luxury Brilliant Brazilian Chestnut Deluxe, too, if you're in luck, so feel free to head over there if you want more choices."

Henrik gazed at her in silence, suppressing the urge to ask if she thought she was being funny, and then he gave a small sigh and went over to get himself a cup of coffee. He chose the fullest pot and filled a blue earthenware cup to the brim. He returned to the table as Hassan brought over a golden-brown cinnamon bun with plenty of pearl sugar left on it. Henrik sat down, blew gently on the coffee, then tasted it. The cup felt rough against his lips. He was expecting the familiar taste of tannin, but the flavor was smooth, rounded.

"Good coffee." He met Nora's gaze.

"You sound surprised. Medium roast is seriously underappreciated."

"Bad coffee is unfortunately the norm." He took a bite of the bun, which was—delicious. It had a buttery filling, crisp bottom, and soft, moist dough that wasn't too chewy. Cinnamon buns could sometimes be too much; you didn't want to feel you'd eaten a greasy sandwich overflowing with filling. This one was kind of on the big side, though.

"Nice bun. But cut down on the size."

She stared at him, clearly offended. Then she fixed her eyes on a point somewhere above his head, before looking around the café.

He raised his eyebrows.

"I'm just wondering where the TV crew is. I didn't realize the recording had started."

He said nothing, unmoved by her sarcasm.

"You've just launched straight into it with comments and advice I haven't asked for, so I assume the show is underway."

"I don't know if Elnaz told you how it works, but tomorrow some of our team will be here to carry out research and eat their way through your breads and cakes, looking for things I can focus on. That's how the show works—I come up with suggestions for things you could change, so you'd better get used to having your bakes reviewed by me."

"*Mmm* . . . The thing is, my customers want large cinnamon buns."

"Smaller cakes are on trend right now, people are tired of buns and muffins as big as saucers. They're just vulgar. My family company cut down on the size of the buns we sell in our shop, because customers were complaining that they were too big."

"I assume you haven't cut down on the price?"

This show is going to be anything but straightforward, Henrik thought.

"Anyway, that's not how I work." Nora folded her arms.

"Okay, so how do you work? As I understand it, this place isn't doing too well, so maybe you haven't got it all figured out."

"The last few years have been a bit slow, but business will pick up. I don't need your help."

He put down the bun and met her gaze. "So why did you apply to be on the show if you're getting along fine on your own?"

She glanced out the window, then back at him. "I won't stand for you making me look stupid. It might work with other participants, but I'm not having it."

He looked searchingly at her. "Can I ask a question? Do you even want to be on the show?"

Her expression was one of irritation, even hostility, but then she softened. Sighed. "To be honest, no, I don't. Who really wants to take part in your show?"

"Lots of people, actually—we receive hundreds of applications, and the Christmas special is even more popular."

After a brief silence, she said, "I just don't want to be portrayed as an idiot on national TV." She took a deep breath. "It was my friend who applied on my behalf, but . . ." Another sigh. "I accept that the publicity will give me the chance to fix a few things."

He nodded. "I appreciate your honesty, but if you don't want to do it, there are plenty of others who would be only too happy to step in." He took another sip of his coffee. "Unfortunately I don't have time to sit here trying to convince a baker who's down on their luck to take part in my show. All we have to do is call the next person in line." He slammed down his cup.

Nora stared at him, then closed her mouth.

"Get in touch with the producer when you've made your decision, and then we can save everyone a lot of time and trouble." He wrapped the remains of his cinnamon bun in a clean napkin and walked out.

3

1945

The train slowed down with a loud hiss and a series of jerks. After one final jolt, the train came to a stop. Tuula lost her balance for a second but quickly straightened up, holding both children's hands tightly so that they wouldn't fall. The doors opened, and she let the other passengers get off first, even though she'd been on her feet since the previous station for fear of missing her stop. With a child's hand in each of hers, she carefully made her way down the steep steps onto the platform, and then she went back on her own, grabbed their suitcase, and heaved it out. Even though they had packed in a hurry, the bag was heavy. It contained everything they owned. She took a deep breath, clearing her lungs after the stuffy air inside the carriage. She inhaled the smell of brakes and dust.

A dozen or so children alighted from the next carriage. A boy who couldn't have been any older than Matias ran off down the platform. A woman with her hair in a neat bun set off after him as he shouted for his mom. She was presumably from the children's home. Tuula felt as if her heart would break. Instinctively she clutched Matias's and Ritva's small hands even more tightly as the woman caught up with the child.

"Ow," Ritva said eventually, and Tuula loosened her grip. She had lost so much. Her husband. Her home. Her homeland. But she had the children, and they had her. She consoled herself with the thought that all the children now standing in a neat line on the platform would no doubt be reunited with their parents as soon as this terrible war was over.

They made their way into the arrivals hall. The smells—fried food from the railroad café next door, dust from the road outside, and years of dirt ingrained in the floor—were the same as at home. And yet everything was so different. Different signs, different words, and everyone around her was speaking a different language with a different melody.

As they walked through the small arrivals hall, the smell of food grew stronger and her tummy rumbled; they had been given a meal in the camp where they first arrived, but not this kind of food. Not the kind she was used to from home, decent food like pork and onion sauce with potatoes, fried sausages with white cabbage, or the meatballs she had made with carrots from the garden in the weeks before they fled. Rationing had been hard with the war raging, but they had managed to get by with their own produce and supplies from nearby farms.

Their footsteps echoed beneath the vaulted ceiling as they made their way outside. Aino was waiting in the sunshine, and the relief at seeing that frizzy blonde hair almost made Tuula's knees buckle. She took a deep breath just as Aino caught sight of them. Her kind gray eyes lit up as she hurried over and gave Tuula a big hug.

"Goodness, look how you've grown!" Aino smiled warmly, patted the children's cheeks, then hugged them both too. "I haven't seen you since you were a baby," she said to Matias as she ruffled his hair.

Aino and Heikki never had children of their own, and they had always helped Tuula out when they were neighbors in Rovaniemi. Aino had been a tremendous support when Ritva was born, because Tuula's mother lived far away and her sister had had her hands full with her own family. Tuula had missed her friends terribly when they moved to Sweden. It was shortly after her beloved Juhani went to war, and Tuula had been left alone with a newborn and a two-year-old. She had consoled herself with the thought that Juhani would be home soon, not knowing back then that she would end up a widow. For some reason the possibility had never occurred to her, even though women were being widowed all the time. It had seemed too unreal to contemplate. Too sad.

Aino picked up Tuula's suitcase.

"No, you're not carrying it—give it to me," Tuula protested.

"Out of the question—you've had a long, hard journey. You hold on to your children. So how was the trip?"

"Fine." Tuula knew that Aino was referring to the journey from the reception camp, but memories of the tumultuous hours after they'd been told they were being evacuated flickered through her mind. She had gathered up the few possessions they were able to take before leaving her home—and her whole life—behind.

"The apartment isn't far," Aino said. "And I've got some good news—you can start at the bakery tomorrow."

"Really?" Tuula smiled gratefully. She had hardly any money left, and she needed to start working as soon as possible. She looked at Aino. "What about the children?"

"The school is expecting Ritva tomorrow, and the nursery has a place for Matias."

After the sheer hell of recent days, Tuula felt a spark of hope. The future hadn't seemed so bright for a long time.

They turned onto the main road, passing low concrete buildings, red-painted terraced wooden houses, and a grocery store. They reached a café, where several people were enjoying coffee and buns at outdoor tables. Tuula could feel their eyes on her.

"Fucking Finns," hissed a man cycling by.

Tuula gave a start, but out of the corner of her eye she saw Aino walking with a straight back and her head held high. She appeared to take no notice of the man who had left the acrid stench of sweat in his wake.

"Some people aren't very welcoming," Aino said as she turned onto a smaller road. "It's best to simply ignore them."

Tuula gave a brief nod.

A small group of children was kicking a ball against a garden wall, and Matias almost twisted his head right around watching them.

Aino stopped by a wooden fence in front of a yellow house. A white gate hung crookedly from its hinges, and a climbing rose had entwined itself over the fence. She lifted the hasp, opened the gate, and led the way into a small courtyard anchored by a fine oak tree, its branches providing shade for the house. "You're in the lodge over there, and we're one story below. That could be useful if you need help with the children or anything." Once again Aino looked at the children and smiled.

They crossed the gravel yard, opened the heavy wooden door, and climbed the creaking stairs. Aino showed them where she and Heikki lived. "He works in the mine," she said with pride in her voice. Aino and Heikki had always worked hard, as had most people Tuula knew back home. She was shocked to discover that many Swedes thought Finns did nothing but drink and fight.

Tuula's apartment was tiny—the four of them could barely fit in the narrow hallway. Tuula followed Aino into the kitchen.

"The toilet is down in the yard—I forgot to show you. But there's running water and electricity." There was a decent oven on one side of the room, and a tiled stove in the corner that would keep heating costs down when the weather turned colder.

Tuula looked around. The pale-blue wallpaper was peeling off in places, the paint was flaking, and the windows looked as if they hadn't been cleaned since the First World War. But it was a home, and they would be safe here, at least as long as Sweden stayed out of the war.

"And the bedroom is in there." Aino nodded toward the room next door, then turned back to Tuula. "I'll let you unpack."

"Thank you for your help, Aino. Thank you for everything." Tuula seized both of her friend's hands.

"No problem. We have to help old friends, don't we? Come and have something to eat later. Six o'clock."

Tuula shook her head. "You're too generous."

"Nonsense. You unpack and get yourself sorted, and we'll see you in a few hours."

When Aino had gone, Tuula unpacked their few possessions. She placed the children's clothes in the shabby chest of drawers in the bedroom, and handed each of them a toy; that was all she had managed to grab before they left the house in Rovaniemi. Matias immediately wanted to run down and join the children in the street with his soccer ball.

"You can play in the yard, but not in the street."

Matias nodded, looking downcast. Tuula didn't want to let him out of her sight, but they had to try to live as normal a life as possible. At least she could see the courtyard from the kitchen window.

She looked around with a deep sigh. How she missed the spacious house they had left behind, with its vegetable garden and all her flowers and the meadow just outside the window. But she was lucky to have her own apartment and a job. It was more than many of the others in the camp had, so she couldn't justify feeling sorry for herself.

Matias ran outside, and Tuula unpacked her own clothes. Last of all she took out the glass jar containing her sourdough starter, carefully wrapped in her woolen pants and sweater. She placed the jar on the kitchen counter.

She would have to spend the few kronor she had on flour to feed it. It was her mother's sourdough. It had survived for so long, and it was the very first thing she had packed before they fled. She opened the lid and inhaled the mild, sour aroma that reminded her of home.

As well as being a precious memory, the dough would provide them with delicious and substantial bread. Only flour and water were required, and then she could introduce variations based on what was available, such as rye or crushed oats.

"Do you want to come with me to buy some flour?" she asked. Ritva put down her wooden horse, nodded, and got to her feet.

They went down to the courtyard and Tuula called to Matias, who was kicking his ball against the wall of the house. He picked it up and ran to join them. As they walked through the village, Tuula realized she was keeping her head down in an attempt to avoid people's gazes.

She picked up a few basics at the store: eggs, milk, cheese, butter. And flour. When she got home, she fed the starter and made two loaves while the children played outside. She left the bread to proof, then took one down to Aino and Heikki so they could bake it later and have fresh bread for breakfast.

After dinner she tucked the children into bed, then slid the remaining loaf into the oven. As the wonderful smell spread through the kitchen, she allowed herself to be transported back to her hometown. The town that had been laid to waste by the war, according to what she had heard. A pang of homesickness squeezed her heart, and yet she felt a strange sense of calm. She closed her eyes and inhaled the smell of the bread once again. She could see their red house, Juhani sitting on the front porch with a thick slice of bread in his hand.

4

Henrik Fucking Eklund. He had been every bit as supercilious as she had expected. Okay, so she might not have been particularly cooperative, but the way he had criticized her cinnamon buns and then walked out was just arrogant. Nora was in the meeting room at the bank, waiting for her personal banker.

She took out her phone while she was waiting. Wondered whether to message Bea about the meeting, but decided she didn't really want to talk about Henrik Eklund.

I see Maryam and Tess have dropped out of floorball tonight. Are you going? she wrote instead, hoping that the practice session would be on; she needed an outlet for her aggression.

Sorry, Ahmat is working, Bea replied. Nora wasn't surprised. She made it to practice more than the others, despite the long hours she worked at the patisserie. The four of them had originally met when they found themselves on the same indoor floorball team in high school and quickly became a close-knit gang. Nora had been the most athletic and played the longest. She had joined the club's women's team and played pretty seriously until the patisserie became too much for her mother to run alone. A couple of years ago, she and her friends had put together a group who played four against four one evening a week in a school gym that they rented out for next to nothing.

In that case maybe I'll skip too. Then again, if no one is there the pace will be more manageable . . . 🙂

However much Nora needed and enjoyed the exercise, she mainly participated to see her friends. Bea, Tess, and Maryam all had relationships and families of their own, and floorball practice was the one night of the week when Nora recaptured a small part of the friendship of their youth.

She sent the message, and Anna came into the room. She was about Nora's age, and was responsible for Nymans' account. She had a cup of coffee in each hand and a laptop tucked under one arm. She passed one cup to Nora, put the other down on the table, placed the laptop beside it, then squeezed her heavily pregnant belly between the table and the chair.

"Thanks—you didn't need to do that. I could have fetched the coffee." Nora put down her phone.

"It's fine, it's good for me to keep moving." Anna smiled and adjusted her chair, then opened the laptop and started tapping away at the keys.

"I believe you wanted to discuss the patisserie's financing?" Anna fished up her glasses, which were hanging from a cord around her neck. Did people really use that kind of thing these days? Maybe it was coming back into fashion.

Nora cleared her throat, took a deep breath. "I did. The thing is, I need a little more credit. I invested in a new oven last summer, and I need some extra money to cover the Christmas season, which always involves considerable expenditure."

Anna nodded, her expression serious as she made notes on the computer. She frowned, considered for a moment, then looked up at Nora. "I'm sorry, but we can't raise your overdraft limit any further. You have no security, and you've already borrowed the maximum you can against the business. I see here that you own the property, including the apartment above the patisserie." Anna paused and studied the data on the screen. "But I'm afraid you can't borrow any more."

"So what does that mean?"

"It means that your account is in the red, so you don't have any funds available."

"So I don't have any money *at all*?"

Anna shook her head. "What's the outlook for the next month in terms of your income?"

"Obviously I hope to make a profit." Nora sighed. "The problem is that I need the money soon, as I said, I have a lot of outgoing expenses coming up . . ." Nora broke off. "Are you sure I can't increase my overdraft limit?"

"I'm afraid not." Anna clasped her hands together. "Unless of course you can show me evidence of a major change in income streams in the near future—substantial regular orders, for example, a contract with a business client, something along those lines. Then I might be able to arrange something."

Nora thought hard. Her shoulders slumped.

"I'm as disappointed as you are," Anna added sympathetically.

Nora was pretty sure this wasn't true.

Anna sighed. "It's terrible to see a small business owner having to beg, but there's nothing I can do."

Suddenly Nora couldn't breathe. She couldn't buy supplies or pay her staff. What was she supposed to do? Close? Was she really going to have to put an end to her grandmother's life's work, a business that had meant everything to Nora's mother when she inherited it? Was the patisserie going to fold on Nora's watch?

"But that means I can't stay open." Nora could hear the desperation in her voice. "If you could just increase my limit by a small amount, and give me a few months' grace on the repayments, I can fix this. I *will* fix this. I've done it before." Nora was referring to when she took over the patisserie after her mother fell ill. There were already financial problems, but her mother had never said anything, and Nora had to bite the bullet. Nora had done the hard work of trimming staff, checking every purchase, and launching new breads and cakes. She had marketed their sourdough loaves harder than ever, because sourdough was hot at the time. Well, to be fair, the sourdough trend had already peaked, and Nymans was late to the party, but even so . . . She had managed the transition without any major changes, doing her best to retain as much as possible, because that was what her mother had wanted. It was what Nora had wanted. Nymans had flourished for a few years. Then that hip bakery had opened nearby and lured away customers with its croissants and cardamom buns, and the supermarket started producing fantastic cakes and sandwiches. Espresso House had lured away the high-end coffee crowd. A series of unfortunate circumstances had brought her to this point, but she knew she could turn the ship around again.

Anna heaved another sigh. "I know you've done it before, but I can't see what's going to change. Things have been going downhill for almost two years, and if you don't have a plan to turn things around, then I'm afraid we can't help you."

"I'm going to be on a TV show," Nora blurted out. "*Let's Get Baking*. Maybe you've heard of it?" She couldn't believe what she'd just said.

Anna raised her eyebrows. "*Let's Get Baking*?" She was clearly interested.

"Yes, and according to the production company, bakeries that have taken part have doubled their sales figures during the first month of recording." She had read that in the email thread between Bea and the company that Bea had forwarded to her.

Anna nodded slowly.

"And I'm going to be in the Christmas special, which is their most popular slot. Filming starts very soon, and it will air in mid-December."

Anna leaned back in her chair and smiled. "That definitely changes things. That show is incredibly popular."

"They only choose businesses that meet their high quality criteria, and all of them have experienced an upswing. Several have even become tourist attractions as a result of appearing on the show."

"Exactly. I went to the one just outside Gothenburg, the old guy who had an inner courtyard with lots of different berries, it was fantastic. We had to stand in line to get a table." Anna straightened up. "Amazing jelly. If that's the case, I can increase your credit limit by another hundred thousand, but I'll need something in writing from the production company."

Nora did a rapid mental calculation. That would keep the business afloat for another couple of months.

"Thank you." But even as she said it, she couldn't believe what she had just promised. She really needed to replace the ventilation system; she had been planning to borrow the money, but that was out of the question for the moment. She wasn't even sure it was possible. She and Henrik hadn't exactly gotten along.

She took a deep breath and gave Anna a big smile. She would just have to call the producer and sort it out.

The bank and a ridiculous TV show were going to save the patisserie. Nora felt as if she had sold her soul twice over.

After closing the café that evening, Nora made ten sourdough loaves. Whenever she was feeling frustrated or simply in need of solace, she baked something with her sourdough starter. It didn't matter if Renée had already produced enough earlier, still she stood there kneading and shaping. If there was too much, she would give a loaf to a regular customer or a friend.

The fresh, sharp aroma and the feeling of the cold, soft dough on her fingers were the purest form of therapy. It took her straight back to the times she had baked with her mother, and all the tension left her body as she worked. The sourdough had meant so much to her mom, who had often said it was a link to her childhood. It meant just as much to Nora and reminded her of everything she had once had: a family, parents who loved her unconditionally, a sense of belonging so complete that she never questioned it—or imagined that it could be taken from her.

Hugs should be soft and kisses hard. That was exactly what her mom had been like: soft and hard. She was either loving, or arguing. Not so different from Nora, which was probably why they had often clashed.

Without her father as a buffer, Nora's relationship with her mother had become even more volatile after his death. The quarrels were worse, but their connection was stronger. What bound them together was that they both missed Nora's father. And they both loved the act of baking and the patisserie itself.

Nora thought about her mother often. Her loud laughter and early mornings. Floral dresses in the summer. The jeans and T-shirts she wore the rest of the year. Nora had kept a couple of her favorite dresses, and they made her think of vacations.

In the aftermath of her mother's death, Nora had felt angry more than anything. So angry. Then grief would take over for a while, but then she always reverted to anger. And it had been like that ever since; she was angry most of the time, angry about what she had lost. The fact that she would never get to know her parents better, watch them grow old, share her life with them.

She shaped the loaves and left them to cold proof overnight. She tidied up, locked the door, and headed for the grocery store. She planned to buy herself some Brillat-Savarin, a soft cheese that was so creamy it simply oozed out, accompanied by a mellow red wine. She wanted to watch the party leaders' debate, and at least one episode of the baking competition she had missed that fall, when Sweden's most prominent bakers tackled classic cakes and pastries. As long as Henrik Eklund wasn't one of the judges. Shit, maybe he was? No, she didn't think so. She would probably fall asleep on the sofa anyway. Every evening for the last month she had promised herself a TV evening with charcuterie, cheese, wine, and the baking show, but she had always ended up working late or falling asleep over the cheese.

It was dark by now. The stores along the main street had just closed, but the restaurants were open, casting a warm glow over the sidewalks. Espresso House was still open, of course. They could afford to keep generous hours. The same applied to the hip bakery; it was impossible for her to compete.

She hadn't managed to get ahold of the producer earlier, so she tried Elnaz instead. She hadn't answered, but she'd sent a text promising to contact Nora later.

Had she sabotaged her chances? Would Henrik refuse to work with her? Why had she messed up so badly?

However, the meeting with Elnaz had gone well. They were about the same age, and she seemed to understand Nora's reluctance. Maybe she was used to slightly difficult owners. She gave the impression of being good at dealing with people, while Henrik appeared to assume that everyone would be charmed by the fact that he had bothered to show up. He clearly didn't understand that some people might not love having their business dissected by His Highness in a prime-time slot. As soon as he walked in, Nora sensed that he thought she ought to worship the ground he walked on and fall all over herself with gratitude that he was paying her poor little patisserie a visit.

In the grocery store she made a beeline for the deli section and chose the softest piece of Brillat-Savarin she could find.

"You know we have a special offer on cheese?" Maggan smiled at her from behind the counter. "And I've got that Spanish ham you like—it's just come in." She picked up the enormous Iberico ham and cut Nora a generous slice. Nora placed it on her tongue, closed her eyes, and reveled in the delicious umami flavor.

"I'll take four ounces."

As Maggan went back to the slicer, Nora's thoughts returned to the meeting earlier that day. She couldn't stop brooding about the way Henrik Eklund had strolled in, looking as if he *owned* the place. Unbearably self-confident. She also had to admit that he was unbearably good-looking. Considerably more attractive in real life than on TV.

Casually dressed in a checked shirt and blue jeans, he was quite capable of pulling off the lumberjack look, even if he was probably incapable of chopping wood, like the city boy he was. Not that Nora was particularly adept with an axe herself. In fact, she'd never used one.

His firm handshake was . . . pleasant. And to be fair, he had introduced himself with his full name, as if she didn't know who he was. Maybe that was a sign of a certain level of humility. And he had a nice smile—a smile she had seen many times on TV, in that commercial for flour, and in photos of red carpet events that appeared in the gossip magazines she read in the hair salon. She was struck by his white, even teeth behind that thick, dark beard.

Maybe she had been even more unbearable than him, come to think of it. She sighed and took out her phone. One missed call: Elnaz.

Maggan brought over the ham slices and wrapped the package in stiff paper.

"I'll take two ounces of the truffle salami too," Nora said. "I just need to make a quick call." She gave Maggan an apologetic look and moved away. Elnaz answered immediately. The hum of voices could be heard in the background.

"Hi, Nora. Wait a second, I'll go somewhere quieter. There you go, that's better."

"Hi, I just wanted to say that the meeting with Henrik didn't go too well . . . And I'd like to apologize. If there's any doubt about my desire to participate in the show, I can assure you that I really want to do it." She did her best to sound enthusiastic.

"That's great, thank you. But what happened during the meeting? I spoke to Henrik a little while ago, and he didn't mention anything."

Shit, had she said too much?

"Oh, okay, good, I was afraid I'd given him the impression that I didn't want to do it."

"But you do? Or have you changed your mind for some reason?" Not surprisingly, Elnaz sounded confused.

Nora took a deep breath. "I definitely want to do it. Henrik and I just had a bit of a misunderstanding, so I wanted to be clear and let you know that I *do* want to be in the show."

"Great. I've spoken to the producer, and we need to get started pretty soon—next week, in fact."

"Next week?"

"Yes, both Henrik and I will be recording *Christmas with the Eklunds* in a couple of weeks, so there will be a break then, but we need to get going right away if we're going to fit it all in."

Next week! Nora's entire body screamed in protest. She just wanted to bake her bread and cakes, make cookies, and chat with her customers. But then she reminded herself that the patisserie's entire future was at stake.

"Next week is fine."

"Excellent. I'll sort out the contracts—there's a confidentiality agreement, rights, and so on. We'll book you in for a lunch so that we can go through everything and get your signature, okay?"

"Absolutely. Sounds good."

"The producer will be in touch. I'm really looking forward to this, Nora. You're going to be great on TV. Have a nice evening!"

Nora slipped her phone into her pocket and returned to the deli counter, where Maggan was weighing the little plastic box of salami. She sealed the lid with a sticker and handed it over. Then she smiled.

"I heard that Henrik Eklund was in town." She lowered her voice. "Is it true what everyone's saying? That you're going to be on *Let's Get Baking*?" She looked expectantly at Nora. The rumors had certainly spread fast.

"It's true," Nora said without further comment. Had she already broken some kind of confidentiality agreement? Was she allowed to say anything at all? Oh well—she hadn't signed anything yet. Let them sue her.

"Wow, maybe I can be on TV too? I mean, you'll have customers in the café when they're filming, won't you?"

"I expect that'll be okay," Nora said, though she had no idea. "I'm not sure how it works."

Maggan beamed, as if the fact that a TV crew was coming to their little town put her on the path to a life of unending glamour.

"This is amazing! Aren't you looking forward to it? It's not just good for the patisserie, I think it'll be great for the whole town. To think you were chosen out of all the applicants!" Nora knew she was right—this was an incredible opportunity.

She returned Maggan's smile. "Absolutely. It's unbelievable. So cool." She almost meant it.

Nora lived in the apartment above the patisserie that had once belonged to her grandmother. She had made some minor renovations, while keeping the turn-of-the-century details. The leaded windows were now double glazed, and the depressing kitchen tiles had been replaced by gleaming white subway tiles. The thick natural stone counter had cost a fortune, but it also served as a baking table when she was trying out new recipes. The dark cabinets were back in fashion. She had sanded and polished the beautiful wooden floors, and repainted all the walls pale gray.

Some of her grandmother's furniture, like the half-moon-shaped hall table and the teak TV unit, was still here. She had also moved a few pieces from her childhood home, including the not particularly attractive pine dining table around which the family had gathered each evening. No matter how tired she was, she still sat there for a little while every evening with a cup of tea.

When she got home, she changed into yoga pants and a sweatshirt, then arranged her cheese plate, along with a spoonful of the jelly she had made from currants in Bea's garden, and broke off some shards of the crispbread she had baked earlier that day.

As she opened the cabinet to pull out a wineglass, it occurred to her that she'd forgotten to buy any wine. She scanned her shelves and breathed a sigh of relief when she spied a bottle at the back. Nora had intended to save it for a special occasion, but her friend Tess always said you should drink good wine on an ordinary rainy Tuesday.

And today was a rainy Tuesday. Nora reached for the bottle and poured herself a glass. She carried her meal into the living room and was about to turn on the TV to watch the party leaders' debate when she got a text from Ahmat, Bea's husband.

I'm working tonight so I'll miss the debate—do you want to save it until tomorrow and come here to watch it?

She smiled and replied: Sure—it's been a long time since I argued with anyone, and I really need an outlet for my aggression.

In addition to their love for Bea, she and Ahmat shared a keen interest in politics, and they always had lively discussions.

OK—I'll clear away anything breakable. And I'll use plenty of bubble wrap on the display cabinet.

Ha ha. For the thousandth time, it fell off the table.

During a leaders' debate a couple of years ago, Nora had waved her arms during a heated argument with Ahmat, and one of Bea's china cats had ended up on the floor. He had never let her forget it.

Admit it—you were grateful! she added.

Eternally grateful. That cat was terrible.

She took a sip of her wine and switched on the television. *Oh wow,* she thought as the wine hit her palate—strawberries, raspberries, black pepper, something herbal, and . . . cedar wood? She sank deeper into the cushions and scrolled through the channels looking for the baking competition. Instead she landed on *Let's Get Baking*. It was probably a good idea to take a look. She ought to be prepared if she was going to be on the show. She took another big sip of wine.

It started off pretty well, with a sob story about a widower running a bakery in Österlen. He and his wife had had the business for fifteen years, but when she fell ill, the bakery had suffered.

Soon Henrik took over. A montage showed him baking on the big stone slab in the bakery. The camera did a close-up of his biceps as he kneaded the dough, then moved up over his broad shoulders and fixed on his face, which was furrowed with concentration. Henrik Eklund was hot, she had to admit that. Bearded, dark, tall, and well built.

As she had expected, he treated the widower like a child as he explained how the finances in a bakery work. Then the camera followed him as he walked around, inspecting the layout and the big ovens. He somehow got the idea that there might be a stone oven buried behind the walls of the picturesque Skåne long house. The widower dug out old drawings and photographs, after which Henrik visited the town's archive department and found even older drawings and plans. And what do you know, there was indeed a real treasure hidden away.

The next day a team of builders arrived, knocked down a wall, and found the oven. Henrik explained to the widower that he could create something unique, selling stone-baked bread and nurturing the tradition that his bakery and the town had inherited. As if Henrik, a Stockholmer through and through, would know more about Österlen's food culture than a local resident . . .

But Henrik was popular with the viewers. The only thing that made him human was his highly publicized breakup with TV sommelier Bente Hammar. They had been something of a power couple, but then she had apparently cheated on him. This had made Henrik even more popular—out of sympathy, presumably.

Nora grabbed her phone and popped on to Tinder, mostly out of habit. She already knew everything that was on offer in Västervik, but then a pretty cute guy popped up. Age thirty, about ten miles away. She swiped right. A match. She assumed he was studying at the college outside town. She had once met up with a student there, then wondered what the hell she was doing with her life when she woke up in his dorm room to discover him sitting on a dilapidated sofa with his friends, strumming away on a guitar and discussing utilitarianism and the nature of goodness.

In the summer it was simpler, because people were only passing through. There was a wider choice, and none of them wanted anything long term, which suited her perfectly.

The guy she had matched with hadn't messaged her yet, and she didn't message him either. She pressed "Play." The episode ended with Henrik being hailed as the messiah, and the hint of optimism she had felt earlier died away. Was this what was going to happen to her? She knew her business better than anyone, and she certainly didn't want to play dumb on TV. Was it too late to pull out? She hadn't signed anything yet. It was perfectly possible to ditch the whole thing; recording wasn't due to start until next week. She thought about what Elnaz had said, that she would come across well on TV. She had taken it as a compliment, but maybe it was an insult? Did she mean that Nora was the perfect target for Henrik's cruel humor?

She lay down on the sofa and gazed out into the November darkness. The rain hammered against the windowpane. The fruity red wine had made both her body and mind feel deliciously soft. The street outside was deserted, and the patisserie sign in the window below cast a red fluorescent glow on the facade of the building opposite. That sign was a part of the fabric of the town. It appeared on many postcards, along with the pretzel that hung above the door.

That was when she realized what was at stake. If she didn't fix the patisserie now, she would lose it.

Nora had her pride—but what would that be worth if she no longer had her business?

5

The cold stung Henrik's cheeks as he waited for the landlord to let him in. He wasn't wearing warm enough clothes for this unusually cold November evening, but the place was around the corner from his apartment, exactly as he had imagined when he dreamed of one day having his own bakery.

He had had his eye on the property for a while. Located right in the middle of the Vasastan district of Stockholm on a small street just off Odenplan, it was a stone's throw from the subway station and the busy life of the city. It currently housed a real estate office, which was a huge waste of its potential. With its tall arched windows that let in a fantastic amount of light and its open layout, it would make an amazing bakery, with plenty of room for customers to sit and chat over a cup of coffee and a delicious cinnamon bun.

He had stopped in once on the pretext of asking the agent about an apartment, and had been blown away by the place. When it subsequently became available to rent, he took it as a sign that he had to act. The landlord had shown him around the previous week, and he'd determined that it wouldn't cost much to convert it to a bakery. The idea was that his father, Camilla, and Tom should have taken a look earlier in the day, but only Camilla and Tom had shown up. At the last minute and with no explanation, Hasse had informed his son that he had to postpone the meeting. As usual. Hasse Eklund often did exactly what he wanted, and he expected the rest of the family to fall in line. However, he was coming over this evening.

Henrik thought the bakery would make an excellent addition to the family firm in which Henrik, his two siblings, and their father were all active shareholders and board members. At one point both Henrik and his father had had more executive roles within the company, and before that Hasse had worked hard to expand the business, and their bread and pastries could now be found in virtually every food outlet in Sweden. Then he had become a popular TV baker, and worked twice as hard as before. Henrik had been the company's production manager for many years before his own TV career took off. His sister, Camilla, acted as agent for both Henrik and his father; Tom was the only one who still worked for the firm on a daily basis, as business manager.

Although Eklunds sold mass-produced bread, Henrik had thought for a while that they ought to open a physical bakery too. That had always been his dream, and this location was perfect. He looked forward to showing it to his father so that he could visualize everything Henrik proposed to do.

The landlord appeared, a bunch of keys ready in his hand.

"Hi—I hope you haven't had to wait for too long."

Standing outside in the cold hadn't exactly been pleasant, but Henrik smiled and said it was fine.

The landlord unlocked the door, and they went inside.

"I thought I'd leave you to it and come back a little later if that's okay? I just need to stop by the office."

"No problem." Henrik actually preferred to show his father around on his own. He should be here any second.

The landlord left, and Henrik took off his coat and draped it over one of the chairs in the sparsely furnished reception area. He wandered around, picturing how the bakery would look. Tiled walls, rustic oak shelves stacked with loaves of bread and rolls, wooden chairs with upholstered seats in muted colors, comfortable sofas and round tables for larger groups, large potted plants, modern art on the walls. He wanted something tasteful but livelier than the industrial-chic trend that had been in vogue for a few years now.

He sat down and opened his laptop to review the numbers one more time. Where the hell was his dad? They were running out of time. Tomorrow was the first day of recording for the Christmas special, and Henrik had to go home and pick up his suitcase before catching the night train to Västervik.

He called his father, but the call was rejected. Then a text message came through: Sorry—running late. I'll be there in half an hour.

Half an hour? He glanced at his watch. Shit, there was no way he'd make his train, which meant he'd be late for tomorrow's recording. Well, it couldn't be helped. He had to show his father the property and present his proposal tonight; the landlord wasn't willing to wait another week.

Some people might think the dream of opening a bakery was silly, but Henrik wanted to get back to the essence of baking, not just running a bread production company and being a TV personality. His most cherished childhood memories were the hours he had spent baking with his grandfather during summer vacations at his grandparents' lakeside country home. He'd kneaded and proofed dough. And made cinnamon buns. And made batter and baked cakes. His love for baking came from his grandfather. Everyone thought it was down to Henrik's father, but the truth was that they had never baked together when he was a child. Hasse was too busy working or hanging out with other celebrities.

His grandfather had often talked about the café the family had run alongside the bakery when he was younger, when the family firm was a smaller enterprise, and Grandfather himself helped out in the bakery. There was a kind of romantic nostalgia in his tales of cycling to work before dawn, preparing the first dough as the sun rose, and ending the day serving customers in the village café. When the family's large-scale production operation had grown, the family had chosen to focus entirely on that. They kept the bakery, but sold the café in Almtorp in Bergslagen where everything had begun, which meant that Grandfather moved farther away from the essence of it all, as he put it. And that was what Henrik longed for, more and more: the essence of it all. Henrik thought a bakery with a café reminiscent of the one his grandfather used to run would give the company a little more heart. It would also enable him to meet the people who bought his bread and to bake real bread in his own oven. Bread that would be eaten by customers and not just by a production team after the cameras had stopped filming. He would do more than simply sit in endless meetings about improving the marketing and maximizing the sales of factory-produced bread.

Eklunds' strong brand name would give the bakery an enormous advantage, but he was a little nervous. Given the family's reputation, he couldn't open an ordinary café or bakery—people would expect something special. At the same time, he didn't want anything too grandiose; he thought he'd landed on a concept that was just right. Camilla and Tom had been enthusiastic, which left only his father.

He flicked through his business plan, which had all the numbers that his mother and her boyfriend, Vanja, had already reviewed. Vanja was a high-ranking bank director, and his mother now worked for an investment bank. In other words, he had been given two expert opinions. They both thought his calculations were sound, the business plan was solid, and the location was perfect. Henrik couldn't think of anything that would make his father say no. However, Hasse was always the one who came up with suggestions within the family firm, and usually everyone agreed with him. That was how it had worked so far. Hasse had taken the company to where it was today; it was thanks to him that the expansion during the eighties and nineties had happened so fast, which was why he thought he had the monopoly on running Eklunds—everyone simply had to go along with whatever he wanted to do. And now for once Henrik had been working on an idea that hadn't come from Hasse, which could be seen as an attempt to undermine his father and his role—Henrik was well aware of the implications. That was why his planning had been so meticulous—he wanted to be sure that Hasse couldn't say no.

The door opened and his father swept in, a faint smile visible behind the graying beard. His glasses immediately steamed up; he took them off, rubbed them quickly on the lapel of his coat, put them back on, and patted Henrik on the shoulder. "Okay, what's so important? Let's hear it."

His cheerful demeanor gave Henrik hope. Maybe he'd misjudged his father?

Henrik made them both a coffee from the agency's machine, and then they sat down and Henrik handed over the business plan. He explained his vision while his father perused the document.

"So I'm thinking that the bakery will be our hub, a meeting place for the family and a flagship for Eklunds," Henrik said in conclusion.

"A flagship for Eklunds? What do you think Almtorp is?" Hasse stared at Henrik. Almtorp was the small town in Bergslagen where the head office had always been located.

"Of course. But it's not a place where our customers can go, it's just an office. It would be easier for us to meet up here. We could try out new recipes, talk to customers, maybe even run classes or training courses."

Hasse nodded slowly while Henrik was talking—which was encouraging. Had he been worrying for no reason?

Hasse finished his coffee and slowly put down the cup, but deliberately remained silent for a few seconds. "To be perfectly honest, this feels like we're going back fifty years in the company's development."

Henrik didn't know what to say, but soon regained his composure. "What do you mean?"

"This was how Eklunds began, with a little café—why would we revert to that now that we have a national baking empire?"

"This isn't a step back, it's an extension of what we're doing today. Something that will give Eklunds heart, a way of enabling us to connect with our customers," Henrik persisted. "Camilla and Tom like the idea."

Hasse still looked skeptical.

"It won't mean more work for you—the idea is for me to run this on my own," Henrik added.

His father let out a bark of laughter. "Seriously? You think you're capable of running this on your own?"

Like an insufficiently proofed dough, Henrik deflated. Why had he even bothered to bring his father here? Hasse had never believed in anything Henrik did. Hasse had always made clear that he felt Henrik's various successes had only been a result of the work Hasse himself had done to build the family business. He'd never even acknowledged his son's success with *Let's Get Baking*—or the boost in sales that Eklunds had seen thanks to that.

If Henrik couldn't convince his father about this new opportunity, there was still another option.

"If you don't like the idea, I assume I can present my proposal to the board and ask them to vote on it."

Hasse stared coldly at him. Henrik had crossed a line. The question of voting always infuriated his father. Hasse had assumed that he would inherit the entire business from his father, but Henrik's grandfather had left equal shares to his son and his three grandchildren. This meant that Hasse had no official decision-making advantage over Henrik, Camilla, or Tom. But he had unofficial, implicit power over all of them—and always had. Henrik was suggesting they might vote against Hasse, which none of the siblings had ever done. So far, any new ideas that any of them had brought up had been vaguely discussed until Hasse crushed them. Henrik was determined not to give up this time. He knew this was a good plan, and he refused to let it go.

"Feel free to suggest a vote," his father said, still staring at him. "But I will not hesitate to remind everyone about the Coffeepot."

Henrik didn't say a word. The Coffeepot was a failed project that Henrik had set up on his own—a small hole-in-the-wall street café that catered to stressed inner-city workers. It hadn't been the success he had hoped for. He preferred to forget the whole thing, but his father enjoyed reminding him of this proof of his lack of business acumen.

Hasse got to his feet, put on his coat, and headed for the door. "By the way, I have something I'd like to discuss at the next board meeting. I was going to wait to tell you all then, but Camilla already knows, so I might as well share it with you." There was something unpleasant about his smile, and Henrik realized that he wasn't going to like what his father was about to say. "I'm in line for a new TV show."

"Oh—tell me more."

"It's a show featuring me, with Anita as my sidekick." Hasse had met Anita when he was given the honor of making a dessert for the Nobel banquet. He had worked with the legendary gourmand Anita Roslund. A romance had sparked somewhere between the fresh cloudberries and chocolate Florentines, and before long they were a couple. They had now been married for fifteen years, and she somehow managed to put up with him, even though her own career had gone downhill ever since she met him. She had set aside her own projects and ambitions to support him—just as Henrik's mother had done, until one day she decided she had had enough.

"The idea is that I will go through the ingredients listed on the most common baked goods on the supermarket shelves, and look at exactly what's in them. Then I will make a product, a genuine product, under the name of Eklunds. *By Hasse for Eklunds.*" Another unpleasant smile. "The production company has already given it the green light."

"That's great—congratulations," Henrik said, and he meant it. His father's career as a celebrity baker had stalled somewhat. He had judged a few baking competitions, and he had published a new cookbook a couple of years ago that had sold reasonably well. This new show might be good for the company.

"Thank you. It's going to get the prime-time slot next fall."

Fall? But that was when *Let's Get Baking* came out. Was there really room for more than one baking show in the autumn schedule?

"I hope the Christmas special gets good viewer ratings this year," Hasse added.

"*Let's Get Baking* always gets good ratings."

"*Mm*—I suppose it depends how you define *good.* I heard that TV24 is unhappy with the numbers this year, and that it's down to the Christmas special to save your beloved show." There was no mistaking the malice in Hasse's eyes.

Henrik was taken aback. What was he talking about? Where had he heard that? Henrik knew the numbers, and they were the same as they had been in previous years.

"Your show is starting to become a dated concept; they want something new and fresh, which was why I pitched *By Hasse for Eklunds.*" He laughed. "Don't you understand why they've brought in Don as the executive producer for your show? They're trying to revamp it as a kind of docusoap. The final attempt to save it." Hasse sighed, then smiled again. "They want my show to go on at eight o'clock on Wednesday evenings," he informed Henrik with an apologetic look that was far from sincere.

"But *Let's Get Baking* is on at eight o'clock on Wednesdays," Henrik said.

His father shrugged. "That's what they suggested."

Henrik didn't say a word. He simply wondered what had turned his father into the type of person who was deliberately nasty to his own son.

Hasse glanced around. "Nice place, by the way."

The door closed behind him, leaving Henrik standing in the middle of the room.

6

1945

The village was still shrouded in darkness as Nils Eklund cycled to the bakery in the morning. Was it even morning yet? It was more like the middle of the night since it was only three thirty. But he liked to get there before the bakers and other employees arrived, so that he could plan the day.

Nils was the foreman in the family bakery. There were six bakers, two packers, and two drivers who delivered the bread in the company vans. Another packer was due to start today.

Nils was also responsible for the café in the village, and the smaller bakery in Sala, a few miles away. The family bakery was known for its cinnamon buns, but it was becoming increasingly difficult to meet the demand, because the raw materials were scarce due to the war. At the moment they were mainly producing bread and rolls, because sugar was in short supply.

He unlocked the heavy wooden door and pushed it open, knowing that as soon as the ovens got going, it would become unbearably hot. He switched on the lights, blinking as his eyes adjusted to the brightness, then went through the bakery and into the office next door. He picked up his black notebook and pen and returned to the bakery to go through the stock on the shelves. They would need more sugar to fill this week's orders; he would check with his father. He made his plans for the day, then wrote up a list of what was to be baked on the chalkboard on the wall. He went back into his office and checked the following week's orders, making a note of what to buy. When the bakers arrived a few minutes later, they called out *hello* and went to change. Before long, he heard the sound of sacks of flour thudding onto the baking table and the clatter of rolling pins. The workday had begun.

An hour later, when the smell of freshly baked bread reached the office, the packers arrived. Aino was first as usual, and she had brought the new employee with her. Nils could see only the back of her head through the window. Aino had assured him that Tuula was conscientious and spoke Swedish, which had made the decision to take her on very simple. Aino was one of the most dedicated workers Nils had ever met, and if she said someone was good, then he had every reason to believe it to be true.

He got up and went to welcome the newest member of the staff, but stopped dead when he saw her. It was as if all his senses had short-circuited. Everything within him was flashing and pulsating. Jesus, was it really possible to feel like this? With one look? Just from looking at someone? She was the most beautiful woman he had ever set eyes on. Her thick blonde hair fell to her shoulders in soft curls, and the morning sunshine flooding in made her hair appear golden. And her clear blue eyes radiated warmth, but also something else—melancholy.

She looked up at him and held out her hand. "Tuula Anttila."

"Nils Eklund." When he shook her hand, he got the strangest feeling; he didn't want to let go. He cleared his throat in an attempt to pull himself together. "Welcome. I'm the bakery foreman. Aino has told me how hardworking you are, so I'm very pleased to have you here." He cleared his throat again; he didn't want to go back to the office yet. "Shall I show you around?"

Aino raised her eyebrows. Nils usually left that kind of thing to one of the other packers, or maybe one of the bakers.

"I think Aino has her hands full today," he explained. "There are a lot of orders going out, so I'm happy to give you the guided tour."

"Thank you, that would be very kind." Tuula spoke slowly, articulating every syllable with care in her lilting accent. He had never heard anyone speak Swedish so beautifully.

"Shall I take Tuula to the changing room first?" Aino suggested.

"Oh—yes, good idea." He couldn't really show her the ladies' changing room. He slipped into the office; the changing room was next door, and it would look weird if he hung around outside.

The two women reappeared a few minutes later, wearing their white overalls and caps.

"The uniform is a perfect fit!" he exclaimed enthusiastically. Tuula smiled, while Aino looked as if she was about to burst out laughing. He smiled nervously. What was he doing? He cleared his throat yet again; at this rate she would assume he was suffering from some kind of lung disease. "Shall we start with the bakery?"

"Sure." Tuula nodded and he led the way.

Did she like it? Was she as impressed as he had been the first time he saw the place? The walls were covered in small, square tiles; wooden baking tables ran the length of one wall, and a large brick oven that had been made to order and transported all the way from Roslagen was installed at one end of the room. "We bake bread and other products. Our cinnamon buns have become very popular. The red-hot surface of the brick oven makes the underside of the buns crispy."

Tuula walked toward the oven and inspected it. "Wonderful."

Nils nodded. It was his pride and joy, presiding over the room like a gigantic trophy.

"And here we have our bakers." He waved in the direction of the men kneading the dough in the heat. They held out their floury hands one by one and greeted Tuula.

Just then, Lydia, the third packer, came through the door.

"This is Lydia, and this is Tuula, your new colleague."

Lydia smiled warmly. "Pleased to meet you. And how nice for us to have some help, *herr* Eklund."

"I know how hard you work," Nils assured her.

They continued to the packing section. Daylight flooded in through the tall, arched windows and the open doors. Out here the smell of freshly baked bread was less noticeable, and the cool, dewy morning air made its presence felt.

"This is where you make up the cardboard boxes, then pack the bread and buns." He saw her gazing out through the doors; for a second she didn't appear to be listening.

"I'm so sorry," she said quickly. "My children are on their own, and they're leaving for their first day of school in a little while. My daughter is seven, so she's looking after her little brother." She sounded apologetic, as if she didn't want to bother him.

She had children. So she must be married. It was obvious really—such a beautiful woman couldn't possibly be single. He glanced down at her hand and saw a ring.

"There's only me to look after them," she added. "My husband died in the war."

"Oh—I'm so sorry."

"I'm just a little bit anxious since it's their first day."

Nils nodded. "I understand perfectly."

He was a bachelor, but his father had big plans for him and his future marriage. Until now he had gone along with those plans, despite the fact that he wasn't entirely convinced about the marriage.

His father had always favored Nils over his brother, Stig, because Nils was more like Father. They understood each other, they thought along the same lines, and they both shared a burning passion for baking. Stig had never been interested in baking or taking over the business and had gone on to become an accountant. Father was proud of Stig, of course, but Nils was the apple of his eye, the son who would one day inherit the bakery. However, that did involve certain sacrifices.

They continued the tour. "Because we're a large-scale operation, we deliver to other cafés and stores," Nils explained. "We've just opened another bakery a few miles away, and my father is planning to freeze bread and cinnamon buns so that we can deliver to a wider area."

Tuula nodded, clearly impressed.

Father's plans were ambitious to say the least, and included a freezer room for which he had commissioned architectural drawings. A company that supplied berries and vegetables had just started building an enormous freezer room. Nils and his father had found a suitable location, but in order to convert the premises they would need permission from the local council. And this was where Nils and his future came into play. The chairman of the council had a daughter, who happened to be an old school friend of Nils's. She had apparently taken a fancy to Nils, which suited his father perfectly. If Nils married the chairman's daughter, then they would get the permission they needed in order to expand both the bakeries and the company as a whole.

Nils wasn't convinced. Birgit was pleasant enough, but they weren't in love. He had always thought that you ought to feel something more when you got married. He didn't know what real love felt like, but he had seen the way his mother and father looked at each other . . . And it was obvious that Stig and his wife were deeply in love. Nils wanted his children to be raised by parents who felt that way about each other.

"We've just sealed an important deal with a store over in Avesta that wants to sell our bread, so we're going to need to increase our production rate. So there's plenty of work for packers; the problem at the moment is the raw materials," Nils went on, pushing thoughts of marriage aside.

They continued out through the arched doors. "This is the loading dock," he said with a sweep of his hand. "We have two trucks, and the drivers start in an hour, when the first batch of loaves has been baked and packed." Tuula nodded as he talked, taking it all in. "We also have a café in the village that sells our bread. You ought to try it sometime—our coffee is very good."

"I walked past it yesterday—it looked nice."

He'd been there almost all day yesterday, and she'd walked past? From now on he would keep an eye out for her.

He turned back to the packing room, where Aino had started assembling boxes. "It's probably easier if Aino takes you through what to do."

Tuula smiled. "Thank you for showing me around."

"It was a pleasure."

Such a pleasure. Nils headed for his office.

He got next to nothing done for the rest of the day. He kept finding himself peering into the bakery through the small window in his office, hoping to catch sight of Tuula. What the hell was wrong with him?

7

Nora had worked day and night all weekend, preparing for the arrival of the TV crew on Monday. According to the schedule she had received, they would spend the day going through the patisserie and would discuss what it would be like once they started filming. When she got up on Monday morning after only three hours' sleep, she was almost too tired to feel nervous. She met her gaze in the mirror, and like a clichéd advertising slogan, she thought: *Just do it.* Her blue eyes were dull, and there were dark circles beneath them. Thank goodness there would be no filming today.

Renée would bake most of the bread. Hassan was coming in early to prepare the sandwiches, make the coffee, and set everything out before the TV crew arrived at eight. The store was opening a little later today so that the production team could work undisturbed.

The smell of newly baked bread met Nora as soon as she opened the door. How she loved that smell—which she associated with a deep sense of security, her childhood, and her parents. Renée emerged from the bakery with a tray of warm rolls and tipped them into a basket, the flour swirling up and dusting her curly red hair. She looked at Nora and smiled.

"Isn't it exciting? It starts today!"

Nora managed a smile in return. *Just do it.* She said hi to Hassan, then took a cup from the shelf, filled it to the brim with freshly brewed coffee, and took a big gulp.

She helped Renée and Hassan with the final preparations, and soon the patisserie was full of camera people sorting through equipment and setting up lighting, presumably to test things out before filming began tomorrow.

Then Elnaz arrived. "Nora—great to see you." Then a look of horror crossed her face. "Oh wow . . . It's good we have Sara—she's fantastic at getting rid of dark circles. Let's have you go straight to makeup." She pointed to a corner table, where a tall woman with a big, bushy hairstyle was setting out approximately four hundred different items.

"Makeup? But we're not filming today, are we?"

"Yes! I thought we made that clear to you."

"No, I thought you were just doing a rehearsal today."

"Yes, but then we're going to start filming."

Nora ran a hand through her tousled hair.

"It's fine—the more harassed you look, the more authentic it will be." Elnaz winked as if she were joking, but Nora wasn't convinced.

Sara, the stylist, introduced herself and asked Nora to sit down. She dragged a brush through Nora's hair while Nora cursed silently to herself. Of course they were going to film today. What had she been thinking? After all, they didn't have much time. She must have misread the schedule. She'd been hoping for a gentle introduction, but that obviously wasn't going to happen.

Filming starts today! she wrote to Bea as Sara continued to battle with her hair.

What? But I'm at work—I wanted to be there, playing a fantastic, slightly eccentric regular customer.

We've got plenty of those, Nora informed her.

By the way, I saw my grandmother yesterday and she told me to tell you that she thinks you need to find someone soon. And I quote: She has a lovely apartment, she's funny, and she runs the best patisserie in town. Please note—these are not my words, but you know what she's like—she'll go crazy if I don't pass on her advice word for word.

Nice of her, Nora wrote. But you can tell her that guys don't like smart girls. They just want girls who'll laugh at their jokes. Please note: You're cool and Ahmat is the exception that proves the rule. Your grandma and I are in agreement on that point: You've found the only good one.

There was a short delay before Bea responded.

There's a good man out there for you, and he'll laugh at all your bad jokes.

Bea's grandmother had taken on the role of Nora's substitute grandma when she and Bea became friends. Nora's own maternal grandmother had died when Nora was little, and her grandfather had passed away before Nora was born. Nora and Bea had often cycled to Bea's grandma's house after school, where they would eat syrup bread with cheese and orange marmalade, accompanied by a cup of tea.

The fact was that Nora wasn't looking for a relationship. Sometimes she felt a bit . . . left behind since it wasn't all that common to be over thirty and not even in a relationship. But she didn't have time to date. Occasionally she wondered whether she might have had a family of her own by now if one of her parents had lived. Then the fear of losing someone wouldn't be so overwhelming. But there was no time to think about any of that now.

A man came over to her. He was a few years older than Nora, dressed entirely in black, and wearing glasses with thick black frames. He had a headset over his black cap and an iPad in his hand.

"Hi—my name's Ted and I'm the producer." They shook hands. "I've worked on *Let's Get Baking* for a couple of seasons now, so just ask if there's anything you want to know."

Elnaz had explained that Ted was responsible for content, staffing, and the budget, while Elnaz was responsible for what happened on-site.

"Ted, have you heard anything?" Elnaz asked, marching over to join them.

He shook his head, and Elnaz frowned. "I'll try calling him again. Don will be here soon." She disappeared into the bakery, while Ted started going through the papers clipped to his tablet, making the odd note.

Nora looked up at Sara. "Is something wrong?"

"Nobody can get ahold of Henrik. He was supposed to arrive last night, but he didn't show up."

So he was a real diva. She knew it.

"And Don, the executive producer, is due to arrive any minute."

"The executive producer?" Elnaz had explained the different roles, but Nora was still confused.

"He works for the TV company—he's the one who commissions the show from the production company, so he has the final say on everything," Sara clarified.

"And how about you? Do you work for the production company?"

Sara shook her head. "I'm freelance."

It was going to be impossible to keep on top of everyone's roles and responsibilities.

"Hi, Don!" Nora heard Elnaz say from behind them, loudly and with a hint of hysteria.

A man with a shaved head wearing designer jeans, a tight white shirt, and a dark-colored woolen coat had entered the patisserie. He looked over at Nora.

"So here's our baker. How are you feeling on this first day of filming?"

"I . . . It's all very new to me." She didn't really know what she was expected to say, but it didn't matter because he had already turned away.

"And where is Henrik?" Don looked around.

"He's on his way," Elnaz replied, sounding distressed.

Ted reappeared, clutching his phone. Don's presence seemed to have put them all on edge. And what had happened to Henrik? Maybe he'd changed his mind about doing the show with her—but could he do that at this late stage?

"Okay, I'm going to pop over to Espresso House and grab a coffee in the meantime," Don said. Nora wanted to shoot him. "I love their dark roast," he added with a smile.

While Sara worked her magic on Nora's face, the rest of the team came over to say hi. There was a sound technician and four camera operators, all women of different ages.

Nora went through the episode list once again. They would be filming four episodes. Two episodes of the *Let's Get Baking* Christmas special would air each week over a two-week period. Elnaz had told her that each episode involved approximately three days' filming, and that the filming would continue through November, with breaks when Henrik and Elnaz were filming *Christmas with the Eklunds*.

The atmosphere felt increasingly fraught. Elnaz was stomping around with her phone clamped to her ear, while Ted scribbled frenetically on his iPad. What if the whole show was postponed? She really needed this.

Elnaz gave her a strained smile. "Good to see you're going through the schedule—do you have any questions?"

"Where's Henrik?"

"We don't know. I'm sure he'll be here soon. But we can talk about the day while we're waiting. We've made a few changes. The plan is for Henrik to go through all your baked goods today and for you to tell him something about the history of the patisserie. Tomorrow he'll look at the raw materials, what you use for baking, then you'll go through the bakery itself—the ovens, the equipment, and so on. We'll use all of that material for episode one. Then we'll spend a couple of days making some changes in here, and we'll ask you to put up Christmas decorations and do the Christmas baking. Oh, and we'd like a section on bread that we plan to film later this week."

Those were *major* changes.

"We're keeping the final scene as is, featuring the gingerbread house competition in the square. It's going to be fantastic!" Elnaz said firmly.

If the star of the show condescends to turn up, Nora thought.

Just then the door flew open and Henrik appeared, in blue jeans, a checked shirt, and a sheepskin coat. A collective sigh of relief passed through the room.

Elnaz hurried over. "Where have you been?"

Henrik didn't answer. He simply glanced at her and headed in Nora's direction. He took off his coat, hung it over the back of a chair next to her, then poured himself a cup of black coffee. Elnaz rolled her eyes and pursed her lips. Nora knew exactly how she was feeling. The fact that Henrik couldn't even bring himself to answer Elnaz only reinforced Nora's view of Henrik as a diva.

He looked at Nora. "So you decided to do the show after all?"

"Yes . . . I mean, I always wanted to do it."

He stared at her without saying a word, as if to underscore the fact that she had said something altogether different the last time they met.

One last flick of the powder brush, and Sara was done with Nora. She nodded to Henrik. "Your turn."

He gave Nora a thin-lipped smile as she vacated the chair and he took her place. Ted joined him, and they spoke quietly. The producer seemed to be issuing instructions.

Nora looked around. The patisserie had been transformed into a film set—two powerful spotlights had been set up, and thick cables snaked across the floor at the far end of the room. Two static cameras had been installed in the café, and an operator was ready with a moving camera. The space behind the shelf where the coffee and cups were kept was occupied by a large sound desk and a man wearing headphones.

"There are a lot of customers waiting outside," Henrik said, glancing up at Nora.

What was he talking about? She went over to the window and peered out. A long line snaked down the street. She hadn't seen this many customers in years. *Oh, so now it suits them to show up!* she thought acidly.

Elnaz joined her. "Henrik is ready. If you open up, we'll film a few people ordering and settling in with their morning coffee."

"You mean you're going to start filming *now*? Don't we need to go through anything beforehand?"

"No, not unless you have questions." Nora had a hundred questions, but chose to stay quiet. "Okay, so we'll start with you unlocking the door so the customers can come in, then we'll start filming—we'll tell you when. We'll also film you and Henrik saying hi to each other. The next scene will be the two of you going through the patisserie together, him trying your cakes and so on. We'll let you know when we break."

Elnaz had already explained that a film crew would sit down and speak to Nora and Henrik separately. These clips were used in all reality shows, with the participants ostensibly sitting alone in front of the camera and discussing their experiences and reflections. The aim was to capture the participants' emotions. Nora, however, had no desire to talk about her emotions.

"Don't worry," Elnaz added, as if she were aware of Nora's hesitation. "Ted and I will give you instructions as we go along. All you have to do now is open up."

Nora did as she was told. At the front of the line stood Maggan from the deli counter. She gave Nora a cheery nod as she walked in, followed by Ingemar. She grabbed hold of Ingemar's hand. "Let's sit here," she said, claiming the table nearest the cameras by draping her leopard-print coat over the back of the chair before heading for the counter and placing their order with Hassan.

Henrik was now wearing an apron. He stared at the waiting customers, then moved closer to the counter, listening as Ingemar ordered.

Nora looked inquiringly at Ted. "Do I just carry on as normal?"

"Absolutely. In a few minutes we'll do some filming here in the café, then we'll do the tour of the whole place with you and Henrik."

Nora went and stood next to Hassan.

"My usual, please," Ingemar said. "A cheese roll and a coffee."

"That will be twenty-five kronor," Hassan replied, sliding a roll onto a plate.

"Sorry, what did you say?" Henrik was frowning at Hassan.

"I . . . er . . ." Hassan glanced uncertainly at Nora. "Twenty-five kronor."

"I see. Twenty-five kronor. Right." Henrik folded his arms.

Nora rolled her eyes and turned to Maggan, who ordered a prawn sandwich and a coffee.

Ingemar dug into his pockets. Eventually he produced a wallet, then put it away. "The thing is, I have a tab here . . ." He looked at Nora. "Nora writes down what I owe, then I pay when I can afford it."

"It's okay, this is on me," Maggan said, and Nora let out a long breath. No doubt Henrik would have some snide response.

"Wait," Henrik said. "Can you do that again?" He waved to Elnaz. "We ought to film this."

Elnaz nodded to the camera operator, who pointed one of the static cameras straight at the till. Elnaz clapped her hands to indicate that they were rolling.

Henrik smiled at Ingemar. "Did you say you have a tab here at Nymans?"

Nora put Maggan's sandwich on a plate, then turned her attention to Ingemar. "Are you really okay with them filming this, Ingemar?"

"We have permission from all the customers," Ted said quickly. "There's a guy outside sorting it out before they come in."

"I've got nothing against being on TV." Ingemar's eyes were sparkling.

"There you go," Henrik said with a triumphant look at Nora. "Don't worry, this is a good thing—it builds character."

"Excellent, let's go again," Ted said.

Ingemar smiled at Henrik. "Yes, I have a tab here at Nymans. Sometimes I'm a bit short on money, you know how it is, and then

Nora lets me have credit. She's great. She understands people in this town."

The camera was pointed at Nora. The merciless glare of the spotlights was shining straight in her face, and she realized why Elnaz had looked so horrified earlier. There was no hiding anything in that light.

8

1945

Tuula had made it to the weekend, but she wasn't looking forward to it. She loved going to work, and although she looked forward to spending time with the children, her first free day brought a sense of emptiness. There had been something invigorating about going back to work. Back home in Rovaniemi she had worked hard in a small hotel before the children came along: serving meals, cleaning the rooms, and sometimes baking. She had loved baking the most of all—kneading dough and spending time alone in the peaceful kitchen, with the warm oven and the smell of the bread. Working hadn't just been about earning a living, it had given her a sense of community, of belonging, of normality. And now she had a job in a bakery! She could hardly believe her good fortune. It didn't even matter that she wasn't baking herself; it was simply a lovely place to spend her days. There was the almost mushroomy smell of the yeast and the flour when the bakers opened a new sack and tipped it out onto the benches. And finally the aroma of freshly baked bread. There was nothing better.

After breakfast, she and the children strolled along the river before going to the café. Would Nils be there? She knew that he spent a lot of time there, pitching in and checking on things. He seemed to love his work. When he wasn't busy in his office, he came out and helped the bakers. She liked seeing him knead the dough, and sometimes allowed herself to watch him for a moment when she went into the bakery to collect the loaves for packing.

She hadn't felt attracted to any man since Juhani, but she wasn't the only one sighing over Nils. According to Aino he was seen as a real catch. Her little crush felt perfectly innocent; Nils Eklund, the golden boy of the village, would never notice a war widow with two children. Especially not a Finn. She knew what some people around her said about the Finns, the same thing she had heard ever since she arrived in Sweden. There were nice people, too, of course, in fact most of those she had met were friendly and helpful. But prejudice existed—the assertion that the Finns did nothing but drink and fight, that they were different, not like the Swedes, even though the two countries lay side by side and couldn't have been more alike. However, some Swedes seemed to regard the Finns as a completely different race. She'd heard rumors that some men had visited the camp she was in, measured skulls and noses and closely examined bodies.

The idea that Nils Eklund would want anything to do with her was ridiculous, so she didn't think it mattered if she let herself swoon a bit over his chocolate-brown eyes, his broad shoulders, his olive-colored skin, and the dark hair curling at the nape of his neck.

The mild March weather that had met them on their arrival at the railroad station had lasted. Spring was in the air as they walked through the village down to the river. She gazed at the large, colorfully painted houses. Tuula had left behind a decent house that she loved, but it hadn't been as beautiful as these, with their decorative carving. At home her life had focused on the practical. Neither she nor Juhani came from an affluent background, but they had managed fine on Juhani's salary as a farm foreman. They had never been able to afford anything luxurious or frivolous, though—no gold-rimmed china for them.

The rich, round aroma of coffee reached her nostrils from some distance away, along with the smell of bread. Sweetened bread. Something she hadn't experienced much in the past few years.

The café had round metal tables outside, with floral-patterned chairs. They looked new, which suggested that Eklunds was doing well. All the tables were full, so they went inside. Tuula took in the checked tile flooring, square tables, well-upholstered chairs, and bare white walls.

She was headed toward an empty table in the far corner when she spotted Nils standing behind the counter. His face lit up when he saw her. He raised his hand to greet her, but then one of the staff asked him a question and he turned away. She headed for the empty table.

Two couples were seated at the next table, but were using the empty one for their coats and the women's purses. One of the women smiled apologetically and was about to move her purse when Matias inhaled sharply. He had noticed the display shelves, and pointed to them.

"Look, Ritva, they've got buns!" he said excitedly in Finnish. The woman stopped, her expression darkened, and she left her purse where it was. She looked Tuula up and down, then turned away, nose in the air.

"Excuse me, is this table free?" Tuula asked anyway, thinking they couldn't deny her if she asked them directly.

The group didn't even glance up at her. She stood there at a loss, feeling the eyes of other customers on her. Some of them looked uncomfortable, and she wanted the checked floor to open up and swallow her.

"*Fru* Anttila, may I take your order?" Nils was suddenly right behind her. "Please sit down." As he gestured toward the table, the others obediently moved their things. Nils demonstratively pushed the table farther away and adjusted the chairs. "There you go. Everyone is welcome here, and if anyone has a problem with that, they can go elsewhere." He spoke loudly, staring at the group seated at the other table. None of them met his gaze, but Tuula looked at him gratefully. She wanted to hug him and cry at the same time. It was extraordinary after all this time—after the flight from Finland, after living in the camp in Sweden—to have someone stand up for her and her children.

Nils went back to the counter, beckoning Tuula and the children to follow him. The hum of conversation in the café resumed, and from the corner of her eye Tuula saw the group at the neighboring table preparing to leave.

"So who do we have here?" Nils crouched down so that he was the same height as the children.

"Matias." The boy straightened his shoulders and held out his hand, while Ritva clutched Tuula's hand tightly and seemed to want to disappear behind her.

"And this is Ritva," Tuula said. "Children, this is *herr* Eklund, the owner of the bakery where I work," she went on in Finnish. "Their Swedish isn't very good yet," she explained to Nils.

"I can understand that—you haven't been here long, have you?"

"We've been in Sweden since the beginning of the year, but we started practicing our Swedish during the journey, so they know a little bit."

"And how come you speak Swedish so well?" His warm gaze was as soft as a pat of butter melting in the sunshine.

"My mother spoke Swedish with me when I was a child."

Nils smiled. "Like I said, you're very impressive." He went behind the counter. "What can I get you?"

"I thought I'd let the children try your cinnamon buns—two of those, please. A bottle of soda with two glasses, and a coffee for me."

"You don't want a cinnamon bun?"

"No thank you—I'll finish off theirs." Tuula knew that the children would eat up every crumb, but the fact was that she couldn't afford any more. She had spent her first week's wages on food, and one or two other things they needed for the apartment.

"You have to try one as well," Nils insisted, putting three buns on three plates. "My treat, of course."

"There's really no need . . . ," Tuula protested.

"I disagree—there have to be some perks to working at the bakery. And I noticed a young gentleman looking at the cookies." He smiled at Matias. "Which ones do you want to try? Choose whatever you like."

Tuula looked down at the children. "Two each," she said quickly in Finnish. They obediently went over to the glass display case and pointed at what they wanted. Nils added a chocolate slice and a jitterbug. *They'll have a stomachache at this rate,* Tuula thought, but she couldn't help smiling.

"If you go and sit down, Anna will bring your coffee," Nils said, nodding to a tall, dark-haired woman who smiled at Tuula.

They sat down at their table, and Tuula watched the children tuck in to their treats. A moment later Anna came over with a pot of coffee and a cup. Tuula nodded her thanks. She added a drop of milk, then tasted the hot coffee. It was rich and mellow, without a trace of bitterness. And then she took a bite of the cinnamon bun. She closed her eyes. It was heavenly. Crisp and sweet, but also soft and buttery, with the perfect touch of cinnamon.

"Do you like it?"

She looked straight up into Nils's brown eyes. "It's fantastic."

He pulled out the chair opposite. "Do you mind if I join you?"

"Of course not."

"So how are you settling into the village?"

She knew she shouldn't be completely honest on this occasion. "Really well. We've got everything we need, and I'm so grateful for the job—it's saved us all." Though that was all true, she left out the hostility she felt from some locals. Could a place where you weren't welcome ever feel like home?

"You're a very conscientious worker, I'm very pleased to have you with us." Tuula thought she detected a warm undertone, as if he was hinting at something more, but no doubt it was her imagination. The idea that he might mean something else was out of the question.

"Thanks." She smiled.

"And those people who treated you so badly—don't worry about them."

"I'll try not to."

"I will never allow anyone to treat you or your children that way." His tone was serious, and those lovely eyes were fixed on her; she believed him. She mustn't let her imagination run away with her, but she couldn't help dreaming.

9

When the line of customers had dwindled, Henrik watched as Nora began to arrange the small rolls in the wicker baskets on the bench behind her, occasionally stopping to assist a customer. She had seemed tense at first, as all the participants did when filming first started, but then she appeared to forget about the cameras and the crew circling around her.

The door opened and Don slipped in, carrying a large cardboard cup from Espresso House. Henrik hadn't realized he was going to be here today. His presence suggested that TV24 was taking the production very seriously. Unless there was another reason, of course.

Henrik had wanted to ignore his father's comment about the viewer ratings. He had enough to think about now that his plans for the bakery were probably doomed, but could those numbers be the reason Don was here on the very first day of filming? Looking back on it, the production team had seemed more stressed during the planning meetings than they had in the past—but why hadn't anyone said anything to him?

Don went behind the cameras, held up a hand to greet Henrik, and joined Ted in the corner. They spoke quietly, presumably discussing the filming. *Something needs to happen.* That was how Don had put it when they were talking about the Christmas special. *More reality.*

Nora continued to work beneath Henrik's watchful gaze.

"I think we'll do the scene where Henrik comes in and introduces himself," Elnaz said after a little while.

Henrik nodded. "No problem."

"Introduces himself?" Nora was confused.

"Yes, it's for the viewers really. Henrik comes in and introduces himself, as if you've never met before," Elnaz clarified.

"But we have met. Are we supposed to pretend?"

Henrik allowed himself an eye roll. "I really don't have time for this."

"Time? I have to understand what we're supposed to be filming."

"We're already behind," Henrik snapped.

"I wasn't the one who arrived late." Nora turned her attention back to the rolls.

"The viewers have to feel as if they're with you on the whole journey," Elnaz said, putting an end to their bickering.

"Okay—what do you want me to do?"

"A simple way of greeting someone is to hold out your hand, then shake my hand," Henrik said. Jesus, how stupid was she? "And you say your name. And maybe *nice to meet you.*"

Nora narrowed her eyes.

Henrik put on his coat and went outside, leaving Nora by the counter.

How was he going to get through today? He had been awake all night, thinking about the disastrous meeting with his father. Eventually he had gotten up and made dough using the sourdough starter he kept at home. Because he was leaving early in the morning, he had left the proofed loaves for his neighbors, a very nice family whose children loved Henrik's bread. They would be able to bake them for breakfast.

Baking and kneading was the most effective way he knew of relieving frustration, but the benefit had been temporary. His anxiety had come surging back once he was on the train.

He had decided he wasn't simply going to give up on the bakery idea. He had emailed the external chair of the board, stating that he had an agenda item for the next meeting: the opening of a bakery to be known as Eklunds. If the other shareholders took his side, then his father couldn't stop it from happening. He was also concerned about the viewer ratings, however much he tried to push the thought aside. He would have to speak to Elnaz as soon as he had a chance.

A chilly sea breeze made him shiver. Winter down south really was colder.

He went back inside and Nora beamed at him. "Well, hi there!" she said loudly. "Welcome!"

Elnaz frowned. "Cut. There's no need to overdo it."

"You told me to pretend."

"Just say hi—even you ought to be able to manage that," Henrik said. "And maybe you could try to be pleasant, unlike the first time we actually met."

He went outside, feeling her death stare on the back of his neck. He reentered the café. At first her expression was mutinous, but then she gave him a welcoming smile. *Well done.*

"Hi, Henrik Eklund." He held out his hand, and she did the same.

"Nora Jansson. Welcome to Nymans." Her hand was unexpectedly warm, and the feeling of her fingers lingered after he had let go.

"Cut. Perfect, we can use that." Elnaz held up her pad and appeared to tick off the scene—one of many. "We could keep going from there, with Henrik ordering coffee and something to eat—if that's okay."

Henrik was expecting an objection from Nora, but she simply nodded.

"Excellent—let's go."

When the camera started rolling, Henrik examined the cakes and sandwiches laid out in the glass display case. "I'd like a cheese roll, please."

"No problem." She picked up a roll with the tongs and placed it on a white porcelain plate. White was fine, but he would probably encourage her to swap them out for stoneware. The coffee cups were a good shape, but they ought to be gray instead of that dated dark blue.

"And a cinnamon bun. And a macaron and maybe a cookie. Which would you recommend? No, wait—I want to try a piece of that shortbread. I didn't think anyone under ninety-three made it anymore." He let out a little snort. Nora's eyes narrowed again. He decided to keep the thread going. "How many kinds of cookies do you actually bake?"

"Thirteen," she said proudly.

"Wow. And you sell out of all of them?"

She looked wary. "Most of them."

"How much time do you spend making cookies?"

"For God's sake, this is a patisserie. I spend *some* time making cookies. Is that really what the show is going to be about? Cookies?"

Henrik looked wearily at Elnaz, who quickly smiled. "It's fine, I think we've got enough."

Henrik picked up his tray while Nora remained where she was. The scene was to begin with him on his own, and he went over to a table. One of the production assistants followed him with a cup of coffee—just a dash of milk, exactly the way he liked it when he was having something to eat. If he wasn't eating, he preferred black coffee.

Ted had finished his conversation with Don and joined the camera operator. Henrik began with the cheese roll. The bread was perhaps a little dry, but generally okay. The cheese, however, was uninspiring, and there wasn't enough butter. He took a bite of the cinnamon bun, which was delicious. He already knew that, but as he'd already pointed out, it was unnecessarily large.

He took a sip of his coffee and almost spat it out. He looked straight into the camera. "That's disgusting! Undrinkable."

"Good," Ted said, pushing a plug of snuff farther up behind his top lip. "If you know what you want to say, we can bring Nora in."

"Can we take a short break?" Nora called from behind the counter. "I need to fix up an order that's just come in."

"Fine—I need a break too," Henrik said.

Elnaz slipped into the seat next to Henrik. "Can we have a chat? Why were you so late this morning?" she asked as the others headed for the coffee machine.

"Something came up last night—I thought I emailed you?"

"I didn't get an email." Elnaz was clearly annoyed. "We were trying to reach you all morning, but you didn't answer."

"Like I said, something came up, maybe I forgot to send you an email, and . . . I apologize, but I switched off my phone."

"You know the TV24 team is stressed, especially since *Christmas with the Eklunds* is going to be recorded in the middle of all this. We need every minute we can get."

His father was the cause of all his problems—how the hell was it possible for him to ruin so much?

"Actually I was going to ask you something about TV24," Henrik began, but Ted reappeared just then.

"Okay, let's get back to it."

"I'll catch you later," Henrik said to Elnaz. What he had to say could wait.

Ted waved to Nora, who was busy making notes and flicking through a pad at the counter.

"Ready?" Henrik shouted.

"In a minute."

Henrik looked at the production assistant, a young guy who was in his first season with *Let's Get Baking*. "Could you please go and fetch her?"

Nora sighed loudly. "I'm perfectly capable of walking across the room, you don't need to send a runner." She put the pad in a drawer and stomped over to the table.

"Great." Elnaz checked her notes, then turned to Henrik. "It would be good if you could complain a little more about the coffee—mention the soul of the patisserie, that kind of thing."

"That's exactly what I was intending to do."

"Super." Elnaz gave him a thumbs-up.

Being patronizing and critical about bakeries on TV wasn't much fun. Henrik felt like a complete shit about it, but that was what the viewers wanted: he had to criticize, but not go too far. *Let's Get Baking* wasn't in the business of humiliating the participants, but in order for something to change, he had to be a bit sharp now and then.

Nora sat down opposite him, and Elnaz gave Henrik the signal to begin. Don and Ted were beside her, keeping a close eye on things.

Henrik held up the cheese roll. "The cheese is sweaty, and there's hardly any butter on this."

Nora was immediately on the defensive. "The cheese has been on that roll since five o'clock this morning; we have to start preparing early to get everything done. And the butter . . ."

"Yeah, yeah. The rolls are too small, the bread is tasteless and dry. There's nothing exciting about them. I could find more appealing rolls in the supermarket. Prepacked." Nora inhaled sharply. His criticism had hit home.

"As I said, in order to get everything done today, we made the rolls very early. And I use plenty of butter—that one must have been a mistake."

"All I'm hearing is excuses. I mean, you offer sixteen different cookies—you clearly have time to make those."

"Thirteen."

"Sorry?"

"Thirteen different cookies. According to my great-grandmother's tradition, there must be thirteen different types of cookies on offer."

"And then there are the buns." Henrik ignored what she'd said, took a bite. "They're delicious, but the size is grotesque. Meanwhile, this cheese roll isn't going to fill anyone up. What's your thinking there?"

"I don't know how things are done in Stockholm—I imagine you serve mainly date balls and raw beans dipped in stevia with your coffee—but here in Småland we like decent-size cinnamon buns. They're supposed to be big."

"Oh really? And do people usually eat the whole bun?"

Nora hesitated. "Some do," she said quietly.

"Do you realize how much raw material you're wasting?" He leaned across the table to drive his point home. "This isn't Wayne's Coffee in the year 2000. Grotesquely huge cakes and buns went out of fashion twenty years ago."

She opened her mouth, presumably to defend herself, then closed it again.

"Okay. And this coffee." He leaned back. "It's like walking into a small-town cop shop. Pure tannin."

"You liked it last time."

Henrik didn't say anything, he merely glanced up at Ted and Elnaz.

"We'll cut that," Ted responded. "Carry on."

Nora frowned at him. "Sorry? Cut what?"

"There is no last time," Elnaz explained. "Henrik has only just arrived here."

Nora sighed. "Okay."

Jesus, Henrik thought. If every scene was going to turn into a debate, they'd never stick to the schedule.

"Before you go on," Ted broke in, looking a little uncomfortable. He turned briefly to Don, who looked expectantly at him. Ted cleared his throat and came up to the table. He pointed at Nora. "Maybe you could pull back your T-shirt to make it a little . . ." He looked around the café, then beckoned to the stylist. "Sara, can you fix this T-shirt?"

Nora inhaled sharply and her eyes widened. Sara positioned herself behind Nora and pulled at the T-shirt, her expression inquiring.

"That's it!" Ted exclaimed when the fabric stretched across Nora's breasts. Sara let go of the T-shirt, unable to hide her skepticism.

"Are you kidding me?" Nora couldn't believe what had just happened.

"Is that really necessary?" Henrik intervened. Okay, so they wanted more reality, but this wasn't *Paradise Hotel.*

"A bit more," Ted said, once again looking at Don, who nodded encouragingly. Sara shook her head, while Nora frowned and pulled the T-shirt back to its original loose fit.

Don sighed, and Ted stepped forward as if he were about to deal with the T-shirt himself.

"Enough," Henrik and Elnaz said simultaneously. Ted backed away, and Don held up his hands in a gesture of resignation. Ted signaled to the camera operator to resume filming.

"You can't serve coffee with this amount of tannin in it. You'll give your customers a gastric ulcer!" Henrik focused on what he wanted to say in an effort to forget the incident. Don had definitely overstepped the mark. Thank goodness he had decided to let the matter go; maybe he had realized how ridiculous it was.

"I am your customer and I want quality coffee," he continued, relieved to have sidestepped an uncomfortable situation.

"Actually, I'd quite like to give some of my customers a gastric ulcer." Nora stared meaningfully at him. "A gastric ulcer that bleeds slowly, for a long time."

Ted was grinning, looking very pleased with himself. Had he deliberately provoked Nora? Don looked equally smug. Henrik clamped his lips together, scratched his head, and waited for Elnaz or Ted to step in. But maybe this was exactly the kind of thing they wanted?

"Can you tell me a little more about the patisserie and what makes it unique?"

For the first time Nora's eyes lit up. "Nymans is a family business that has been passed down through the generations on my mother's side. My great-grandmother worked here, then my grandmother, and she eventually took over when the owner got too old. My grandfather had no interest in baking, but he helped out and was kind of there in the background." She pointed to a black-and-white photograph of a woman standing between two bakers. "It was a big deal for a woman to run a patisserie in those days. Mom followed in their footsteps. When

I was a kid, we were here all the time. It was my second home." She smiled at the memory.

"So your parents ran the place together?"

"Yes. Until my father died, seventeen years ago."

Seventeen years. Henrik did the math. She couldn't have been very old—barely sixteen?

Her voice was steady, but there was sadness in her eyes. He sensed that she'd had to grow up quickly, a bit like he did, even if it was for different reasons.

"I understand. And now you run the business alone?" He didn't ask about her mother. When he was doing his research, he had come across an article in the local paper, saying that Nymans' owner had died of breast cancer eight years ago.

"I do. I have no brothers or sisters, so after Mom died, there was only me." She gave a quick smile, smoothing over any awkwardness. Then she straightened her shoulders, as if to say, *Don't feel sorry for me.*

He nodded. "Were you always going to take over?"

"Absolutely—it's what I've always wanted." Her tone left no room for doubt. "My great-grandmother lived for her work, and my grandmother had to fight to be allowed to run the business, then Mom carried on the tradition. It was incredibly important to her that Nymans should stay in the family."

"Okay." He sensed that there was more to it. It must be tough for Nora to run the place alone, without a partner or relative to share the burden. "What are you most proud of, apart from the fact that it's been in the family for generations?" he asked, changing the subject.

"Our customers. The sense of community. Some of them have been coming here for decades. It makes them feel secure. They meet up with friends, have a chat, hang out. Or they chat with me." She smiled again, and he could tell that this meant at least as much to her as it did to the customers. He understood perfectly; that was one of the reasons he wanted his own bakery.

"Okay. Let's take a short break," Ted said.

Don cleared his throat. "Henrik, do you have a minute?"

"Of course." Henrik followed him to the very far end of the baking room by the dishwasher.

Don turned around. "She's a feisty one—we like that. And there's definitely chemistry between you. She's going to make great TV. I want Elnaz and Ted to try out a few different angles, but based on the little I've seen, I think this is going to be very good."

The feedback was positive, and Henrik really hoped he was right. And yet something felt . . . off. And that business with the T-shirt . . . What did Don have in mind for the show?

"What do you mean exactly by 'try out different angles'? In the past we've picked up on a storyline and built on it, like if a participant was sick and struggling to cope."

"Yes, and of course that's worked. But I think we can boost the show's ratings by exploiting what Nora's got, drawing out genuine emotions." He raised a hand, demonstrating the heights he expected the show to reach.

Henrik wasn't completely convinced, but he had to trust Don, who was the executive producer. He was the one who was backing the show, the one who knew what worked in people's living rooms.

"Sounds good. But anything like that business with the T-shirt or showing breasts is out of the question," Henrik said firmly.

Don laughed. "I never said anything about showing breasts, I just thought the T-shirt didn't look quite right." Henrik didn't answer. "Oh, come on—it was kind of cool, don't you think?"

Henrik stared at him. "Not particularly."

"Come on, relax." Don shook his head, turned, and headed back to the café.

"Ready to get back to it?" Ted said. "I thought Henrik could go through the rest of the baked goods you have on display."

"Why? So that he can patronize me for selling something as old-fashioned as Danish pastries?" Nora folded her arms. "I haven't jumped on the trend for raw raspberry pies made of beans and sprinkled with quinoa."

Henrik sighed. "Have you had anything to eat?"

Nora frowned. "What are you talking about?"

"You seem out of sorts."

"Okay, okay." Elnaz raised her hands in an attempt to shut them up. "I have a lovely surprise for you!" Her voice was exaggeratedly cheerful. "I'm going to ask the production assistant to book a table somewhere nice this evening. I'm assuming you're free, Henrik, but how about you, Nora? To celebrate the start of filming." She beamed at Nora, who looked as if Elnaz had just suggested meeting up to share an insect buffet.

"I'm busy." No hesitation. "I'm . . . babysitting. My friend is a police officer, and she works shifts."

That was fine by Henrik. He had no desire to spend his evening with Nora.

10

Slottsholmen was deserted, and the sea appeared as no more than a dark silhouette in the distance. Across the water the lights of the town sparkled, with Saint Gertrude's church lit up like a stately crown jewel. Nora was strolling over to the hotel, where she was due to meet Tess and several friends. She took out her earbuds—she was listening to one of her favorite political podcasts—and listened to the sound of the wind whipping across the waters of Skeppsbrofjärden.

The ruin of Stegeholm castle was no more than a shadow in the distance; the town's music festival took place there every year. Västervik was completely different in the summer: sunny, with offshore breezes that smelled of seaweed, burning sunsets, and a horizon that stretched for miles.

A few months ago, she and Bea and her other friends from high school had cycled down to the castle ruin with a picnic basket and blankets. It was the only fun thing Nora had done all summer, given that it was the patisserie's busy season. But that evening had been magical, with the sound of guitars and beautiful voices, the evening sun on her face, a beer in her hand, and easygoing conversation. If there was one thing that could make her relax, it was the company of her friends. They did their best to be there for her—especially Bea—which included making their families, friends, and acquaintances shop at Nymans instead of some soulless coffee shop chain.

When Tess had suggested meeting up at Slottsholmen this evening, Nora had jumped at the chance to see her gang. A glass of wine with friends was exactly what she needed. After a quick shower, she had changed into black jeans and a white silk blouse, with big hoop earrings. She had blow-dried her hair, put on some mascara and a slick of red lipstick. She felt like a new person.

A gust of wind tugged at her scarf. She pushed her hands deep in her pockets and lowered her head against the weather as she ran the last few yards to the hotel entrance.

She walked into the warm lobby and made her way to the restaurant. The loud laughter made it easy to locate her friends. They were over in the corner, their table already crowded with plates and glasses of wine. Nora had had some leftover soup back at home. She hadn't eaten out in ages, as she simply couldn't afford it.

She joined the group, hugged everyone, and sank down in an empty chair.

"Chablis for you." Tess handed her a glass.

"Just what I need." Nora took a big gulp. It was crisp and ice-cold. Tess always chose delicious wines.

"We've ordered lots of food," Bea informed her.

"It's okay, I had something at home and . . ."

"Just eat," Maryam said, pushing a plate of Skagen toast toward her. "It's on us." Nora inhaled her perfume. She was the principal of a junior high school, but as soon as she left work for the day, she sprayed herself with the latest scent. Her collection was almost as impressive as Tess's wine cellar.

"They have oysters," Tess announced. She was the bon vivant of the group. Her impressive manor house had a pool and a fantastic sea view, as well as several stables and a huge wine cellar. When Nora needed to rest, she stayed over with Tess, enjoying the food, wine, and tranquility of her home. She had a feeling it would soon be time for another visit.

The waiter arrived with a tray of oysters on ice, and a bottle of Tabasco.

Nora couldn't resist. She picked up an oyster, added a few drops of Tabasco, closed her eyes, and savored the saltiness and the heat.

When she had turned thirty a couple of years ago (God—almost *three* years ago!) the girls had surprised her with a weekend in London. It was late spring, warm and sunny. They drank beer in gastropubs, shopped for Marc Jacobs purses, accompanied Maryam to various perfumeries, and ate oysters in the sunshine at a bar on the Portobello Road. They ordered oysters with Tabasco whenever they got the chance, and even if the feeling wasn't quite the same in late fall in Sweden, those flavors took her straight back to that wonderful weekend.

Then she took a bite of the Skagen toast, a heavenly crispy bread fried in butter, topped with creamy but fresh-tasting shrimp, crème fraîche, lemon, and dill. Followed by another sip of Chablis. She looked at her friends. "Thank you so much—I'll repay you one day."

They protested loudly.

"Forget it," Bea said. "We know how hard you've been working lately—well, for the last few years—and you deserve a treat."

What would she do without them?

"If anyone deserves a special night out for hard work, it's you," Nora said to Bea. "You haven't exactly been taking it easy." Bea had recently been promoted. "The only thing I don't like about it is that you always have to put yourself at risk."

"That's because I'm a police officer."

"I don't know how you do it." Nora shook her head. "I liked it so much better when you were pregnant with Svea and confined to desk duties."

Bea laughed. "I nearly died of boredom—it definitely wasn't my thing." She looked at Nora, smiling but with a seriousness in her eyes. She had been there through every family loss Nora had suffered, and knew how much sorrow she carried within her. It wasn't easy to be best friends with someone who was paranoid and overprotective, but Nora did her best not to show how anxious she was when Bea was working.

"Okay, we want to hear all about the TV show," Tess said, leaning across the table. "What's Henrik Eklund really like?" Her green eyes sparkled at the thought of him.

"Where do I start?" A purely rhetorical question. Nora took the wineglass that Tess had refilled, looked down into it as if the words might be swimming around in the ice-cold Chablis, which in a way they were, and took a generous sip. "Henrik Eklund is repulsive, every bit as vile as he is on TV." Tess suddenly looked shocked; she seemed to be staring at something behind Nora.

"But good-looking?" Maryam asked. She was sitting next to Nora, who rolled her eyes.

"What's with the *but*? There's no contradiction—good-looking men are usually smug shits, in my experience."

Tess quickly shook her head, her red curls bobbing. She looked almost panic-stricken. What was her problem?

"What? Henrik Eklund is a smug shit," Nora reiterated.

Now Bea was smiling at a point beyond Nora's shoulder. The smile was broad and entirely insincere, and Tess was shaking her head again. What the hell was wrong with them?

"He's awful, a real diva," Nora continued blithely. "He showed up late this morning on the first day of filming. And he's incompetent to boot."

"Nora," Bea said tentatively.

"What?" Nora spread her hands wide. "It's true. He complained about my cheese rolls and the size of the cinnamon buns, just because he's a raw-food-munching idiot." She let out a snort. "I'd like to bet that he never even eats real bread."

"Nora," Bea said, louder this time, looking meaningly at Nora, then beyond her shoulder.

Nora heard someone clear their throat. Right behind her.

It couldn't be . . . no . . . could it?

She turned around.

Yes indeed, His Highness Henrik Eklund was standing behind her.

He held up his hand. "I just came to say hello, but you seem to be busy explaining something. Don't let me disturb you." His tone was acerbic. Obviously he was going to be furious about this. *And,* Nora thought, *who wouldn't be?*

"I . . . I didn't mean . . . I was talking about . . ." She fell silent. "I was talking about a friend that we . . ." Her eyes darted around—hello, couldn't one of the girls step in?

"It's cool." He smiled, glanced at her friends and then back at her. "Aren't you going to introduce us?"

"Oh yes, of course." She stood up. "This is Henrik Eklund," she announced with a sweep of her hand, as if she were hosting some kind of gala. *Ridiculous.* Then she introduced her friends, one by one. The atmosphere was still strained, she could see that Bea wanted the floor to open up and swallow her, but that was nothing compared to the way Nora was feeling. This couldn't get any worse.

"But where are the children?" Henrik asked.

"The children?" Apparently it could get worse. "They . . . They're . . . I . . ." She broke off as a series of potential lies flashed through her mind. "The parents had a change of plan and I . . ."

"It's fine, I won't tell the others." Henrik leaned a little closer. "I get it—it's nice to have some free time." She could feel his breath tickling her cheek, and she shivered. A very pleasant shiver.

She cleared her throat and he leaned back.

"So where are the others?" she asked, wondering how she could have been so stupid. How could she have come to Slottsholmen for dinner when they were staying here, for fuck's sake. She was lucky that Henrik was the only one around.

"They're at another restaurant. We had a drink here in the hotel bar, and I stupidly forgot my wallet. That's why I came back."

"Yes, that was stupid." She let out a shrill laugh.

"It's fine." He leaned in again so that his mouth was close to her ear, so close that she could smell him—like a pine forest on a hot summer's day, mixed with freshly baked gingerbread cookies. And something else—she didn't know what it was, but it was incredibly masculine. His scent, along with the taste of the oyster lingering on her tongue, gave her a tingle deep in her belly. "I promise I won't say anything to the others," he said quietly. His warm breath and his deep voice made her shiver again, and something inside her vibrated. The feeling died a quick death as soon as she met his gaze, which was cold and anything but sensual. He must really loathe her.

"I'd better go." He turned to her friends and said, "Good to meet you," before he walked away.

Oh God. This was definitely a disaster—she could see it in their eyes.

"I don't suppose that will have improved your working relationship," Bea said.

Nora sank down onto her chair, stared gloomily out the window, and took an enormous swig of her wine.

11

The air was dry and chilly, making Henrik's nostrils sting as he walked. On the other side of the water, he could see the illuminated silhouette of the town. He had enjoyed seeing Nora caught out. He had found her comments about him quite amusing, but lying to Elnaz was unacceptable, and reinforced his view that she was ungrateful. Participants usually appreciated and enjoyed dinners with the team, but Nora behaved as if they ought to be paying her to be on the show.

He reached the restaurant, the Smugglers, which was housed in a red wooden building reminiscent of an old warehouse. The team had been allocated a long table in a separate room upstairs.

The food was just being served when Henrik arrived; he was greeted by the smell of burning candles and a variety of dishes. The predinner drink had probably turned into several drinks by now, because the hum of conversation was loud. The mood was also more relaxed now that Don had gone back to Stockholm. Henrik felt much more relaxed now that he was with the crew he'd worked with for years.

He sat down next to Elnaz, thinking this might be a good opportunity to have a chat with her, as he hadn't managed to speak to her alone during filming.

Halfway through the first course he turned to her. "Hey, I heard from my dad that TV24 is launching a new baking show on Wednesdays next fall. Please tell me I misunderstood him."

Elnaz didn't say a word and didn't meet his eye.

"He went on to say that TV24's unhappy with this year's viewer ratings for *Let's Get Baking*," Henrik went on. "Be straight with me—we've worked together for a while now, and I consider this show our baby, not just mine."

"I only found out about the ratings a couple of days ago," Elnaz said eventually, looking apologetic. "Hasn't Camilla discussed it with you?"

He shook his head. "I've been trying to get ahold of her, but she's Dad's agent, too, so I suspect she's avoiding me."

"You mean the show they're commissioning is your dad's?"

He nodded.

"I had no idea."

"Is TV24 planning to scrap *Let's Get Baking*?"

"Nothing has been decided yet. All I know is that they're looking around. And I'm sorry you found out that way." Elnaz frowned. "What I don't understand is why your dad wants to compete with you. It seems crazy—you're part of the same company, the same family."

Henrik shrugged. There was a great deal about his father and his behavior that was impossible to explain. "It's fine," was all he said.

"Ideally, the Christmas special will give the show a boost," Elnaz said after a moment. "We need to add something new this year, something that gets people talking." There was a sudden spark in her eyes. "Maybe people are getting tired of the same old same old? Which is why Nora Jansson is the perfect fit."

Her tone was teasing, insinuating. She used the same tone whenever they'd finished dinner together on location—when she always suggested that he should try out what the town had to offer. And she wasn't talking about the food, but more . . . nocturnal activities.

"What do you mean?" He took a spoonful of the artichoke soup, which was delicious. Another nice thing about Västervik was the number of good restaurants. He tried the wine, a dry Riesling with the perfect blend of sweetness and acidity.

"The bakers we've worked with so far have been great people, with good background stories that were both entertaining and sympathetic.

But a lot of them have been men." Elnaz paused. "And the women who've appeared on the show were a little too old for you. Nora's about your age. She's attractive, and she would probably be charming if she dropped her guard a little."

"You want me to stage a romance?" Henrik asked, even though he understood exactly what Elnaz meant. He just wanted to make her come straight out with it so that she could hear for herself what a stupid idea it was.

"A romance wouldn't be such a bad thing, would it? I mean, it doesn't have to be real. It just needs to be suggestive enough for the viewers to believe something is going on."

Henrik sighed and took another sip of his wine. Then he looked at Elnaz. "And is Nora on board with this romance?"

"I haven't said anything to her. I'm thinking it could just be something understated. You don't have to fall in love—maybe just flirt a little, give the viewers hope."

"I'm not sure—it doesn't feel right."

"Don't worry—all you have to do is gaze at her for a few extra seconds, maybe make a nice remark after you've been all critical. Enemies to lovers . . . We'll take care of the rest."

Henrik took a deep breath.

"I know what you're thinking, Henrik, but this is exactly what we need to give the show a boost. The heartbroken celebrity baker, trying to recover after his breakup with the beautiful sommelier."

He was taken aback. No one on the production team had ever mentioned the situation with his ex.

Henrik and Bente had fallen in love on prime-time TV when they appeared on several episodes of a morning show, marrying cakes and puddings with dessert wines and demonstrating how rustic bread with a few drops of olive oil and a pinch of sea salt could make the perfect appetizer when accompanied by a good Italian wine. Henrik's Italian bread and Bente's favorite Barbaresco had found their way into many Swedish homes, along with their love story. The press adored the two of them together—but had adored their painful separation even more. When Bente cheated on him, they both became fodder for the gossip columns. The interest and speculation made him more popular than ever, and *Let's Get Baking*'s ratings had actually gone up.

He knew the production team was well aware of what had happened, but no one had ever said a word about it.

He merely nodded. The main course arrived, and Elnaz started chatting with one of the camera operators. Henrik wasn't sure what he thought about all of this; first Don's talk about angles, and now Elnaz's attempt to turn *Let's Get Baking* into a dating show, which he hadn't expected of her. He might have expected it of Ted, who was notorious for ruthlessly pushing ahead with no scruples, but he hadn't yet witnessed any situations where the producers' conscience and moral compass were tested. It seemed that was about to change.

The following morning, Nora could barely look Henrik in the eye when she arrived at the patisserie. He thought she deserved to be a bit embarrassed after the previous evening.

"I thought we could start with some clips about what we discussed yesterday," Ted said when everyone had gathered. Nora was asked to go in the bakery while Ted sat down at Henrik's table.

"Tell us what you think about the patisserie."

"I definitely think the patisserie has potential," Henrik began. He had to speak in full sentences for editing purposes, because the viewers wouldn't hear the producer's questions and instructions when the show aired. "But what I said to Nora is true. She has too many different items on offer, too many cakes and cookies, when she should be focusing on the products that have the most potential. She has too many irons in the fire but not enough good bread in the oven, so to speak."

"Mmm . . ." Ted didn't look happy, possibly because of the awful analogy. "Does it annoy you that she's let things get to this point?"

Henrik realized where Ted was going with his extremely leading question, and he was completely on board. "I do find it frustrating that she's taken over such a fine, well-established business, only to let it slip through her fingers." He raised his voice, frowned. "Not looking after such a gem really does infuriate me."

"Excellent." Ted nodded to the cameraman to stop filming. "Okay, let's take a walk around."

Henrik followed the team into the bakery, where Nora had clearly just finished her clip for the camera. Her cheeks were pink, and her eyes were a little shiny; presumably she had been furiously complaining about Henrik's feedback on her bread and cakes.

Definitely genuine feelings. Exactly what the production company wanted.

Filming resumed and Henrik looked around. Everything was kind of shabby, but the appliances and ovens were of good quality, and the equipment was clean and well maintained. He continued into the cool room. In the middle of the room was a tray of loaves, and he immediately recognized the smell of sourdough. He often baked using a sourdough starter at home, and his grandfather had taught him a lot about it. His father had a complicated relationship with sourdough, which might sound surprising, but in spite of everything Hasse was both a baker and a baker's son—he took dough seriously. Besides, he had a complicated relationship with most things.

Henrik didn't know much about his father's childhood, apart from the fact that he had grown up as an only child with a single mother. Strangely enough, Henrik's paternal grandparents had separated—not a formal legal arrangement, but they lived apart, and Hasse had stayed with his mother. He never talked about it, but Henrik's grandmother wasn't a particularly loving person, and one of the elderly ladies who had worked at Eklunds forever had hinted that Hasse had been beaten as a child. When Henrik thought about that he felt a degree of sympathy for him, but then his father had done little to ensure that his own children had a happy childhood. Though he had never hit them, he had made no effort to be affectionate with them. He seemed to think it was enough that he had helped his father build up a baking empire. In his world, that was worth more than any amount of love.

Henrik continued going through the produce in the cool room, starting with the bottom shelves: decent butter, milk, whipping cream, fresh vegetables, cheese, and other toppings such as liver pâté, ham, turkey, Brie, and salami, all of good quality. Nothing out of the ordinary. But then he took a closer look. The higher shelves were packed with inexplicable jars, tins, and packets. He picked up a can of condensed milk and held it out to Nora. "How often do you use this?" Then ricotta cheese. "And this? It's nearly out of date." He shook his head, moved on to several rock-hard tubes of pasta coloring. "You've got way too much stuff in here. You're wasting money on unnecessary things."

"I need the condensed milk for cookies. And the ricotta for cakes with . . ."

"You're not listening to me," Henrik interrupted.

Nora frowned. "Both the cookies and the cakes sell very well."

Henrik didn't answer. Instead he returned to the bakery and walked over to an old bread maker. "Wow, I haven't seen one of these since I was with my grandfather in Eklunds' first bakery—it closed thirty years ago."

He gazed at the single hot plate. "Everything is very clean and well maintained, but the whole place reminds me of the former Soviet Union. It's like being in an abandoned café in Chernobyl, where time has stood still."

Nora rolled her eyes.

"Some new equipment wouldn't hurt," Henrik added.

Nora looked around as if she, too, were assessing the place. "I agree, but I can't afford it, which is why I'm doing the show. And I'm not interested in some luxury renovation just so that it will look all shiny and new. If I were investing in anything, it would be in important items like the ventilation system, which is ancient."

Henrik clamped his lips together. She wasn't making this easy. The bakers were usually amenable to his suggestions, open to new ideas, eager for his help. Sometimes they would moan about the fact that things had gone so badly, which was Henrik's cue to offer a few words of consolation.

Several large loaves of bread were laid out on three trays. Henrik went over to them.

"That's our sourdough," Nora explained.

He reached for a knife and sliced through the crust, glanced around for butter. Nora handed him a carton and he spread a nice, thick layer on it. Took a bite. Absolutely delicious. And somehow . . . familiar.

"This bread is excellent," he said before he had time to think. Maybe he shouldn't come across as too positive; that didn't make for good TV. On the other hand, he had to give at least some praise. Otherwise his criticism wouldn't be as credible. If there was one thing that deserved his strictly rationed praise, it was this sourdough.

"It's one of our popular items." She looked proud. "The starter has a wonderful history." Her face lit up as she reached for a large glass jar on a shelf and unscrewed the tight-fitting lid. "It's more than a hundred years old. We even celebrated its hundredth birthday. It originally comes from . . ."

"You know those stories are often made up?" Henrik broke in with a supercilious smile. "I mean, I have nothing against sourdough, I love sourdough, I often bake it myself. But I can't tell you how many times I've heard about how the starter has been passed down through generations, and I doubt whether any of those stories are true." He had an old starter that he used only at home that his grandfather had given to him, but his father had insisted that its alleged history was nonsense, that it hadn't existed for anywhere near as long as his grandfather claimed. And to be fair, Grandfather had been a real romantic, so it was more than likely a tale he simply *wanted* to believe. All the same, Henrik had kept it alive. It had been important to his grandfather, for reasons Henrik had learned by a circuitous route. These days the kneading and baking of two large sourdough loaves was a part of his weekend routine.

The light in Nora's eyes died away, and she frowned. She inhaled as if she was about to say something, but then she exhaled and remained silent.

"These red plastic trays." He went over to a pile in the corner and picked one up. "Do you use them to display your cakes and cookies?"

She looked up at him. "Yes? I realize you don't think they're trendy, but they're practical."

"Practical isn't always best. Is this Nymans patisserie in Västervik, or a downtown McDonald's?" Henrik waved the red plastic tray around as he spoke, and then he put it down, grabbed a wooden cutting board, and quickly arranged a few rolls on it. "There you go, that looks much better."

"How lucky I am to have a celebrity baker come here and show me that I can put things on cutting boards." Nora gave an entirely artificial smile.

Henrik had no intention of letting her sarcasm go. "You know what?" He folded his arms. "I'm here to help you. I haven't traveled all this way to listen to your sassy remarks." He stared at her, his expression stern. This was partly for the camera, but also because that was how he felt. He had to show both Nora and the viewers who was in charge. "If you don't want my help, I can leave." He waved a hand toward the door.

Nora didn't say anything.

"Time for an interview clip," Ted decided.

Henrik and Ted's team went into the bakery, where Henrik spent several minutes complaining about Nora's lack of respect and the fact that he had better things to do than put up with crap from someone who was running her business into the ground.

After a few minutes, Nora appeared. She barely glanced at Henrik, and he guessed that Elnaz had been firing her up. It would take only a tiny spark to set the air around her alight; she was practically surrounded by lightning bolts. He was nowhere near as angry—this was only a game—but he suddenly realized how unfair this was. She really *was* furious. For her these were *genuine feelings*, just like Don wanted. This was about her life's work, while he was simply playing up to the cameras. He quickly pushed the thought aside—she knew what she was getting into, so surely she ought to understand the game too?

◆ ◆ ◆

Lunch was served—minestrone with pasta salad. Nora sat as far as possible from Henrik and refused to look in his direction. Elnaz ran through the filming schedule again, highlighting a couple of changes. The next few weeks were going to be hectic.

"And what about the renovations?" Henrik asked. "Are we going to have time to get them done?" He glanced around the room. No doubt the decor had once been attractive in a cozy kind of way, but now the faded red curtains and cracked floor tiles were simply depressing. The pale wood furniture had yellowed over the years, and some of the vinyl cushions on the benches had been repaired with tape.

"Renovations?" Nora asked, still without looking at him.

"Yes—hasn't Elnaz discussed them with you?"

"I mentioned that we were planning to freshen the place up a little. We thought we might make a few minor adjustments in here," Elnaz replied.

"Freshening up is a start," Henrik said. "But what's really needed is a total renovation."

Nora inhaled sharply. "It's perfectly fine as is. Everything is good quality."

Henrik looked around again. "It's hard to even tell what color the walls once were. Have they always been a dirty yellow? And the curtains—I can understand it if they haven't been washed for a while, because they'd probably fall apart."

Nora's eyes narrowed. "This renovation fever you Stockholmers suffer from isn't really my thing. Ripping out stuff that works—it's just ignorant."

"The colors will be brighter and better on TV," Elnaz said quickly. "And Henrik is only talking about small updates like repainting, in the same color scheme of course . . ."

"New curtains, repaint the ceiling, replace the furniture, fix the floors," Henrik said. "Get rid of those shabby glass shelves and the wooden shelves where the coffee cups are."

Nora scowled at him. "There's nothing wrong with the floor in here. Why does everything have to be shiny and new? When things work perfectly well?"

"Because . . . ," Henrik began.

"It looks better on TV." Nora finished the sentence for him. She shook her head. "I don't want you to touch a thing."

Elnaz exchanged a glance with Henrik, then looked at Nora. "The viewers love the part when we redo the café. And you'll get it all done for free."

Nora chewed her salad, looking far from convinced.

"Then you can put up the Christmas decorations," Elnaz continued.

"Christmas decorations? It's only November!"

Henrik closed his eyes, wanting to take several deep breaths. Preferably into a paper bag. And bang his head against a wall, because he was on the verge of a nervous breakdown. Was it really possible for someone to object to every single thing?

"We have to put up Christmas decorations," he said wearily. "It's a Christmas special. The viewers have to believe it's Christmas. The production team will help you—we have a good event planning company that we hire for this kind of thing. They'll make Nymans look super festive in no time."

"An event planning company?" Nora's expression was skeptical. Then she shook her head again. "No—I always do the Christmas decorations myself."

Ted looked from one to the other. "Why aren't we filming this?" He beckoned to one of the camera operators, then turned to Henrik and Nora. "Could you please do that again?"

Nora had had enough. She got to her feet, picked up her plate, and disappeared into the bakery.

"I don't think she wants to," Henrik said.

12

1945

Nils cycled through the village, past the rows of wooden houses, across the red wooden bridge, then continued along the river, its fast-flowing waters sparkling in the afternoon sun. The air was chilly, but the sun was warm on his back. He had been so happy when Tuula came into the café today, and he had enjoyed talking to her and meeting her children.

He was disheartened about the people who had treated them so poorly. Of course he knew what the village gossips said about the Finns, he knew they weren't popular, but to treat them as if they were of a lower status was an entirely different matter. Personally, he had always thought that Finland's cause was Sweden's cause, that it was a given for Sweden to help Finland, and therefore the Finns were welcome here. It was vital to support those who came. They were Sweden's brothers and sisters who were suffering the trials of war, and yet the Swedes, whose homeland was cowardly enough to remain neutral throughout, had the gall to think they were superior. It was ridiculous. He was appalled that Tuula had been exposed to the hostility of his countrymen. However, he knew that people in the village listened to him, so he would speak well of them whenever he got the chance, and would do his best to make sure that Tuula and her family were treated with respect.

He could see the tiled roof of his parents' home. He loved the yellow house with the white eaves where he had spent most of his childhood.

He opened the white gate, parked his bike, and walked past the apple trees that were perfect for climbing to the front door. Nils had loved growing up here. He could hear birdsong from the tops of the trees that shaded the veranda in the lush garden.

He usually felt a sense of calm when he visited his parents, but today his stomach was churning. His father had had a successful meeting with the local council the previous week, and as a result he had invited Folke Berglund, the chair of the council, over to celebrate, along with his wife and daughter. Nils's mother loved entertaining, and she had no doubt put their housekeeper to work to produce a magnificent dinner.

He opened the door and called out. His mother hurried into the hallway. "How lovely to see you, Nils."

He kissed her lightly on the cheek.

"Stig and Marianne will be here soon—they managed to get a babysitter."

A second later his father appeared, smiling proudly when he saw Nils, which always made Nils stand a little taller.

Nils and his father had always worked well together. Father had started the business with the café, then added the bakery. Nils had expanded the business by working out agreements with local retailers, enabling the family to develop their large-scale production. It had all been very successful, and it was understood that Nils would one day take over.

Nils heard footsteps, then the door opened and his brother and sister-in-law appeared. Stig's face lit up when he saw Nils.

"It's been too long," he said, patting his brother on the shoulder.

The housekeeper hurried into the hallway and helped Stig and Marianne with their coats. Stig gave her a grateful smile, then turned to his father. "I was wondering if you'd like me to take over the Nymans accounting. I'm doing pretty well, but I'm feeling that it might be time to move on. *Herr* Franzén isn't likely to retire anytime soon, so I'm kind of stuck where I am."

Nils was heading for the living room, and almost stopped dead. What was his brother proposing? Stig had spoken as though this was no big deal, but this was a major change of plan—was he actually suggesting that he should leave the accounting firm where he worked, and join the family business instead?

"Oh, wouldn't that be wonderful?" His mother clapped her hands together and beamed. "If Stig could work with the two of you!"

His father looked thoughtful for a moment, then smiled. Nils felt a strange sense of unease.

"Yes . . . why not? We're expanding all the time, and it would be useful to have someone who understands finances. Someone we can trust. Come down to the office tomorrow and we'll talk it through."

Why did Nils feel this way? Shouldn't he be overjoyed at the prospect of working with his beloved brother?

He and his brother had never competed with each other, largely because they had always had different interests. Stig had been a model student in school, while Nils was the one with good business sense and a love of baking. He had spent all his free time helping out at the café as a child. When he saw Stig's satisfied expression, he realized what the weird feeling was about. Father had always put Nils first, and his role as successor had been self-evident. If Stig was joining the firm, that changed things completely.

The doorbell rang, and his mother hurried to open the door and welcome Folke Berglund, who was followed by his wife and daughter. Many people found Birgit attractive, with her thick blonde hair, tidy features, and slim figure. She was undeniably pretty, but it was obvious to Nils when their eyes met that there was no spark there. He didn't know what made him so averse to her company, but he found her somehow unpleasant.

The situation wasn't improved by the fact that all four parents watched them expectantly as they greeted each other.

"Perhaps we should go into the living room and have a drink," his mother suggested.

The sun was shining in through the veranda windows, casting long golden stripes over the well-stocked bookshelves. His father served aperitifs in the coupe glasses that were only taken out of the display cabinet when there were guests.

"Welcome, everyone! We're here to celebrate this evening," his father announced when everyone had a drink.

Birgit looked at Nils over the rim of her glass as she took a sip, and fluttered her long eyelashes at him.

"Another piece of good news is that my eldest son wants to join the family firm," his father added. He looked at Stig. "You don't mind me telling everyone?"

"Of course not," Stig replied with a grin.

"Maybe we'll all be part of the family firm soon," Father went on. He smiled meaningfully at Folke, while Birgit smiled at Nils in the same way. He immediately felt all eyes on him, as if he and Birgit were about to get married on the spot.

But all he could think about was Tuula. She was the one he wanted. When she smiled, he thought about sunshine; when she laughed, he thought of beautiful music. There was *something* there.

Dinner went well. His father and Folke Berglund discussed business matters, and Nils joined in their conversation. Stig made a number of useful contributions, while Birgit chatted with Marianne and his mother. There was apple compote for dessert, followed by coffee and liqueurs. Then it was time for the guests to depart. Nils decided to leave, too, as he had an early start in the bakery the following morning as usual.

They were all standing in the hallway with their coats on when Father cleared his throat. "Our guests live in the same direction as you, don't they, Nils?" He looked at Folke, then Birgit, and finally Nils. Expectant, but with a sly smile.

"That's right," Birgit replied.

Nils ought to offer to accompany the family home—to do anything else would be rude—but he didn't want to. He didn't want to give her false hope, and he didn't want his father and Folke to think their scheme was going to succeed. If he was going to put a stop to these wedding plans, then now was the time to do it.

"Unfortunately I have to stop by the bakery. I just remembered I need to check how many sacks of flour we have left."

"Surely you can do that tomorrow?" His father wasn't pleased.

"Yes, but if we're short, I can bring some over from the café first thing tomorrow, which will save me valuable time."

Father looked puzzled, and then his expression hardened. Nils didn't care—he was not going to walk Birgit home.

When Nils set off on his bike ten minutes later, after awkward goodbyes and handshakes, it was already dark. He could smell the fresh water and brushwood from the river, a smell that grew stronger as the days grew warmer, bringing a hint of spring.

The evening had taken too many unexpected turns. First Stig, then Nils's decision to make it clear that he was not interested in a relationship with Birgit. How was this going to affect his future prospects? Was the bakery still his? But then he thought about Tuula, and he felt for the first time that the family firm and his long-held plans were no longer so important.

13

Henrik poured himself a large cup of coffee, closed his eyes, and inhaled the rich aroma. Roasted coffee beans—was there anything better? Freshly baked bread, maybe—he couldn't decide between the two. He headed over to the hotel breakfast buffet, helped himself to a bowl of yogurt, and topped it with fresh berries and muesli with plenty of nuts. Then he joined Ted at a corner table by the window. It normally had a view of the sea, but at this predawn hour, the water was nothing more than a dark, shapeless mass. A week of filming had passed, and things had gone relatively smoothly. Nora's opposition to almost everything he suggested made for more conflict, which Ted seemed to like. Henrik might have gone in a little harder than in previous seasons, but he didn't think he'd ever crossed the line.

He went back to the counter to fetch some bread and felt a hand on his elbow. He turned to see Elnaz smiling at him, holding a cup of coffee. "It's going well so far."

"Thanks, I'm glad you're pleased." He reached for a white porcelain plate, then picked up a fresh roll and a croissant that was still warm. Elnaz hadn't moved. "Was there something else?"

"Like I said, filming is going well. But . . . I wish you could be a bit more flirtatious." She gave a wry smile. "Something needs to happen between you two."

Henrik sighed. "Why does this make me feel dirty?"

"What's the problem? You've fallen in love on TV before."

"With Bente it was real. There's a difference when you're pretending to flirt with someone."

"We've talked about this. When the baker is a single woman around your age, the viewers are going to expect something. Christmastime and all that. Magic—you know."

"Magic," Henrik repeated.

"Think of the ratings." Elnaz took a sip of her coffee.

"But won't it look weird if I criticize her and then start flirting?"

"I think that's exactly what the viewers want. Like I said before, everyone loves a good enemies-to-lovers story."

Half an hour later, Henrik arrived at the patisserie. Filming began as soon as Sara had finished his makeup.

He started by going through the cookie selection. Took a bite of a vanilla and chocolate checkerboard cookie that melted in the mouth, but was still crunchy. "Not bad, I have to say. And this is a classic. Everyone likes these." Then he tried a raspberry jelly cookie. The jelly was hard, almost impossible to chew. He spat it into a napkin and looked at Nora. "What's your insurance situation?"

"Insurance?" She folded her arms defensively. She was wearing a black T-shirt with the same straight, slightly trendy cut as before, and black jeans. He couldn't help but notice that her outfit highlighted her blonde hair and red lips, which were currently pursed to indicate her displeasure.

"Yes—does your policy cover dental costs for broken teeth? How long has this cookie been sitting here?"

Elnaz was glaring at him, but how was he supposed to flirt with the baker when the whole premise of the show was to cut the participants down to size?

"What do you mean . . . I . . ." She broke off and shook her head. "I don't usually have stale cookies for sale—there must have been a mistake." She snatched it out of his hand, took a bite, and made a face as she chewed and swallowed. "Like I said, a mistake." Henrik had won that battle.

Nora folded her arms again. "Any more unnecessarily nasty comments?"

"I'm not nasty, I'm just honest."

"I'm just honest," Nora repeated with a snort. "You do know it's only unpleasant people who have to make that excuse to justify what they say."

"Thanks, good job," Ted said, looking ridiculously pleased. "We'll do an interview clip, then you two can take a break while we talk to some of the customers."

Henrik used his interview time to rant about how crazy it was to have eighteen different cookies for sale—or maybe it was thirteen—and how appalling it was that Nora didn't focus on a few best-selling items. Not much flirting there. He just didn't know how to do it, it felt totally unnatural.

When they'd finished, he looked at Ted. "Have you and Elnaz agreed on the angle?"

"You mean the fact that she wants more flirting and romance?"

"Exactly."

Ted shrugged and sipped his coffee. "I know she thinks it's a good idea, but I'd rather go down a different route." He drummed his fingers on the table. "As Don says, Nora is pretty feisty, and that can make for very good TV."

Henrik also took a sip of his coffee. Clearly Ted and Elnaz weren't entirely in agreement—should he be worried? Then again, it wasn't his problem. It wasn't up to him to make decisions, he simply followed their directives. But he was the face of the show . . .

"Hi there!" a familiar voice called out, and Henrik turned to see Don walking in. He was wearing a woolen hat on his shaven head, and a thick winter coat. Henrik was surprised to see him. And judging by the reaction of the team, the others were too.

Henrik went over and shook his hand. "I didn't know you were coming."

"Just a quick visit, I didn't have a chance to give anyone a heads-up. Do you have time for dinner tomorrow?"

"Sure." Henrik swallowed hard. Was that when Don was going to drop the bombshell about the ratings? What if he said that TV24 intended to cancel the show?

"Great, I've already booked a table. Guldkant, seven o'clock." Don looked at Elnaz and Ted. "Could we have a few minutes in private? You too, Henrik."

They went into the bakery, and Don leaned against one of the tables with his arms folded.

"So I've seen the first clips from this week's filming." He sighed heavily, then took off his hat. "It's the most boring crap I've ever seen. We've talked about feelings. You've got a gold mine out there with her—she's an emotional person, you can see it from a mile off. Create situations that give her an outlet for those emotions."

Elnaz's expression was skeptical, but she didn't raise any objections. Henrik kept quiet, too, even though this didn't feel right. Of course he wanted to make good TV, but he still thought it was wrong to go beyond factually criticizing the patisserie. The idea of provoking feelings and reactions as Don was suggesting was another matter altogether.

"I've checked the schedule; we can let you have a few more days of filming. This will give you a chance to fix things."

They returned to the café. It was time for the team to interview some of the customers. Ted and the camera operator went over to a table where the man and woman from the first day were sitting. He was the one who'd said he had a tab, and that Nora allowed him to pay when he could afford it. Don sat down at a table nearby, picking the spot with the best view. Henrik noticed that Elnaz was looking kind of anxious while Ted gave nothing away—but then he was always like that. Always kind of switched off. Maybe that was how he survived in an industry where genuine feelings were hard currency.

Nora marched toward Ted and her customers.

"I think they want to film in peace," Henrik said as she passed him.

"I just want to hear what they're saying."

Henrik followed her, and they both stopped behind the camera. Ingemar was dressed entirely in beige, while Maggan was his polar opposite: a leopard-print coat, lips painted a bright pink that clashed with her vibrant red hair.

"Tell us what you think about Nymans," Ted instructed them. Nora was listening attentively.

"I think everything is delicious," Ingemar said.

"The bread's too hard," Maggan announced. "Nora does certain things very well, the croissants are very good, for example. But some of the bread is kind of tasteless." She glanced apologetically at Nora. "I'm sorry, but it's true. And some of the cookies I've bought have been stale."

Henrik had to stop himself from giving Nora a triumphant look. He could feel the tension radiating from her body. She smelled amazing; he'd thought the same when he was whispering in her ear that evening in the hotel restaurant. As if she had just stepped out of the shower, mixed with a subtle scent of lavender. She smelled even better than freshly baked bread.

"The rolls are good, the price is good," Ingemar piped up again. "But the coffee can be . . . a little bitter sometimes," he added hesitantly. Unlike Maggan he didn't look at Nora, but kept his eyes fixed on the table.

"The coffee?" Nora exclaimed. "Why haven't you said anything?"

"I'm sorry, but should she really be here when you're talking to the customers?" Henrik said.

"Because I . . . ," Ingemar stammered. "Because you're so kind to me, and I didn't want to complain." He still managed to avoid looking at Nora.

"No, she shouldn't be here," Ted agreed wearily, rubbing his eyes. "Nora, can you please go and take a break somewhere else?"

Nora sighed loudly and stomped off into the bakery.

When they had finished filming, the camera team followed her. Nora ignored them as she peered into the oven, then lifted out a tray.

"We thought Henrik could go through the bread now. What you bake and how," Ted said, glancing over at the table where the production assistant had laid out a selection of loaves on red-and-white-checked kitchen towels.

"Bread is a specialty of mine, so you might find it interesting," Henrik said.

Filming began, and Henrik noticed a rich smell coming from a tray Nora that had just taken out of the oven. Ignoring Ted's instructions and the script, he went over to check out the thin square of crispbread, baked to a perfect golden brown.

"What's this?"

"Sourdough crispbread."

He broke off a piece, tasted it. "This is delicious." For a moment he forgot all about the show and Don's demands—this was special. Discovering something unique in a patisserie was always delightful, and he was going to savor this moment.

It was the best crispbread he had ever eaten. But he couldn't come straight out and tell her that—she would be unbearable.

"I don't sell it in the store—I only make it for myself."

"Why don't you sell it?"

"Because people around here aren't interested in buying expensive crispbread when they can buy Wasa instead."

"I think you're misjudging the residents of Västervik. From the little I've seen of this town, people seem to enjoy the good things in life—and are prepared to spend money on them. I think you could sell this."

"Sell crispbread," she said calmly.

"Yes, and it's made from your sourdough, so it feels rustic, authentic. That's what you're after, isn't it?"

She didn't say anything, but she nodded hesitantly.

"I want you to try something. Wait there." He went over to the bench where he'd left his backpack and took out a jar of marmalade that he'd bought at a specialty shop back in Stockholm. He broke off another piece of crispbread, added a slice of ordinary cheese, then some of the marmalade. Without thinking, he brought the crispbread to her mouth. She was so surprised she took a bite. His fingers brushed her lips, and a strange tingling sensation shot all the way up his arm. He hadn't considered the intimate sensuality of what he was doing. Nora, however, seemed unmoved. She munched away, then looked at him.

"Delicious."

"Isn't it?" He nodded, took a bite for himself. The crispbread's mild but well-rounded flavor was the perfect pairing for the bittersweet marmalade and the savory creaminess of the cheese.

He could feel Ted's skeptical gaze, and he heard Don clear his throat. No doubt Ted was ready to shout *cut* at any second. He had to change course—and fast.

"I really think the locals would love this," he said with conviction. "They could buy it to add a touch of luxury to their weekend breakfast, or a Friday night cheese platter, or to give as a gift with a good jar of marmalade. Better than this tough, uninspiring object." He held up a roll.

"But our rolls . . ."

"Are uninspiring. At least . . . these rolls are uninspiring. If you made them from your sourdough, I'm pretty sure they would be something else." He leaned back against the table, folded his arms. "What do you want your customers to think of your patisserie?"

"Authentic and classic."

"Authentic. And would you say that rolls made from mass-produced flour are authentic?" He almost thought he heard Ted heave a sigh of relief now that he was back on track.

Nora didn't answer.

"How about trying something more specialized? Flour made from different grains, for example? You could try baking with flour produced by local farmers—I think that could work."

"Cut—let's move on," Ted said.

Henrik thought the scene had gone well, but judging by Don's grim expression, he knew it was a long way from what TV24 wanted.

14

They were about to start interviewing Nora when they were interrupted by Don, who had followed them into the bakery. Nora got a pit in her stomach whenever she saw him. She had noticed that some of the others—Elnaz and Henrik in particular—didn't seem to enjoy his presence much either.

He inspected her face, and then he turned away and yelled, "Sara, get in here!"

Nora sighed. What now?

Sara came in, and Don stepped aside.

"Can we do something about the wrinkles on her forehead?"

Nora blinked. Was this a joke?

Sara hurried off and immediately returned with powder and a brush, which she quickly swept across Nora's forehead. Don scrutinized Nora's face again. "I suppose that's the best we can hope for." He met her gaze. "I don't suppose you've considered fillers?" He narrowed his eyes, still studying her.

Nora couldn't speak.

"Enough, Don," Sara snapped.

"What? It's just a suggestion."

By now Nora had regained her equilibrium. "Why haven't you mentioned Henrik's wrinkles?"

Don shrugged. "Because they're masculine."

"So you think wrinkles are unfeminine?"

He looked at her apologetically. Both Sara and Elnaz were staring at him, waiting for a response.

"This isn't some kind of antifeminist thing," he said quickly. "I think fillers and other interventions actually favor feminism. They even out inequalities and give everyone the same chance, regardless of age or appearance."

Once again Nora was at a loss for words.

"It might be a little skewed, but that's the way society works," Don continued. "It was just a suggestion, I meant well." He held up his hands in a gesture of resignation.

"Okay, let's do this," Elnaz said firmly, glaring at Don as she signaled to the cameraman.

"So how did you feel when Henrik criticized your rolls?" Elnaz looked apologetic, but Nora wasn't sure whether it was because of Don or Henrik or even genuine. "And don't forget to speak in full sentences so that the viewers can get the context."

Elnaz's questions were always tough, and Nora never managed to conceal her emotions. However, she and Henrik had shot a pleasant scene, so this interview for the camera shouldn't be too bad. The problem was that she felt like a wreck. They had filmed until midnight yesterday, and then she'd had to wake up three hours later to prepare for the day. She was exhausted, and the constant criticism and relentless scrutiny—of the patisserie and now her appearance—didn't help.

"Of course I don't love his critiques. But he has a point—the rolls could be improved."

"Is that really what your customers want? Or does Henrik have a cynical, urban snob's view of what you do?"

Nora cleared her throat. "This idea of rustic life seems to be something of an obsession in Stockholm. Everything has to appear simpler—purer—but in reality, it involves a lot more work." She sighed. "What can be simpler and purer than a bread roll? But that's not good enough. It has to be made with flour from ancient grains, wood-fired, goodness knows what else. I don't suppose Henrik has ever baked an honest, plain roll in his entire life," she added with a snort. "And all his remarks about too wide a selection . . . Maybe a celebrity baker is happy to serve raw food balls laid out on a thick stone slab in a venue with a concrete floor and walls, but in this town, people want the classics. And plenty of choice." She thought about everything Henrik had said during filming. Too many cookies, too many ingredients, ugly setting, shabby utensils, tasteless bread. "You know what? I'm furious. He shows up here with all his opinions on what I do, and it's not even constructive criticism. I can take that, but this is just whining and complaining. I'm absolutely livid." She had worked herself up into a rage.

"This seems to be very important to you—the bread you bake?" Elnaz was gazing at her with a look that was meant to inspire confidence.

"It was . . ." Nora paused. "Those rolls were my dad's favorite."

"But the sourdough seems even more important. Can you tell us about it?"

"As I tried to tell Henrik—who, I might add, wouldn't even listen to me—my sourdough has a very special history. It's a hundred years old and . . ."

"No, I want to know what it means to *you*. I think you said it was the bread that you and your parents always baked together? And don't forget to use full sentences."

"The sourdough means a great deal to me. We baked it all the time, both at home and here, and we made it all kinds of ways—crispbread and loaves, with wheat flour and rye flour, but always with the same starter, and that smell . . ." She closed her eyes for a few seconds, smiling at the memory. "I could pick it up as far away as the main square when I was on my way here, and I knew that the sourdough loaves were in the oven. We always had it with breakfast. The smell, the taste . . . It means home, it means . . ." She broke off. Maybe it was the lack of sleep and all the emotional strain of the past few days, but she felt suddenly overwhelmed by her grief and the enormity of her loss. *It means Mom and Dad,* she thought. She shook her head, fighting back the tears.

"It means . . . ?" Elnaz prompted her.

"The sourdough bread means home to me. It means security and . . . unconditional love." She didn't know why she added those final words, but that was what she missed most of all—the love her parents had given her, the love that had been taken away from her much too soon.

"Thanks, that's great," Elnaz said. "I think Henrik wants to talk to you in the bakery."

On the way Nora was stopped by Hassan, who was about to go on his break. "Do you have a minute?" He looked down at the floor.

"Sure." She could see it was important.

"It's just . . . I should have been paid on Friday, but there haven't been any deposits into my account."

"What?" Nora frowned. Thank goodness Don couldn't see her—the unfiltered sight of all those wrinkles would probably give him palpitations. "That's odd, all the payments should have gone through. I'll look into it right away."

"Thanks, Nora."

She took out her phone and logged on to her bank account. It was empty, and there was no sign of the increased overdraft that Anna had promised. Had they canceled her overdraft protection? Surely not—but if so, how many payments hadn't gone through?

Her head was spinning, and she felt a growing sense of panic as she walked into the bakery. Elnaz showed her where to sit, directly opposite Henrik. She said something, but Nora wasn't paying attention. She still couldn't make sense of the figures she'd just seen.

They started filming, and Henrik placed a bundle of papers in front of her. "What are these?"

She looked down. Invoices from her wholesaler—Jonathan and his father. Where had he gotten hold of them? He must have taken them out of the folders she kept behind the counter.

"Er . . . invoices."

"Exactly, itemized invoices, and this list . . ." He shook his head. "Your expenses are unbelievable. And when I look at your overhead . . ."

With a flourish he produced another sheet of paper. "It's obvious that you have a major problem."

What was she supposed to say? She had no idea what she'd been thinking during all those months while things had been going downhill. She'd just kept telling herself that it would all sort itself out. She'd been counting on a miracle.

"Do you realize that you've driven this place into the ground?"

She simply stared at him, trying to quell the rising tide of panic. Her mind swirled with memories of her parents, the sourdough, all the happy times in this place, Henrik's words. Was it true? Had she driven the business into the ground?

She suddenly saw everything so clearly, as if a curtain had been raised, exposing her failure. Could she have saved the patisserie if she'd acted earlier? She'd seen those invoices and the overhead each month with her own eyes; she'd spoken to the accountant, been in those meetings. She'd done her best, hadn't she? Maybe she should have stomped on the emergency brake weeks ago. How could this have happened? Why had she done this? Why hadn't she seen the magnitude of the problem until now?

Henrik's words echoed in her mind: *driven this place into the ground.* She wasn't sure whether he had actually said them again, or if they were just reverberating in her head.

"You continued to spend even though your overhead . . ." That was his voice, and it was filling her head.

Continued to spend. Driven this place into the ground.

Suddenly she couldn't breathe. Her hands were tingling. Oh no, this couldn't happen now, not in front of Henrik and the production team, not on camera. *Not now. Not now.* It had happened to her only once before, but she recognized the signs. Maybe she could stop it?

She tried to take a deep breath, but her heart was beating faster and faster until it was pounding. The tingling in her hands spread up her arms to her neck, and her throat constricted.

"Can't breathe," she gasped, bending forward and clutching at her throat. "Can't get any air. Can't breathe." She was desperate for air. She heard a strange noise, unaware that it was coming from her, and her whole body was suffused with pain. Then everything went black, and she felt as if she were drowning.

15

1945

Ritva ran up to Tuula as she was about to head out to work. There were tears running down her daughter's cheeks.

"Mommy, can't I come to work with you today?"

Tuula crouched down next to the child. "I'm sorry, sweetheart, but you can't. You have to go to school." It was hard to say those words; every cell in her body protested.

When Tuula had gotten home the day before, she had found Ritva in floods of tears on the sofa. Eventually it emerged that Ritva's classmates had laughed at her in school. Little by little Tuula had coaxed more details from her. Ritva had found it difficult to pronounce the teacher's name, so he had forced her to say it over and over again, but she still couldn't get the consonants right. In the end he had grabbed her by the shoulder straps of her dress, lifted her off the floor, and held her there, legs dangling, while the children ran around her shouting made-up Finnish words. And the teacher let them do it. Ritva told her mother that the children had been mocking her from the start, she had no one to play with, and the teacher did nothing to help.

Her heart broke as she pictured Ritva sitting at her desk, trying to answer the teacher's questions, spending recess alone and then bullied by her classmates. Unable to hold back her own tears, Tuula had gone into the bedroom so that the children wouldn't see her cry.

She felt so powerless. Given the teacher's attitude, she didn't think it would help to speak to him. It might even make things worse. All she could do was surround her with love and make sure she understood that the fault didn't lie with her.

Tuula bent down and hugged her, then took her tearstained face in her hands. "I'll see you this afternoon—I can't wait." She gave her daughter another hug, then hugged Matias as well before she left the house. She wished she could take Ritva to school, but the timing just didn't work. Ritva had been so proud when Tuula gave her her own key to the apartment, so that she could take her brother to daycare and then walk to school on her own. There was no sign of that pride now; the spark in her eyes had been completely extinguished.

At work it was impossible not to think about Ritva and the situation in school. Aino kept looking questioningly at her, but didn't say anything until their coffee break. When they had settled down with freshly baked Danishes and a cup of coffee, Aino turned to her friend.

"What's wrong, Tuula? Has something happened?"

The words came pouring out. Aino placed a comforting hand on her shoulder, and Lydia, who had come out for a smoke, sat down beside them with a worried look on her face.

"Sweetheart, what's happened?" Lydia took Tuula's hand and held it.

"What is it?" This time it was Nils's voice.

Tuula glanced up at him, and the others looked in surprise at their boss.

"Sorry—maybe it's none of my business," he said quickly.

Tuula shook her head. "It's fine. Nothing for you to worry about." She didn't want to burden Lydia and Nils with her troubles.

Nils and Lydia didn't leave.

"*Fru* Anttila's daughter is having problems at school," Aino said eventually.

"Oh?" Nils said.

"Tuula, what's this about? We want to know because we care," Lydia assured her.

"It's . . . the children are bullying poor Ritva. And the teacher . . ." Tuula's voice broke, and Aino took over, relaying what she had just heard.

The tears poured down Tuula's face. Suddenly, everything had caught up with her. When Juhani died, she had been inconsolable at first, but then she had pulled herself together for the children's sake and had hardly shed a tear since. Not even when her mother died shortly afterward due to complications from pneumonia; nor when her sister, the last remaining member of her family who was still alive apart from the children, left with her family to travel into the war zones as a nurse.

"It's barbaric," Lydia snapped. "Is that how we treat refugees in this village? Children who've lost their father, then been forced to leave everything behind?"

"I apologize for crying like this," Tuula said with some difficulty. "It won't affect my work, I can promise you that."

"I don't doubt that for a second." Nils looked pensive. He placed a hand on her shoulder, but then snatched it away as if her skin had burned him. She felt the same; his gentle touch had seared itself into her flesh. Out of the corner of her eye she saw Aino and Lydia exchange a glance.

Nils cleared his throat. "So the teacher allows this to happen?"

Tuula nodded.

"Is it *herr* Nilsson?"

Another nod.

Nils took a deep breath and straightened his shoulders. He disappeared into his office, then returned a moment later, pulling on his cap and jacket.

"*Herr* Eklund, wait, you . . ." Tuula stood up. She didn't want to him to feel obliged to solve her problems. It didn't feel right.

But Lydia grabbed Tuula's hand and stood up too. "Let him go. If there's anyone who can help your daughter, it's *herr* Eklund."

He jumped on his bike and pedaled away so fast that the dry gravel whirled up around the wheels, leaving a cloud of dust behind him as he disappeared around the corner.

The three women returned to the bakery and continued packing bread. Nils walked in a short while later and went straight over to Tuula.

"I trust that *herr* Nilsson will not upset Ritva again. If he does, or if the children are nasty to her, please let me know right away."

Tuula nodded cautiously.

"I've known Nilsson since we were kids. He's just a coward who takes out his own shortcomings on the children." He shook his head. "I hope he'll leave your daughter in peace from now on." He gave her a brief nod, and before Tuula could speak he retreated to his office. She could have kicked herself—she hadn't even managed to say thank you.

Ritva had an easier time of it for the next few days. Although she still didn't have any friends, she was no longer being bullied, and the teacher had stopped mocking her. Tuula wanted to thank Nils, but couldn't find the right moment. He spent most of his time in the office, and she didn't want to disturb him.

One day, however, she summoned her courage. She tapped on Nils's door a minute or so after he came back from lunch.

"Come in."

She took off her cap and opened the door. "I'm sorry to disturb you."

"You're not disturbing me," Nils said, smiling at her. That smile—it lit up his whole face and made her go weak at the knees.

She pulled herself together. "I wanted to thank you for speaking to the teacher, and helping Ritva."

"Has the situation improved?"

Tuula nodded. "She doesn't have any friends yet, but the children leave her in peace."

Nils's smile faded. "I'm so pleased I could help. I do hope that she'll soon start making friends."

"Thank you." Tuula turned to leave.

"By the way, I heard you were curious about the ovens. There was talk of a recipe you wanted to try out?"

Tuula stopped, turned back. "I do apologize, *herr* Eklund. It's just something I mentioned to Aino and Lydia. I . . . you . . ." She didn't know what to say. She hadn't thought anyone was listening to their conversation the other day.

"Sorry if I was too direct," Nils said. "But one of the bakers told me about your sourdough. He said you had a starter at home, and a special recipe?"

It was probably best to be honest. "Yes, I was asking about the ovens. I thought it would be exciting to see how the bread would turn out, given how hot they can get," she admitted.

"Would you like to try?"

Even though she had been brought up *not to be any trouble*, it was too tempting an offer to refuse.

"Yes, please! Back home I used to bake in the kitchen at the hotel, but I've never tried such fine ovens as these. Ever since you showed them to me, I haven't been able to stop thinking about it."

"I'm glad you're interested." The silence grew between them, and their eyes met. Tuula looked away, embarrassed. His expression . . . once again she felt weak at the knees.

"I'll bring the dough tomorrow," she said eventually.

When she left the office, she stood for a moment with her back against the door. She closed her eyes and took a deep breath to slow down her racing heart.

After dinner that evening, Tuula prepared the dough so that it could proof overnight. She hoped it wouldn't sink too much during her walk to the bakery.

In the morning she carefully transferred it to a bowl and covered it with a dishcloth. When she arrived at work she shaped the dough into a loaf, placed it on a tray the bakers weren't using, then set it aside to proof again.

After the bakers had left and she, Aino, and Lydia had finished packing the last of the loaves, the other two women went home, leaving only Tuula and Nils. Nils emerged from his office just as she entered the bakery.

"Thank you so much for letting me use an oven."

"I'll show you how it works." He smiled at her, and she tried to ignore the strange feeling in her heart.

He switched on the oven.

"You don't need to do that—I can use the residual heat from the day's baking," she protested.

"But then you won't get to see how hot these ovens can get—and that was the idea, wasn't it?"

"Thank you." Tuula gave him a grateful smile and uncovered the loaf she had made.

He nodded appreciatively. "So this is the famous recipe. What kind of bread is it?"

"This is rye bread, made with the sourdough starter my mother gave me."

"You brought a sourdough starter from Finland?"

"I did."

"How exciting."

When the oven was hot enough, Nils opened the door, and Tuula slid in the tray.

"It won't take long—that's the advantage of this oven," Nils said as he closed the door. "Are the children with Aino, or are they okay on their own?"

"They're with Aino. We were neighbors back in Rovaniemi, and she was a huge help with Ritva back then."

Nils nodded. "I like her a great deal. She's kind, sensible, and the most loyal employee you could imagine."

Tuula agreed. "And a loyal friend."

"That's good—we all need friends."

She peered in through the glass door of the oven.

Nils cleared his throat. "I wanted to say that if you ever need my help again—if anyone is unkind to you or your children—just tell me. I'll do whatever I can."

"Thank you," Tuula replied, although she knew she would find it hard to ask.

"Are you okay?" Nils asked after a while, looking searchingly at her. She hadn't realized she'd gone quiet.

"I'm fine. I was just lost in my thoughts." She checked the oven again. "I think it's ready, judging by the color." She opened the door, Nils handed her a glove, and she took out the tray. The loaf smelled amazing, rich and tempting. That was what she loved most about her rye bread—the richness. It was best enjoyed when it was freshly baked, with plenty of butter on it. After the butter shortages during the war, it would be pure joy to taste this bread with real butter.

"It should be eaten fresh," she said, tapping the crust.

"Can I show you something while it cools?"

"Of course." Tuula was puzzled, but Nils had a cunning smile on his face.

"I've been experimenting with a new wheat dough for our buns. I've changed the filling too." He went over to the shelves where the buns were proofing, and picked up a tray of large, unbaked cinnamon buns. "What do you think?"

"They look fantastic."

He nodded. "I hope they'll turn out well. I wanted to make them a little fluffier." He replaced the tray. "I'm going to leave them to proof until first thing tomorrow morning, then bake them." He glanced over at the loaf. "Do you think we could try your bread now?"

"Perfect timing."

He fetched a knife, cut two slices, took a packet of butter from the refrigerator, and spread a generous amount on each slice.

Tuula took a bite. It was heavenly. The crust had turned out thick and crisp, while the inside was silky soft—these ovens were phenomenal. And then there was the delicious taste of rye.

"This is amazing." Nils looked at Tuula. "Absolutely amazing."

"The heat definitely did the trick."

"We could sell this bread, you know."

She smiled hesitantly, unsure if he was serious.

"Sorry, don't take that the wrong way—I'm not talking about stealing your recipe or anything, but this could be a real hit. Finnish rye bread."

Her smile broadened. "Do you think so?"

"I'm sure of it."

"My fellow countrymen would certainly love genuine Finnish rye bread."

He gazed at her for a long time. "If I can persuade my father to add this to our selection, would you be able to bake it for us?"

"Of course."

"As a baker?"

"You mean you'd employ me as a baker? Here?" She couldn't hide her astonishment.

"Exactly. Naturally you'd be paid more."

She didn't know what to say. "But that's . . . It's too much."

"Not at all. This bread would be a real asset to our business." He placed a hand on her shoulder, and this time he left it there. They were standing very close to each other, and it was already very hot in the bakery. But Tuula suddenly felt even hotter. She longed for the coolness of the spring evening outside, but didn't want to move away from his touch. After a while he removed his hand and finished off his slice of bread. "I'll speak to my father. I assume you're walking home—do you mind if I walk with you?"

Tuula inhaled sharply, and her heart beat faster. "Not at all, no."

They cleared up, and Tuula changed out of her uniform. Nils locked up, collected his bike from the rack, and wheeled it onto the road. They set off side by side. It was still light, a sign that summer was on its way.

"So you're from Rovaniemi?"

"That's right."

"Do you miss it?"

"I do, but at the same time I really want us to make a new life here. There's nothing left up there. As I'm sure you've heard, the Germans burned everything, *herr* Eklund."

"I have. And there's no need to call me *herr* Eklund—it's Nils."

She smiled. "Nils. It's strange—in a way I'm grieving for what we left behind, and yet I don't want to go back." When she found out what had happened to her hometown, she became all the more determined to create a fresh start for her family.

"I don't think it's strange at all. It's hard to yearn for something that no longer exists."

"True."

Nils asked questions about the bread she had baked in Finland, and they became absorbed in details about different kinds of flour and proofing times. All too soon they had reached her street, and she stopped. "This is where I live."

"And I live down by the square."

"Thank you for your company, *herr* . . ." She broke off. "Thank you for your company, Nils."

"No, thank you. It was good to have the chance to get to know you a little better."

16

Could a sourdough starter be the closest thing you had to a family? Was it weird to think that way? It probably wasn't fair to Bea, her best friend. Nora's mind was whirling as she fed her beloved starter with flour and water. She stopped for a moment, inhaled the smell, allowed herself to simply be in the moment.

It was the morning after that horrible panic attack. She felt exhausted but calm, as though a violent storm had passed through her. And yet she couldn't relax.

The production team had rushed to help her, and she had come around with her head on Henrik's lap and Elnaz looking down at her. It was so humiliating! Thank goodness Hassan had been sitting beside her. He had held her hand, and it had been good to see a familiar face. They had led her into the changing room, where she had sunk down onto a bench. Elnaz and Hassan had eventually helped her up to her apartment. They had tried to persuade her to call someone to come and stay with her, but Nora just wanted to be left in peace.

She had slept deeply but had vivid dreams. She was woken by a text from Elnaz, wondering how she was feeling and telling her she didn't need to come in for filming until lunchtime, and then only if she was up to it. They would spend the morning filming material around the town, plus a couple of scenes with Henrik on his own, so none of the team would be in the patisserie.

Henrik sent a message too: Hope you're feeling better! Henrik

Was she feeling better? She didn't know. It was as if she had been sedated.

After a quiet morning at home, she stood holding the sourdough starter in its jar. The glass beneath her fingertips was reassuring, but she decided she had too many other things to do, so she put it down. She really ought to call the bank and ask about her overdraft protection. She owed Hassan money, but she couldn't face it. Instead she logged on and transferred the money to Hassan from her own personal account, which she could just about afford to do. Then she sent him a text to let him know that the payment had gone through.

She then got to work, doing a lot of preparation for the week ahead, which meant she wouldn't have to call in the extra baker she sometimes used, which would save on expenses.

The afternoon's filming was a lot less dramatic than the day before. They discussed the renovations for the café, and then she and Henrik baked some cookies. They didn't talk much—the team was mainly looking for footage that could be used in montages at a later stage. Even Ted kept quiet, and fortunately Don wasn't there.

Elnaz took her aside when they'd finished filming, asked how she was feeling, and informed her that the production company was happy to arrange for her to see a counselor if that would be helpful, but Nora smoothed the whole thing over. She couldn't open up to these people—they weren't her friends and didn't want what was best for her. They would always put the show first.

There was to be a break in filming for a few days so that the renovations could be done. Henrik and Elnaz would head out to record *Christmas with the Eklunds* during that time. The thought of a break made everything seem a little easier, and there wouldn't be much more filming after that. The thought of having to close for the renovations made her feel slightly panic-stricken again—that was the last thing the business needed—but she had no choice.

Although Nora was still exhausted when the workday ended, she showered and changed; packed her bike basket with cheese, marmalade, and crispbread; and cycled over to Bea's, who had invited her to dinner. They were going to dig out the patisserie's Christmas decorations, which she stored there after having an issue with dampness at the patisserie.

Nora let herself in when she arrived and stepped into the hallway, littered with muddy Wellingtons, winter boots, hats and gloves, and padded dungarees. The others were seated at the table, where dinner was already loudly underway. Max hurtled over to Nora and gave her a hug. Svea was in her high chair, and Nora ruffled her dark curls before she sat down.

Ahmat, Bea's husband, served Nora a generous portion of lentil stew. Nora took the plate and inhaled the aroma of the spices.

She usually joined them for dinner at least once a week. She was immensely grateful that there was always room for her; they were the nearest thing she had to a family. She adored the children, and had liked Ahmat from the moment she met him, even though they rarely agreed when it came to politics. They often had heated discussions—the kind you can only have with someone you're very close to.

However—and this was hard for her to admit, even to herself—sometimes the gratitude stuck in her throat. She knew Bea felt that she belonged there, but the constant sense of having to feel grateful could be wearing. Since she had no plans to build a family of her own, she was very glad that she could borrow theirs, so to speak.

After dinner, Nora produced the goodies she had brought. Bea made tea, they put everything on a tray, and then they pulled on their jackets and headed out to the shed to find the decorations.

"It feels so weird to be doing this in November," Nora said. "I mean . . . what's everyone going to think?"

"Stop sounding like my anxious granny," Bea replied. "Nobody's going to think anything—everyone knows it's for the TV show."

"But the leaves have only just fallen from the trees."

Bea gave her a reproachful look. "For God's sake, Nora—it's for TV! Let it go." Her tone was teasing, but she looked concerned as she unlocked the door of the shed. Nora set the tray down, and they started to take down and go through the boxes. Nora pulled down a box with an audible sigh.

"Are you okay? You look a little . . . pale."

"I'm fine, it's just a bit much with all the filming and keeping the business going at the same time."

"You're not yourself. You don't usually care what people think, not like that."

"It's hard to be myself when there are cameras in my face all day every day." Nora couldn't bring herself to tell Bea what had happened, even though she knew she should. She put some marmalade on a piece of crispbread and took a bite.

"How's filming going?"

Nora shook her head. "That Henrik Eklund is such a pompous asshole. That incident at the hotel was kind of embarrassing, but everything I said was true. When he starts criticizing me, I just want to slash my throat with a bread knife and put an end to my suffering."

"Surely it can't be that bad?" Bea said with a wry smile.

"He always takes it too far. He seems to be doing his best to make me look incompetent." Nora took a sip of her tea, then opened the box to discover the brass Advent candleholders.

"How so?" Bea asked, helping herself to some crispbread.

"Something . . ." Nora took a deep breath. She knew Bea wouldn't give up until she knew what was going on, and she was incapable of keeping secrets from her friend. "Something happened yesterday. The producers are very good at getting me to open up, and I started talking about Mom and Dad . . . All the old memories came flooding back, I'd hardly slept, and then Henrik launched into an attack on my finances, said I'd run the business into the ground, and I . . . broke down."

"In what way?"

Nora said nothing. She just looked at Bea.

"Oh, Nora." Bea gave her a hug, held her close. "And what did they do? Did they help you?"

"Yes, they did." She had no intention of revealing how traumatic it had been to find herself surrounded by strangers when she was at her most vulnerable.

"So what happens now?" Bea let go of her.

Nora shrugged. "The plan is to carry on filming. They offered me counseling, but I've had my share of therapy, so I said no."

"But they were the ones who provoked this reaction?"

"Yes. Although there's other stuff going on too. Financial pressures, lack of sleep, too much work . . ."

"I'm so sorry I applied on your behalf," Bea said quietly. "I didn't know . . ." She broke off. "I didn't realize it would be like this."

"It's not your fault," Nora said, placing a hand on Bea's arm. "I've got a few days' break from filming, and hopefully things will feel better after that."

The fact was that she needed *Let's Get Baking*. Her daily earnings had broken record after record since filming began, and if that continued for even a little while longer, she might be able to save the business. She pushed aside her worries about her overdraft situation. She would call the bank tomorrow—no doubt it was some kind of technical glitch. She looked at Bea. "Can't we talk about something else? Something more fun? For example, who had the bad taste to buy this bauble?" Nora held up a gigantic neon-green ornament depicting female bikini-clad Santas.

Bea laughed. "What can I say in my defense? It cost a fortune! I was in London, young and in love, on my first trip with Ahmat. I wanted to show him that I was edgy and cool, but a thoughtful friend at the same time, so I bought you a ridiculously expensive and kitschy ornament."

Nora laughed and put it back. She couldn't put it up in the café, but it always had pride of place on her Christmas tree at home.

Bea sipped her tea and opened another box. "Speaking of Christmas, we're going to my sister's place this year."

"Are you sure it's okay if I come along?" Nora had asked the same question every year since her mother died, and Bea always said yes. She still had to ask, though, and there it was again, that persistent gratitude.

She was afraid of coming across as ungrateful if she didn't ask and simply took it for granted.

Bea looked at her. "Don't be silly—you're as much a part of our Christmas celebrations as Donald Duck on TV."

Nora smiled and hoped it was true. Maybe it was, but it didn't stop her feeling like a fifth wheel.

Bea handed Nora a box. "Could that be a contributing factor to yesterday's panic attack?"

"What do you mean?"

"The theme for the show—Christmas. And the fact that Christmas is getting closer," Bea said as she tried to untangle a string of fairy lights.

"I don't know what you're talking about—you know I love Christmas." Nora cut a piece of Brie and put it on some crispbread, then popped the whole lot in her mouth.

Bea's expression was skeptical. "I know you love the *idea* of Christmas, but not necessarily the day itself." She picked away at a stubborn knot.

"The idea of Christmas? You mean the birth of Jesus? That's the idea of Christmas, isn't it?"

"Stop it—you know exactly what I mean." Bea opened a box filled with tinsel and garlands and passed it to Nora. "I should never have applied for you to take part in the Christmas special."

"Yes, you should have. And despite what you think, I have absolutely no problem with Christmas."

It had always been her favorite holiday. She and her parents made their own gingerbread cookie dough, chocolate cookies, and other specialties. They also made their own candy—marzipan, mint kisses, chocolate truffles, and more. Her parents baked gingerbread cookies day and night since Nymans was known for having the best in town. They decorated the entire café. They set out angel chimes, and placed Advent candleholders in the windows. A huge Advent star hung in the window by the door, and bags of gingerbread cookies were on display to tempt customers inside.

On the second Sunday of Advent, they held a gingerbread house competition and attended a Christmas buffet at the beautiful Gränsö castle. On the third Sunday, they drank mulled wine and bought their Christmas trees: one for the patisserie and one for the apartment. In the evening they made marzipan pigs, which they dipped in chocolate.

They celebrated Christmas Eve as traditionally as possible, with ham and all the trimmings, and Donald Duck on TV.

That last Christmas had been pure agony. Her mother had been in palliative care for a couple of months and moved into hospice shortly before Christmas. Nora couldn't do much to re-create any of their Christmas traditions, but she took samples of all the goodies she baked nonetheless. She couldn't take the Christmas tree to the hospice, so it was standing in Nora's rented apartment, scrawny and bare, when she got home hours after her mother had passed away.

These days she did most of the Christmas preparations herself, although she usually invited the girls over one evening in the last week before Advent. They would celebrate with mulled wine and put up the last of the decorations in the patisserie. She would have to invite them over a little earlier this year. Everything was going to be different.

Since her mother's death, she hadn't felt the same sense of anticipation before Christmas; instead, she became increasingly anxious as the holiday approached. Maybe Bea was right—she loved the *idea* of Christmas. She loved the lights and candles brightening the winter darkness, the music, the glitter, the mulled wine, the sense of togetherness. But the pain of her mother's death was a constant presence, and of course she became increasingly aware that she lacked a family of her own.

Nora looked at her friend. "I love Christmas," she said firmly.

17

Nora's panic attack had shocked Henrik. He thought he had acted appropriately under the circumstances; he knew that Elnaz was going to talk to Nora and offer counseling, but maybe he ought to do something else as well. In the end he sent a text message. Should he apologize?

When they were filming without Nora the following day, Ted insisted that Henrik do a piece for the camera about what had happened, as if they planned to include Nora's panic attack in the show. Henrik naturally questioned this, but Ted reassured him that they would show only the conversation beforehand, not the attack itself.

Henrik was still ashamed of himself for going along with it. He talked about how Nora drove herself too hard because she had no boundaries. "And," he had said in conclusion, "if someone is in such a fragile mental state, then maybe they shouldn't be running their own business."

How could he have said that? Surely he had gone too far? But Ted had been pleased, and in the end it was all about making Don and TV24 happy. What the hell was happening to Henrik's show if they were putting the participants in situations that provoked panic attacks? Don had been across the room when Nora collapsed, and Henrik had seen his expression. He had looked shocked, but also delighted in a bloodthirsty way, like someone watching a gladiator fight.

On their way back to the hotel that evening, Elnaz took him aside.

"Did you think what happened yesterday was okay?"

Henrik gazed out across the inlet. He could just make out the circular jetty that was apparently known as Myntbryggan. The sun had gone down, leaving behind pink streaks across the sky and casting a golden glow across the surface of the water. A thin mist was rising in the chilly air.

He turned to Elnaz. "What do you think?"

She didn't say anything for a few seconds. "I thought you were going to try flirting with Nora? You do realize Don is going to want to highlight the hysterical-woman angle with manipulated emotions, if you don't give him anything else?"

"So pretending to flirt with her isn't manipulating her emotions?" Henrik pushed his hands deep into the pockets of his sheepskin jacket.

"It's not about pretending or manipulating, it's just being a little flirtatious with an attractive woman—that's not such a terrible thing, is it?"

Nora was attractive, he couldn't deny that. He had gazed at those incredibly long legs more than once, and then there were those alarmingly blue eyes that constantly threw murderous looks at him. He shook his head. "Surely that's irrelevant? Ted just asked me to talk about Nora's reaction yesterday. What do you want me to do? Ted gives me one set of instructions, then you come along and say something different. Then there's the fact that Nora is furious all the time. I have no idea how I'm supposed to flirt with her convincingly."

Elnaz shook her head. She sighed, a distant look in her eyes as if she were thinking. "Maybe the two of you ought to meet up on your own; it might make the vibe between you a little more relaxed. Ask her out for a glass of wine; try to build some bridges."

"I'm not sure a glass of wine will help when my very existence infuriates her. She seems to think it's *my* fault that she's run her place into the ground."

"That's exactly the kind of thing you mustn't say. I know how Ted thinks, but we've got a lot of footage of you being supercritical—I'm afraid the viewers will begin to have a negative impression of *you* if we carry on like this. Everyone loves Henrik Eklund, and I'd prefer that it stay that way. A little romance would make you more human; they don't want to see that superior being anymore." They had reached the hotel, and the last rays of sun had been swallowed up by the dark-blue twilight.

Elnaz had a point, of course.

"Invite her out for a glass of wine tomorrow evening and talk about something else. Just try to get her to like you a little bit so that we can get on with filming. Okay?"

In order to clear his head before dinner with Don, Henrik took a walk through town. He stopped outside the bookstore and decided to go inside. It was a light, airy space, with bookshelves lining the walls from floor to ceiling. Henrik's latest book was a bestseller. Thanks to his TV success over the past few years, sales had been excellent. Then again, success might be fleeting—he was nervous about meeting Don.

He wandered over to the cookbook section. He couldn't see his father's latest work, but the classic *Home Baking with Hasse* was there. It had been reprinted several times, with a new edition published last year. Henrik picked up a copy, leafed through the pages. He stopped on a picture of his father and thought of how he'd outright rejected his proposal for a café. The book really was a classic, containing recipes and photographs of bread, cakes, and Danish pastries. There were also a few pictures of his father in the big rustic kitchen at the mansion.

The recipe for Eklunds' cinnamon buns was one of the first in the book. The buns were their pride and joy, and they were the key to the company's original success.

It had all begun with Great-Grandfather, who had started his own bakery, which then grew. Henrik's grandfather had gone into the business as soon as he left school, and the two of them had expanded the bakery, delivering bread and buns all over Västmanland, Uppland, and

Dalarna. By the end of the 1970s the firm had grown so much that Eklunds' cinnamon buns were the most popular store-bought bun. Thanks to the technique of baking at a high temperature and then immediately freezing them, they seemed as if they were freshly made when customers bought them at the store.

The love of baking had been passed down to Henrik's father, then to Henrik and Tom. Even though they had so much in common, there had always been quarrels and rifts within the family. Hasse thought his children should earn their place in the firm, because that was what he had had to do. He had created a public profile, made a name for himself, and the expansion of mass-produced loaves and cinnamon buns had proceeded at warp speed when Hasse took over. He thought his children had had everything served up on a silver platter. He had assumed that he would eventually have sole control of the business, given that he was an only child. When Grandfather split everything equally between Hasse, Henrik, Tom, and Camilla, the shaky relationships within the family had reached an unprecedented level of difficulty.

Henrik had always gotten along better with his grandfather, who adored his grandchildren. On one occasion when Henrik was a teenager and his father had made some disparaging remark to Henrik over dinner at the summer cottage in Bergslagen, in front of the whole family—Hasse's specialty was making condescending comments when everyone was listening—Grandfather had taken Henrik on a fishing trip. In the little skiff on the quiet waters of the lake, with only eight hundred mosquitoes for company, he had confided in Henrik that he and his father had also had their difficulties. The conflicts between them had escalated, and by the time Great-Grandfather died, the two of them were only colleagues rather than father and son. They discussed business, nothing else. They never saw each other outside of work. Henrik didn't know what those conflicts were about, and it didn't matter; he had understood that he didn't have to be friends with his father, that it was okay for a family relationship to be poor. And now it felt as if everything he had fought for, all his dreams, was slipping through his fingers because of his father.

Henrik had spoken to the landlord, who told him that there was another interested party coming to look at the place in a couple of weeks. The board meeting would be taking place around the same time, so Henrik still had a chance of securing the lease unless the other party was superquick.

"It's Henrik Eklund, isn't it?"

A voice interrupted Henrik's train of thought, and he turned to see the bookstore owner smiling at him.

"It is." He held out his hand.

"Malin—I just wanted to say hello. I heard you were in town."

"That's right—I've been here for a few days now."

"Your book is very popular. I love the apple cake, my kids are crazy for it. I make it all the time."

Henrik smiled. "I'm glad you like it—it's always good to hear that." It was true—he was always pleased when people appreciated his recipes.

"I wonder if you'd be interested in taking part in an author's event here? We run them from time to time, and they're very well attended."

He considered for a moment. He wasn't sure he had time; filming days were busy, and he was traveling back to Stockholm soon to record *Christmas with the Eklunds*. But he enjoyed meeting his viewers and readers, and maybe the production team would be interested in including it as part of the show?

"Of course I understand if it's not possible, but I thought it was worth asking," Malin said.

Something about her cheerful demeanor and warm smile made it hard to refuse.

"Why not? It sounds great—would you mind if we filmed it for the TV show?"

"That would be fun! We could make it a mulled wine evening—we could buy some snacks and treats from Nymans too. Maybe you could bake your delicious gingerbread cookies?"

"I'd love to."

"We usually hold our author events on Wednesdays—would that work for you?"

"Let me double-check the schedule with the production team—I'll ask them to contact you."

"Wonderful!" Malin clapped her hands with delight.

Outside the snow had begun to fall, thick, heavy flakes drifting slowly to the ground. The world was like a snow globe that had just been shaken. Henrik made his way to the restaurant. An open fire was crackling inside, and Don was already waiting at a corner table with a lowball glass in front of him. He stood up and held out his hand as Henrik approached.

"I'm drinking an old-fashioned—what would you like?"

Henrik shook hands, then turned to the waitress, who had just arrived with their menus. "I'll have the same, please."

"Good to see you," Don said, rubbing a hand over his bald head. "Okay, let's cut to the chase. I want to start by saying that *Let's Get Baking* is a good show. We've had several fantastic seasons. But as I mentioned earlier, we need to liven it up this season. We want something to *happen*, which is why I think we have to make the best possible use of Nora Jansson."

"Are you sure? *Let's Get Baking* has been popular for several years now, and the concept works."

"What can I say? The competition is fierce, and we need higher viewer ratings. We need something extra to make the show stand out, something that makes viewers *engage*. And Nora has character. Feisty as fuck. It could work."

"And is there a particular reason why you're so focused on the ratings right now?"

"We're always focused on ratings."

"I heard through the grapevine that you're not happy with the numbers."

Don put down his glass. "Okay, I'll be honest with you. TV24 isn't too happy with the fall season's ratings."

Although Henrik had already heard the same thing from his father, and Elnaz had confirmed it, he still found it tough to hear it from Don—who actually represented TV24.

"Why haven't you said anything until now?"

"We didn't want to make things worse; the plan is to work on taking the show to a new level. Obviously we were going to share our thoughts with you. I was planning to bring it up with Camilla, but since we're sitting here, I decided I might as well talk to you about it directly."

Henrik nodded, studying the young executive producer. Don looked significantly older than he was, with his shaven head and slightly old-mannish clothing. He was ambitious and would no doubt be working on the channel's biggest shows in a few years. His penchant for creating controversy might cause him some trouble, though, especially if he refused to drop the reality thread. "While we're being so honest, are you lining up any new shows for next fall?" Henrik asked.

Don's pause and sharp intake of breath confirmed Henrik's fears.

"We're in discussions with a production company about a new baking show, yes. But nothing has been decided yet." Don leaned closer. "I mean, what can I say? The success of the Christmas special is crucial. We have to give viewers what they want." He sat back and finished off his drink. "So it's in both our interests to make this year's Christmas special as good as it can be." He grinned at Henrik, picked up the menu. "Agreed?"

Henrik nodded slowly, even though he didn't quite know why. Had he just agreed to try to make *Let's Get Baking* the next big reality show?

Ahmat offered to drive Nora home with all the decorations, but she needed the ride home in the cold November night to clear her mind. Bea promised to bring the boxes over later in the week.

The sky was clear and filled with stars. Nora cycled fast, enjoying the feeling of the icy air tearing at her lungs.

When she reached the kiosk on the corner next to the patisserie, she slowed down. **Celebrity Baker Chooses Västervik** said the placard for one of the evening papers. So her participation in the show had hit the headlines in town.

She was about to stop when she saw a man standing outside the patisserie, looking up at her windows. Unfortunately, it was Mange Lund, a guy she'd hooked up with now and again. He'd wanted something more serious, which had made her break off the whole thing. She braked sharply, then turned into the first alleyway she came to. Someone appeared out of nowhere. She braked again, lost her balance, and wobbled precariously.

"Whoa!" The deep voice belonged to the man she had almost crashed into; fortunately, he caught her and stopped her from falling.

Unfortunately, he turned out to be Henrik Eklund.

She couldn't help registering how solid his torso was. He held her firmly to keep the bike from tipping over.

"Sorry," she whispered. She freed herself from his grip and got off, her legs trembling.

"Are you okay?"

"Ssh!" She put a finger to her lips.

"Why are we whispering?"

"Because there's someone I don't want to talk to just around the corner." She moved over to the wall, where the glow of the streetlamps didn't quite reach and she was hidden by the shadows. Henrik followed her, raised his eyebrows. "And what is this someone doing there?"

"I think he's checking to see if I'm home."

Henrik's eyes widened. "That doesn't sound too threatening."

"No, it's just . . . he . . ." She hesitated. "He might have a reason for coming over. I stopped contacting him, and I haven't answered his calls, and . . ."

Henrik was grinning now. "I understand—it's kind of awkward."

Nora shrugged, feeling stupid. What could she say? She'd simply been too much of a coward to have that conversation with Mange.

"So what are you doing out and about?" she asked quietly.

"I've just had dinner with Don, and I thought I'd take a walk around town."

"Not much happens at this hour in November."

"That's okay. I like the quiet."

She nodded. "That's what I like about this town too—you can find peace and quiet, but still have people around you. It's an unbeatable combination." They fell silent, and she expected him to bring up yesterday's incident. "I'm sorry I lied the other day," she said quickly, in an attempt to divert him.

"Lied about what?"

"About dinner—when I said I was babysitting. Going out for dinner with you and the production team would have felt like hanging out with my kidnappers."

"You mean we've *kidnapped* you and your patisserie?" He was smiling.

"Something like that."

"And having dinner with us would equate to some kind of Stockholm Syndrome?"

She couldn't help laughing, then suddenly realized she was laughing with Henrik Eklund—the man she had regarded as her enemy.

Henrik's expression grew serious. "Listen, what happened yesterday . . . I apologize for pushing you too far. I didn't understand what was going on until it was too late."

"Neither did I. You're not going to use any of that, are you?"

He hesitated briefly. "No, of course not. I'll make sure of it. This process is intense when you're not used to it—long days with cameras in your face, irritating features producers, and a sour-faced executive producer to boot."

His phone buzzed, and Nora sighed with relief—the last thing she wanted was to discuss her panic attack with him. He read the message and frowned.

"Is everything okay?"

"Yes." He slipped his phone back in his pocket. "It's just something I'm not too happy about."

She nodded, but couldn't help feeling curious. Surely his celebrity baker life must be worry-free?

"A difficult TV-something?"

He gave a wry smile. "A difficult TV-something with my family."

"Oh?" She was surprised.

He shrugged. "We're about to start filming *Christmas with the Eklunds*, and the situation is a little . . . strained."

Nora was even more surprised. The Eklund family seemed so perfect on TV. "I guess it can be tricky when you spend so much time working together."

He nodded thoughtfully, then looked at her. "Is this really what you want?"

"The show?" She frowned. This was getting tedious—he knew she didn't want to be on his show, but she had no choice.

"No, I mean the patisserie. Is it really what you want?"

"What do you mean?"

"Has running this place always been your dream? Is this where you saw yourself ten years ago? Or are you doing it for someone else's sake?" His questions seemed honest, with no hint of cynicism. "Sometimes it sounds as if you're doing things out of a sense of duty, as if you're baking for someone else. Is that the case with the patisserie too?"

"This is definitely what I want," she said, perhaps a little too quickly. "And is this what you want?" she countered. "Baking on TV?" Maybe that would show him how dumb his question was. Of course he wanted to be a celebrity, of course she wanted to run her business.

"I don't actually know," he replied to her amazement. He said nothing for a moment. "I want to bake, but I don't know if I want to do it on TV." He looked up at the starlit sky. "Or at least not only on TV. The fact is, I'd really love to do something along the lines of what you do. To have my own bakery. That was how our family business started, and I long to bake that way again, to sell what I make and interact with the customers. I'd love to go back to the heart of what we used to do."

Nora nodded. "Having your own place is fantastic, but at the same time you're . . . vulnerable. As you know, taking part in your show wasn't my choice. And running the patisserie is hard work. But surely you have every opportunity in the world to open up a place of your own? Why don't you just do it?" He was in a healthy financial position, with a well-known name and reputation—he'd be able to draw plenty of customers. What was stopping him?

"Actually, I've set some plans in motion. I want Eklunds to open a bakery, and I've already produced a business plan."

"How exciting—so what's the problem?"

"The formalities—getting the board's approval and so on."

She still didn't understand why he didn't just do it.

"So why not do it yourself, without the family firm?"

He stared at her in silence, as if the idea had never occurred to him. "I . . . I think it would make sense to do it within Eklunds somehow, since that was how it all started." He smiled. "So there's nothing else you'd rather be doing?"

She sensed he was trying to change the subject. She considered her answer. "I've always been interested in politics."

"Politics?" She had taken him by surprise.

She nodded. "The patisserie means everything to me, and it's what I want to do, but . . . If I hadn't ended up there, I might have gone into politics, one way or another."

He narrowed his eyes. "With the Center Party?"

"I have no intention of sharing my political views." She laughed again. "What are you basing that assumption on?"

"You're the owner of a small business out in the country."

"Not exactly out in the country. And maybe I wouldn't want to work for any party, but instead get a job as a civil servant. I might have studied political science in college. That guy on TV24—Hermansson—has a dream job analyzing and commenting on politics. Not that I want to become famous," she added quickly.

"Don't worry. I know that fame isn't high on your list of priorities." He glanced in the direction of the main street. "Do you think your admirer's left by now?"

"Probably."

She left her bike propped up against the wall, took a few steps, and peered around the corner of the building. The street was deserted. A bitterly cold wind was blowing up from the harbor, the wet surface of the asphalt had hardened but was not yet frozen, and she suddenly shivered. She went back to Henrik and retrieved her bike.

He walked her to her door. The air was cold and clear, with a hint of woodsmoke from someone's stove.

"I was wondering if you'd like to join me for a glass of wine tomorrow after filming?" he asked. "I thought it might be nice to meet up and talk about something different."

Why would he want to do that? Nora was under the impression that he disliked her at least as much as she disliked him.

"It was Elnaz's idea," he added. "She felt it would improve our relationship, and I agree. It's always easier on camera if you get to know each other off camera."

"Okay." Nora knew that saying no wasn't an option, after lying about the reason why she couldn't have dinner with the team, then making such nasty remarks about him.

"Good. Cool." He didn't sound entirely convinced. "Any suggestions as to where we should go?"

"How about Harry's?"

"Perfect."

He said good night, and as Nora was locking up her bike, she reflected on what had just happened. She was going to have a glass of wine with Henrik Eklund. For some reason the prospect didn't seem quite as bad as it would have a few days ago. Maybe it wouldn't be completely unbearable.

18

1945

Nils was sitting opposite his father, and between them, on Father's enormous desk, lay a warm, fresh loaf of Tuula's rye bread. The crown of one of the tall willows outside the window cast flickering shadows across the surface every time the wind took hold of the lush green foliage. The branches scraped the glass, and the sunlight filtered down through the leaves, brightening the dark decor of the office. The rich aroma of Tuula's bread filled the air. His father picked up the slice Nils had cut for him. Tuula had baked the loaf only a little while ago, and Nils had wrapped it in a kitchen towel so that it would be as fresh as possible when he served it to his father. He had cycled to the family firm's head office with it tucked beneath his arm, steering with one hand. The office was on the village's main street, not far from the bakery. The butter melted as he spread it on the slice.

His father took a bite, then closed his eyes. Took another bite, swallowed, looked up at Nils. "I've always thought that Finnish rye bread tastes like it's been made from tree bark, but this . . ." He paused for another bite. "This is delicious. It would go perfectly with herring, or a mature cheese." He shook his head, taken aback by how good it was. "And you said it was baked by the Finnish woman who's just started in packing?"

Nils nodded. "If we decide to sell the bread, I thought I could promote her to baker. Back home she worked in a small hotel, where she baked a lot."

His father frowned, clasped his hands together, and leaned back in his chair. "I definitely think we should add it to our offering, but can we really promote someone at this point? A woman? And a Finn?"

"It doesn't feel right to take her recipe and bake the bread if she's not involved. Plus she's the one who has the skill."

His father cleared his throat. Cut another slice and buttered it. "I don't believe women belong in bakeries, and as for Finns . . ." He shook his head slowly. "You know what they say about the Finns here in the village. Malmsten down at the sawmill, he's had all kinds of trouble with them. They drink and fight, and the police have been called out several times to the places where they live. They show up drunk to work; it's a serious issue."

Nils straightened his shoulders and took a deep breath. "I do know what people say about the Finns here, but I've heard plenty of other stories, too, so I think there might have been a certain amount of exaggeration."

"Oh? So you're saying I'm exaggerating?" His father looked indignant—he wasn't used to Nils contradicting him.

"No, not that *you're* exaggerating, but the people you've spoken to. This woman is incredibly conscientious, just like the friend who recommended her. And I know the foreman at the mine—they've got some very hardworking Finnish men there, so some of what you've heard is clearly not true. Anyway, I can't sell this bread if I don't promote her. That would mean stealing the recipe from her."

"My son." His father leaned across the desk. "In business it is sometimes necessary to steal. And a Finnish woman isn't in a position to fight back, so you're risking nothing."

His father was wrong there—Nils was risking a great deal. He had no intention of treating Tuula that way. He shook his head. "No. I'm not going to bake that bread, and I'm not going to ask her for the recipe unless she becomes a baker with us."

His father gazed at him in silence for a few seconds. "So there will be no Finnish rye bread unless she's promoted. Have I understood you correctly?"

Nils took a deep breath. He wasn't used to setting himself against his father. They often discussed his suggestions, but Father always had the final word. "You have."

Father sighed. "Well . . . People have started to talk about the end of the war. Demand will rise, and we'll have to increase our production, which means we'll need a couple more bakers. I still don't think women belong in a bakery in that capacity, but . . . okay."

"Thank you, Father. I really appreciate it." Nils got to his feet. "I'd better get back to the bakery."

"I'm keeping this." Father grabbed hold of the loaf.

"You do that." Nils smiled and headed for the door, feeling excited. He couldn't wait to give Tuula the good news.

"Before you go . . ."

Nils stopped, then turned around.

"This idea of frozen food looks as if it might become a reality. I've heard from my contacts that there are plans to start selling frozen berries and vegetables. And I'm all for it—so I'm going to need that permission from the local council. Just imagine, a huge freezer room!"

Nils shuffled uncomfortably from one foot to the other while his father was talking, and then came the inevitable question. "Have you asked Birgit out?"

He shook his head.

Father sighed again. "I don't want to force you into anything, but can you please explain why not? She's a nice girl from a good family. And she's . . . very attractive, as far as I can see. Can't you just invite her out for dinner?"

Nils had already tried his father's patience sufficiently, and didn't want to discuss the matter any further, but he couldn't simply give in. "I . . . I'll think about it."

Father nodded slowly, but as Nils closed the door behind him, he saw that his father was shaking his head.

He didn't want to have dinner with Birgit; he didn't want to spend any time with her. They had nothing in common. And someone else was filling his thoughts. He wanted to be with her right now, tell her the big news.

He got on his bike and pedaled through the village as fast as he could. He heard a cry of delight from an open window, and wobbled alarmingly. Another whoop of joy, then a cheer, and within seconds everyone seemed to be laughing and shouting. Someone ran out into the street, quickly followed by others.

"The war is over!" Wilhelmsson yelled, hurtling out of his grocery store, hands in the air. "It's peace!"

Nils jumped off his bike. "Seriously? Peace?"

"Yes—the Germans have surrendered!"

Nils laughed and gave Wilhelmsson a hug. Soon the street was full of people celebrating; he greeted those he knew and smiled at everyone. Dizzy with joy, he got back on his bike and set off for the bakery. Suddenly everything seemed easy. Only now did he understand how much the ever-present dark shadow of the war had affected him. He had tried his best to live a normal life, but it was suddenly so much easier to breathe, as if a deep-seated mortal fear had finally released him from its grip.

The news had already reached the bakery; he heard the cheers as he rounded the corner and saw everyone out on the loading dock. He dropped his bike and ran to join them. He hugged Fritiofsson, the baker who had been with him the longest. One of the drivers was dancing around in circles. Lydia was weeping with joy, and Nils caught Tuula's eye before they all cheered in unison.

"Take the rest of the day off," Nils yelled when the cheers subsided.

"But I've got loaves in the oven," said Wingård, one of the bakers.

"Okay—as soon as they're ready, you can go. Any customers waiting for bread can wait until tomorrow." He looked at the drivers. "You too—we'll deliver tomorrow. In you go, get changed, go home, and celebrate with your families."

Another burst of cheering ensued. The staff began to head inside.

"Tuula, do you have a second?" he asked. Tuula stopped and nodded. They found themselves alone.

"Peace—can you believe it?" he said with a smile.

Tuula shook her head and returned his smile, but then her eyes filled with tears. She smoothed down her cap, and he could see that she was making a huge effort not to cry. Was she thinking about everything that the war had destroyed? Old memories brought to life? Maybe she was remembering her late husband and her ruined hometown. She laughed, but the tears began to flow. He took a step toward her, reached out, and gently wiped her cheeks. He didn't know what came over him, but a second later he was kissing her, tasting the salt of her tears. And coffee. Salt and coffee, along with the sweetness that was Tuula. She tasted divine.

"Forgive me. I'm so sorry." He stepped back, looked up at her in surprise, and said, "But the war is over." Then he realized what had just happened. Oh God, was this even permissible? He was her boss, after all.

"I . . . I apologize. I . . . Sorry, I didn't mean to kiss you." He backed away, keen to make sure she didn't feel pressured.

She smiled. "It's fine."

Nils cleared his throat, tried to pull himself together. "The reason I asked you to stay behind is that I have something to tell you. My father wants to sell your bread, and you're going to be the one to bake it. You're going to be a baker."

"Seriously?" Her hands flew to her mouth. "Do you mean it?"

He nodded. "You're going to be a baker, and your pay will go up accordingly." She threw her arms around his neck, and now she was the one kissing him. He held her close, wanted her kisses to go on forever. The scent of her filled his nostrils—the Danish pastries she had just been packing, butter and cardamom and something else he couldn't put his finger on, but something fresh, like the aroma in the kitchen when his mother was making an elderflower cordial.

Someone coughed discreetly behind them. They quickly let go of each other, and Tuula looked anxiously over her shoulder. Lydia was coming toward them, carrying a box of bread. "I thought I might take this to the grocery store so they can sell it, as it's not going to be delivered—is that okay with you, *herr* Eklund?"

"Of course—good idea."

Lydia's smile broadened and she winked. "I haven't seen a thing." She walked past, then turned and waved goodbye.

Tuula looked at Nils, and after a second they both started to laugh.

"I play soccer," he said.

"Oh?" She raised her eyebrows inquiringly.

"Would you like to come and watch? There's a match tonight. Bring the children."

"Lovely—why not?"

"Fantastic." He was filled with excitement. "Down on Bredåsen—seven o'clock."

Tuula walked through the village in the spring evening. The atmosphere was relaxed, and the celebrations were still going on. People were sitting outside the café, and there was dancing and singing in front of the hotel. The hawthorn had just blossomed, and its intoxicating perfume filled the air.

She was holding Ritva's and Matias's hands. Matias had his soccer ball tucked under his arm, and occasionally let go of his mother's hand so that he could kick the ball and run after it.

No one was giving them dirty looks or calling them names tonight—everyone was too busy rejoicing.

Tuula wore a thin spring dress, pale gray with narrow blue stripes, which she had bought with her first paycheck. She was pleased with the dress and the jacket she had borrowed from Aino since she couldn't afford a spring coat just yet. With her raise, she would soon be in a position to expand her spring wardrobe—soon she was dreaming of the clothing she would be able to buy.

Then she thought back to what had happened earlier. What on earth had come over her? She had kissed her boss. The owner's son! It was crazy. But he had kissed her first, and invited her to the soccer match. Lydia had seen the whole thing . . . But Lydia was one of the kindest people she had ever met. She wouldn't make life difficult for them.

The match had already begun. Twenty or so spectators were sitting on the narrow wooden benches, shouting encouragement and clapping. Tuula and the children sat at the far end at the back. No one seemed to notice them. She wondered if things would change now that the war was over. There had been so much tension over the past few years. Perhaps attitudes toward the refugees would change. She could only hope.

Her heart sank when she saw one of Nils's teammates. It was the man who had cycled past them on the very first day. She had seen him in the village several times since then, and he had always hissed at her: *fucking Finnish bitch*. He glanced up at them, and she turned her head away, not wanting to provoke a reaction.

A moment later Nils spotted them. His face lit up and he waved, and then he raced across the pitch and fired a shot at the goal, but missed.

"Nooo!" Matias howled. Tuula smiled and put her arm around his shoulders.

Nils came over to them at halftime. As usual Ritva suddenly became shy, shuffling closer to her mother and saying hello to Nils with her head down, while Matias immediately began chattering about the game in broken Swedish.

"So you like soccer?" Nils asked.

Matias nodded eagerly.

"Would you like to come down to kick the ball?"

Matias leaped to his feet and followed Nils onto the field.

The two of them passed the ball back and forth, and Nils let Matias dribble past him and try to score. When the referee blew his whistle, indicating that the second half was about to begin, Matias hurried back to Tuula. He was panting and his face was red from the exertion, but his eyes were shining and he was beaming from ear to ear.

The match ended in a tie, but both teams acted as if they had won. Today everyone felt as if they had won, and maybe they had—the end of the war was a victory for them all.

Matias ran down onto the pitch again, and this time Tuula and Ritva followed him. Nils and Matias resumed their game, and some of the other team members joined in, including the man who always swore at Tuula. He passed the ball to Matias a few times, even if he wasn't smiling and joking with him like the others were. Tuula kept a wary eye on him. She couldn't relax, but he kept quiet.

Maybe, just maybe they could be accepted here? Maybe they could build a normal life here after all? That little spark of hope spread a warm, liberating glow through her chest.

She realized how late it was. The children needed their sleep, and she had to be up early. She stepped onto the field and waved to Matias. "Matias! We have to go now!"

The boy didn't hear at first, so she raised her voice and called to him again. He came running over, rosy-faced and sweaty. There was a chill in the air, and when she patted his cheek, she could feel how cold he was.

Nils followed him. "Thanks for coming."

"Thanks for inviting us."

"Mm." Nils swallowed hard and looked down at the ground, then looked up at Tuula again. Those sparkling brown eyes made her head spin. Or was it the scent of the hawthorn? Or the day's joyous news? More likely it was just charismatic Nils Eklund's presence. "I was wondering what you're doing on Saturday evening."

"What I'm doing on Saturday evening?"

"Yes—do you have plans?"

Tuula shook her head. "No plans. I'll be at home with the children as usual."

"Maybe Aino could watch them? I'd like to invite you to dinner at the Stadshotell."

"I'd love to come," she replied, much too quickly, before she even had time to think. The evening sun, turning the sky a warm shade of peach, the scents, the atmosphere in the air—it was all so intoxicating. And being so close to Nils, of course. His dark hair, damp after all his exertions, the smell of him. He smelled like the air around them, but stronger. And of sweat, but it wasn't unpleasant, a mixture of salt and something that made her think of a forest at dawn. He smelled like a man.

She hadn't been near a man since Juhani went to war. She hadn't been near anyone except her children for such a long time. And now Nils was standing before her, making her feel as if she had drunk the neighbors' schnapps. She wanted nothing more than to have dinner with him.

Nils smiled. "Fantastic. I'll book a table for seven thirty. I'll pick you up at seven fifteen."

She nodded. "See you tomorrow."

He laughed. "See you tomorrow—at work." He looked at the children. "Good to meet you again." He patted Matias on the shoulder. "Well played!"

19

The following morning, Nora called the bank before she went down to the patisserie. A strange sense of relief flooded through her when it went to voice mail. Thank goodness she didn't have to deal with her overdraft situation just yet.

Filming was much less dramatic today. They continued to talk about bread and various sandwich combinations. Henrik was critical as always, but unusually sympathetic. Nora thought everyone was behaving as if she were a ticking time bomb.

When the team had left, her sense of calm returned. She was about to get a full week away from filming, and she just wanted to be left in peace, pretend that nothing had changed. The renovations were due to start the day after tomorrow, but for now she could go back to business as usual.

She told Hassan and Emil that they could go home. Then she refilled the coffee machine, tidied up the display counter, and served a few late-afternoon customers—enjoying these tasks without a camera in her face, without Henrik observing every move she made.

There were only a couple of people left in the café, so Nora poured herself a cup of coffee and sat down in the kitchen.

She sipped her coffee, which tasted excellent. Henrik must have gotten a bad batch.

She knew she ought to call the bank again.

The phone rang for a while, and someone finally answered.

"Göran Fredriksson."

"Oh, hi, my name is Nora Jansson. I wanted to speak to Anna Bäckström—isn't this her number?"

"It is, but Anna has just had a baby, so all her calls are being forwarded to me."

"Okay. So the thing is, my overdraft protection doesn't seem to be working—I don't understand what's happened."

"If I can just ask you a couple of security questions to confirm your identity, I'll look into it right away."

"No problem."

She did as he asked, and she heard him tapping away on his keyboard. "Let's see . . . Ah." Silence on the other end of the line. An alarming silence. "You're . . . the Nora Jansson who owns Nymans. I was going to contact you this week, ask you to come in for a meeting."

"Oh?"

"I don't like to do this over the phone, but I've looked at your overdraft situation. None of the overages have been paid back, and in fact the amount has increased significantly over the last month. That's why the protection has been withdrawn."

"But . . . when I spoke to Anna recently, she agreed to raise the limit, because I'm taking part in a TV show that will significantly boost my income."

"A TV show?"

"Yes—*Let's Get Baking*. It's already brought in more customers."

"So Anna said you could delay repaying your debt because of this . . . TV show?"

"Exactly."

"I see. I'm sure it's because she was pregnant, not thinking straight. She needs approval from the board to increase your limit in a case like this, and as far as I can see, the figures don't add up. So unfortunately I've had to lower your overdraft limit, and stop any further withdrawals until you can make the necessary repayments."

"You mean I have no credit? You can't do that . . . I have salaries to pay and invoices for all my pre-Christmas orders. I won't have anything left."

"If you can't cover your expenses, you won't be able to continue to run your business. I suggest you close the patisserie before you incur further debts."

She was sure he was smiling.

"We're turning things around. I've already noticed an uptick in sales."

"I'm afraid there's not a thing I can do for you right now. Not until you come back to me with a financial projection that makes sense, or repay seventy-five percent of your overdraft debt."

"Seventy-five percent! But that's impossible, where am I supposed to get that kind of money?"

Göran sighed loudly. "I'm afraid you'll have to discuss that with your accountant." He paused, sighed again. "It's after five, I have to go. Get in touch when you have a solution."

With trembling hands, Nora fetched the broom and started to sweep the floor, and then she began to prep for the next day. Without feeling, without thinking, she moved from one task to the next, anything to avoid plunging into an abyss of fear and anxiety. She mixed dough while listening for the doorbell and new customers. When they arrived, she went and served them. At six thirty she locked the door, swept the floor, and wiped down all the benches and work surfaces. She worked mechanically, eyes fixed on the cloth as she moved it back and forth across the tables.

She switched off the lights, went up to her apartment, and stepped into the shower. Only then, with the water flowing over her body, did she allow her mind to return to the conversation with the bank. She couldn't absorb the full implications of what Göran Fredriksson had said, so she focused on the TV show. She ought to cancel her drinks with Henrik tonight, contact the producer and let them know she was going to have to close the patisserie. There would be no TV show. Her body began to shake as the realization hit her. Would she really have to close?

She took a deep breath. She would speak to her accountant, review her income this month; maybe there was a solution. But she had run the numbers and knew that even if business had increased over the last week or so, she was nowhere near being able to repay 75 percent of her overdraft.

Her legs were trembling as she switched off the water, wrapped a towel around her body, padded across the cold, drafty floor, and sank down on her bed. She dried her hair with the towel. *One thing at a time.* She would meet Henrik tonight, tell him. Then she would call Elnaz.

While she put on her makeup—she didn't want to look as bad as she felt—she wolfed down some leftover pasta salad. She scrutinized herself in the mirror. She looked pretty tired, and the lines Don had pointed out on her forehead were deeper than ever.

She pulled on a pair of dark-blue jeans and a white cotton shirt that she loved. She piled her hair on top of her head in a loose bun and put on an extra slick of red lipstick, as if the color might give her strength, before she put on her quilted jacket and set off to walk the short distance to Harry's.

On the other side of Fiskartorget, the water was shimmering in the glow of the streetlamps along the quayside; its dark, rippling surface looked like liquid gold. She took a second to inhale the fresh, salty air. The endless darkness of the sea calmed the storm within her.

Henrik was already there, taking a selfie with one arm around an older woman. The woman beamed and gave him a hug, just as he spotted Nora. He nodded to her, handed back the phone, and came over. He offered his hand as Nora leaned in to hug him, so they collided and she fell against his arm. He caught her, and she smiled as he awkwardly patted her shoulder. It might have been meant as a response to her attempt at a hug, but it came across as a gesture of consolation more than anything.

"What would you like to drink?"

"A glass of red would be good, but I can go and order . . ."

"No, no, let me do it. You sit down."

She did as she was told and sat down in a leather armchair as he went to the bar. She gazed at him. Blue jeans and a cotton checked shirt. Leather boots. Well built, bearded, and a baker . . . He was everything she dreamed of in a man, at least on paper. It was a shame he was such an arrogant shit.

"Hi, Nora." A male voice interrupted her train of thought. She glanced up. The Veg Guy. Had he come to present her with all his unpaid invoices?

"Hi, how are you?" She got up and gave him a half-hearted hug.

"I'm good. I heard you're going to be on *Let's Get Baking*?"

"I am—we started filming a little while ago."

"Fantastic."

"Listen, I'm sorry I haven't paid the last few invoices, but . . ." She wondered what to say. She might never be able to pay. Ever. Hopefully there would be something left for her creditors when the business was wound up. Both Jonathan and his father had been good to her. "But it's all in hand," she said, dredging up a smile.

"No problem. Now you're on *Let's Get Baking*, business is bound to take off."

She nodded. "Let's hope so."

There was a brief silence. Jonathan looked as if he was working up the nerve to say something else, but then Henrik reappeared with their wine.

"Oh, you're here with Henrik Eklund?" Jonathan was clearly impressed. He held out his hand. "Hi there, Jonathan, I'm a big fan."

Henrik put down the glasses and shook his hand. "Good to hear."

"I won't disturb you. Nice to meet you." Jonathan cleared his throat and turned to Nora. "See you soon."

"Another of your admirers?" Henrik said when Jonathan had gone.

She shook her head. "I wouldn't call him an admirer."

"It's just the way he looked at you."

"He wants his invoices paid. And possibly a roll in the hay. Nothing more." Nora smiled, then realized how it sounded.

"He wants to be paid for a fuck?"

"No, that's not what I meant . . ." She laughed. "I mean he might want to sleep with me. For free. There's nothing else between us."

"Okay, *skål*." They clinked glasses. "*Skål* for a fuck. Congratulations."

She narrowed her eyes, then laughed again. "*Skål.*"

"Here's to working together in harmony."

Her smile dissolved into a frown.

"Okay, so maybe we're not there yet," Henrik conceded. "But I do want us to work well together, which is why I invited you out this evening." He sipped his wine. "I really am sorry about what happened the other day, and I apologize if I pushed too hard. I promise that the rest of the filming will be a more pleasant experience."

"It's fine. I know I might have been a little difficult at times . . ." She took a big gulp of her wine. It felt rough against her tongue, but she was incapable of tasting anything. She should have gone for sparkling instead—it was easier to knock back. "I . . . I need to tell you something. I'm afraid the show isn't going to happen." She swallowed hard. "I'm going to speak to Elnaz tomorrow."

"Oh?" She had taken him by surprise. "Why? Have you changed your mind again? It's too late to pull out now, and if this is about the incident the other day, I've . . ."

"No, it's not that. I spoke to the bank." Another gulp of wine. "They've frozen my overdraft limit, which means I can't afford to buy anything or pay anyone. I can't even afford to stay open for another week. And if we have to close for the renovations, there won't be any money coming in at all." Though she felt ashamed, saying the words out loud brought an enormous sense of relief.

He nodded slowly, gazing into the distance as if he were letting it all sink in. Would he get mad? Give her another lecture on how worthless she was, running her business into the ground?

"There has to be a way to fix this," he said, much to her surprise.

"But how? I simply don't have the money."

He looked at her. "Give me a week. The production company will lose a fortune if we have to cancel the show after all the time and money we've invested in it. We have to figure out a way to make it work. I'll speak to them and see what we can do."

"That's very kind of you, but . . . I don't know if I've got a week. The invoices are piling up. To avoid a complete disaster, I'll have to close *within* a week!"

"Did Elnaz mention the meet and greet at the bookstore next week?"

Nora nodded.

"Apparently the tickets sold out in a day. The plan is for you to do the catering—I can try to get you paid in advance. Meanwhile, I'll see what I can do on my end, okay?"

"That sounds amazing." She released a long breath and smiled at him. "Thank you. But the renovations . . . having to stay closed . . . I don't know if . . ."

"Of course we'll compensate you for the days you lose to the renovations. I'm pretty sure that's in the contract. But again I can arrange for you to have the money now. That will give you a few days' grace."

"Thank you," she said again, more hesitantly this time.

"There's no need to thank me—I want the show to go ahead, so this is not an act of charity."

"I realize you're not doing this for my sake," Nora said quickly. "But thanks anyway—this might just be my salvation." She shook her head. "I really can't understand how it's come to this."

"I can," he said, looking her directly in the eye.

"Oh? Because I serve bad coffee?" she said, half joking.

He made a face. "No. And by the way, all that business with the coffee—I have to confess that was all scripted by Ted."

"What?"

"I'm afraid so. You serve excellent coffee."

She was so relieved—she had begun to wonder. Although lying to her wasn't fair.

"It's come to this because of the selection you offer." Henrik's expression was serious. "I'm not saying that just to make you mad, but because it's true."

She didn't say anything for a while. "Not *just* to make me mad—but that's part of it?"

"Okay, yes." He smiled, but immediately grew serious again. "Even if I pushed too hard the other day."

She met his gaze. "You did go too hard. I don't know what the production company wants, but it was a terrible experience, and even though the last thing I want to do is to close my business, I have to admit that the bank's decision felt like a way out. No more filming."

"I promise things will be better from now on. You have my word on that." He sipped his wine, leaned a little closer.

She picked up his smell and shivered. He was good-looking, that was why he had this effect on her, she told herself. And because she hadn't had sex with anyone since the Veg Guy, hadn't even been anywhere near a man in ages. Her primitive self had no defense against the handsome, divine-smelling man before her. But her rational self knew all too well that he was unbearable.

"I'll ask the production team to help you with your current financial difficulties, but in return you have to promise to listen to what I say. Your offering is too broad, and your purchase list is too long. Seriously."

Nora remained silent. She didn't like the fact that he was right.

"Can I ask a question?" he went on. "I get that this is what you want to do—apart from being a famous political pundit on TV." He gave her a teasing smile, then grew serious once more. "But if you had opened Nymans yourself, without any traditions to consider, would it have looked the same? Would you have offered so many different kinds of cakes and cookies?"

She thought for a moment. "Probably not," she said, to her own surprise.

"So why not do it your way? The fact that your parents and your grandmother did it one way shouldn't stop you, should it?"

Nora took another sip of wine, tried to marshal her thoughts. "You know how people find it difficult to throw things away after someone has died, or can't bring themselves to sell a house?" She kept her eyes fixed on the flickering candle flame as she spoke. "That's kind of how I feel. There's a memory attached to every single cake or cookie. I remember icing the Catalans with my grandma. I remember my dad eating the ends of the Brussels cookie dough when he thought no one was looking. Mom's favorite was the Mazarin tart. It makes me think of them, keeps their memory alive."

"Just because you change something doesn't mean you'll forget them."

"I know. But they're my family, and I've lost every single one of them. This is all I have left." She felt the familiar lump in her throat, and her eyes filled with tears. She turned her head away, pretended to look out the window, then drank some more wine in an attempt to pull herself together before she went on. "I know you think I'm incompetent, but I'm not stupid. It has struck me that I ought to simplify things."

"So why haven't you done it?"

She shook her head. "I tried once, but . . . everything went wrong." She didn't really want to revisit those memories, but she felt she had to make him understand. "Mom always insisted on keeping things exactly as they were. When I took on a bigger role in running the business and saw the numbers, I suggested a total rethink. That was just before she got sick."

"She didn't like the idea?"

"No. I was seduced by the idea of a sort of rustic industrial direction, with a few decent loaves and cakes and stone ovens, but that's not

Nymans. And Mom took it really badly. I think she felt that Nymans—the place that had been her dream, our life, the place I had grown up with—was no longer good enough for me. Then she got sick, like I said. When she got her cancer diagnosis, we hadn't spoken to each other for several weeks. The diagnosis brought us back together, of course, but we never brought up my suggestion again. Then she died, and somehow it seemed important to keep it exactly the way it was when she passed." Nora shook her head slowly. "I can't believe it might be too late."

Henrik gazed at her, then placed his hand on hers. Her whole body reacted to his touch, but she managed to maintain a cool facade.

"It will be fine." He squeezed her hand and looked at her with those dark-brown eyes. His hand was big, warm, and rough, yet somehow soft too.

After a while, he let go—slowly, hesitantly.

Nora cleared her throat. The unexpected touch had made her head spin.

"The bookstore would like you to serve something filling," he said quickly. Had he been affected, too, or was she imagining a hint of nerves? "Maybe your crispbread? And your sourdough? They want mulled wine, and they're expecting my gingerbread cookies."

She suddenly realized that he *was* nervous. She'd made *Henrik Eklund* nervous! There was something quite sweet about it.

He sipped his wine, straightened his shoulders. "I make them with brown butter." His usual self-confidence was back.

"The most important thing with gingerbread cookies is to use classic spices and to toast them." Her voice was steady. She had no intention of letting him see how his touch had affected her.

He stared at her for a few seconds. "You make your crispbread and your sourdough. But they're expecting *my* gingerbread cookies." He picked up his phone. "I'll send you the recipe."

Nora rolled her eyes. The dynamic between them was restored.

20

When Henrik arrived in Stockholm the following day, he stepped out into a city covered in a blanket of snow, with big, thick flakes swirling down from a dark-gray sky. Filming of the family Christmas show was due to begin that afternoon, starting with the arrival of the siblings at Hasse and Anita's home. The snow would provide the perfect backdrop.

Darkness had already fallen as a cab took him out to Saltsjöbaden, but the snow brightened the late afternoon. His father's yellow three-story mansion was situated by the bay, which was completely still. A gigantic Advent star hung in the bay window on the ground floor, its glow making the snow on the ground outside sparkle.

Henrik's brother and sister and their families were already settled in; their arrival scenes had been filmed earlier, which left only Henrik. The stylist quickly powdered his face in the hallway, but he kept his coat on and his duffel bag over his shoulder. Everything must appear genuine. He went back outside, down the steps, then turned around and came back up again, wearing a smile that was anything but genuine. The viewers would never notice. The snow crunched beneath his feet. He knocked on the door, one camera behind him and one to the side. The door opened, and as the children came hurtling out his artificial smile was momentarily replaced by a real one. It was impossible not to feel joyful with Theodor, Alma, and William running toward him. Hasse and Anita appeared behind them. Anita exclaimed "Hi!" in a happy, surprised tone, while Hasse beamed and enveloped him in a bear hug.

"Henrik—how wonderful to see you."

Henrik stepped into the hallway and gave Anita a hug. As he brushed the snow from his shoulders, Camilla and her husband, Antonio, appeared, followed by Tom. They all hugged him and fired off warm smiles in front of the cameras. Then the director shouted "Cut!" Henrik's scene was done.

He took off his jacket and shoes and looked inquiringly at Tom. "Where's Ellen?"

"She had a work thing that she couldn't change," his brother replied quietly.

"She's known about this for six months!" their father bellowed from the kitchen.

Tom shrugged. "Yes, but the filming was brought forward. So it is what it is."

Henrik headed into one of the guest rooms to change. He sank down on the neatly made single bed. The whole place felt so alien. It was hard to believe he'd grown up here. Everything was familiar, yet strange. The apartment his mother shared with Vanja on Mariatorget felt more like home, even though Henrik had never lived there. He was always welcome and felt relaxed there. He stayed where he was for a few minutes, told himself this was going to be fine. He would play his part, as he always did. He took a deep breath, stood up, and joined the others.

While Hasse and Anita continued their preparations in the kitchen, Henrik sat down in a corner of his father's study where his makeup was carefully applied. From then on, the action took place in the large living room with a view over the bay. The open fire was crackling in the hearth, and an enormous silver tray on the dining table was laid out with champagne glasses and an array of canapés—Hasselback potatoes with caviar and sour cream, Asian prawn toasts on salad leaves, goat cheese with green cabbage, all framed by the flickering flames of tall candles.

This was supposed to be two days before Christmas Eve. The following day would be filled with intense Christmas preparations, and then on Christmas Eve, they would film the big celebration.

Hasse and Anita took their places next to the table. Tom sat down in one of the armchairs with both children on his lap, and Camilla and her family occupied the sofa. The production assistant suggested that Henrik might like to perch on the arm of the sofa, in an effort to look relaxed.

"I'm pleased to hear that Ellen will be joining us tomorrow. At least two of you are sticking with your partners and raising your families." Hasse stared at Henrik, then continued. "I'm afraid it's going to look pretty sad that you're here alone."

"Sad?"

"Yes, you're nearly forty. No children, not even a partner these days."

This was seen as a huge failure in his father's eyes—the breakup, but also the infidelity that had preceded it. When Henrik had seen the photos of Bente and Frederic in the South of France, his father's words, which became Henrik's own, had echoed in his mind: *it was only to be expected.* Seeing those pictures had confirmed Henrik's impression that he wasn't good enough. Even though Bente denied that she had cheated on him, he didn't doubt for a second what had happened, because why would someone like Bente be faithful to him? And the photographs would have convinced anyone. She was looking at Frederic in a way that she never looked at Henrik. That had hurt.

"Well, I'll just have to smile a lot so that it looks less sad," Henrik said acidly.

His father didn't respond, and Elnaz appeared just then. The camera operators and sound technicians took their places, and Elnaz told Hasse that it was time to welcome everyone.

Filming began and Anita served champagne. The air was filled with the smell of burning birch logs, and the clementines that one of the production assistants had peeled and handed out to the children.

"I'm delighted to welcome all my wonderful children and grandchildren home," Hasse said, spreading his arms wide and beaming. Then everyone chatted and drank champagne, laughing and smiling warmly at one another. Henrik had done this so many times that it was easy enough to pretend that they were having a lovely time. Unlike with *Let's Get Baking*, *Christmas with the Eklunds* didn't require genuine emotions.

"Actually, I have a surprise for you, children," Hasse said after a while. They all fell silent. "Anita's son Niklas and his family will be here on Christmas Eve as usual, of course, but we're also expecting someone else." He paused dramatically. The only sound was the crackling of the fire. "Your mom is coming. And Vanja."

No one spoke—this was unbelievable. Was it some kind of weird joke? Why had his mother agreed to such a thing? Then there was a burst of happy chatter, which was exactly what was supposed to happen, and they all looked at one another, nodding and smiling.

"And I have another little surprise," Anita informed them. "I'm using a new rub on the ham this year."

Loud protests broke out, exactly as they had been instructed in the script they had received a few weeks ago.

"I promise it will be delicious," Anita assured them with a twinkle in her eye.

When the filming ended, Hasse and Anita disappeared into the kitchen, and Antonio disappeared upstairs with the children. The siblings stayed where they were and exchanged glances. "So, Mom?" Camilla said.

Henrik shook his head. Their mom made every effort to avoid their dad.

"So it will be Mom, Vanja, Niklas, and his family," Tom said.

"Like we're one of those great big happy celebrity influencer families." Henrik was finding it hard to summon a smile.

"More like a Lars Norén play," Camilla remarked, which made her brothers laugh. Henrik sometimes forgot how things could be when it was just the three of them. Without Hasse constantly making them compete for his favor and playing them against each other, the dynamic shifted, and they could actually have fun together.

They had a quick bite to eat, and then it was time to bake gingerbread cookies with the children. This was a simple scene, and it was a relief to focus on the children rather than Hasse. As the snow fell outside the window, they rolled out the dough, cut out hearts and stars, and drank mulled wine. They also made a big gingerbread house meant to represent the mansion itself, complete with an Advent star shining in the window.

When the scene was over, Henrik declined the invitation to stay for a drink. He and his father hadn't had a proper conversation since they had looked at the space for Henrik's bakery, and he couldn't bear the strained atmosphere for a second longer. Tom, Camilla, and Antonio needed to get their children to bed, so they all left together.

In the cab Henrik caught himself smiling broadly at the driver, the same fake smile he'd put on for the filming, as if he couldn't let go of his role. He sank back against the leather seat and opened the window. The driver gave him an irritated glance, but he needed a burst of oxygen, if only for a few seconds. The chilly winter air rushed into the cab, and Henrik tried to stop thinking about the day. He closed the window and sank farther into his seat, utterly exhausted.

When he got home, he took a hot shower, then took out a little of his grandfather's sourdough starter. He added some flour and kneaded the dough until his arms felt numb. Kneaded and kneaded, as if he were letting out all his pent-up emotions. He put the dough in a bowl, covered it with a kitchen towel, and left it to proof. Then he opened his laptop; he had a promise to keep.

When he told Nora he would help her, he had mentioned compensation from the production company, but he knew that was never going to happen.

He took out his phone and logged on to the Eklunds business account. He was impressed by everything that Nora had achieved. Regardless of what he said during filming, he didn't know anyone more motivated and hardworking. Her vulnerability had been a complete revelation. When he had placed his hand on hers at Harry's, he realized he was taking a risk, and half expected her to bawl him out. But there had been something wonderful about what they had shared in that moment, and the feeling of her skin beneath his fingertips had affected him in an unexpected way. He had wanted to lean in closer, inhale the smell of her. And that confused him.

Her vulnerability had made her more human, and he liked that. After everything she had gone through, she deserved some help. No one had ever supported Henrik's dreams, and if he could help someone else, then he was going to do it. As he entered the sum of money, it occurred to him that he probably wouldn't have done this for any other participant, even if they'd needed it. There was something special about Nora.

21

1945

Tuula went into the butcher's and was met by the metallic smell of meat. It was chilly in here, a sharp contrast to the early-summer warmth that had swept into the village over the last twenty-four hours. She joined the line; there were only three people in front of her. She was planning to buy a steak and cook it for Aino and Heikki to thank them for watching the children this evening so that she could have dinner with Nils.

She had left Matias at home in the yard, playing marbles with some of the other boys on their street. Ritva, however, was still struggling to make friends. Tuula had found her trying to hide her tears the night before. The children had teased her, and the teacher had done nothing. Tuula was distraught, and the faint spark of hope she had felt was instantly extinguished. Instead, her mind swirled with anxious thoughts as she waited her turn. She had urged Ritva to keep a low profile, keep to herself and avoid the other children, but was their life always going to be like this?

When it was her turn, the assistant turned to a man who stood behind Tuula. "What can I get you, sir?"

The man was confused, and gestured in Tuula's direction. "I think this lady was before me."

The assistant ignored Tuula and kept her eyes focused on the man. Tuula had no idea what to do. She eventually stepped back to allow the man to go ahead. She stood there waiting as the assistant served the next customer. And the next.

The insults that were sometimes flung at her in the village were nothing compared to this humiliation. She wanted to protest, but she didn't want to draw even more attention to herself. Yet that made her despise herself. Why was she accepting this?

Forty minutes later the store was empty, and Tuula walked up to the counter. She cleared her throat. "I'd like a pound of beef, please."

The assistant still refused to look at her. She began wiping down the counter with a frayed cloth.

"Excuse me," Tuula ventured, but to no avail. Rage and humiliation surged through her, but Tuula suppressed her feelings. "Excuse me," she said again, her voice trembling.

At long last the assistant went over to a piece of meat on the shelf behind her, chopped off the end with the most bone and gristle, wrapped it, and weighed it.

The assistant slammed the package down on the counter without making eye contact, then nodded toward the price label to indicate that Tuula could work out the cost for herself. Tuula handed over a coin. She should have received some change, but she couldn't bear to stay in this woman's presence for a second longer. She picked up her meat and hurried outside, tears pricking behind her eyelids.

She almost felt like laughing scornfully at herself—how could she have imagined that she and the children would be able to live a normal life here? They would always be regarded as second-class citizens. The fucking Finns weren't wanted here.

And tonight she was having dinner with Nils Eklund, the golden boy of the village. Who did she think she was?

She turned her face up to the bright summer sun, as if she could burn away her tears. There was no way she could go out with him.

When she got home, Matias was still playing with the boys. Ritva was sitting in the yard doing homework. Tuula hurried upstairs and switched on the oven. She had spent so long at the butcher's that she was now running late. She placed the beef in a roasting tin, added seasoning, sliced a couple of onions and put them in beside the meat, dotted the whole thing with butter, and put it in the oven. It wasn't the best cut of beef, but hopefully there would be enough for everyone.

Then she sank down at the kitchen table. She really ought to get ready. Aino had lent her a pair of pumps, and they were standing in the corner like a bad joke. What was the point of wearing nice shoes when everyone thought she was the most repulsive creature in the world?

She had intended to wear her thin cotton dress with the pumps and Aino's spring coat. She also had some hair curlers that Aino had borrowed from Lydia, and if Aino had time she was going to come down and help her with them.

It was time to do her hair, change her clothes, apply her eyebrow pencil and mascara. A dab of rouge on her cheekbones, a slick of lipstick. The lipstick was one of the last things she had tossed into her suitcase before she left home. She had felt incredibly vain, thinking about lipstick in the middle of a raging war, with a dead husband, and two small children to take care of. But it carried the hope of normality, a faint promise of a life where it might be possible to think of such trivialities.

That hope now seemed very distant.

There was a knock on the door, and she pulled herself together.

A beaming Aino was waiting outside. "Something smells delicious!" she said as she came in.

"There's a pot roast in the oven—you can take it downstairs if you'd rather eat at home."

"Thank you! So? Are you excited? I am!" Aino's smile suddenly vanished. "But you haven't changed! Or done your hair! I mean, you're beautiful as you are, but I thought . . . You need to hurry, he'll be here soon to pick you up."

"I can't go." Tuula swallowed hard. "I'll have to let him know."

"Let him know? How are you going to do that?"

"I'll have to go over there, or maybe you could do it for me."

"But why? He'll be here in half an hour—you can't cancel now."

"I just don't think it's a good idea."

Aino took hold of both of Tuula's hands and looked her in the eye. "Is this because of Juhani? Don't you think he'd want you to be happy? Say it's time to move on?"

"It's not that, it's . . . I don't belong here. What will people think of me and Nils? Nobody wants me here—can I really expose Nils to that?"

"Oh, Tuula—Nils is a grown man, he can make up his own mind. He likes you. Don't pay any attention to what other people in the village think of you. They're nothing but country bumpkins if you ask me." Aino smiled. "If they haven't got anything else to talk about apart from you and Nils, then let them carry on."

She pushed Tuula into a chair, fetched a brush, and attacked Tuula's hair. "That's better! Now go and get changed. Then I'll put your hair up while you do your face."

There was no point in arguing. Tuula went into her room and slipped on her cotton dress and a cardigan. Then she sat down in front of the mirror in her bedroom and did her makeup while Aino swept up her hair. At the last second Tuula removed the curlers, put on Aino's coat, and said good night to the children. At seven fifteen she was outside, waiting for Nils.

And there he was, wearing a gray suit with a dark-blue tie and hat, looking as stylish as ever. He smiled warmly at her. As they walked down the main street, she could feel people watching, but Nils acted as if everything was fine, cheerfully greeting everyone they met. They made their way down to the river, then across the bridge toward the square. The familiar tang of the sea was in the air, and Tuula thought she could smell the blossoms from the gardens they passed.

When they reached the restaurant, Nils opened the heavy door for her. The heels of Tuula's pumps sank into the thick red carpet in the foyer. Tuula tensed as they approached the maître d', but he welcomed them effusively and then showed them to their table in the dining room. Tall windows ran the length of the walls, lined with heavy green velvet drapes. A huge crystal chandelier hung in the middle of the room, and Tuula could hear the sound of silver cutlery on bone china, and the clink of crystal glasses. It was the most elegant place she had ever been.

Nils pulled out her chair, and she sat down on the soft leather seat. He sat down opposite her and ordered a glass of sherry for each of them. Tuula took the menu from the maître d' and studied it. They both chose a traditional dish of sprats with eggs on crispbread as an appetizer; then Nils ordered sirloin steak and persuaded Tuula to do the same.

As they sipped their sherry from small crystal glasses, Nils asked Tuula about Finland and her hometown, and she regaled him with memories. The sherry was very warming.

"Thank you for inviting us to the game on Monday. Matias has been talking about it all week."

"You're welcome." He smiled. "Do you have any hobbies?"

Hobbies. That is something for people with spare time, she thought. Back home she had had her hands full looking after the children, working in the hotel, and running her household. There must have been things she enjoyed doing before Juhani left, but she could hardly remember those days now. She had enjoyed her garden, when it hadn't just been about survival. She loved growing flowers—fragrant climbing sweet peas, clematis, delphiniums, marguerite daisies, foxgloves, and columbine, among so many others. And she had read novels, especially in the fall and winter, when it was dark outside and the garden was dormant.

She looked at Nils. "I haven't really had much time for hobbies since the war started."

"No, of course not. I'm sorry, it was a thoughtless question."

"Not at all. Things were different before the war. I always enjoyed my garden. And I love reading."

"Have you visited the library here in the village?"

"Not yet."

"You should go—it's not very big, but they have a good selection. And then of course there's the bookstore on the main street."

The appetizer that was set before her was delicious. Tuula could barely speak while she was eating, and tried not to gobble it up in seconds. She carefully put down her knife and fork while she was chewing, and made an effort to chat.

The waiter wheeled the main course over on a cart. He lifted the cloche, sliced the steak, transferred it to a warm plate, and placed it in front of Tuula. He did the same for Nils, then served up boiled potatoes and a generous helping of sauce.

The meat was tender and the potatoes perfectly cooked. Nils had ordered red wine, and Tuula was beginning to feel the effects of the alcohol. She restricted herself to a few small sips.

They enjoyed pears poached with cinnamon and served with whipped cream for dessert, followed by coffee. By the time they had finished eating, Tuula was so full she was afraid she wouldn't be able to get up from her chair.

Nils paid the bill, then looked at her. "I know you have to get home to the children, but shall we go for a little walk first?"

"I'd love to—I should walk off some of our dinner!"

Twilight was falling, but the sky was still light. As they crossed the square, Nils took her hand. As they walked side by side, her shoulder touched his upper arm, making her feel safe and secure.

He showed her the apartment where he and his brother had been born, where they had played hide-and-seek while his mother did the shopping, where he had learned to ride a bike, and where they bought ice cream in the summer. Where you could clamber down into the river for a quick dip. She loved seeing the village from his perspective; it made the place feel a little more like hers.

They stopped by the entrance to her house, and Nils looked at her.

"Thank you for this evening, Tuula."

"No, thank you. Thank you for dinner—I've really enjoyed myself."

"Me too. It's . . ." Nils broke off, gazed up at the sky and the stars as if he were hoping to find the words written there. "It's so easy to talk to you, to spend time with you. You make me feel good."

Tuula smiled. She felt exactly the same way about him.

He bent down and kissed her with those soft, warm lips. Yes, he definitely made her feel alive.

22

Henrik brought both sourdough loaves over to his father's house the following morning. His father wasn't impressed.

"Are you still using that old starter?" he asked, distaste written all over his face.

"Indeed I am. It makes the most delicious bread."

"I love sourdough!" Anita said. "I've never understood what you've got against it, Hasse."

Hasse shrugged. "I just think it's overrated." He turned his head away. "That starter and the whole history behind it almost cost your grandfather the business," he muttered.

"That smells delicious—can I have some?" Elnaz asked as she entered the kitchen. Henrik smiled as she cut herself a slice of bread and spread it generously with butter. She smiled back. "I love your sourdough." Hasse scowled at them.

"So it's time to trim the tree," Elnaz informed them through a mouthful of bread.

They had their makeup done in Hasse's study. Ellen showed up just in time, and smiled stiffly when Tom gave her a rather clumsy kiss on the cheek. Then they all took up their positions around the tree, surrounded by boxes of tinsel, fairy lights, and ornaments. Then they set to work decorating the tree, listening to Christmas music and enjoying Christmas treats as they did so. The children had fun, and Henrik found he was able to relax as he stepped into his role as the cheerful son of Hasse Eklund.

Then it was time for Henrik and his father to bake their saffron buns. Before the cameras, they got along just fine, agreeing on the elasticity of the dough, the amount of saffron to include, and the fact that the milk shouldn't be too hot. Hasse came up with an anecdote about when Henrik was a little boy and didn't have the patience to wait for the dough to proof. Henrik listened with half an ear, but smiled anyway. He knew most of it wasn't true; Hasse had no special memories of his children, because he had never spent any time with them.

Hasse patted Henrik on the shoulder as he told his stories, gazing at him as if his son was very special. Love in front of the cameras was so unconditional! The worst thing was that Henrik always treasured those brief moments when his father was like this. He was doing it even now, but then he reminded himself that this was the same person who'd decided to compete with his own son's TV show just because Henrik had stood up to him.

They paused for a coffee break in the middle of the scene.

Hasse stared at Henrik as they helped themselves to the refreshments provided by the production team. "So have you found something else to do?"

"Sorry?"

"In the fall." The loving expression was completely gone.

"There are no plans to cancel *Let's Get Baking*." Henrik sat down at the table and sipped his coffee. He hoped his father would go and sit in the armchair by the bay window as far from him as possible.

"No?" Hasse narrowed his eyes and took the chair opposite Henrik.

Tom joined them, but Hasse didn't care. Maybe he wanted Tom to hear this.

"This is what I was afraid of," he went on. "You don't have enough backbone."

Henrik looked wearily at him. "What do you mean?"

"You've had everything served up to you on a silver platter. A job, a business. Fame. All I've ever wanted from my children is for them to put in a little effort, and it's a great disappointment to me that you can't come up with something to do on your own terms." He got to his feet, picked up his empty plate, and left the room.

Henrik couldn't bring himself to look at his brother and instead focused on his meatball sandwich. But he had lost his appetite.

When filming resumed, they took out the dough that had been prepared the previous day and checked its elasticity.

"Perfect!" Hasse exclaimed, laughing heartily. "No one makes better saffron dough than you, Henrik." He smiled warmly and leaned closer. "Don't tell Tom," he added quietly, but loudly enough for sound to pick it up. Henrik grinned, even though he felt nauseated. How long could he put up with this nonsense?

Filming finally came to a close with Camilla arranging the floral centerpiece for the dining table. Henrik could hardly wait to get home. He was supposed to meet up with the guys; they had been friends since high school and went out for a meal on a regular basis, even though he couldn't always make it. He sent a text, made his excuses. He just couldn't face it. Instead he went out for a run in the cold night air, then took a long, hot shower, poured himself a whiskey, and fell asleep in front of an old episode of *Seinfeld*.

The following morning, he was right back at it. When he arrived at the mansion, they all changed into pajamas so it would look as if they'd slept over. The first scene featured Christmas breakfast with rice pudding, and ham on freshly baked wort bread. They all praised Anita's new rub, which made her happy.

Then they filmed lunch. Anita's son, Niklas, and his family showed up, and they filmed Henrik, Camilla, and Tom carving the ham and piling meatballs and potatoes on gold-trimmed serving dishes that had come from his grandfather's childhood home. Henrik cut generous slices of the previous day's sourdough. He really wanted to tell the production team the story of the starter; he knew they would love it. But of course he kept quiet.

When his mother and Vanja arrived, the atmosphere grew chilly. His parents greeted each other with a formal handshake and awkward air kisses. Vanja followed suit. If there was anyone who loathed Hasse more than Henrik's mom, it was Vanja. Henrik couldn't understand why they had agreed to be in the show at all.

They were filmed watching *Donald Duck and His Friends Wish You a Merry Christmas* as a family. (Recorded, of course.) Then they went for a festive walk together before dinner.

The snow lay thick on the ground, creating a magical atmosphere. Darkness was falling and the air was chilly. All the moisture had frozen, forming tiny, shimmering ice crystals everywhere.

Henrik walked alongside his mother, but the cameras were on so they couldn't talk about anything personal. He watched his father, walking out in front of the group between Camilla and Niklas, chatting and laughing like a jovial patriarch. The production team only wanted to film a short section of the walk, but it was good to get out of the stuffy house.

"Have you talked about the board meeting?" his mother said once the cameras were far enough away. Her words formed little white clouds in the cold. Henrik had told her about his disastrous conversation with his father, and she had given him lots of encouragement.

He shook his head. "As far as I know, Camilla and Tom are still in favor, but I haven't discussed it any more with Dad."

The evening ended with a traditional lutefisk. Hasse shared his personal recipe, of course. The fish preparation had already been filmed that morning, so all that was left was for Tom and Henrik to whip up a white sauce. Though it was a short scene, Henrik found it increasingly difficult to keep up the facade. He tried to play along and chat about any of the approved conversation topics, but the pretense had become almost physically painful to him. How much of his life was a sham?

When they had finished, Elnaz came over to him.

"Don has seen the latest clips from *Let's Get Baking*, and he wants to talk to us and Ted—do you have a few minutes?"

He followed her upstairs to his old bedroom, which had long ago been converted into a library, and Elnaz got them all on speakerphone.

"Okay, Don, we're all here."

"I'll come straight to the point. This is the most boring crap I've ever seen—I don't feel *anything*. Watching paint dry would be more exciting. I want to *feel* something, for fuck's sake. Do you understand?"

"I like this flirting idea," Elnaz said, managing a strained smile. "Henrik and Nora went out for a drink the other night, and you had a nice time, didn't you?"

"Yeees . . . ," Henrik began.

"If you're going down the romance route, something has to fucking happen. Fireworks. A nuclear explosion, okay?" Don broke in.

"No problem," Elnaz said, looking encouragingly at Henrik.

"No problem," he heard himself parrot.

"I'd like to see a few scenes where you try to provoke Nora," Don went on. "See what you get. I think you might be sitting on something really good, and you're just wasting it. Fiery characters always make good TV."

Henrik hated the way Don talked about Nora.

They ended the call, and Elnaz looked wearily at Henrik.

"Like I said before, that angle doesn't feel right. I've had enough of humiliation TV. But I still like the idea of a flirtation. A romance," Elnaz said.

Henrik realized he had had enough. He was already pretending to be part of a loving family—he couldn't bring himself to pretend to be in love as well.

"I don't know, I . . . Do you really think it will work?"

"Are you ready?" The production assistant had appeared in the doorway. "We need to get going again. It's your scene, Henrik—dessert wine and Christmas desserts."

Henrik breathed a sigh of relief at the reprieve. He and Elnaz hadn't finished their discussion, but he couldn't think about that right now. He stood up and left the room.

The adults gathered to sip dessert wine in the living room. The open fire was crackling, and the snow was still falling. It was as if everything had been perfectly staged for a cozy family celebration.

"So how's business, Vanja?" Hasse asked, rolling his cognac around in his glass. He wasn't a big fan of dessert wine.

"Fine."

"I hear you've taken a look at Henrik's proposal for a bakery."

"That's correct. Or rather one of my colleagues did. It was a solid business plan."

Hasse snorted. "I regard the fact that the bank approved the plan as pure nepotism."

"As I said, it was a colleague who checked it over," Vanja replied calmly.

"Henrik makes a good saffron dough, but he's no entrepreneur," Hasse continued.

As usual, no one said a word, once Hasse got going.

Henrik sat very still, hardly daring to breathe, as if his breath might ignite the tense atmosphere. He kept his eyes fixed on the dancing flames.

"Enough, Hasse," his mother said.

"Don't you dare tell me what I can say and do in my own house!" Hasse roared.

"The way you speak to your children . . . ," Vanja began, but Henrik's mother placed a hand on his arm and he fell silent.

She looked at her ex-husband. "Vanja is right. The way you speak to *my* children—I'm tired of hearing it."

"So what are you doing here? In my house?"

Mom swallowed hard but didn't reply.

"Henrik needs to hear the truth. The reason I'm hard on them is because they haven't had to learn a thing for themselves. They were born into all this, the celebrity status, the money. If you take a chance on every crazy idea, you'll run the family firm into the ground. Henrik is too much like his grandfather in that respect. Henrik proved he's no businessman with that fiasco with the Coffeepot. He can bake, and he's good on TV, but he will *never* run a business successfully."

Henrik recoiled as if he had been slapped across the face. Why was he so shocked, though? Hasse had never believed in him.

A second later Elnaz came in, all smiles. "Everyone ready?"

"Absolutely." Henrik did his best to bury his humiliation. God knows he was used to it by now—it shouldn't be hard. He took a big gulp of the wine, which was so sweet that his whole mouth tingled. Then he stood up and took a deep breath. The smell of burning wood stung his nostrils.

As filming began, he made a decision. He was going to fight back, Hasse wasn't going to get his new show in the fall. The *Let's Get Baking* Christmas special was going to be the best Christmas special ever. Longtime viewers would be surprised, and the buzz would attract new viewers. He was going to make sure everyone was talking about it.

He'd been faking things his whole life, so he might as well keep going. If a hot romance was what they wanted, then he would give it to them.

23

While Henrik was away in Stockholm, Nora worked hard to prepare for the bookstore event. Though the café was closed for the renovations, she was able to work in the bakery kitchen. The night before, she made Henrik's gingerbread cookies. She noted that there was no allspice in the recipe and thought it couldn't hurt to add a little. She would, however, use brown butter as per the recipe, and see how it turned out.

The wonderful smell of toasted cloves, ginger, allspice, cardamom, and cinnamon filled the air. She put a large chunk of butter in a saucepan, whisking it constantly to make sure it didn't burn, and the slightly nutty aroma mixed with the spices was something else. This was going to be good.

Once the cookies were in the oven, she turned up the volume on the Christmas music she had put on to get her in a festive mood and sat down with a list of everything she baked and sold. She wanted to surprise Henrik with a shorter list when he returned. She had also been in touch with Jonathan—the Veg Guy—about local grain, and was planning to experiment with an exciting new sourdough. She was going to try to do things her way and see how it turned out.

She returned the following day and worked to the accompaniment of the carpenters hammering and sawing away in the café area. They had put up a heavy curtain over the entrance, and she had to make a real effort not to pull the curtain aside and take a peek. She buttered the crispbread and added thick slices of Christmas cheese, with small wedges of fresh figs on top. Sliced the sourdough and topped it with a tangy mixture of stewed apple, crème fraiche, and blue cheese, garnished with toasted crushed almonds. Then she prepped for the next day, when the café was due to reopen.

The changes would bring results, but only gradually, and the bookstore event would provide a welcome bonus, but not enough to save her. She dreaded broaching the subject with Henrik tonight—but she really needed his help.

Later that afternoon Nora brought the food she'd prepared over to the bookstore. Like Nymans, it was a local institution. She set it all out on a long table, alongside large thermoses of mulled wine. The store was decorated with amaryllis and Christmas roses, and Advent stars shone in every window.

People started to arrive, and the TV crew filmed them as they helped themselves to food. When the star of the show arrived a few minutes later, the hum of conversation stopped for a few seconds and everyone simply stared at him. Including Nora. God, she'd forgotten how gorgeous he was. He pulled off his hat; the wet snow falling outside had made his dark hair go curly. He met her gaze and gave her a quick smile, but there was something different about him. She didn't know what it was, but he looked tense.

A lady came over to speak to him, and he seemed to relax. She understood why he dreamed of running his own bakery—he really did seem to enjoy talking to people. And baking on TV wasn't the same as being a professional baker. Whatever she had thought about Henrik in the past, he clearly loved baking.

He headed over to the makeshift stage and draped his jacket over an empty chair. Nora noticed that it was dripping, and a little puddle formed on the floor. Then he positioned himself front and center, and everyone sat down. Malin, the store owner, introduced him. As soon as he started talking about himself, his baking, and his latest book, the tension in his face disappeared. Nora couldn't deny that he was made for the limelight. He was putting on a performance, and now that it didn't involve her patisserie, she could see the magic—and why everyone loved him so much. The audience was spellbound. He made them laugh, even flirted a little with the ladies near the front. She caught herself smiling as he talked. He definitely had that charisma that only a real TV star had.

"I love Västervik, and I feel very much at home here," he said about the filming. He glanced over at Nora. "Almost *too* much." The look he gave her made her heart flip. The whole audience turned to her; they clearly understood the point he was making, because everyone laughed. What had she missed? She had made both the filming and his life in Västervik pure hell. Yes, things had been a little more pleasant recently, and there had been the odd touch now and again, maybe a look here and there, but nothing on the level he was insinuating. Was this some new message for the cameras?

"And tomorrow is the grand reopening of the patisserie," he went on. "Newly renovated, and with lots of delicious baked goods, needless to say. We look forward to seeing you all there."

A long line formed in front of the table where Henrik was signing copies of his book. When there weren't too many people left, Nora bought a copy and joined the line. When it was her turn, Henrik glanced up in surprise. "You didn't pay for that, did you?"

"I spent the very last of my hard-earned cash on it," she replied, holding it out with a smile.

Henrik wrote something. She took it back and read: *To Nora, wishing you many happy hours with this book. Hopefully together with me. Henrik*

She looked at him, and he met her gaze with a smile, which made her heart race. What was going on? And why was she reacting like this?

There were people waiting behind her, and she stepped aside. Read the dedication again. *Hopefully together with me.* He hated her, and the feeling was mutual. She couldn't help it if she thought he was good-looking.

When the signing was over, Henrik got up and mingled with the guests. He tried the canapés, and she watched as he picked up one of her gingerbread cookies and took a bite. He chewed slowly, then looked surprised. He took another bite.

She smiled to herself as she went over to him. "So what do you think?"

"It tastes like my gingerbread cookies, and yet not."

"A little better, perhaps?"

Yet another bite, followed by a smile. "Okay, I admit it—a little better." Nora realized that she had rarely seen him smile. Not like this, straight at her. Her heart flipped again and she inhaled sharply.

"What did you do?" he asked when he'd finished the cookie.

"I toasted the spices and added a pinch of allspice."

"Delicious." Another smile. "Did you miss me while I was away?"

"I'm not sure if you can miss an irritating mosquito."

He laughed. "Is that how you see me?"

"Maybe more like an angry wasp. But I know you can be quite nice when you want to make the effort."

He gave a brief nod. "Thanks. I think. And right back at you."

So was it possible for the two of them to be nice to each other?

She cleared her throat. She hated having to bring this up, but she had no choice. "This evening has helped my financial situation, and I'm very grateful for that, but I still don't know how I'm going to survive until . . ."

"I told you not to worry—I still have a couple of days to fix things, don't I?"

She nodded, then sighed. "I don't know, maybe I ought to say something to the producer. It doesn't feel right to keep quiet."

"Like I said, don't worry—I'll speak to Elnaz. I have a plan, but I have to get a couple of things in place before I bring it up with them. Then I promise I'll tell you everything."

"Right now I'm not sure I can last the week," she said quietly, leaning closer to him. "My accountant advised me to close before my financial difficulties escalate further."

"Don't do that. Trust me, okay?" His expression was serious.

"But I . . ."

And then he bent down and kissed her—in front of everyone, in front of the cameras. It was a long kiss. He pulled her close and she didn't break free. The ground beneath her feet appeared to have given way, and her entire body was throbbing. She wanted that kiss to go on forever.

When he finally let go, she opened her eyes and stared at him.

"It was the only way to shut you up," he said, then moved away to talk to an elderly couple. Nora glanced around; yes, the TV cameras were pointing straight at her.

She stood there with her legs trembling. What the hell had come over Henrik Eklund?

"The light is so good today that we thought we'd start out here." Elnaz nodded to the camera operator to start filming.

It was the following morning. They were standing outside the café, and Nora was about to see the results of the renovation for the first time.

Henrik was standing right behind her; she could feel his presence, like a warm barrier. She hardly dared look at him, which annoyed her. That kiss . . . She had felt something, so how could he behave as if nothing had happened? She had been so overwhelmed that she hadn't been able to stop thinking about it. What if it wasn't just for the TV show? What if he'd kissed her because he wanted to? And then she got annoyed at herself for thinking about it so much. She never brooded over anything as trivial as a kiss. Then again, she had never kissed anyone she had to see every day.

They unlocked the door and she stepped inside, full of anticipation. The first thing that hit her was the smell of fresh paint and sawdust. She ignored the camera that was following her and looked around. What she saw made her gasp and forget her agitation over Henrik.

Everything was reminiscent of the way the café had looked in its early days, but with a fresh, modern twist. The wallpaper was still there, but the vanilla trim that had yellowed over the years had been painted a crisp white, and the wall behind the counter was now covered in small square tiles. Black shelves affixed to the wall provided space for the bread to be displayed, and beneath them a pale wooden countertop ran the length of the entire wall. The long glass counter had been replaced by three freestanding glass cubes framed in the same pale wood. The cubes contained glass shelves and wooden trays where all the cakes, cookies, and sandwiches were laid out.

Renée stood behind the counter, beaming with pride. "Isn't it wonderful?" Nora nodded in agreement.

The café area was now equipped with rustic wooden furniture. The benches that lined the walls had been varnished and reupholstered in strawberry-red fabric.

Blown away, Nora turned to Henrik. "It's fantastic!"

He pulled off his hat. Once again the dampness had made his hair curl, and she felt a strong desire to touch it. She remembered the feeling of his rough beard on her chin when he kissed her, and suddenly her whole body was tingling.

He looked around. "It is, isn't it?"

Nora cleared her throat and pushed aside all thoughts of Henrik's beard, which she also thought was fantastic. And that kiss, which was more than fantastic. "I love it," she said sincerely.

Henrik went over to a table and sat down, and she took a seat opposite him. Someone had already made coffee, and a production assistant brought them each a cup.

"We found pictures from the opening in 1940. The wall was tiled, and there were black shelves," Henrik explained.

Nora nodded. "The place has been renovated a few times over the years, and not always for the better."

"We thought we'd give you something new that felt well planned and classic. The fact that we did it all in one go meant we could bring a coherence to it that it lacked before."

Elnaz came over and asked Nora to record a piece directly for the camera. Nora practically skipped into the bakery. The renovation was better than she could ever have imagined.

They sat down in front of a static camera. Elnaz was grinning.

"So can you tell us what actually happened yesterday?"

Nora stared at her. Of course they were bound to ask about the kiss. She cleared her throat. "Henrik kissed me yesterday—I'm assuming it was for the TV cameras."

Elnaz frowned. "You can't say that."

"But it's true."

Elnaz shook her head. "I don't know anything about that, but I do know there's a spark between you two. How was the kiss?"

"The kiss was . . ." Nora looked down at the floor. Why lie? It wasn't as if she was swearing her undying love for Henrik by telling the truth. "The kiss was good. Absolutely amazing, in fact. But don't tell Henrik," she said with a wink, which made Elnaz smile again.

"That's great—we'll save the rest for tomorrow."

They returned to the café, and Nora sat down with Henrik again.

"Are you putting up the Christmas decorations this evening?" Elnaz asked as she joined them with a cup of coffee. Renée brought over a tray of cheese rolls baked according to Nora's new recipe: sourdough made with spelt flour from a farmer a few miles to the north.

Nora took a bite. It was perfection. "I was going to do it later in the week—I thought that was what we'd agreed on?" She'd already arranged to decorate the café with her friends as they did every year, with mulled wine and Christmas music to set the mood.

"We really need to get it done tonight if we're going to fit everything in," Elnaz insisted.

Tonight? Well, she would make it work, but it would be impossible to gather all her friends on such short notice.

"What colors do you go for?" Henrik asked, trying a cheese roll. Nora frowned at him. What kind of a dumb question was that? She was about to give a snippy answer when he smiled at her. "What's this?" He held up the roll.

"My new sourdough. Made with local spelt flour."

He nodded. "It's delicious."

"The usual colors—red and green, gold. Are you worried about my poor taste in Christmas decorations?"

"No, no, I'm sure it'll be fine." Henrik's expression was cool.

Cool. How could he possibly be cool after that damned kiss? She regretted what she'd said to Elnaz, or rather to the camera. *To the entire Swedish nation.*

Then she realized that the problem lay not with his reaction, but with hers. The fact that she couldn't forget about it. She simply had to accept that he'd done it for the cameras. This was about ratings, and she needed to get on board with that. But why hadn't he involved her in his plans? Was he hoping that she would simply go along with it? And why had he decided to kiss her?

"Don't tell me you're in the Melania Trump Christmas camp?" she said acidly.

"Melania Trump?"

"Yes—frosty and ethereal and nothing but white, white, white." She narrowed her eyes. "You remember—she created a forest of fir trees dripping with plastic icicles that made the White House look like the white witch's ice castle in Narnia. What she did to Christmas was pure sacrilege. Christmas should be luxurious, warm, and inviting."

"I understand." Henrik nodded calmly, but then exchanged a quick glance with Elnaz, which made Nora even crosser. They really wanted her to believe that Henrik was interested in her, but she was smarter than that. She was mainly disappointed because they had talked so openly and honestly with each other at Harry's—but then the first thing he did was to manipulate her by flirting, then kissing her on camera.

"Do whatever you like," he continued in a disinterested tone.

Nora felt vulnerable and exposed, and wished she hadn't told him so much about her personal life. Elnaz tried to smooth things over. "Have you both read the outline for the Christmas bake?"

"Yes, everything looked fine," Henrik replied. "You've included what I asked for, so I don't have any objections."

Nora took a deep breath. "I have some objections."

"Of course you do," Henrik muttered.

"I don't like the fact that I'm supposed to get the saffron dough wrong, and Henrik has to help me fix it. I've been making saffron dough all my life—why would I get it wrong?"

"We always have a similar feature, it's an integral part of the show. Someone makes crispbread that's too hard, or a gingerbread dough that's too soft. The viewers expect it," Elnaz explained. "It's a way for Henrik to teach both the baker and the audience at the same time." Nora wasn't convinced, and Elnaz leaned closer. "You can't be a super-baker—even though we all know how brilliant you are, it doesn't work on TV."

"I have no intention of pretending to fail at something I can do. I'm not going to play dumb on TV." She could feel her cheeks grow pink with indignation.

"No problem—we can make sure you don't need to pretend," Henrik said.

"What do you mean?" Was he insulting her?

"I mean, we can find something else that I can teach you, so you don't have to pretend you can't do it."

"No thanks."

"Okay, so what do you suggest the show should be about? How fantastic your patisserie is? Why be on the show at all if you can't learn anything from me?"

Nora remained silent for a few seconds. "I'm just sick of playing dumb on TV."

But most of all she was upset because Henrik hadn't kept his promise. Upset and disappointed because he had said that the filming would be better, when in fact he was just exploiting her in front of the cameras. She stood up, grabbed her coat, and walked out.

24

Nora didn't return to filming that day. Fortunately both Hassan and Emil were working, so she could stay away completely. The accountant had told her that wages took priority when a business went bankrupt, so she felt comfortable calling them in. She messaged Elnaz and explained that she needed a break from filming, which no doubt made her very unpopular. Maybe they could film a few scenes with Henrik on his own; it was his show after all. And she would be spending the whole evening putting up decorations, so she would be making her contribution.

She spent the rest of the day doing housework, then took a trip to the liquor store. She browsed the shelves with the evening in mind, and picked up a bottle of ordinary mulled wine and a bottle of that year's special—Forest, with a hint of pine needles and birch resin—which sounded okay. She added a bottle of red for when the sweet taste of the mulled wine got to be a bit too much. She'd sent a message about the change of plan to the girls, and to her surprise both Bea and Maryam were free.

She continued on to the grocery store and bought two blue cheeses to go with the gingerbread cookies, plus a bottle of alcohol-free mulled wine in case any of her friends were pregnant again.

When she got back to her street, she saw two men with a cherry picker hanging up Christmas decorations. Farther along, the lights were already on. Thick fir garlands adorned with red silk ribbon and tiny lights were draped between the buildings, with a gold-colored bell in the center. She put down her bags by the door leading up to her apartment and quickly checked on the patisserie. The production team seemed to have left, but Emil and Hassan were busy serving a long line of customers.

As she walked into her apartment, her phone pinged with a message.

Sorry, but I've been called into work this evening—it sucks! I don't suppose you can postpone? It's our tradition! Bea wrote.

A second later she received a message from Maryam. Arvid has picked up some kind of bug and Stefan has it too. So sorry but won't make it. Please can we do it another day?

Nora felt deflated. Then she took a deep breath; she'd coped with far worse.

No problem. I'd love to postpone, but in TV world it's Christmas tomorrow. I'll pour myself some wine and get those decorations up in record time! she replied.

Take the bottle I gave you, Tess wrote.

I drank that weeks ago, Nora answered with a dancing emoji.

She grabbed the cheeses, one bottle of mulled wine, and the bottle of red and went downstairs. When she walked into the café, Emil's face lit up. "We've had a fantastic day—it might be a record! And this place looks amazing!"

"Brilliant renovation," Hassan said as he swept beneath the tables and chairs.

"It's great, isn't it?" Nora agreed.

"And the new rolls are a hit—we sold out in no time."

The boys helped Nora carry the boxes of decorations into the café. Then she checked the day's take.

"Best day of the year," she said with a big smile. "Well done, both of you."

After the boys left, she locked the door, poured some mulled wine into a pan, and gently warmed it. She put some gingerbread cookies on a plate, the cheeses on another, then carried everything through to the café.

She put on her favorite Christmas playlist and got to work untangling lights and extension cords.

She put a piece of creamy blue cheese on a cookie, popped it in her mouth, and closed her eyes. It reminded her of her mother and that last Christmas. She hadn't been able to eat much by that stage, but Nora had taken this very same cheese and gingerbread cookies to her mother in hospice. Nora had spent those final days keeping vigil. When her mother seemed to be listening, Nora had reminisced about Christmases past. One evening when her mother was sleeping, Nora had felt a surge of rage. She was suddenly furious that her mother wasn't going to be around anymore. Angry that she was going to be left behind. The same feeling overwhelmed her again as she sat in the newly renovated café, but this time her anger was tempered with grief.

"It's all so empty, Mom," she said out loud.

Her eyes filled with tears. Tommy Körberg and Sissel Kyrkjebø sang *Christmas Is Here*, and she let the tears flow. She wiped her eyes, but the tears kept on coming. She'd loved this song ever since she was a little girl. It reminded her of the sense of anticipation she had experienced back then and the wonderful sense of security that her mom and dad gave her. Why had it all been taken away?

25

1945

High summer had come to Bergslagen. The bakery was almost unbearably hot, even though it was still morning. Nils removed a tray from the large oven, puffing and blowing as the heat surged toward him, but then he inhaled the smell of the freshly baked bread. He had spent the last month experimenting with Tuula's sourdough. The Finnish rye bread was wildly popular, and he could see great potential with the sourdough. He had been thinking about what his father had said about frozen food in the future, and had worked out that a small, flat loaf would freeze well. They could freeze the bread immediately after baking and deliver it as a frozen product; when it defrosted, it should taste almost as good as fresh bread.

He gazed at the perfectly golden-brown loaves on the tray. He had used both rye and wheat flour along with Tuula's sourdough, making it a mixture of Tuula's bread and the kind that Nils often baked at home.

The first rays of the sun found their way through the windows. He slid in a tray of bread and rolls; he was happy to help out the bakers, and they would have fresh rolls for breakfast when they arrived.

When the loaves had cooled a little, he tore off a chunk and tasted it. Perfect. The rye had a strong, rich flavor, but there was also a smooth sweetness thanks to a bit of syrup he had added. He let it cool for a bit, then wrapped two of the loaves in a cloth with some butter, and biked over to his father's office.

His father was already hard at work when Nils knocked on the door.

"Come in!" His face lit up when he saw Nils in the doorway. "Is that freshly baked bread I smell?"

"It is. I've been experimenting with *fru* Anttila's sourdough."

"I see." His father's expression darkened. Nils knew he'd heard about him and Tuula, but he hadn't said a word. Yet.

He unpacked the bread, cut a slice, spread it with butter, and passed it to his father.

He heard footsteps behind him.

"I've looked over the designs, Dad." Stig walked in with his nose in a file and didn't look up. "If we make use of the current storage area, we'd have space for another freezer room, which means we can expand our delivery area to include northern Uppland and southern Dalarna. I've been in touch with the local consumer associations and . . ." Only then did he glance up and notice Nils. "Oh, hi. I didn't know you were here." He saw the bread on the desk. "Great—freshly baked bread!"

"Yes—I've been trying out a few new recipes."

As Stig helped himself, Nils suddenly realized what his brother had been talking about.

"Are you planning to launch in Dalarna and northern Uppland?" Nils looked from his father to his brother and back again. He and his father had always planned this kind of thing together—why hadn't they involved him this time?

"We are. It was Stig's idea; it doesn't involve much more travel for our delivery drivers, and there's room in the trucks. We weren't sure about freezer space, but as you just heard, Stig has been working on that."

Nils swallowed hard. So his brother was planning major changes to key parts of the business, while Nils was still slogging away in the bakery. Had he been demoted?

Stig tried the bread. "Wow—this is delicious!"

"Yes." Nils took a deep breath. "I thought it would freeze well, and we could deliver it as a frozen product. Because the loaves are so thin, they'll freeze quickly, and thaw in no time. If we freeze them immediately after baking, the quality will be comparable with fresh bread."

Father tasted. "*Mmm* . . . Not bad. Not bad at all. I like your thinking."

"The only thing I'm not sure about is how we solve the issue of transportation from the bakery to the deep freeze room, if it has to be as fresh as possible," Stig said.

Nils suppressed a sigh. "It only takes a minute in the van to go from the bakery to the freezer, so it can be frozen while it's still steaming from the oven." It bothered him that Stig had opinions—was he going to have to run everything past his brother now? "I've got a good name for this bread too," he continued. "I thought we could call it Tuula's Tasty Bread."

Father coughed, almost choked. "You want me to name our bread after a fucking Finn?"

Nils was shocked. He had never heard his father talk about anyone that way. It seemed to be quite an overreaction. Maybe it was because of the whole Birgit Berglund business. His father hadn't mentioned her name again, but he'd made it clear that Nils was letting him down by refusing to court her.

Father put down the bread. "You know people have seen you two together in the village?"

Nils didn't respond.

Stig discreetly backed out of the room.

"The war is over now, and it's time for us to get moving on things," his father said. "Rationing will come to an end, and we want to be ready." He got to his feet. "Do you understand, Nils? We can take this company far beyond Bergslagen. We can sell our bread and cakes across the country. We've got the operations, we've got the plans, all we need is permission from the local council. Which means I need Berglund."

He walked over to the window, gazed out at the street and the river. Nils looked out too. Storm clouds had gathered. The air in the room was oppressive, suffocating. The rushing waters of the river were dark. His father turned to him. "And what is Berglund going to say when he discovers that you're gallivanting around town with a Finnish widow? Dining at the Stadshotell? Strolling through the streets and sitting in the café?"

Nils took a deep breath, summoning his courage. "To be honest, I don't understand why that's any of Berglund's business."

His father gave a start. "What are you saying?"

"I'm saying that what I choose to do is up to me. How I spend my evenings and weekends, and with whom."

Father took three rapid steps toward Nils. "I've worked tirelessly for years to grow this company. For your sake. For Stig's sake. I do it for this family. I thought we were in agreement that we would do whatever it took to make it a success. And that doesn't mean running around after other women. What's wrong with you? Birgit is a much better bet than that Finn with two kids!" Father slammed his fist down on the desk.

Nils gazed at him steadily. "I have no intention of marrying Birgit."

"But you'd be happy to marry a Finn? Are you going to raise her Finnish brats?" Father snorted, shook his head. "I hoped you'd come to your senses so that I wouldn't have to argue about it." His expression was almost pleading. "We can't afford to lose any more time. The application is all ready to go; all we need is the council's formal approval."

"I don't understand. You and Folke Berglund were celebrating, the council was on board with our plans—what does any of this have to do with me and Birgit?"

Father sighed wearily. "She likes you, and Folke wants to give his little girl whatever she wants. He assumed you would start courting her, but nothing has happened. The council approved our application to carry out alterations, but this is about the change of use so that we can start the deep-freezing side of the operation." He shook his head again. "If we don't get permission, it will be your fault."

"My fault?"

"Yes, because you're refusing to do what you can to help. Instead you're planning to marry *her*."

"I have no idea if I'm going to marry Tuula, I have no idea who I'm going to marry, but what I do know is that the choice will be mine. And Tuula's children are wonderful—I would have no problem with raising them." Nils walked out of his father's office and slammed the door behind him.

◆ ◆ ◆

When the other bakers were leaving for the day, Tuula lingered. Nils saw her through the window, sweeping up flour and glancing toward his office. He'd hidden in there all day, buried himself in work.

Eventually he emerged and gave her a quick kiss on the lips. The packers and drivers were still in the packing room, so he had to be discreet. They didn't mind being seen together around town, but they both felt it was best to keep a low profile at work. They hardly even spoke to each other when anyone else was nearby.

"First time I've seen you today," Tuula said with a smile.

"I had a lot of work to catch up on." His smile was strained. "By the way, I've got a surprise for you. It's just an idea, but I'd like to see what comes of it."

He went over to the second batch of dough, which had been proofing since the day before. "This is made with your sourdough." After kneading it a bit, he shaped the flat loaves and slid the tray into the oven. "I'm trying to persuade my father to sell it."

She nodded encouragingly. "He usually listens to you."

Her face was pink with the warmth of the bakery, and there were tiny beads of sweat along her hairline. He wanted to brush them away. He wanted to take her down to the sea for a swim. Unless she had to hurry home to the children, of course.

"We're . . . We're not exactly getting along at the moment." Nils peered in through the glass door of the oven.

Tuula looked at him searchingly. "Why? Has something happened?" She placed a hand on his shoulder.

"It's nothing, just a disagreement."

"You're not quarreling about me, are you?"

How could she know that? But she wasn't dumb. She knew that people in the village were talking. He still didn't want to worry her.

"No, no, it's just a couple of things to do with the business. Don't worry about it. At least I got him to try the bread, and he liked it. It would be great if we could add it to our offering."

The loaves were ready in no time, and he removed the tray. "I want to call it Tuula's Tasty Bread."

She looked at him, and in a second she was in his arms, kissing him.

As usual he felt as though he were floating. He was so happy with her, so free. Whatever happened with the business, it was worth it. This was what love was supposed to feel like—and now that he had experienced it, he knew he couldn't live without it.

26

Henrik was taking one of his evening strolls around Västervik. It had become something of a habit after dinner with the production team. The air was fresh, and the snow that had fallen earlier had melted away. People complained about the winters in southern Sweden, but he loved them. There was a melancholy beauty to the barren landscape, and the fact that no one expected snow in the south meant that they weren't disappointed when "the real winter" didn't make an appearance. Not being disappointed could be nice sometimes. As he walked through the streets, glistening with rain, he saw a couple out walking their dog, then a group of friends leaving a restaurant. There were people around, but no rushing crowds or traffic.

He found himself outside Nymans and stopped; the lights were on. Of course—Nora was putting up the Christmas decorations tonight. Given what she'd said earlier, he was expecting to see Santa's elves working away inside. Instead he saw Nora sitting alone at a table with a small mug in her hand. She looked lost in thought, and then she rubbed her cheek with one hand as if she was . . . crying? There were several boxes on the floor next to the coffee machines. Advent candle bridges had been placed in the windows, but they weren't lit. She seemed to have a lot left to do. Judging by the number of boxes and her Christmas decorating aspirations, she was probably in for a long night.

He hadn't managed to shake off the feeling after the previous day's kiss. He hadn't planned it. Although he had intended to flirt with her for the sake of the show, it had simply happened. She was standing so close to him, he loved the smell of her, and . . . It had shut her up as well, of course. The sudden and immediate attraction he had felt baffled him. Then there was the fact that the kiss had been fantastic—which didn't make anything any clearer.

His plan had been to continue to flirt lightly with her during filming today, but her objections to the business with the dough had made it impossible. In a way he understood; one minute they were provoking her into outbursts of rage, and then he kissed her, only to ridicule her skill as a baker the very next day.

Nora stood up, put down her mug, and went over to the boxes. Henrik moved closer to the door, and heard the muted sound of holiday music.

The decorations had to get done if they were going to be able to film tomorrow. He had to help her.

He tapped gently on the glass and she looked up, a strand of tinsel in her hand. She peered into the darkness, then raised her eyebrows, dropped the tinsel, and came over to unlock the door.

"Hi—what are you doing here?"

"Hi—would you like some help?"

At first she looked wary and defensive, as she so often did, but then she relaxed and smiled. She had a lovely smile, the kind that lit up her whole face, and he felt a pleasant warmth spread through his body.

"Okay, why not?" she replied, not moving.

"Er . . . Can I come in?"

"Sorry." She shook her head and there it was again, that lovely smile. She held open the door, and as he came in his hand brushed against hers. She quickly pulled away, but that small touch had sent a tingle up his arm and through his body like an electric shock. He closed the door and followed her inside.

"Would you like some of this year's special mulled wine?" She nodded toward a bottle on one of the wooden tables, next to a plate of gingerbread cookies and two cheeses. "I've got red wine, too, and ordinary mulled wine, but that's up in the apartment. My friends were supposed to be here, but something came up for a couple of them, and the others couldn't make it on such short notice."

Henrik felt a pang of guilt, which he didn't like. She had volunteered to be on his show after all; it wasn't his fault that they had to move the decorating schedule up.

She held up the bottle. "Flavored with pine needles and birch sap, apparently."

"Sounds somewhat promising. I haven't been impressed by some of their other experiments."

"Tropical fruits?"

"Exactly—not very Christmassy. More like a trendy summer soda."

She nodded. "I couldn't agree more." Then she looked at him in shock, probably because she was thinking the same he was—that this was the first time they'd agreed on something. She disappeared into the bakery with the bottle.

He plugged in the extension cords that were laying on the table, then connected the candle bridges, illuminating the windows with that soft, warm glow that only Christmas could bring. The effect couldn't have been more different than the harsh light of the gigantic Advent star at his father's house.

"Aren't they lovely?" Nora said when she came back. "We've had them since our very first Christmas here, when my grandmother took over the patisserie. They were made by a factory in town that's long gone. I've had them repaired several times, but I think they're wonderful."

He inspected the brass bridges, with their seven candles lined up on curved arms, adorned with tiny wreaths, each one studded with minute gold-colored pine cones. The central section was made up of three sturdy brass rings. "They're beautiful."

She handed him a steaming mug. He inhaled the aromas of pine and birch, and it made him feel as if he were sitting in a wood-fired sauna in Norrbotten. His mother's family lived near there, and he suddenly longed to visit his relatives up there; it had been a while. He took a sip, savoring the classic mulled wine spices as well as the sharpness of the pine needles and the acidity of the birch sap.

Nora emptied a box onto the table. Advent stars, a porcelain nativity scene, a wooden church, countless elves and Santas, tinsel, lanterns, and candlesticks tumbled out. They set to work, and he followed her instructions without question. It felt good to bury the hatchet temporarily, because he was pretty sure they would have differing views on a number of issues over the next few days.

Nora handed him a pile of red embroidered cloths, which he laid out on the tables. Then came the slightly shabby wooden candlesticks. Henrik set them out and stuck a candle in each one. Not exactly elegant, but certainly very charming. Nora climbed up onto a stool to hang up one of the Advent stars in the side window, then swore. "Damn. It looks like the nails were removed during the renovations." She looked at Henrik. "I'll go and get some more." She headed into the bakery and returned with a toolbox. They hammered in nails, hung the stars, and plugged them in. Finally she picked up a big cardboard star and carefully unfolded it. "This goes in the front window." She climbed onto the stool, but couldn't quite reach. She stretched too far, lost her balance for a second. He caught her, but she pulled away and straightened up.

"Sorry," she said. The wariness was back.

The warmth and feeling of her body lingered, and Henrik took a deep breath.

Nora looked at him and quickly hung the star. Then she climbed down and fetched her empty mug. "I need some more wine—how about you?" Her cheeks were flushed—from the wine, the heat—and maybe what had just happened? Her breathing was rapid; he could see her chest heaving.

"Please." He followed her into the kitchen, and they warmed up the rest of the bottle. As the contents of the pan began to steam, she turned to him.

"Aren't you going to apologize for what happened the other day?"

"You mean yesterday? When you stormed out?"

"No, I mean at the book event." She cleared her throat. "When you kissed me."

He gazed at her for a long time. "Why should I apologize? It was a fantastic kiss." A frank comment, but why lie? He thought about how soft her lips had been and the heat radiating from them. He was suddenly aware that he was standing very close to her. That he could easily kiss her again. Then there was a hissing noise, and Nora gave a start. The wine was boiling furiously, splashing over onto the hot plate. Henrik removed the pan, while Nora grabbed some paper towels and wiped down the stove. They filled the thermos and returned to the café in silence, then poured themselves some wine and sat down.

"I know the production team had something to do with that kiss," Nora said slowly, blowing on her drink as steam curled into the air. "I mean, the idea that you should flirt with me and then kiss me, but . . ."

"Listen," Henrik broke in. "Don't you think this could benefit both of us? A little flirtation, a kiss or two? It would make the show more popular. And like I said, it was a fantastic kiss, wasn't it?"

"It wouldn't be the worst thing," she conceded, but he knew she felt the same way he did. He had seen her reaction, and surely a kiss couldn't feel fantastic for just one person, could it? "It's just that you know so much about me," Nora went on. "My whole situation, the fact that I've made such a mess of things here, and that kiss was so . . . intimate somehow."

He took a cookie and topped it with cheese. He had to take her seriously, though he didn't quite understand which part of the intimacy she didn't like.

"I'm sorry, Nora—I didn't think of it that way. I apologize if you think I crossed a line."

She shook her head. "It's fine. I don't feel like you took advantage of me or anything. And I'm prepared to admit that it was a wonderful kiss." There was a faint glint in her eyes, and they looked at each other in silence for a while. He lost himself in those blue eyes. He inhaled sharply, as if he'd forgotten to breathe.

"I was confused more than anything," Nora went on, "but now I get it. The whole situation is kind of confusing. I don't know what's genuine and what isn't. But now I realize you did it for the cameras, and that's okay."

Henrik nodded slowly. For some reason he felt the need to change the subject. "By the way, the production company has given me the green light for the money." He hadn't mentioned it before because he'd been worried that the transfer wouldn't go through, but he'd checked and the payment had been made today. "You've received enough to cover your staffing costs for the rest of filming and through the end of December."

She looked shocked. "That's too much."

"It certainly is not. The production company will also cover any other expenses you have during filming—ingredients, electricity, whatever you need."

She frowned. "I don't know if that feels right."

"We're doing it to help you, and to make sure we can finish filming. Most of the money is already in your business account."

"But . . ."

"Consider it payment for your participation."

"Do you do that for everyone on the show?"

"No . . ." He hesitated. "We haven't had anyone in this kind of financial trouble before." Then he smiled. "This season is important. Very important for me."

"I can't accept all that money. It's wrong."

"Look, if your business goes bust, the production company stands to lose a great deal more money than what we're investing in you." He realized he needed to be honest, as she had been with him. "The problem is that TV24 isn't satisfied with the ratings. If we have to cancel this project, that will be the end of *Let's Get Baking*." He paused. "So in order to boost the ratings, they've proposed various angles, and the idea that there might be some kind of romance between us is their latest suggestion."

She thought for a moment, sipped her wine. "I'm sorry to hear about the ratings." She took a deep breath. "I'm really grateful for everything you and the team are doing. Even if it's confusing, I'm on board. Sounds like a little flirting could be beneficial for both of us."

"Cool." Henrik held out his mug. "*Skål* to that." Now he had an excuse to kiss her again.

"*Skål.* By the way, how are the plans for your own bakery going?"

"Moving forward. The decision will be made at the board meeting on Monday."

"Seriously?" She smiled. "That's exciting! So after that you can get started?"

He didn't feel particularly excited. "Yes, but only if everyone votes in favor."

"And if they don't?"

"Then it's dead in the water."

"But why can't you open the place on your own?"

He looked at her in surprise.

"Do you really need the board's approval?"

"I . . . It's just that everything I do is with my family. I'd really like for the Eklunds to be on board with it. I already have one failed project behind me, something I started up on my own, and . . . I think it would be better if . . ."

"If you had a big company behind you?" Nora frowned. "Can't you see how ironic it is that you travel around fixing up bakeries all over the country, and yet you're too . . ." She broke off.

"Too much of a coward to open my own?"

"You're very good at telling everybody else what they're doing wrong."

He nodded slowly. "I guess that is kind of ironic."

Although her opinions often irritated him, he appreciated her honesty. She was direct without being nasty or supercilious—something he wasn't used to. This kind of honesty was new to him, and it meant a lot.

He looked at her. He couldn't imagine what it was like not to have any family. He and his siblings had a complicated relationship, but at least they were there. And his mother meant the world to him. Life really wasn't fair, and he hoped he would be able to provide some support to Nora, who was all alone.

They got back to decorating, setting out Santa on his sleigh with his reindeer, and lots of elves in the front window. Then they hung thick wreaths on red silk ribbons on either side of the large Advent star. When they were done, the place looked lovely—festive and cozy. It would go over very well on TV.

As they folded up the empty boxes, Nora said, "All I have to do now is buy a tree, but no one is selling them yet."

"I'm sure I can fix that. What kind do you like? Let me guess—Norway spruce?"

"Actually I love a Nordmann fir, but I usually go for a Norway spruce. It's a classic, and it smells wonderful."

"So I was right?"

She gave a wry smile. "I'd really like a Nordmann, but let's go with the spruce."

"What's stopping you from choosing a Nordmann fir?"

She remained silent for a few seconds, then shrugged. "Because it's always been that way. We've always had a spruce, that's just how it is."

He managed to stop himself from saying that a lot of things had always been that way—this wasn't the time for a snide comment.

"You seem to have plenty of traditions too," she added with a smile. "The Eklund family's fairy-tale Christmases."

The actual Christmas holiday was nothing like the celebration they staged for the cameras in November every year, but he couldn't tell her that.

"Baking gingerbread cookies, the marzipan competition, preparing the ham and all those fun activities like making wreaths and huge flower arrangements," Nora went on without a hint of sarcasm.

It was Henrik's turn to shrug. "Like I said the other day, things in our family are a little . . . tense. It's not like on TV."

"No? I've always envied your wonderful Christmases, a fantastic blended family where everyone loves everyone else."

He snorted. "In reality, we're a blended family where everyone hates everyone else and is jealous of everyone else and . . ." He broke off. What had he just said? Somehow he couldn't stop himself. "Christmas with my father is vile. I've spent the holiday with my mom and her partner for the last couple of years. We don't go over the top with traditions; I have so many terrible memories associated with Christmas that I no longer find it particularly enjoyable."

She gazed at him. "I'm sorry to hear that."

"That's the way it is when Hasse Eklund is your father."

"So . . . how is it?" she asked gently.

Henrik shook his head. "When I was nine years old, Christmas Eve was completely ruined because I spilled some water during lunch. It's always been like that. Everything I did was wrong. I knocked the glass over, and the water went everywhere. It was a pure accident, but my father just kept saying over and over again how clumsy I was. So fucking clumsy."

"And how did you react?"

"I got upset, which he hated. *You're too sensitive, Henrik.*" He imitated his father's deep voice—how often had he heard those words? "That's why I like TV. I can pretend to be someone else. I follow the script, and it all goes according to plan." He cleared his throat; he hadn't intended to reveal so much, or to express such strong feelings. And yet . . . the way they were talking now was genuine. And he loved it.

She nodded. "That makes sense."

"Thank you," he said quietly. "I'll speak to the production team, see if we can get ahold of a tree. Maybe we could trim it in one of the episodes," he added in an attempt to change the subject and shake off the tenderness and intimacy that had infused their conversation. It was all too much.

"Yes, that's fine, but . . ." She looked a little uncertain.

"Let me guess—there's a tradition associated with the tree?" He couldn't help laughing.

She sighed. "It's just that I've always chosen the tree myself. In the middle of the day so you can check it out properly, with a thermos of mulled wine." She glanced at the green thermos on the table. "That thermos. My friend Bea and her family come along, too, and choose their tree at the same time."

"We'll make sure you can do that—it'll work beautifully for the show."

Nora nodded. "Thank you. And thank you for all your help."

Those blue eyes made him think that the honesty and intimacy between them might easily lead to something more.

27

Filming over the next few days was a lot more pleasant. When Nora presented her pared-back list of baked goods—which Henrik had already praised when there were no cameras present—he made a few suggestions and they bickered a little as usual, but they also had some fun. And she found she had nothing against the flirtation—a smile that lasted a fraction of a second too long, a teasing but warm remark. In fact, she had to remind herself that it was just for the show. But she was starting to enjoy spending time with Henrik. For real. Or rather—no, it wasn't for real at all.

On Saturday the production team had arranged for Nora to go and buy a Christmas tree, and then there would be a break in filming because Henrik had to attend the board meeting in Stockholm.

When Nora met up with the team on Saturday morning, Henrik was already there with a dark-blue knapsack over his shoulder. "I've taken care of the mulled wine." He fished out the green thermos. "And some gingerbread cookies." He held up a tin. "So I assume we're good to go."

"Absolutely." The fact that he had remembered these details gave her a lovely warm feeling, but she told herself it was only because she wasn't used to him being so considerate.

It was a windy day, and she was glad she'd chosen her warm quilted jacket. She had also opted for her wool hat, mittens, and thick socks inside her boots. She had made a special effort; she wanted to be warm, but she also wanted to look good.

Henrik was wearing a gray quilted jacket, jeans, a red wool hat, and heavy winter boots. The lumberjack vibe suited him. For the first time she was looking forward to the day's filming. This wasn't going to be about her and her shortcomings; they were just going to buy a Christmas tree, and she couldn't possibly be criticized for that.

"Ready?" Ted said. "I thought we'd start out here. The Christmas lights are already up, and you'll stroll down the main street. We'll film a few scenes with the two of you walking and chatting before we reach the square." The camera operators took up their positions, two in front of them and one behind. Ted waved his hand, and Nora moved a little closer to Henrik. "Off you go," said Ted. "It doesn't matter what you talk about, there won't be any sound. This is just for background and atmosphere." He clapped his hands and filming began.

They set off and turned onto the main street, which was bathed in misty winter sunshine. The street was adorned with white silk ribbons and enormous silver-colored snowflakes.

"Beautiful day," Henrik said, squinting against the low sun.

"It is."

They continued in silence.

"Any plans for the weekend?" Henrik asked eventually.

Nora nodded and smiled. "Yes . . . well no, not really." Her expression was skeptical. "Are you really interested, or are you just asking because they're filming?"

He laughed. "I'm really interested."

She laughed, too, and shook her head at the absurdity of the situation. "I'll be spending most of my time at the patisserie."

"Do you ever get tired of it?"

"Not the work itself, but working such long hours is hard. And of course not knowing if I'll last the month is exhausting. But I'll keep fighting, because I love it."

Henrik nodded thoughtfully.

When they reached the square, a young girl yelped with delight when she saw them. Filming stopped, and the girl hurried over to ask Henrik for a selfie. Meanwhile Nora looked around the square, and was completely blown away by the Christmas world before her.

Elnaz came over to join her. "Our events company worked their magic," she explained, looking pleased with herself.

A proper Christmas market had appeared, with small red booths selling handmade gloves, wooden candlesticks, and other crafts, and plenty of Christmas trees. Fairy lights were looped between the booths, and the sweet smell of roasted almonds hung in the air.

Filming resumed, and Henrik served them both steaming mulled wine from the thermos. They took a stroll around the square so that Nora could inspect the trees. They stopped by a long row propped against a wall.

"How about this one?" Henrik held out a tree.

"Too thin at the bottom."

"Right."

They kept going. The smell of the firs, the dry air, and the taste of mulled wine made it feel exactly like the beginning of Advent. The classic mulled wine Henrik had chosen was perfect for the occasion.

"This one?"

Nora took a sip of her wine, then examined his offering. She sighed. "Too top heavy."

After the sixth tree, Henrik was the one who was sighing. "I'm going to need plenty of energy to get through this."

Elnaz was beaming, delighted that they sounded like an old married couple bickering over the choice of tree. Even Ted looked pleased. And Nora was having a lovely time, much better than she'd expected. Once again she had to remind herself that this wasn't real. But there was nothing wrong with enjoying it; it was a whole lot better than feeling angry all the time.

Henrik went over to the booth selling roasted almonds. A woman in a thick fur coat tipped two scoops into a brown paper cone and handed it to Henrik. He held it out to Nora, who helped herself as she continued toward the next batch of trees, totally focused on her goal. She glanced at the Nordmann firs, their needles gleaming silver-blue in the sunlight, then continued on to the Norway spruces.

She stopped. "That one."

She had found the perfect specimen—bushy from top to bottom, not a single branch out of place. She pulled it out so that she could examine it in all its glory.

"Fantastic," he agreed. "Like something out of a painting by Jenny Nyström."

Nora nodded. All that was missing was the perfect family surrounding the tree.

The stallholder bound the tree in twine and passed it to Henrik. The cameras captured the scene as he hoisted it onto his shoulder, then set off across the square with Nora by his side. Suddenly the tree slipped, but Nora caught it. The needles scratched her face and she shrieked in surprise, which made Henrik laugh. He reclaimed the tree, but a branch got caught in her hair, and he carefully worked it free. Then she felt something wet on her forehead. Was it raining? She looked up at Henrik; he had snowflakes in his thick beard. They both glanced up at the sky, which a few moments ago had been clear blue. Now it was milky white, the snow drifting slowly down from the clouds.

She smiled at him. "This is almost too good to be true!" For a moment she forgot the cameras and lost herself in his brown eyes. She only came to her senses when Ted waved at them to start walking, and they set off carrying the tree between them.

"It's perfect," Henrik said. "Elnaz and Ted will be delighted—this will be great on TV," he whispered.

Nora laughed again, and realized that she hadn't laughed this much during any of the previous filming days. Or for a very long time, to be honest.

As they made their way back to the patisserie, Henrik told her about the time when he, his mom, and her partner, Vanja, went into the forest to chop down a Christmas tree, but were caught red-handed.

They propped the tree against a wall next to the café door. Henrik looked at her for a moment, and she remembered how she had felt when he kissed her at the bookstore.

When the filming ended, the team went inside to warm up, and Nora and Henrik remained outside. Nora couldn't help laughing as Elnaz ran inside, shivering.

"What's so funny?" Henrik wanted to know.

"You guys seem to have underestimated winters in Småland. It can get really cold here."

"I think I've dressed appropriately," he replied, looking down at his clothes.

"Absolutely. This is a good, thick jacket." She placed her hand on his upper arm. A slightly too intimate gesture, but she left her hand there and smiled at him. Oh God, she was flirting and the cameras weren't even there. She took her hand away, but kept smiling. He smiled back.

"Listen, I've got something to tell you—a surprise," he said. "I should probably wait until we start filming again next week to tell you, but . . ." He paused briefly. "No, I can't wait. I have good news. Gunnebo has ordered your Lucia buns for the beginning of Advent."

Nora's hands flew to her face. Gunnebo was the town's biggest employer, and she didn't know whether she ought to celebrate or panic. "Seriously? That's a massive order!"

Henrik nodded. "It is. Apparently someone who organizes their conferences was at the bookstore event, and she loved your food—they want sandwiches and Lucia buns. Not only that, it's a regular order for every Monday throughout December."

Nora laughed and threw her arms around his neck. She felt his rough beard against her cheek. The feeling of a *man* made her body wake up. This was something very different from the Veg Guy and Mange Lund, who seemed like boys in comparison. Much to her surprise, she kissed him. His lips were warm, a sharp contrast to the chilly air, and he kissed her back, hungrily. Pulled her around the corner into the alleyway, pushed her up against the wall of the building, and kept on kissing her. She wrapped her arms around his neck, enjoying the sensation of those soft, wonderful lips as the snowflakes drifted gently down.

When they pulled apart, he looked at her for a long time as he caught his breath. "That was unexpected."

"Yes. But I'm not going to apologize—it was a fantastic kiss."

He laughed. "I agree." He tucked a strand of hair inside her hat. "You've got a lot to do tomorrow, and next week is going to be hectic with filming and lots of baking, so I suggest you go home and have a quiet evening. We've finished filming for today."

Nora went up to the apartment on trembling legs. She had kissed Henrik Eklund. *She* had kissed Henrik Eklund. She would never have imagined such a thing. Never.

Henrik was right; she deserved an evening at home. And she wouldn't give a second's thought to what she had just done. If there was one thing she was good at, it was avoiding thinking about that kind of situation.

Just before closing time, she went down to say hi to Emil and Hassan and cash out. They'd had another good day. If their earnings continued to improve like this, they would soon turn a corner.

When she had locked up, she went to the grocery store and bought a pint of vanilla ice cream and some fresh dumplings. Back at home, she heated up the dumplings, found a Christmas movie to watch—she chose *The Holiday*—and settled in.

When she had finished eating, she paused the movie and returned to the kitchen. She prepared a bowl of ice cream and mixed it with some gingerbread cookie dough crumbles. She couldn't understand why no ice cream maker had come up with this brilliant idea—ice cream with gingerbread cookie dough! There were plenty of cookie dough ice creams out there, but gingerbread had to be the best.

The dough was the one she had used for the cookies at the bookstore event, and she had to admit that her recipe and Henrik's made the perfect combination. The brown butter gave it a nuttier taste and brought out the flavor of the toasted spices. She sat down in front of the TV again and took another spoonful of ice cream. Oh God, were things going to be awkward when they saw each other again next week? She wasn't going to brood about that now. Or the kiss. What would be would be. Fortunately she had a few days to compose herself.

Had she behaved like a fool? Taken liberties? But he'd clearly enjoyed the kiss, hadn't he?

She sighed and lay down on the sofa. Why couldn't she stop thinking about this? Why couldn't she stop thinking about him? Maybe because she hadn't had a quiet evening at home for ages, and seemed to have forgotten how to relax. And maybe because she had chosen to watch one of the most romantic movies ever made! What an idiot.

Why had she kissed him? It was totally inappropriate, given their working relationship. Then again, what normal woman would have been able to resist kissing him today? Not a single one. He had looked so good in that gray quilted jacket, with the tree over his shoulder, and the red woolen hat that brought out the color of his brown eyes. And then there was the beard that made his smile so captivating. And that slightly dangerous, raffish smile.

She sighed loudly. Reminded herself that it *wasn't for real.* They might have kissed each other when the cameras weren't around, but no doubt it was simply an extension of the show as far as Henrik was concerned. A way to keep the flirtation and the spark alive for when filming started again.

She rewound the movie to the point where her mind had begun to wander. The first sight of Kate's cozy, snow-covered cottage. *A place like that would suit Henrik perfectly,* she thought. He seemed more like a country boy than a city dweller. She could picture him in front of an open fire in the evening, with a freshly cut fir tree beside him—a tree he had chopped down himself, of course, not bought from a market. Which wasn't even a real market. And she would fit perfectly right beside him.

28

1945

Tuula saw Nils several evenings a week that summer. She didn't like to leave the children, so he usually came over to her place when they had fallen asleep. Occasionally the children spent the night with Aino and Heikki, and then she and Nils were able to go for walks, have coffee and cakes somewhere, or have dinner at his home.

When the bakery closed for a week in July and everyone was given a week off, Nils suggested that Tuula and her kids accompany him to his summer cottage. "I want to go fishing as soon as we get there!" Matias said when Nils arrived to pick them up. Nils laughed and ruffled his hair, gave Tuula a kiss on the cheek, and patted Ritva's shoulder. Matias had been beside himself with excitement ever since Tuula told them about the vacation. Ritva had been more reserved, but now she, too, was smiling expectantly. A remarkable sense of calm suffused Tuula's body. This was the first time her little family had gone on a long journey together. An enjoyable journey, at least.

Tuula had been concerned about how the children would react when she started seeing Nils. She wasn't worried about them feeling that their own father was being replaced—Ritva hardly knew her father, and Matias didn't remember him at all. In fact, she was certain that it would be good for them to have Nils in their lives. But she was anxious about change. They had already been through so much, and for the first time in a long time their lives were stable. She could only hope that Nils would strengthen and contribute to that stability. To Tuula he meant security, and she thought he would be a good male role model for the children. Maybe she was jumping the gun, but their relationship felt so right. Someone who was so assured, so comfortable in their own skin would never desert her. She felt sure they would stay together.

The only fly in the ointment was that she had heard the gossip in the village. Things hadn't improved after the incident last week. Tensions between the Swedes and the Finns remained high, and she worried whether Nils would cope with that. She glanced at him as he confidently drove along. If not, surely he would have left her already?

They traveled through the undulating landscape, past fields of wheat, huge meadows, and evergreen and deciduous forests. Nils stopped at a country store to buy groceries when they were only a few minutes from the cottage. They all went inside, and Tuula found herself hoping the children wouldn't say anything. They usually spoke Swedish now, but of course they still had a Finnish accent. As long as the children kept quiet, no one would realize where they were from. With a bit of luck, they would be able to escape the stares and the gossip for a while. When the children started chattering away inside the store, she held her breath—but no one paid any attention to them. Tuula was ashamed of her thoughts. Who would accept them if Tuula herself didn't stand up for her own children?

The cottage lay by a lake, surrounded by dense forest, with no close neighbors. The children ran straight down to the lake for a swim. Tuula followed with their towels, and when Nils had carried their luggage and groceries inside, he joined them with a basket containing sponge cake, coffee, and juice. When the children had finished swimming, they wrapped themselves in their towels and sat down. They munched on slices of sponge cake and giggled as the crumbs they dropped were borne away by hungry forest ants. Tuula savored her coffee, which tasted particularly good here in the shade of the tall pine trees, beside the sparkling waters of the lake, and with the rays of the sun warming her legs.

After their picnic, they went for a walk in the forest and picked blueberries and wild strawberries. That night, Tuula and Nils prepared dinner together. They enjoyed fried herring and boiled potatoes and blueberries with cream for dessert. Then they all took an evening dip.

The children fell asleep early, and Tuula and Nils sat on the veranda watching the sun go down behind the treetops on the far side of the lake. Nils fetched two glasses of cognac. They finished off the rest of the sponge cake, with whipped cream and the remaining berries.

"Do your parents know we're here?" Tuula asked. The question had been nagging away at her. It wasn't just the talk in the village that bothered her, but what they said—that Nils's parents would never accept her.

Nils hesitated, then looked her in the eye. "I considered telling them that I was coming out here with friends, but I didn't want to lie about it—about you."

"And what did they say?"

"Mom didn't say anything, but Dad yelled enough for both of them. But this is my grandfather's house, which he left to me and Stig. My parents have looked after it over the years, but they have their own summer cottage. They don't have any jurisdiction over this place, so they can't stop me from being here."

Tuula nodded. She appreciated his honesty, even if the answer was upsetting. "Do you and your father usually get along well?"

He nodded. "We've never had anything to fall out about. We generally agree about most things as far as the business is concerned."

Never had anything to fall out about, she thought. Until now. She was overcome by a feeling of sorrow with a pang of bitterness, which took the joy out of the carefree summer evening. She knew she was the reason why Nils was at odds with his father.

As if he could read her mind, Nils put his index finger under her chin. "You're not the problem. The problem is my father and his expectations."

"Expectations? What does he expect of you?" Tuula just wanted to understand. She gazed at him in the golden light of the setting sun. He was wearing a white, short-sleeved polo shirt that showed off his muscular arms. He had a baker's arms and broad shoulders, and his body was athletic—maybe thanks to the soccer. She had never seen his body properly, so to speak, but had admired him in his clothes many times.

"They had a girl in mind for me. The daughter of one of my father's business associates."

"So you're . . . promised to someone else?" The thought made her head spin. She couldn't imagine him with another girl—he belonged to her. The very idea of someone else touching that firm upper body . . . the soft skin at the nape of his neck . . .

"No, no, absolutely not." His dark-brown eyes almost glowed in the light. "It's just . . . My father wants me to ask her out. He'd *like* me to marry her to smooth the path for some of his business dealings."

"I don't want to get in the way," she said quietly. *The daughter of one of his father's business associates.* Of course she would be a better partner for Nils. Tuula stretched her legs.

He placed his hand on her thigh and stroked it gently. "You're not getting in the way. I didn't want to ask her out, and when you came into my life, it made my decision even simpler. You have to believe me when I say she is nothing to me."

He leaned forward; she could smell his aftershave, his tanned skin. He kissed her softly, tentatively, and she responded in kind.

What was she going to do with this information? Now she knew his parents would never accept her and the children. His kiss deepened, as if to convince her, and she relaxed and pressed her body closer to his as his kisses became hungrier.

They had kissed like this before, but she had always stopped him before they took the next step. But here, with the lake and the forest as their only audience, and the cognac making her whole body feel pleasantly relaxed, she allowed herself to give in to the tingling sensation in her breast. It quickly spread down into her belly and beyond. She eagerly ran her hands over his shoulders and his arms, slipping them under his polo shirt, across his hard stomach. He kissed her neck as he continued to caress her thigh.

Eventually he pulled her to her feet and they staggered, still kissing, into the cottage and toward his bedroom. He undid a few buttons on her shirt, and then his warm hands were inside, stroking her shoulders.

She wanted this, but she couldn't help worrying that the children might wake up.

He sensed her hesitation, stopped, and looked at her.

"Forgive me if I'm going too fast," he whispered. "I've wanted to do this for such a long time, but I completely understand if you're not ready."

"It's not that, it's the children. I . . ." She glanced at their bedroom door.

"I get it," he interrupted her. "You don't need to explain." He slowly released her, gave her a kiss on the lips, and tucked her hair behind her ears. "It's late, and I'm guessing Matias will want to make an early start on our fishing trip in the morning," he said with a smile.

Tuula nodded slowly as she buttoned up her shirt.

They washed the dishes and tidied the kitchen, and then they said good night and went to their respective rooms. Tuula crawled into bed, but the silence made her feel restless. She tossed and turned, her desire for Nils pulsating through her entire body. She couldn't just lie here. What should she do? Go for a dip in the lake to cool her burning passion? She sighed and sat up in bed. There was only one thing she wanted to do. She got up, opened the door, tiptoed along to the children's room, and pushed the door open a fraction to check that they were both asleep. Then she headed for Nils's bedroom.

He was standing there waiting for her. She threw herself into his arms, kicked the door shut behind her, and at long last they fell into bed together.

She pulled off his shirt and lay down on top of him. Inhaled his smell, kissed his neck. He took off her nightgown and cupped her breasts gently in his hands before he began to stroke them. She rolled onto her back, longing to have him inside her. He settled beside her, caressing her whole body.

What's going on? she thought. Wasn't he going to thrust himself into her? But no, he carried on stroking her slowly, every part of her, and her desire continued to build. His index finger circled her nipples, and she shuddered with pleasure, unable to contain her desire.

"I want to feel every bit of you," he whispered. "And I want you to enjoy it."

His hand moved to her stomach, then to her more intimate parts. He slipped a finger inside her. She whimpered. She wasn't used to this. Juhani had been a tender lover, but it had all been over quite quickly. He had never taken his time like this, and she had never felt such pleasure.

He found the magic spot. Nils took his time, and Tuula's pleasure grew and grew until she could no longer resist him. She pressed herself to him, kissing him and muffling a scream against his neck as the dam broke, leaving her whole body trembling.

She lay beside him, panting. "That was . . . ," she gasped, unable to complete the sentence.

It wasn't long before she wanted more. More of *him*.

She began to kiss him again and ran her hands over his broad chest. Caressed the nape of his neck, his curly hair. She wanted to feel all of him. Her hands moved down to his manhood. She wanted him, wanted him inside her.

"Please," she whispered.

In the half light she saw his eyes sparkle, and those soft, full lips smiling. He rolled on top of her, kissing her as he entered her. He began to move rhythmically, and she heard herself moaning with each thrust. She pressed her hips against his, wanting him deeper inside her. He started to stroke that magic spot again, moving faster and faster as she responded. Then he let out a groan and gasped. She felt him grow inside her, and her pleasure spilled over again. Two more hard thrusts, and then he collapsed on top of her.

She would never be able to make love with another man. Not as long as Nils Eklund existed.

The days they spent at the cottage were like a long, blissful dream. The sun never stopped shining, they swam in the mornings, had lunch on the terrace, and in the afternoons they went for walks in the forest or Nils took the children fishing. They cooked and baked together. Tried out new recipes for bread and buns. Ate Tuula's Tasty Bread for breakfast with butter and thick slices of cheese, made sandwiches with it for afternoon picnics. She didn't want to return to Almtorp, and felt a pang of anxiety whenever she thought about the village. She worried the hatred toward the Finns would escalate when she was back.

On their last afternoon, Tuula had just put a batch of rolls in the oven and was standing on the terrace. Nils and the children were down on the jetty catching roach. She listened to the sound of a woodpecker hammering on a nearby tree as the smell of the bread reached her nostrils. She felt a strange sense of calm. Happiness, maybe? Perhaps she could begin to leave all her past difficulties behind her. Being here in this cottage with Nils and the children, it was as if she had become a different person, not the Tuula who was constantly thinking about the war, who lay awake at night thinking about her hometown and the house she had left behind. Her friends. Her mother and father. And Juhani, dead in a trench.

Here she was Tuula who had brought a pile of novels on vacation with her. Tuula who worked as a baker, swam in a lake, and spent her free time coming up with new recipes for cookies, buns, and bread. Tuula who weeded the flower beds around the cottage and packed picnic baskets for afternoon outings. Tuula who was in love.

Because it was true. She was in love with Nils. Everything was so easy, so carefree with him. He enjoyed beautiful sunsets, excellent dinners at the Stadshotell, a fun soccer match. And it allowed her to forget the war. Nils's main aim in life seemed to be to make her happy. He wasn't carrying any hidden trauma, he made her feel safe, and for the first time in several years, she was happy.

29

The buzzing of his phone woke Henrik. He had been lost in a wonderful dream about Nora, where they were doing considerably more than kissing. He blinked, looked around, and grabbed his phone from the nightstand. The message was something about a change to the board meeting. He would read it later. He put down the phone and sank back against the pillows, went back to thinking about Nora. That kiss yesterday had been unexpected. He had nothing against the idea that a flirtation for the cameras was on the way to becoming . . . what? Something real?

Suddenly he realized what he had just seen on his phone. He picked it up again, opened the message. The board meeting had been brought forward from Monday to tomorrow. *Tomorrow.* Or rather today—since it was the middle of the night.

What the hell was going on? Why had the meeting time been changed? It was normally the chair's PA who sent out the meeting information, but for some reason this message had come from Hasse himself.

He sent a message to his father: What's this about? Then he changed his ticket to the morning train.

Hasse replied when Henrik was standing at the snow-covered train station a few hours later. A message about the change of date had gone out earlier in the week—hadn't Henrik received it?

A knot formed in his stomach. Something wasn't right. He took a deep breath; maybe he was just being paranoid? However, bearing in mind the way his father had treated him recently, it seemed entirely possible that Hasse had deliberately withheld the details about the new time in order to unsettle him.

The train was delayed because of the snow. When it finally set off, it made good progress at first, and Henrik began to feel a little more optimistic that he would make it. He wanted to speak to everyone ahead of time and make sure they were still in favor of his plans. He knew that his father could get everyone in the room to do exactly as he wanted. Henrik needed some time to convince his fellow board members to stand up for him before the time came to vote.

When the train reached Nyköping, it slowed down, then crawled through the snowy landscape. Henrik nervously checked his watch. He was going to be at least half an hour late for the meeting.

A year. He had spent a whole year developing this bakery plan. He'd run the numbers, prepared the business plan, and put considerable time into creating his product line. He had searched for the right location and commissioned architectural drawings, organized fabric and paint samples, and created mood boards. And now he was going to lose it all. He knew they wouldn't wait for him if he was late. They would simply make their decision, make a note of his absence, then move on to the next item on the agenda.

He sighed as the train stopped yet again. He sent a message to Anders, the chair of the board, explaining that he was on the train from Västervik but was delayed because of the weather. He asked him to move the bakery discussion to the end of the agenda.

The train set off at a snail's pace; when they reached a tunnel, it stopped altogether. "Unfortunately we have to wait for an X2000," the driver informed everyone. Henrik shook his head. The meeting was starting right now. He wasn't going to make it; he would have to call his father.

No network coverage. What the hell? He was beginning to panic. He was going to miss the meeting. He was going to miss everything. He got up and walked through the carriage in an attempt find a cell phone signal. Eventually he spotted one tiny bar in the corner of the screen. He called his father's number. Stuttering signals rang out, and then it went to voice mail. He swore out loud and tried his sister. Camilla answered almost straightaway.

"Hello? Hello? Henrik?"

"Hi—can you hear me?"

"Hello?"

"Can you hear me?"

"I can't hear you properly. Everyone is here. We . . ." Camilla's voice disappeared. "Without . . ." She was gone again.

"Camilla? I'm here. Hello?" Henrik was almost yelling, even though he knew perfectly well that it wasn't going to do any good. His fellow passengers scowled at him.

He lost the connection altogether as the train began to move. He returned to his seat and tried again, but this time Camilla rejected the call. Then a text message came through: We have to begin. There's a lot on the agenda and we don't have time for technical glitches.

Those were his father's words. He could imagine Hasse snapping at Camilla.

When the train finally reached Stockholm, he ran out and grabbed a cab. The traffic was flowing well, and he arrived in minutes. He hurried upstairs, hoping the other agenda items had taken a lot of time.

He flung open the door. Tall candles were burning on the table, and the dark walls and tiled stove made everything extremely atmospheric. It was a lovely place for a winter lunch, but right now it felt more like a medieval torture chamber.

"Nice of you to join us." Hasse stared at Henrik over the top of his glasses. He was seated at the head of the table, of course. Camilla glanced up at him, then immediately looked down again. Tom was on Hasse's left-hand side. "However, you're in luck," Hasse added.

"We had a lot to get through," Anders explained, "but we put the bakery last on the agenda, and we've just reached it."

Henrik took a deep breath and sat down. He took out his laptop, typed in his password with trembling fingers, and found the relevant document. For some reason the program containing his presentation and all his notes refused to cooperate. He clicked frenetically on the window, but to no avail. He looked around the table. Hasse gazed wearily back at him. His siblings were concentrating on their printouts.

He was precisely the worthless waste of space his father thought he was, meeting every single one of Hasse's low expectations.

He reached for one of the printouts on the table. He didn't have his notes for support, but he knew most of his presentation by heart.

And yet he stammered and stuttered when he began to speak. When he reached the last page, he understood why. As he looked around the room, it was clear that everyone had already made their decision. He could feel it, and he could see it in his father's eyes. Henrik's presentation was merely a formality.

He thought about Nora and how capable and determined she was. To her the idea of running a business alone was perfectly simple and straightforward, while he couldn't even manage a fucking presentation. Was his father right when he said Henrik had had everything served up to him on a plate? Was that why he was so incompetent?

"Time to vote," Anders said. "All those in favor?" Anders held up his hand, as did Henrik, even though the vote was humiliating at best. He looked at his siblings. Tom leaned back on his chair, glanced at Henrik, then stared at the wall. Camilla was still focused on the presentation before her. The only one who met Henrik's gaze was his father, who kept his eyes fixed on Henrik without saying a word.

No more hands were raised. Henrik couldn't bear it for another second.

Anders didn't seem surprised by the result. It was obvious they had discussed the matter before Henrik arrived. It was a small consolation that Hasse hadn't managed to browbeat the board's external chair, but it didn't help.

"We had a brief discussion about this earlier," Hasse said. "You were late, so we went ahead without you. We all know you have no business acumen—you've already proved that in the past. So we simply dare not take the risk."

A waiter came in with a plate of beef Rydberg and put it down in front of Henrik. He had hardly touched his breakfast on the train, but the sight of the food made him feel nauseated.

Once again he thought about Nora and how driven she was. He ought to be able to do this, to ignore his father's words. He looked around at his family. "You do realize what an opportunity this was? We could have rented the perfect location at an unbelievable price—we'll never find anything like it again."

"As I said, it feels way too risky," Hasse said firmly.

No one else spoke for a few seconds.

"I need to pick up the kids," Tom said eventually.

"Okay, meeting closed." Anders looked sympathetically at Henrik, who got to his feet and left the room without looking at any of them.

"So why were you late?" Hasse caught up with him as he was walking down the stairs.

"I was in Västervik filming the Christmas special."

"You like your little towns, don't you?" Hasse chortled, but Henrik merely glared at him. "I believe there's been some buzz about your show," Hasse went on. "Even before the premiere."

Henrik simply nodded.

"Smart move, setting up a romance with the owner." Hasse was grinning now.

"We do what we have to, don't we? It will make good TV," Henrik replied dryly. "Just like we all pretend to love each other when we're filming *Christmas with the Eklunds*."

"Absolutely." Hasse was still smiling. "I admire you, I really do—not many people would go that far to save a show."

"Just like you've pretended to care about your kids all our lives, purely to satisfy a TV audience." Henrik no longer gave a fuck about what he said. He was so sick of his father's power games, of being so dependent on him. He didn't want to do this any longer.

When they reached the bottom of the stairs, Hasse patted Henrik on the shoulder. "Believe what you want, but I've given my children everything." He paused, looked at Henrik. "And never forget that the three of you need me. I'm the one who's made the company what it is today, and I'm the one who makes the decisions."

Henrik walked away without a word and hailed a cab. As if the day couldn't get any worse, he saw that he had a missed call from Don at TV24. There was also a text message.

> I've looked through what's been filmed so far and I've never seen anything more boring. What's happened? When I was there and the girl broke down, I thought we had something. But the romance thread is putting me to SLEEP. I'm dying of boredom here. I've spoken to Elnaz and Ted. Call me. You need to fix this.

30

Tuesday was a glorious winter's day. The snow that had fallen over the weekend sparkled in the sunshine.

Nora sensed the muted atmosphere as soon as she arrived for filming. Ted and Elnaz were involved in a quiet discussion, and Henrik only glanced at her. There was something evasive in his expression. He smiled, but the smile didn't reach his eyes.

She smiled back anyway. "Hi."

"Hi."

What was going on?

"How did the meeting go?" she asked as they walked over to the makeup corner.

"Not great, I'm afraid."

"I'm sorry to hear that."

He simply shrugged in response. A second later Elnaz came over and led him into the bakery, talking in a low voice. Nora felt a knot in her stomach; she didn't like this. She had finally felt as if they were all on the same side, and now everything seemed to have gone sideways.

When Henrik and Elnaz reappeared, Ted went through the day's schedule. They were going to discuss the selection of baked goods that Nora sold in the run-up to Christmas. When everyone was ready, she and Henrik took their places by the display counter.

"Okay, so today we're going to take a look at your product range in the lead-up to Christmas," Henrik began. "And I understand you've secured a large order from a local company for Lucia buns, so we have a lot to do."

"Exactly. It's the first Sunday in Advent this weekend, so people are going to want Lucia buns starting in a couple of days. I need to do as much preparation as I can."

"So . . ." Henrik set off toward one of the tables, and Nora followed him. "What do you usually bake for Christmas?" He pulled out a chair and sat down. "What does your December assortment look like?"

Nora sat down opposite him and opened up her big black recipe notebook. She flicked through yellowing pages spattered with years of cake batter and the odd greasy butter stain. It had been her great-grandmother's book originally; she had used it when she first got a job here at Nymans, and the family had continued to collect recipes in it over the years. "The first Sunday in Advent is one of our busiest days, and I usually bake quite an assortment. Wafer rolls, doughnuts, almond pastries, chocolate cookies, gingerbread cookies of course, toffee cookies . . ."

"I get it—lots of cookies." Henrik's expression was grim, but Nora smiled at him. Nothing could upset her when it came to baking for Christmas.

"Exactly. And lots of other things, of course."

"I see. I know how many different cakes and cookies you usually have on offer, this is going to be something of a cookie explosion. Sounds like you're planning to fill the shelves with even more products?"

She didn't like his tone or his cold and impersonal demeanor. There was no sign of the warmth that had sprung up between them. What was going on?

She looked him straight in the eye. "Correct. But I've always done it this way. Just as my mother and grandmother did it before me."

"Don't you understand that it's your ideas about tradition that have caused so many of your problems?" His tone was exaggeratedly sympathetic, as if he really cared about her. She took a deep breath, attempting to suppress the anger that was bubbling up inside her. Apparently there was something that could upset her when it came to baking for Christmas, and that was a pompous Henrik Eklund.

"Things don't always have to stay the same," he went on. "Not if it's at the expense of the patisserie's very existence. What would your mother say about this?"

"About what?"

"About the fact that you've let your patisserie fall apart."

Nora gripped the edge of the table. She had told him why tradition was important to her. Told him that every single cake and cookie was a link to the people she loved and remembered. Explained how important it was for her to bake those particular items because somehow it made her feel less lonely. How could he use her revelations against her?

"It's a way of remembering the people I've lost," she replied grimly.

"Oh, so you're doing it to honor your mother's memory." Henrik laughed. "We've already talked about this. You seem to think you're doing your mother a favor by making this place into some kind of mausoleum in her honor. But you're running your business into the ground. That's not honoring her memory, Nora. On the contrary. It's dishonoring her memory."

She stared at him in silence. *Dishonoring.* She couldn't believe that he was using things against her that she'd told him in confidence. *Mausoleum.* She snorted. How could he think it was perfectly acceptable to poke his nose into her life and her unhappiness, pretend to listen and understand, only to exploit it all and make sensationalist TV? Worst of all, she was dependent on his help if the patisserie was going to last the month.

She stood up and ripped off her apron. "Enough." She threw the apron at Henrik. "I'm sure this will make fucking great TV," she yelled. Elnaz was looking at the floor, but Nora couldn't help noticing the satisfied expression on Ted's face as she headed for the door, with the cameras following her.

Don's words echoed in Henrik's mind. Don had probably really wanted to see another panic attack, but Nora's walkout was probably the next best thing on Don's scale of humiliation. Henrik's words had come straight from Don, and he had followed Ted's instructions to the letter. And it felt completely wrong. When he called Don, his emotions had been all over the place. After the confrontation with his father, Henrik had been willing to do anything to boost ratings and show up his father. But now . . . Okay, so it was important to save the show, but did he want to continue with *Let's Get Baking* if its main aim had become the manipulation and humiliation of the participants? Nora had been brave enough to open up to him, and he had behaved with cruel disregard for her feelings.

He took a deep breath, leaped to his feet, and ran after her.

"Nora, wait. I . . . I'm so sorry." He shouted the words, and she stopped as she reached the door. Slowly turned around.

Henrik looked at Ted. "I refuse to do this anymore. I don't want a show where we deliberately provoke people and mess with their feelings. I'm done."

"But Henrik, Don and TV24 . . ."

"I don't give a shit about Don. I'm not doing it, okay? We've already got enough material. We're dropping that thread right now. I suggest we redo the scene, and this time I refuse to mention Nora's family."

Everyone listened in silence.

"TV24 won't like it—they specifically asked for something stronger," Ted replied eventually.

Henrik understood the dilemma, but surely this approach wasn't the answer.

"I want to do the scene differently," Henrik insisted.

"Differently?" Nora was staring straight at him. "You mean without cutting me down and making nasty remarks about my family? Is that even possible?" He realized how much he had hurt her by dragging her mother into the conversation.

"I understand why you're upset, but I'd like us to give it one more go. Please stay."

"What do you have in mind?"

"I thought we could take a look at your list and I'll suggest scrapping a few cookies, but that's all. No nastiness."

Ted sighed loudly, but Henrik ignored him. What could Ted do? Without Henrik there was no show.

Nora nodded slowly and went back to the table. Picked up her apron and put it on before sitting down.

Filming began. "Your list of baked goods is too long," Henrik began. Nora's shoulders tensed and she was immediately on the defensive, but Henrik tried to give her a reassuring look. This was a fine balancing act. He had to keep Nora on his side, while giving the producers something with an edge.

He picked up Nora's list and suggested a few items that could be dropped, like candy canes (who the hell had time to make their own candy canes?), marzipan balls, and a dozen or so cakes and cookies. Then he met her gaze. "We talked about this, how you'd be better off offering a smaller selection." Before she had time to sigh wearily, he went on. "I'm giving you this advice with your best interests at heart, because I . . ." *Care about you,* he was on the point of saying, but he didn't. Did he? "Because I care about you." There, he'd said it. They were supposed to be faking a little romance, so why not? However, as he spoke the words, he realized that he actually meant them. It was true. He did care about her, he wanted things to go well for her, and he wanted her to be happy. Because he cared about her.

With that realization, a very strange feeling came over him.

When they had finished filming, Ted looked at him and shook his head. "Don will go crazy."

"Like I said, I don't give a shit about Don," Henrik replied.

31

Nora glanced up at the clock as they finished filming for the day. It was already seven thirty.

They had prepared several batches of saffron dough, and Henrik hadn't criticized her once. In fact they had worked together in total harmony and had a really nice time. Hassan and Emil had closed the café and gone home. Nora had to stay to work on the Lucia buns. It was going to be a long night.

"There's still a lot to do," Henrik said, as if he had read her mind. "I'll stay and help."

Elnaz gave them a meaningful look as she put on her jacket.

Once the TV team had left, there was an awkward silence between them; they were suddenly very aware that they were alone. The last time that had happened, they had kissed. However, Nora couldn't forget what Henrik had said earlier.

After a while, Henrik spoke. "Once again, I'm really sorry for what I said about your mother."

Nora looked at him warily. "What made you change your mind?"

"I didn't want to be fake or a complete shit any longer."

"It's about time."

"I want to stick to what's authentic." He looked at her for a long time. She shivered, but she had no intention of letting him off the hook so easily.

"So you're done with humiliating and ridiculing people?"

He didn't answer. Instead he picked up a bag of flour, scattered a generous amount across the baking table, then tipped out a batch of golden-yellow saffron dough. He began to knead by hand, ignoring the mixer, and Nora did the same by his side.

"I realize it's hard for you to understand all these twists and turns, and I truly apologize for everything I've put you through," he said as he worked. Nora couldn't take her eyes off his muscular forearms. "But . . ." He broke off, looked up at the ceiling. "How can I explain without it sounding totally sick?" he said, mostly to himself. He looked at her, honesty shining from those dark-brown eyes. "This is the way it's been my entire adult life—a pretense in front of the cameras, while something completely different is going on behind the scenes. I play a role in *Let's Get Baking*. Our aim is to get a bit of a rise out of people—although I have to admit we've never taken it so far in the past." He sighed.

"So why did you go along with it this time?"

He shook his head. "I don't know. I don't really understand it myself . . ."

"Is it just because of the ratings?" She was genuinely interested; she wanted to know what drove him to behave the way he did.

"Yes, that's part of it. But another reason why I've accepted Don's ideas is that my father is trying to blast me out of the water. He's sold a new show to TV24, which is apparently going to air next fall at the same time as *Let's Get Baking*—in the slot we've had for almost five years. That's no excuse for the way I've behaved, but it's the truth."

Nora nodded slowly. Somewhere deep down she had known that there was something else behind it all. She respected the fact that Henrik wanted to save his show—after all, she was prepared to go to more or less any lengths to save her business—but she had sensed there was more to it.

"Do you really need your father? Do you need the company?" she asked. "It sounds like a toxic relationship you ought to get out of."

He shrugged, continued kneading. "Baking and my job have always been my passion, and the family business has been a part of that. It's what puts fire in my belly, what I live for." He thought for a moment. "Without Eklunds and my family, I wouldn't be here. It's my father's work that's built my career and made me who I am."

"I don't agree. You've become who you are thanks to your own TV show. Not Eklunds."

He remained silent for a long time, considering what she had said.

"Are you okay?" she prompted him eventually.

Then he looked at her. "Thank you for listening. I have to say it's fantastic to stand here and bake with someone like this. To *talk*."

"Don't you talk best when you're kneading dough? I'm sure I've heard you say that several times." She gave him a teasing smile, knowing perfectly well that it was just something he said for TV.

"That's kind of the Eklund family mantra on TV," he conceded. "*We talk things through over a bubbling boeuf bourguignon,* and *conversation flows freely when we all crowd into the kitchen for family dinners,* and *kneading a batch of dough solves every problem.*"

"You do realize that's how everyone thinks of your family? I've always assumed that you all hang out together on weekends, trying out new recipes. Baking vanilla and rhubarb buns, then eating them in Hasse and Anita's lush lilac arbor with homemade raspberry juice."

"Sometimes we do just that," he said with a weary smile. "But only for the cameras."

Living life in the public eye as Henrik did, constantly playing a role, must be exhausting. Nora thought about his ex-girlfriend and how the media had gone crazy over their breakup. She realized she wasn't comfortable with the idea of his ex. It didn't exactly make sense since this thing between her and Henrik was nothing more than a flirtation for the show. His attractive ex *shouldn't* bother her. And yet she found it hard to let go of the knowledge that Bente Hammar had cheated on Henrik, and that maybe he still hadn't gotten over the beautiful, bohemian, enchanting Bente.

They began to shape the dough into S-shaped buns and arranged them in rows on the baking trays, working methodically and settling into a good rhythm.

"I don't think I've ever enjoyed working with a participant as much as this," he said after a while. Nora grabbed a handful of raisins and placed two on each bun, then moved on to the next tray. And the next. She was getting close to him, and when he didn't step aside, she looked up at him. She was right beside him now, and he looked down at her. She wanted to kiss him, taste him, feel that rough beard against her cheek. Oh God, she really wanted to kiss him. Instead she turned and quickly brushed each finished bun with lightly beaten egg, then slid the first tray into the oven.

Henrik followed her example, and soon all the trays were in the oven.

They continued shaping buns, working methodically in silence. The heat was making Nora perspire, and she could feel how pink her cheeks were. The cold outside meant the windows steamed up, condensation trickling down the glass.

"What would you have been doing this evening if you weren't working?" Henrik asked after a while.

Nora sighed and looked up at the ceiling, trying to think. "I guess I'd have watched a movie, maybe met up with my friends. Or stayed home with a glass of wine."

"A glass of wine would go down pretty well right now."

She smiled tentatively. "I have a bottle of wine up in the apartment—shall I go and get it?"

"Great idea—why not? Lucia buns with wine."

She ran upstairs, taking the opportunity to drag a brush through her hair and freshen up her mascara. She grabbed the bottle, then at the last minute dashed into the bathroom and slipped a couple of condoms in her pocket. *Please don't jinx this now.*

She went back down to the patisserie and poured the wine into two tumblers. They raised their glasses in a toast and took a sip before carrying on with their work. The silence between them was tense, as if each of them was waiting for the other to make the first move. After the second glass of wine and the third batch of baking, Henrik turned to her.

"Nora . . ." He looked at her with those dark eyes, and she held her breath.

"Yes?" A second later she was in his arms, and they were kissing hungrily.

He pushed her up against the baking table. His hands were inside her top. She untied her apron, took it off, did the same with his. She fumbled with his T-shirt, slipped her hands inside it. His skin felt burning hot beneath her fingers. His upper body was soft and hard at the same time, and she caressed his broad shoulders before pulling off his T-shirt. They carried on kissing, his beard scratching her cheeks, his hands gentle as they moved over her body. She kissed his neck and inhaled the smell of him, which made her feel a little dizzy, and then she focused on the sensation of his touch. He stroked her breasts outside her bra, then continued downward. He took hold of her T-shirt, pulled it off. Given the heat of the room, she felt pure relief, and his kisses on her hot skin were almost cool.

The edge of the table was chafing her back and she shifted her position slightly, but then he lifted her onto the table, slipped down her jeans in a single movement, left her sitting there in nothing but her underwear. He stopped and looked at her.

"God, you're beautiful," he said.

She gazed at him standing in front of her, bare-chested. He was muscular and broad-shouldered but not bulky. He just looked strong. *And. Absolutely. Fucking. Fantastic.* She wanted to feel every inch of him. She drew him close, caressed his hairy chest, his back. His hands were inside her bra now, stroking her breasts as she undid his jeans. She pushed them down, along with his underwear. He was touching her panties now, his fingers finding their way beneath the lace. She whimpered, wanting more, wanting him to touch her where it was most sensitive.

She ran her hands slowly up and down the soft skin of his cock. He let out a small groan, and now he was exploring her most intimate places. She laughed when he stroked her clitoris, and soon her whole body was trembling.

He pulled her close, yanked off her panties. Then he stopped. "Shit, I haven't . . ."

Nora took a deep breath. "Pass me my jeans." He grinned, picked them up, and handed them to her. She took a condom out of the pocket, opened it slowly. He put his lips to her ear, whispered, "So you planned this?"

She smiled. "Well, I was hoping . . ."

She slid the condom over his cock with a smooth movement that made him moan.

He thrust into her, moved slowly inside her, then faster, stroking her clitoris all the time.

They both came quickly, neither waiting for the other.

He slumped over her, and she sank back against the table with her head on the bag of flour behind her. Henrik was breathing heavily, and then after a moment he kissed her gently on the neck and lifted her off the table. They sank down onto the floor. Fortunately Emil had both swept and mopped before he left.

"Is it the booze and the crap ventilation system, or is it very hot in here?" he said.

Nora laughed and kissed him. "It's definitely not your sense of humor that makes you so sexy."

"So you think I'm sexy?"

"Is there a woman in this country who doesn't?" She rolled her eyes. It was a well-known fact that he was handsome, and to hear him fishing for compliments was . . . kind of sweet. She kissed him again, she couldn't get enough of those wonderful lips, the feeling of that prickly beard against her chin.

"It's just that you gave me a different impression—that you thought I was the most hateful person on the planet."

"You can be hateful and sexy at the same time."

Nora's head was spinning from the physical exertion involved in both sex and baking, the stuffy air inside the bakery, and the emotions sizzling between them. Henrik suggested a walk, and she quickly agreed.

Västervik was dark and deserted. Not many people were out and about at three o'clock in the morning in the middle of the week. They wandered along the main street, over cobblestones still covered in snow. They carried on toward the sea. The sky was clear, studded with stars.

The nearer they got to Henrik's hotel, the more her heart raced. She really wanted to spend the night with him. She wanted to have him, over and over again. She turned toward him and saw that he was watching her, which made her feel warm inside.

Henrik was different from all the other men she had known, but this could never turn into something serious. Filming would soon be over, and he would go home to Stockholm. She wasn't into serious relationships, and she was pretty sure he couldn't be over Bente yet. Maybe Nora was just some kind of rebound for him? Oddly enough, the thought was painful. However, there was one way to numb the pain. She stopped and kissed him, in the darkness and the icy cold. Her desire sparked to life again, pushing aside all other thoughts and feelings.

32

Nora was woken by the sound of her phone pinging with a text message. It was from Bea, saying that she was home. Nora breathed a sigh of relief.

Henrik drew her close. "What was that about? It's the middle of the night."

"It's Bea—I always ask her to text me when she gets home from her night shift, so I know."

"So you know . . . ?"

"That she's safe. She's a cop, and I worry when she works nights." The room was cool; Nora shivered and curled up next to Henrik with her head resting on his shoulder. She drew the thick quilt up to her chin.

"Is Västervik such a dangerous place?"

"I'm sure I have no real reason to be anxious, but I've gotten so much bad news over the years . . ." She sighed. "It's not easy when you care about someone. I'm terrified of getting a terrible shock, like when my father died."

Henrik cleared his throat. Pulled her close. "Can I ask what happened?"

Nora swallowed hard, took a deep breath. Remembered thinking that things were different with Henrik. She wanted to share this with him.

It was just that every time she touched on the deaths of her parents, the pain overwhelmed her again. But she also knew that talking about it eased something inside her a little. "It was an ordinary day. He was driving to Kalmar to look at a new industrial mixer." She paused. Henrik placed his hand on hers. She could barely make out the contours of his face in the darkness. "A truck was on the wrong side of the road. Mom got the news while I was at indoor floorball training, so a friend of hers came to pick me up. Mom was a wreck when I arrived home. Apparently Dad died instantaneously." She shook her head slowly. "I experienced an indescribable, almost physical pain. I thought I would never feel anything like it again. But . . . I was wrong." Henrik kissed her head, gently stroked her shoulders. "When my mom died, the pain was agonizing and drawn out. Every time we were given bad news about the progression of her illness, it was like hearing about my dad's death all over again. And yet I couldn't help hoping for better news next time—only to be disappointed. So . . . I guess I'm always expecting the worst."

"I'm so sorry for everything you've been through. It's . . ." He broke off. "I don't know what to say, but it seems terribly unfair."

Nora nodded, and they lay in silence for a while. She loved being in his arms, her head resting on his shoulder.

"I've been thinking," Henrik said after a while. "You said you had a story about your sourdough, and I never let you tell me what it was."

Nora turned her head, looked up at him in surprise. "You've been thinking about my sourdough?"

He shrugged. "I'm a baker, that means I think about stuff like an old sourdough starter."

She smiled. "It belonged to my great-grandmother." She told him the story her grandmother had told her many times, of how the sourdough had been passed down and survived so much.

"Interesting." She thought she heard a slight tremble in his voice. "I'll ask production if we can include the story somewhere; I think it would be a good addition."

Filming with Nora in the days following their night together was . . . strange, but in a very pleasant way, Henrik thought. Everything they had shared with each other that night gave rise to a burning, intimate attraction he had never felt before.

They ended the week with a simple *see you around*. He went to the hotel, and Nora stayed to lock up. Which seemed a little . . . flat. But what else could he have done? It would be obviously a good idea to let things settle, especially as she was a participant in his show, and they still had a few more days' filming to complete.

As usual the team had dinner at the hotel. Since Sunday was going to be a day off, the atmosphere was more relaxed. Elnaz suggested they all go for a drink after they'd eaten. Much to his surprise Henrik found himself agreeing—for the simple (yet in a way quite complicated) reason that he would otherwise have spent the evening in his room, thinking about Nora. He might even have called her.

Once they'd settled in at a nearby bar, he accompanied Elnaz to the bar to order drinks for everyone.

"What did you think of the first scenes? Honestly?" Elnaz asked while they were waiting. Henrik had seen the early clips just before dinner.

"I thought they looked really good—including the material for the press launch."

"Oh, I can't wait!" Elnaz replied with a smile. The launch of the Christmas special was something they all looked forward to. It was a big deal because it was the last big push before everyone disappeared for the holidays. "But I can't wait to have some time off either," Elnaz added.

"You deserve it. You've worked hard this season. God knows it hasn't been easy, but I think we've ended up with something good. I'm very pleased with what I saw earlier." He meant every word. The new season had remained true to the spirit of *Let's Get Baking*, but with a little more chemistry, more feeling, more of a spark—with that hint of a flirtation between him and Nora in the background, in spite of their frequent bickering. He thought it was a fair portrayal; there was nothing that cast Nora in a dubious light. She came across as a serious and highly skilled baker who took great pride in her profession.

Elnaz nodded. "I agree. And we'll have the gingerbread house competition to round things off, maybe with a kiss in front of the cameras in the square?" She winked at him. "I've always said that flirting was a better direction than the hysterical-female angle."

Henrik smiled at her. Of course romance was preferable.

"This is taking forever," Elnaz said. "I'll just run to the bathroom."

Henrik picked up a menu while he was waiting and read through the wine list, and then he looked around the room. Anything to distract himself from thoughts of Nora.

It didn't work. He took out his phone.

What are you doing? He sent the message before he had time to change his mind.

"Hey." Elnaz was back. "What do you think of her?" She nodded toward a girl farther along the bar, then smiled at her. The girl returned the smile.

"I think she looks about half your age," Henrik said with a grin.

"What's that got to do with anything?"

"Nothing. As long as she's reached the age of consent."

Elnaz glanced at the menu in his hand. "Are you ordering wine?"

"No, it's just habit—I always check out the wine list. It got to be a habit when I was with Bente."

"Are you still in touch?"

Henrik shook his head. "She cheated on me. Why would I keep in touch with a cheating ex who humiliated me in front of the entire population of Sweden?"

"Cheated on you? But . . . Didn't you know . . ." Elnaz looked confused. "Didn't Bente tell you what happened?"

"What are you talking about?"

"She never cheated on you."

"I don't know what you mean. Of course she said she didn't cheat on me, but the pictures were very convincing. Why should I believe her?" The photographs were taken at an outdoor café at a castle in the South of France, Bente sitting opposite her ex-boyfriend Frederic on those rustic French cast iron chairs at a round marble table. In the distance there were rows of vines growing on undulating hills, and Bente was positively glowing with love.

"Because it was true." Elnaz rolled her eyes. "Nothing happened with Frederic."

"How can you know that for sure?" Henrik felt a twinge of doubt. Elnaz had been the producer on Bente's show, so maybe she did know something he didn't.

"I was with her all the time. They only saw each other that one time at the café. I was there, and they did absolutely nothing. There was no kiss. Okay, I saw the way she looked at him, but she didn't betray your trust. I'm not saying you don't have the right to be angry because she did look as if she was in love in those photos, but she didn't cheat on you in the physical sense. Some idiot in production leaked the pictures, and they were taken completely out of context." When Henrik didn't respond, she went on. "They met briefly at the vineyard. I saw him arrive, they talked about what was going to be filmed, he presented his wine, and then they chatted for a few minutes after filming wrapped for the day. Then he left. And shortly afterward, so did we. Bente and I were sharing a hotel room, because the company always tries to cut costs as soon as there's foreign travel involved. She had no opportunity to cheat on you."

"But the photographs, they . . ."

"I know. They looked compromising. But she was never unfaithful. I've always thought that the press was really hard on her, they were very unfair, and you . . ."

"Didn't say a word."

"Exactly, and I never understood why."

So what Bente had told him was true? Once he'd seen the pictures, he'd never thought there was a reason to question the narrative. He also knew the history between Bente and Frederic. She had fallen in love with him when she was working as a sommelier in Paris, but it had never turned into anything serious—at least not on his side. Frederic was the love of Bente's life, and when she told Henrik how much Frederic had hurt her, he had known that the relationship was unresolved; Bente still had feelings for her ex. As far as Henrik was concerned, the photographs were proof enough. He had never discussed the matter with anyone else—including Elnaz, precisely because she knew Bente, too, which put her in a difficult position. Plus he was a very private person, and didn't want to share his emotions.

Now he felt like an idiot. The depth of his misunderstanding was hard to take in. Not because he believed that he and Bente would still have been a couple today—their relationship had been going downhill for a while at that point—but he cringed at the memory of everything that had happened afterward . . . Bente had been trashed by the media, and Henrik had said nothing. He had never stood up for her; he was much too hurt. And maybe he had enjoyed her treatment by the press just a little, which wasn't a very pleasant realization.

Nora leaned back in her chair; she couldn't manage one more slice of truffle salami. She had invited the girls over for snacks and wine, and much to her surprise they had all shown up. As a thank-you for the dinner they had treated her to recently, she had bought good red wine, Pata Negra ham, bresaola, truffle salami, and a selection of cheeses. She took another sip of her wine.

Nora was glad she had asked them over, mainly because they were good company of course, but also because it forced her to think about something other than Henrik Eklund for a few hours. The strange, warm feeling she had felt ever since that night with him had lingered.

It was as if those amazing orgasms were still in her body. Or was her body preparing for more?

"Can I put on a playlist?" Maryam said when Nora's Spotify list ended.

"Absolutely. My phone's over there." Nora picked up the bottle of wine and refilled her glass. Took another sip, let the warm, spicy flavors roll around her mouth.

"You've got a message," Maryam said, waving Nora's phone in the air.

"Who from? We're all here."

"Someone who's wondering what you're doing." Maryam handed her the phone.

What are you doing?

When Nora saw that it was from Henrik, her heart started pounding.

What are you doing? She read the message several times. Who would have thought that four little words could start a mini-tornado swirling around in her belly?

Having dinner with some friends. How about you?

Elnaz has dragged me and the production team out to check out the town. Can't you come and join us?

"Who's it from?" Bea was staring at her. Jesus, why did Bea have to be so nosy?

"Henrik. He's out on the town and wants me to join him."

"So you know each other well enough to exchange texts?"

"Apparently."

"Hang on, has something happened between you two?" Bea's eyes widened.

Nora didn't answer. She didn't know why she hadn't told her friends about what had happened. But for some reason she wanted to keep it to herself.

Bea slapped her on the arm. "Spill!"

"Okay, so that night we made Lucia buns, we ended up having sex."

"Like you do! It's a well-known fact that making Lucia buns always ends with sex," Bea said, looking shocked. Then she grinned. "Details, please! How did it happen? I thought you hated him!"

"Yes, I know, but . . . it just happened. I mean, we've been getting along better recently—much better. We've talked a lot, and the filming began to go better. Once his arrogant TV persona disappeared, everything changed."

"So where is he now?" Maryam asked.

"Let me find out." She tapped out a quick message and received a reply within seconds. "Guldkant."

"So let's go!" Tess said.

Maryam clapped her hands. "Let's do it—it's been a long time since we had a proper night out!"

"Fine by me," Nora said, trying to keep her cool. She didn't want to give her friends any false hope. They always hoped that her next relationship would be The One, but they had to realize that she and Henrik Eklund weren't ever going to be a real thing.

"I'll just . . . get changed."

She went into her bedroom and grabbed the black, high-waisted jeans that showed off her butt to its best advantage. She kept her wine-red blouse on; it was very Christmassy.

"Oh, you've gone for your butt-hugging jeans," Bea said when Nora emerged. "Someone has plans for tonight."

"Shut up."

"Ha—who do you think you're fooling? You always wear those jeans when you're planning to take someone home," Maryam said.

Nora went into the bathroom, painted her lips dark red, and swept her hair up into a high ponytail. Then she changed her mind and let her hair hang loose over her shoulders. She sprayed on the most sensual perfume she owned.

Then she and her friends set out. The bar was buzzing when they arrived. Nora looked around, trying not to appear too eager—though in her mind, she felt like a celebrity-baker-seeking missile.

And there he was. Standing at the bar. He had already seen her, and when she met his eyes, he smiled, held her gaze for a long time. The world around her seemed to tremble, then suddenly began to spin. Just from the way he looked at her. If she didn't know better, she'd think that what she saw there was genuine feeling. It couldn't be, though, right? It was just an extension of the flirtation they'd begun for the cameras. But if that were the case, what did her reaction mean? She decided these thoughts were way too complicated for her wine-befuddled brain, so she simply walked straight up to him.

She gave him a quick hug, and he held her for a fraction of a second too long. Then he greeted her friends, ordered a bottle of champagne, and made sure everyone had a glass.

Standing right next to him, Nora was hyperaware of his smell, the smell that had enveloped her whole body that night. Her legs trembled, just because of his proximity, and she realized she had been fooling herself. Of course she intended to spend the night with him, she *had to* have sex with him again. Tonight.

The girls made for the dance floor, and Henrik followed. As they started to dance, Nora found it hard to tear her eyes away from his tall figure, those broad shoulders. The thick hair that sometimes flopped forward, only for him to push it back again. And that irresistible beard. She reached out and stroked it just to feel its roughness against her fingertips. A shudder passed through her entire body, and he grabbed her wrist, drew her close, danced with his hips touching hers.

An old Ace of Base track was playing, which made her smile. When he sang every single word while swaying in time to the music, she couldn't help laughing. He pulled her even closer, as close as it was possible to be. She wound her arms around his neck. Felt his breath on her face. *Oh God.*

When the song ended, Nora let go of Henrik and danced for a while with her friends.

Elnaz appeared with a tray of shot glasses containing a luminous green concoction and passed the tray around. Everyone knocked them back, and Henrik drew Nora close once more.

"Where were we?" he murmured in her ear, and his deep voice vibrated through her very bones.

Nora looked around; the girls had gone back to the bar with Elnaz. She met Henrik's gaze, let herself get lost in those dark-brown eyes. They were dancing close together again, his hands in her hair. Her silk blouse was no barrier to the heat emanating through his cotton shirt. He was so close, but though they didn't kiss, the heat whirled around Nora's body like a hurricane. She wanted him. So she leaned forward and kissed him. Her tongue slowly played with his, and he responded by kissing her hard. They carried on kissing. When a new song came on, they were no longer dancing, just swaying to the music while they made out. Making out was so underrated!

"Get a room!" Elnaz's voice brought them back to reality, and when Nora looked around she could see that everyone was staring at them. She turned back to Henrik, eyes wide with horror, but he simply smiled, and then they both burst out laughing.

They were still laughing as they collected their jackets and left the club. Out in the street the cold struck them, along with a swirling wind coming off the sea.

"That might have been a step too far," Henrik said. "After all I'm almost forty, not sixteen." He looked at her. "But I couldn't help it."

She gazed at him. "Almost forty . . . I'm so glad there's someone out on the town tonight who's older than me."

He punched her lightly on the shoulder, then put his arm around her.

They walked in the dry winter cold to his hotel, and they had barely gotten through the door of his room when they ripped off each other's clothes and tumbled onto the bed.

33

1945

The week in the cottage had been fantastic, and Nils had no desire to return home to reality. But on Sunday afternoon they packed the car and set off.

When they reached the village, he stopped outside Tuula's house. He helped them unload their things and gave Tuula a long kiss when the children weren't looking. She had crept into his room every night, where they had made love before she tiptoed back to her own room.

Nils drove home feeling very pleased with himself. He unpacked the car, then jumped on his bike and cycled to his parents' house for Sunday dinner.

Stig, Marianne, and the children were already in the garden sipping drinks when he arrived. His father barely glanced at him as he made his way through the apple trees, but the children came rushing over and threw their arms around him. When dinner was ready, his father took him aside before they went in. "Could I have a word with you?"

Nils nodded, and his father led him into the trees so that they wouldn't be disturbed. He stopped and swirled his sherry glass in his fingers. "The council reviewed our application and rejected it."

"I'm very sorry to hear that," Nils replied honestly.

"They didn't actually say as much, but I suspect it's because they don't like this . . ." Father waved his hand in the air, trying to find the right word. "This . . . relationship of yours. They said they found the whole thing very odd, and they weren't sure they could rely on me, given my family's connections."

"Connections? We're not talking about something dangerous here—she's an ordinary woman, a decent woman, not a criminal!"

"They weren't my words. Plus Karlsson is on the council, and he canceled our contract last week."

Karlsson ran a general store outside the village, and they'd been supplying him with bread for years. Nils's father was looking at him as if he expected him to say something. Apologize, perhaps? But Nils had no intention of pacifying his father. Instead he gazed toward the river in the distance. It was a beautiful evening, and a number of people were out strolling. They looked happy and carefree—exactly how he had felt in the cottage with Tuula.

They heard footsteps on the wooden porch. "Are you two coming?" Nils's mother called out. His father merely looked at him, his expression grim, before turning and walking away.

They ate dinner in silence. Nils could understand his father's disappointment and frustration that the business had suffered a setback because of him, but he couldn't accept that he and Tuula were the source of the problem. It was other people who were in the wrong, all those people who felt they had the right to an opinion on Nils's private life. The atmosphere was tense, and he left early.

On the way home he stopped by to see Tuula.

"The children have just fallen asleep," she said. The kitchen window was open. A gentle breeze made the thin curtain flutter, carrying with it the scent of the roses blooming down in the courtyard. There was a cup of tea on the table by the window, and an open book on the embroidered runner. A loose bouquet of cornflowers and daisies stood in a jug in the middle of the table. The apartment had seen better days, but Tuula had made it pretty and welcoming. It was so much cozier than his own apartment; this felt more like a home.

"I bumped into our landlord earlier, and he told me about a vacant apartment in the building next door," Tuula said. "A bigger apartment—with a living room! And I think I can afford it. The children would have their own room, and there's a bathroom." Her eyes were sparkling.

"Sounds perfect for you." Maybe perfect for the four of them? Or she and the children could move in with him. He was about to suggest it, but Tuula carried on talking.

"It's all thanks to you, for taking a chance on me and my bread. I wouldn't be able to afford it without my baker's wage."

Nils shook his head. "It's all down to you—you're driven. And talented."

Tuula picked up a bottle of water from the counter and removed the cork. "Apparently the water has been smelling funny recently, so I don't dare use it. Aino left me a note, and some bottles of water from the well next door. She and Heikki have gone down to Småland for a few days." She poured the water into a pan on the stove and heated it up. "Unfortunately Matias drank a glass before I saw the note, but he seems fine so far." She made Nils a cup of tea and they sat down at the table.

"I can go down and take a look," Nils offered.

"No, it's too dark now. The landlord said he'd check our well tomorrow afternoon. How was dinner at your parents'?"

He didn't answer right away; he couldn't tell her what his father had said. "It was . . . fine."

She looked at him for a long time before she spoke. "Listen, Nils. I really appreciate the fact that you're so open with me. And I know you well enough by now to see there's something wrong. Don't worry, I can take it, whatever it is that happened over dinner."

"I . . ." He broke off, sighed deeply. Stirred his tea. He really wanted to protect Tuula from all this, but he had to be honest with her. "As you know, my father applied for permission to put up a building with a freezer room, but his application was rejected. He blames us and our relationship. And one of our clients canceled his contract with us. But they're just narrow-minded old men, the lot of them."

Tuula looked down at the table, then up at him. "I'm so sorry to hear that."

"If we got married, people wouldn't be able to say anything." The words just came out.

Her eyes widened. "Is that a proposal?"

Nils nodded; he had surprised himself. "I think so."

She blinked a couple of times, then shook her head. "No, I don't want you to ask like that. And you've already said that your family isn't happy about us."

"Mommy," a little voice whimpered from the bedroom. "Coming, sweetheart." Seconds later Nils heard someone throwing up. He grabbed a bowl from the sink and hurried after Tuula.

She was sitting on the bed with Matias on her lap. The boy was still retching, and Nils held out the bowl. In the faint glow of the bedside lamp, Nils could see that the child's face was pale. Matias sank back against the pillow. Nils helped Tuula to undress him and change the sheets. Tuula gently cleaned him up and found him a fresh nightshirt.

Nils went into the kitchen and turned on the tap with the intention of rinsing the boy's clothes, but a horrible, almost rotten stench rose from the sink. He bundled everything up in a sheet so he could wash them at home.

"There's obviously something badly wrong," he said when Tuula emerged from the bedroom.

"You mean the water?"

He nodded, pointed to the bundle on the floor. "I'll take everything home, try to get it clean."

"There's no need, I . . ."

"There's every need. Use the bottled water for drinking and cooking."

"Thank you."

"I'll come back and check out the well first thing tomorrow, as soon as it's light."

"Thank you. Maybe I should try to get some sleep now—I think it could be a long night."

Early the next morning, Nils returned, and Tuula showed him the well in a corner of the courtyard. Nils removed the lid, and the stench that met him made him gag and turn his head away. He pulled up his shirt to cover his mouth and nose before he peered inside. What he saw made his stomach turn. He turned away, retching, but nothing came up.

A cadaver of some kind. It was impossible to see *what* it was exactly—the combination of the water and the heat of high summer had made it unrecognizable, but possibly a deer. But one thing was certain. It hadn't gotten into the well by itself—someone must have thrown it in. There was absolutely no doubt about that.

"What is it?" Tuula tried to look over his shoulder, but she, too, had to turn her head away.

"A dead animal." He looked at her. "Don't you worry about it, I know some guys who will take it away for a few kronor, then we'll get someone in to clean the well."

"A dead animal? But how . . ." Then she realized what he had already grasped. Seeing the truth hit home was heartbreaking.

"You can all move in with me until the well is clean and safe."

She didn't say a word; she just stared blankly into space. Then she swallowed hard. "I need to get Matias to the doctor. Right now."

34

Nora lay stretched out on her back, then rolled over onto her stomach close beside him. She was still breathing hard and her back, which was shiny with sweat, was rising and falling rapidly. "No doubt you have a baker in every small town," she said between breaths. She rested her head on his chest. He put his arm around her, held her close.

He looked down at her. "No, only in every medium-size town. So you're the exception."

She laughed and playfully slapped his arm. "Thanks, I'm flattered."

Henrik felt a strange emptiness in his heart, knowing that filming would soon be over. He would leave, with no plans to return to Västervik. This thing between them was so different—definitely not just a fake romance for the cameras. He didn't know what it was, but it seemed too soon to end things, leaving the possibilities unexplored. He tilted her chin up, met her gaze. "I like you, Nora."

She grinned. "I like you too."

"I know this could make things awkward, given that we're working together."

"But you've been in this situation before, haven't you?" she said teasingly.

The question put him on his guard. "What do you mean?"

"I was thinking about Bente."

"Ah." His ex was the last person he wanted to think about right now; he wanted to concentrate on Nora.

"How did you handle it? The cheating? Was it tough to get over her?"

He didn't say anything. He hadn't given any more thought to what Elnaz had told him; Nora had showed up and taken his mind off Bente.

"Sorry." She shook her head. "Maybe that was too personal a question—it's got nothing to do with me."

"No, it's not that, it's . . ." He sat up, looked at her. What the hell was he supposed to say, when he had no idea how to deal with what he had just been told? "I found out this evening that Bente didn't cheat on me."

Nora sat up too. "You found out this evening? But . . . why did it take so long?"

"She swore she hadn't cheated on me at the time, but I refused to believe her."

"Oh my God—so what happened this evening?"

"I'm not sure how much you know about what went on, but photos were taken of Bente and Frederic. Elnaz was there at the time, and she assured me that absolutely nothing went on between Bente and Frederic."

"To think of everything Bente went through . . ."

Henrik nodded. He didn't really want to face up to that, because he was so ashamed of the way the press had treated her. "I have to do something, tell the truth."

"Yes, you do," Nora agreed.

When the news about Bente's infidelity broke, *Let's Get Baking*'s ratings had shot up, and he'd gotten several offers from other shows—judging baking competitions, morning TV appearances. Meanwhile, Bente had lost her TV career outright. And he had kept quiet, watched it happen.

"Why didn't you believe her?"

"I . . . I don't really know. I . . ." He searched for the right words, looked out the window at the darkness. "I guess it reinforced my own self-image. Everything my father had always said about me was confirmed as soon as I found out she'd cheated on me; it was almost as if I'd been waiting for it. In my defense, she looked deeply in love in those photographs. She and Frederic had a long history together. It was just easier to believe that what I'd thought all along was true."

"And what had you thought all along?"

"I guess I'd been waiting for her to realize that she didn't want me."

Nora gazed at him for a long time. "But why? Does that have something to do with your father as well?"

He looked away. She already seemed to know more about him than anyone else ever had.

"Well, as soon as something goes my way, my father tries to take me down a notch. That's what happened with Bente. As soon as my father saw that my relationship with her was boosting my TV career, he told me it would never last. Every time I have an idea of my own, he undermines me."

"In what way?"

"He's . . . He's always found ways to humiliate his children, whenever we've tried to go our own way without his blessing. Like the dog thing." He fell silent, wishing he could take back those words.

"The dog thing?" She raised her eyebrows.

He had never told anyone about it. He had discussed it with his mother once, because she had been there at the time. He looked at Nora, wondering how she would react to this story. Would he come across as trying to win sympathy points? But the story revealed a great deal about both Henrik and his father. The dog thing had become a symbol for all the humiliation and bullying that he and his siblings had endured over the years. Maybe Nora would understand him better if he shared his story?

He would never forget that late-spring day at his childhood home. They had eaten dinner on the patio among the lilacs in the evening sun, seated around the big white wooden table. Henrik was fourteen, Tom was twelve, and Camilla would soon turn nine. Henrik had just finished a school project on political ideologies, and had said at dinner that he believed the significance of money was exaggerated. Henrik put forward the idea that money didn't mean anything. He didn't remember his exact words, but he did remember his father's wolfish grin.

"So money isn't everything?" Hasse stared intently at Henrik, then at Tom, then Camilla. "You do realize you can say that because you grew up with plenty of money?"

Henrik didn't answer.

"So kids—how about a little competition?" Hasse went on.

Henrik never turned down a challenge, but he knew this wasn't going to be fun. Tom and Camilla seemed to feel the same way, judging by their silence.

"Hasse, please." Mom looked up from the boiled cod on her plate.

"Someone could win ten thousand kronor!" Hasse said, ignoring his wife.

"What?" Tom's jaw dropped, and beside him Camilla let out a gasp. Henrik's eyes widened.

"I'd like you to crawl across the garden on all fours, barking like dogs. Fastest wins."

Tom laughed.

"I'm not joking," Hasse said, putting down his knife and fork. The clatter of the cutlery on the plate was the only sound in the still evening air. Hasse wiped his mouth with his napkin, set it down, and looked at them, one after the other. "I'm going to throw a stick, you bark like dogs and go after it on all fours. The one who reaches the stick first and picks it up in their mouth wins."

"Hasse, is this really necessary?" Mom's expression was reproachful.

"It's entirely voluntary." He got to his feet, went over to a lilac bush, broke off a thin branch, and stripped off the leaves and flowers. "Okay, who's in?"

Mom slammed down her knife and fork, stood up, and marched into the house.

The siblings laughed and looked at one another as if it were a game, as if they were trying to convince one another that this would be fun.

Henrik realized that his point about money not being important would be completely lost, but ten thousand kronor was a stunning amount of money. He wouldn't need a summer job, wouldn't even need a part-time job for the rest of the year. And besides, it was just a game, wasn't it?

But he was too old to pretend to be a dog, and Tom would never play a game like that. The only one who still did that kind of thing was Camilla, but she, too, realized that something was amiss, and her eyes darted between her two brothers.

"I am," Tom said.

"Me too." Henrik felt his morale and his values evaporate as he uttered those words.

"And me," Camilla said firmly.

"Good." Hasse positioned himself on the edge of the terrace, took a deep breath, and hurled the stick toward the other side of the garden. They heard a soft thud as it landed on the grass.

No one moved.

Hasse looked at them. "What are you waiting for? Down on all fours—off you go!"

They exchanged dubious looks, and then Tom dropped to the ground and let out a quiet bark.

"Louder—otherwise it doesn't count!" Hasse said.

Henrik dropped to the ground, followed by Camilla. Tom already had a five-yard lead, but Henrik sped across the lawn. "Woof, woof!" He had longer arms and legs than his brother, and quickly reduced the distance between them.

Camilla was some distance behind; he could hear her barking.

The smell of freshly cut grass tickled his nostrils. They had reached the gravel path now; Henrik was only a couple of feet behind Tom.

"Louder!" their father yelled.

The heat of the sun on his back made him sweat, and the gravel was scraping his knees. But he kept going. Why? For the money, or because their father was issuing orders? He didn't really know.

Camilla gave up; the boys were too far ahead.

Henrik extended his arms, moved his legs faster, his knees torn to shreds. He was level with Tom now, and the stick was only a couple of yards away. Henrik hurled himself forward, grabbed it between his teeth, growled when Tom caught up with him, and rolled away so that Tom wouldn't be able to take the stick from him.

Henrik lay on his back on the grass, panting.

The competition was over.

"Congratulations, Henrik." Hasse came and stood over him. "And never forget that people will do anything for money."

When Henrik had finished telling his story, Nora gazed at him, then drew him close. He rested his head against her breast. She didn't say anything, but after revealing something so deeply personal, so humiliating, it was nice just to be near her.

"I guess the point of the story is that my father has made me believe everything he says, made me do virtually whatever he wants. If he says that a project is doomed to failure, then I believe him, and I fail. If he says a relationship won't last, I believe him. I see the slightest setback as confirmation of my incompetence."

Nora shook her head. "And now he wants to kill *Let's Get Baking*?"

Henrik nodded.

"What does your sister think about this? She represents both you and your father, doesn't she?"

"She does. She just says our father has handled all communication with TV24—she hasn't had anything to do with it. I'm guessing she doesn't want to be dragged into our dispute."

"But you haven't let him win—you've fought back. I think you're well on the way to freeing yourself from your father."

He nodded slowly; maybe she was right. Then he realized that she was a big part of it. He had learned so much from her. She was so strong, so capable. And she was right about his father—Henrik's relationship with him was destructive, and he really had to free himself of it.

What was it about Nora that made him open up to her like this? He didn't want to leave Västervik next week. It was too soon. And he didn't want whatever it was that they had between them to end. It had only just begun.

35

Over the next few days, they continued filming the Christmas preparations as the snow melted away. Nora still opposed half of Henrik's ideas in front of the cameras, but the atmosphere between them was different—more highly charged, but also more relaxed and teasing. Henrik told her off from time to time, and Nora came back with a spiky comment or two. Then they would meet up in the changing room and make out in secret.

Orders had come pouring in over the past week, and he could see how happy Nora was. Apart from Gunnebo's standing order, there were other companies who wanted her help. She had started to sell her crispbread, and a number of grocery stores in the town had bought several boxes, so she and Renée had their hands full baking tray after tray. She hardly had time to see Henrik, nor had they had a chance to discuss what would happen when filming was over. The big gingerbread house finale was fast approaching, and Henrik was falling more and more deeply in love.

One evening he managed to take her out for dinner, and of course they ended up in his hotel room. She also came to his hotel on the penultimate day of filming, but it was too late to eat in the restaurant, so they opted for room service instead. She showed up at almost midnight, exhausted after preparing all the orders for the next day. They were due to film the gingerbread house competition in the square in the morning.

Despite her frenetic schedule, he managed to get her to relax, and she slept soundly all night.

They had breakfast in his room, sitting by the window with its sea view. At first there was only darkness, but the sun slowly rose, lighting up the horizon. They were in their underwear, and Henrik realized he would happily sit here with her like this for the rest of his life, eating scrambled eggs with freshly baked bread and drinking strong black coffee. He inhaled sharply. Was that really how he felt? He sipped his coffee and gazed at her in the golden glow of the dawn. Yes . . . it felt so . . . right.

"I've been thinking about the press launch next week," he said. "Maybe we could have dinner that night? The whole team usually goes out to eat together afterward, so we'll have to go with them, but then I wondered if you'd like to stay in Stockholm for a couple of days?"

Her posture changed almost imperceptibly; it was as if she disappeared into her own thoughts for a moment before she looked at him. "That would be difficult—I have the patisserie to run. I can't just take off."

"Okay."

He leaned forward and took her hand. He couldn't help himself, he had to say it. "I'd love to have breakfast with you like this every morning."

She looked shaken. Something changed unmistakably in that moment, and she gave a stiff little smile. He wished he hadn't spoken, but he meant what he'd said. She was special, and he wanted to go on seeing her. Maybe she'd reacted this way because she didn't know where they stood?

"Nora . . . I'm serious. I want to have breakfast with you every day. And not just in some hotel room."

She laughed—but it was a brittle, nervous laugh. "How's that supposed to work? I live in Västervik and you live in Stockholm."

"Maybe we could change that?"

Another fleeting smile. "By the way, do you think Elnaz has met someone down here?"

He frowned. "I don't want to talk about Elnaz, I want to talk about us."

"Us?" She sounded shocked.

"Yes. I know it's early days, but I want to go on seeing you."

"You're right, it's way too early to decide on something like that," she said coldly, taking a gulp of her coffee.

Henrik nodded briefly. He had no intention of pushing her, but her reaction wasn't what he'd expected. Maybe he'd been too direct? The relaxed, easy mood between them was gone.

"I'd better go home," she said. "I need to change my clothes before we start filming."

Henrik nodded again. Nora finished her coffee, then went over to the bed and got dressed. She suddenly seemed in a hurry to leave. His thoughts were whirling as he stood up. What had he done? Why had she reacted this way?

He followed her to the door. Surely he could say goodbye properly without her thinking he was proposing? She turned back and gave him a quick kiss on the lips.

"See you in the square," he said.

"Absolutely." She was already hurrying down the corridor.

36

The square was already crowded when Henrik arrived, and many of the people there were dressed as Santas. Of course, there was a Santa Claus parade today—Nora had told him it was a long-standing local tradition. A large stage had been erected at one end of the square, and fairy lights twinkled everywhere. At the other end there was an ice rink, where skaters were whizzing around and around. Stalls were selling mulled wine, gingerbread cookies, Lucia buns, and hot dogs, all very welcome on such a cold day.

Henrik had been thinking about Nora on his way down. Even an early run in the freezing cold by the water hadn't cleared his head. She confused him. They hadn't known each other very long, but there was something about her. This thing between them was special, and he definitely wanted to see her again. They couldn't simply end it when filming was over, which seemed to be her intention.

The production company truck was parked in a corner of the square, and the team was busy unloading crates containing the various gingerbread house components. Henrik went over to help them. Nora didn't seem to have arrived yet, which at the moment felt like something of a relief after the strange vibe he'd gotten from her earlier.

He soon saw her approaching. She was wearing sturdy winter shoes, her bright-blue quilted jacket, and a woolen hat, with her blonde hair loose over her shoulders. The short walk in the cold had given her rosy cheeks. She looked exactly as she had on the day they bought the

Christmas tree, when she'd kissed him. She gave him a hesitant smile, then headed for Ted and Elnaz over by the stage. Henrik took a deep breath and joined her.

"Okay, we start filming in ten minutes," Ted announced. "You know what to do, but I'll start things off by explaining the competition to the audience, and then you can take it from there."

They waited while everything was arranged, and then Ted stepped onto the stage, followed by Nora and Henrik. Everyone applauded.

"A warm welcome to the gingerbread house competition between Nora Jansson, Västervik's leading baker, and Henrik Eklund, everyone's favorite baker." Ted gestured toward them, and there was plenty of applause and a few whistles. Henrik looked out at the audience and noted the position of the TV cameras. He could see Nora out of the corner of his eye. "Henrik and Nora will each assemble one end of Västervik's beautiful town silhouette. The rules are simple: the one who finishes first is the winner. But of course it has to look good too." Ted turned to them. "Are you ready?"

Henrik nodded, and heard Nora say *yes*.

"Then let's go!"

Henrik turned his attention to the items laid out on the table. He squeezed some glue from a little tube and began to assemble one end of Saint Gertrude's church. For some reason it seemed important to beat Nora; maybe his bruised ego from this morning was speaking up? As if winning would somehow pay her back for being so unresponsive to his feelings. He continued with the church tower—how could there possibly be so many pieces? He had already been working for several minutes and hadn't even finished the first building. He pressed the tower onto the main body of the church, with a large blob of glue to hold it in place.

Encouraged by the shouts of the audience—there was a particularly noisy group of Santas up front—he moved on to the town hall. Its straight lines made it slightly easier, although the roof with its clock tower was tricky. He didn't look at Nora, didn't want to be distracted.

He moved on to the neighboring buildings. One more wall. Shit, the glue wasn't coming out properly. He glanced up and saw that Nora had only a couple of walls of the final building left to do. He squeezed the tube harder, spread a thick line of glue along the wall, fixed it in place, threw down the tube, and raised his arms to the cheers of the audience. It was all a little surreal, with all the Santas in front of him. Nora looked up, smiled to acknowledge her defeat, then calmly finished off her section while Ted congratulated Henrik.

Carefully they carried the two parts of the silhouette to a bench at the front of the stage and joined them together on a wooden tray. They decorated it with frosting and surrounded it with cotton wool to represent snow. It would take pride of place in the main window of the patisserie. Nora tucked a couple of battery-operated strings of fairy lights among the cotton wool and switched them on; the result was magical. An idyllic winter townscape with tiny lights sparkling in the snow.

Henrik suddenly noticed a large dressing on her hand. She held it up when she saw him looking. "I'm blaming my defeat on my injury," she murmured.

"Louder, please," Ted said, holding out the microphone. "What happened?"

"I burned myself with some oil just before I came out."

"Oil?" Henrik raised his eyebrows, and when he saw the little smile playing around the corners of her mouth, he laughed. "Let me guess—you were making deep-fried waffles."

She nodded. "I thought the display counter looked empty without them."

He was still laughing, and Ted looked inquiringly at him. Henrik spoke to the audience. "I thought I'd persuaded Nora to give the waffles a pass this year." He turned to her. "You've worked day and night this week to fill all your orders, and in the short break between filming at the patisserie and this competition, you decided to deep-fry waffles."

A few people laughed. Nora smiled and slowly shook her head at Henrik.

For a second he tried to resist the urge to kiss her, but it was impossible. He wanted to kiss her. He wanted to kiss her in front of everyone. He pulled her to him and gave her a long kiss.

The cheering that followed almost burst his eardrums. He held her tight, kissed her harder. He really was falling in love with this woman.

◆ ◆ ◆

The kiss took Nora by surprise, but she kissed him back. She loved these kisses—they were almost too good to be true—and that was what frightened her.

He pulled away and whispered in her ear, "I want to show everyone exactly how I feel."

The audience was still cheering. She looked at him in embarrassment, but couldn't help smiling.

But they had to talk. She'd been truly stunned by what he said that morning. She hadn't wanted to leave like that, but she needed to be alone. She was entirely unprepared for what Henrik said; she had assumed all along that he was looking for something temporary. Nora had thought he saw her as nothing more than a fling, a bit of fun. The suggestion that they should carry on seeing each other was totally unrealistic.

She looked at him. "Can we talk?"

He gazed at her for a long time. "Sure."

They left the square and walked down to Espresso House. Normally, Nora boycotted the chain, but she needed some caffeine to keep her on her toes. She didn't want to let herself get swept up in any romantic nonsense. She bought a large coffee, blew on it, and took a sip. Reluctantly she had to admit that it tasted pretty good.

They continued strolling, and she took big gulps of her steaming coffee, hoping the caffeine would help her say the right things.

"I'm sorry I just took off this morning, but . . . Why does everything have to happen so fast between us?"

He shook his head gently. "It doesn't have to get serious. Not yet." He held her gaze as he spoke. "What I said this morning, I . . ." He broke off, glanced at the church they were passing, the church he had recently assembled in record time. "I didn't mean we have to become an exclusive couple right away; I just meant I'd like to continue to see you after we finish filming."

That's what she wanted, too, of course, but it was all *too much*. The loneliness she had lived with for so long wasn't easy, but she had gotten used to it. If she let someone in now—really let them in—what would happen?

And yet she had never allowed any man to get as close as Henrik. That had to be significant.

But no, this was too big. Too scary.

"I don't know. Maybe this was just a one-off fling that got out of hand."

He frowned. "A one-off fling that got out of hand? Do you really believe that?"

"I live here in Västervik, and I'm struggling to keep the patisserie going. You live in Stockholm, you have an entire baking empire, and you're famous." She shook her head. "I think you're just imagining that this is worth pursuing. Maybe it's a way of getting over Bente?"

His expression darkened. "This is about you and me, no one else."

"I think you've been seduced by the idea of life in a small town, and your dream of running your own bakery. As soon as you get back to Stockholm, you'll forget about me and all of this."

He gazed at her for a few seconds. "You often talk about what's genuine and authentic, and you seem to believe that anything to do with you and the patisserie is authentic, while everything I stand for is superficial. As far as I'm concerned, what's happened between us is genuine and authentic. And I'm very sorry if you don't feel the same way." He lingered for a moment, then turned and walked away.

Nora continued down toward the shore. She threw her empty coffee cup in a trash can, took a deep breath, and faced the sea. It was ice blue on this beautiful day, the wind had dropped, and feathery clouds were reflected in its glimmering surface.

She walked along the water, then turned back up toward town. She wandered aimlessly, lost in thought. She had meant what she said; she was convinced that she and Henrik were an impossible equation. But she suddenly realized that she was terrified that she wouldn't find it easy to forget him, because what Henrik had said was also true: what had transpired between them *was* genuine.

She felt a sharp, stabbing pain in her chest, an echo of the pain she had felt when she lost her parents. She gave herself a little shake; what was wrong with her? To be fair, this kind of behavior wasn't unfamiliar to her; she often reacted this way when it came to relationships. Most of the men she had met over the years weren't looking for anything serious, but she had always pushed away the ones who were. She didn't give it much thought; that was how she was, and she had never had strong feelings for any of them. But then none of them had opened up to her the way Henrik had, nor had she opened up like that to anyone else.

Everything was so unexpected with Henrik, both his feelings and her own. She realized that she would actually miss him when he left, and that deep down she really wanted to see him again. In which case it was best to squash her emotions now, before they deepened, before they developed into love. Then she wouldn't be too crushed if he forgot about her when he got back to Stockholm. If she could avoid falling in love with him, then she could avoid the risk of any pain.

37

1945

Tuula and the children stayed with Nils until the end of the week. Matias improved after fluid replacement treatment and rest, but Nils had had to drive him the short distance to the doctor's because he could barely stand. Tuula still couldn't get her head around the idea that someone bore them such ill will.

When Aino and Heikki returned home that weekend and Tuula told Aino what had happened, Aino's face lost all its color.

"How much longer can we stay here?" Aino whispered. They were sitting in the shade of the tall oak tree, on rickety wooden chairs that Heikki had bought cheap. They were enveloped in the warm scent of roses. The well was clean now, and there was nothing to remind Tuula of what had been down there.

"What do you mean?" Tuula said.

"Things are completely different in Småland. They live in a bigger community that's more anonymous. There's the odd insult, but no hassle. Nothing like this." Aino took a deep breath. "Nothing approaching pure hatred."

They suddenly heard a scream in the street. Then the door flew open, and Ritva tumbled into the courtyard, sobbing helplessly. Tuula leaped to her feet as the child flew into her mother's arms.

"Sweetheart, what's happened?" She ran her hands over her daughter's body. Was she injured? Her hair was all over the place, her blouse was open, and one sleeve was torn. Then she saw it—a gash across her chest. It was bleeding, and Tuula quickly took off her own blouse and used it as a makeshift dressing.

"Ritva, what happened?"

The child just kept on sobbing.

"Ritva, what happened?" She realized she was shouting in sheer panic.

Aino took Ritva in her arms and tried to soothe her. After a few minutes she was calm enough to talk.

Some boys had followed her to the grocery store. They had wrestled her to the ground, torn her blouse, and yelled at her that she stank. One of the boys had slashed her chest with his pocketknife, then run off.

"They didn't do anything else?" Tuula had to ask the question.

Ritva shook her head.

Tuula was beside herself at the thought of what else might have happened. She and Aino exchanged meaningful glances, both hoping that Ritva didn't understand why. They took her upstairs to the apartment, where she sat in silence, gazing blankly into space. Aino inspected the wound while Tuula fetched warm water and rags.

"It looks clean and it's not very deep. Do you have a dressing?"

Tuula shook her head.

"I'll go and get one from downstairs."

Shortly after Aino had left, there was a knock on the door. It must be Nils—she was supposed to meet him at the café.

She opened the door to let him in. "I'm so sorry, I . . . Something's happened."

"What is it?" Nils looked worried.

"Some boys attacked Ritva, I completely forgot we were meeting up, and . . ."

"How is she?"

"Under the circumstances, she's okay. I think she wants to be left alone right now," she added quietly.

Nils stopped and turned to her. "What did they do?"

"They cut her with a knife. She has a gash across her chest. Thankfully it's not too deep."

Nils went white. "They attacked her with a knife? We have to go to the police!"

Tuula nodded. "You're right." But all she wanted just then was to be with her daughter.

Nils drew her close and hugged her for a long time. Something inside her let go, and for a second she allowed herself to feel weak and vulnerable. She hadn't wanted to break down in front of Ritva, but now the tears came. "I can't stay here," she said eventually. "My children . . ." She didn't finish the sentence, and Nils let her cry, held her and consoled her without saying anything.

Tuula realized that she had reached the end of the road. People talking about her and disliking her was one thing, but the people she loved most were suffering the most. The children above all, but also Nils. His business and his career were being affected, and the situation was no longer tenable for anyone.

"I have to leave." She wiped her eyes and looked up at him.

"Let me come with you."

"But what about the business?"

Nils sighed. "I didn't want to worry you when everything was so chaotic, but my father has given me an ultimatum. He told me to choose between you and the business; otherwise my brother will take over."

"And what's your decision?" Tuula could hardly breathe.

"Naturally I choose you." His eyes filled with tears. "I choose you and the children."

She swallowed hard. She couldn't help thinking about what he'd said at the cottage, that he and his father had never had anything to fall out about. Not until she came into the picture. He'd had a good relationship with his whole family before that. "We can leave tonight," he went on. "We can go as soon as you like, start over somewhere else, as a family."

Tuula's chest was flooded with warmth, but there was pain in it too. She wanted nothing more than to be with Nils and the children. He loved them, she knew that, and they had grown close to him. But if he went away with her, he would be leaving his own family, losing everything he had here. What if he regretted it in the future? What would happen if he fell out of love with her when real life took over? Could she really do that to him?

"Tuula, I mean it. I want to build a life with you. I don't care about the business."

"But you love the business."

"I can start something new, once we're on our feet."

"You can't replace your parents."

She saw something in his eyes. Pain. "No, but I'll have a new family." He smiled as the tears ran down his cheeks. He rested his forehead on hers and they stood there, weeping together and holding each other.

Tuula couldn't persuade Ritva to go to school the following morning, and even though she was a woman of principle—everyone has to go to school—she couldn't bring herself to force her daughter to go. Ritva was allowed to stay home as long as she read her schoolbooks.

Matias went with Tuula to the bakery early in the morning, and during her coffee break, she quickly took him over to daycare.

She got back just as everyone was due to start work again. Oddly, they weren't sitting outside drinking coffee—where were they?

The packing room was empty, so she continued through to the bakery. The whole staff was gathered there, standing or sitting in complete silence. Karl Eklund, Nils's father, stood in the middle of the room. He glanced at Tuula when she came in, but didn't acknowledge her. Tuula went and stood by the wall. Nils was over by the baking tables. She could see that he was trying to look calm, but he folded his arms, then let them fall to his sides, then changed position again.

"I'm afraid I have some bad news," Karl Eklund said at last. "We're going to have to dismiss two people, effective immediately." A low hum of conversation broke out. "Some spirit vinegar has gone missing from the storeroom."

"That's not true, Father," Nils protested. "I did the inventory—no spirit vinegar is missing."

"It is," Karl snapped. "I carried out the inventory myself. Either you were careless, or you were trying to protect someone." He looked around the room. "I know who the guilty parties are." He paused, either to let his words sink in, or to make them nervous. "It pains me to do this, but I have no choice. The first person is Tuula Anttila."

Tuula wanted to laugh at the ridiculous accusation, but she also felt a mixture of anger and relief. She wanted to leave the village, and now she had no choice.

"And the second is Aino Lahti."

Tuula inhaled sharply and looked at her friend. That wasn't fair.

"Where's the proof?" Lydia spoke up.

"The proof?"

"Yes, where's the proof?" Nils folded his arms.

"Do I really need to say it out loud? We all know the Finns can't handle alcohol. It was a mistake on your part, Nils, both to employ Finns in the first place and then to leave something like spirit vinegar out for the taking. They get desperate when they don't have any money."

Tuula had to make a real effort not to laugh. The idea that she and Aino would want to get drunk on spirit vinegar—she'd never heard anything so ridiculous. But she managed to restrain herself; if she so much as smiled right now, it wouldn't go down well.

"That's just plain old prejudice. Has anyone here seen Tuula or Aino stealing?" Lydia looked around the bakery.

"Enough!" Karl roared. "This is my decision, and I won't tolerate anyone contradicting me!"

"I'm just asking, has anyone seen either of them stealing?" Lydia faced down the bakers, the packers, and the drivers. No one said a word.

"Lydia, you don't have to . . . ," Tuula whispered.

"Enough, I said!" Karl's face had reddened with fury. "Or I might decide to let a few more people go!"

Aino took a deep breath. "You know what, *herr* Eklund? No one else needs to go." She took off her cap and headed for the changing room. "We're done here. Tuula and I will pick up our things and leave."

Tuula followed her friend.

"Wait. Please. Aino. Tuula." Nils was coming after them, but Tuula didn't turn around, didn't stop. She had no desire to make a scene—for his sake.

When they emerged from the changing room a few minutes later, Karl Eklund had left. The others were working away in silence as Tuula and Aino walked through the bakery and the packing room.

Lydia was swearing to herself as she slammed the loaves into boxes. "He won't get away with this," she muttered when she saw Tuula and Aino.

Tuula heard footsteps. Nils. She turned to face him.

"Tuula, Aino—I'll speak to my father. I won't allow this."

Tuula shook her head. "We can talk later. Go and reassure everyone else—they're bound to be worried after what just happened. Look after them—Aino and I will be fine."

Nils looked devastated. "I had no idea this was going to happen."

"I know that." Tuula gave him a warm smile.

Nils glanced around, then moved closer to her. He placed both hands on her shoulders. "I know what you're planning to do. And I'm coming with you. I can't stay here under my father's dictatorship."

She took a deep breath. Looked at Aino, who was waiting by the door.

"Come over this evening," she murmured.

38

"*Skål* to *Let's Get Baking*!" Elnaz held out her glass of cava toward Nora, who leaned forward and clinked her glass against Elnaz's. She reached up to touch her hair, which was still warm from the stylist's efforts.

"No no no—don't touch! You'll spoil it. We need some spray, I think." The young woman who had done Nora's hair grabbed a can and enveloped Nora in a fragrant cloud. Nora coughed. Elnaz had suggested they should go to the salon for a blow-dry, because it was more festive than trying to do their own hair in the middle of all the hectic preparations for the press launch. Sara would pick out their clothes and do their makeup.

"Top-up?" The stylist held up the bottle of cava and smiled.

"Not for me, thanks." Nora didn't want to take any risks before the launch; she had drunk just enough to keep her nerves in check. Although she might need a whole bottle before her conversation with Henrik.

She had remained undecided about whether to talk to him until the very last minute. They hadn't been in touch since their walk through town after the gingerbread competition, but he had been on her mind the whole time.

She owed him an explanation, because what she had said wasn't true. What they had wasn't a one-off fling.

And now she was sitting here in Stockholm with a glass of fizzy, ice-cold cava and freshly styled hair, ready for the press launch. After that she hoped to get some time alone with Henrik and ask for a second chance.

"It's going to be a fantastic launch, I can feel it," Elnaz said. Then she suddenly put down her glass. "Hello, what have we here?" She picked up the gossip magazine lying next to Nora's mirror. Nora had hoped that Elnaz wouldn't notice it—which she hadn't, until now.

She held it up, beaming. Henrik Eklund in Love with Small-Town Baker. "Have you read it?"

Nora nodded. She must have read the article twenty times, but it was still just as weird to see her face on the cover—being kissed by Henrik onstage in the middle of her town square.

"I assume that both TV24 and the production team have been high-fiving each other until their palms hurt," Nora said.

"Something like that," Elnaz admitted. "This is the best PR the show could possibly have. We're perfectly positioned for the premiere next week."

Nora nodded; she couldn't help smiling too. After all the twists and turns during filming, she actually felt quite good; it was going to be a really good show.

"Henrik's had a busy time with the press over the past few days," Nora said. She didn't normally gossip like this—maybe it was the cava talking—but she wanted to know what Elnaz thought of the statement Henrik had made earlier in the week.

Elnaz nodded. "I think it was generous of him to do what he did."

Henrik had posted on social media about the part he had played in Bente's downfall. How wrong it had been of him not to defend her when she was attacked by the press. I was feeling hurt and chose to keep quiet. What upsets me most is that my career was boosted by what happened to her, which shows how skewed the TV world can be. I want to apologize to Bente for the fact that I never attempted to stand up for her.

It was the first time he had spoken about their separation, and it had attracted a great deal of attention. Nora couldn't help wondering how Bente had reacted—what if they got back together? Maybe they were already seeing each other. What if Nora was too late?

They finished their drinks and left the salon. The city was shrouded in snow, which made everything eerily quiet. Magnificent thick green garlands, swathes of fir, and shining red ornaments hung down over the street as they walked to the venue where the launch was to take place.

When they arrived, Nora was directed to a small conference room for clothes and makeup. As she made her way along the corridor, she looked around for Henrik. She felt as though she was holding her breath. What should she say when she saw him? Did he even want to talk to her?

Sara was already waiting for her when she arrived; a large mirror was propped against one wall.

"Perfect timing—I've just finished with Henrik."

Nora's heart gave a little leap. He was already here!

"Wow, your hair looks fantastic!" Sara said, then got to work on her makeup. Then it was time to get dressed. "These are the clothes I've picked out for you—what do you think?"

Nora admired the dark-blue velvet pantsuit with a wraparound jacket. It felt festive and upscale, but trendy at the same time.

Nora changed and put on a pair of high-heeled pumps. When she looked in the mirror, she couldn't help smiling. Then Elnaz came in, accompanied by a man about the same age as Nora. "This is Adrian, who handles all the publicity for the show. He'll be running the press launch today."

"We're starting in fifteen minutes, but you're welcome to get something to eat and mingle a bit until then," Adrian said to Nora.

She followed them into the main room, which was already crowded with journalists, photographers, members of the production team, and representatives from TV24. The corner room had amazing views over the waters of Nybroviken and the Royal Dramatic Theater. She looked around. In one corner was a table laden with steaming glasses of mulled wine and soda. Fir garlands and gold ornaments adorned the room, and the large Advent stars hanging in the windows provided a warm glow while Christmas music played in the background.

Elnaz greeted someone she knew, exchanged air-kisses with someone else, then drew Nora in and introduced her. "This is Nora, who's appearing in the Christmas special of *Let's Get Baking*. She's an amazing baker, and a real star on TV."

Nora smiled; she wasn't convinced that this was true, but it sounded good. As they moved slowly through the room, she looked around for Henrik.

When she saw him, she stopped dead. Just seeing him was painful, because she felt so uncertain about their future. He was wearing a white shirt and a pair of dark-blue jeans. His dark hair was carelessly brushed back. How she loved that thick, slightly coarse hair, and the feeling of it beneath her fingers! He was chatting with another man, laughing in a way that lit up his whole face. Then he noticed her, stopped laughing—and smiled.

A moment later, they were standing in front of Henrik. Elnaz gave him a hug, and he and Nora gazed at each other in silence.

The man next to Henrik introduced himself to Nora as the CEO of the production company. When Elnaz started talking to him, Nora took a step closer to Henrik. There was something she had to say.

"I'm sorry for what I said about us," she murmured. "Have you got time to talk after the launch?"

He nodded. "Of course." Then he placed a hand on her shoulder and drew her slowly into a hug. She laid her head on his chest, she could hear the steady beating of his heart, and she let out a long breath. Everything was going to be all right.

A loud voice interrupted them. Nora stepped away and turned around. It was Hasse Eklund.

"Good evening, Henrik." Hasse was beaming. Henrik's expression was uncertain.

"Didn't you know I was coming? They wanted me here—apparently they've included a couple of scenes from *Christmas with the Eklunds*, and thought it would be good if I showed up."

Nora could see the tension in Henrik's body; his entire posture had changed. After everything she had heard about Hasse, she couldn't imagine that his presence here was in any way a good thing. This was Henrik's show, not his.

Then he turned to her. "So you're the one my son is hanging out with these days? If the press is to be believed, that is."

She didn't know how to respond, but Hasse didn't give her the opportunity to come up with anything. "Hasse. Nice to meet you." He held out his hand.

"Nora. Likewise." His handshake was firm.

"I hear that filming was a triumph, thanks to Nora." He looked at Henrik, then back at her. "And your little romance. I hope the season is a success."

Adrian came over. "Time to get started." They followed him to three small tables at the front of the room, and Adrian showed them where to stand.

"Welcome, everyone! I thought we'd start by taking a look at some clips from the show, and then we'll move on to the interviews and any questions you might have." He turned away from the journalists to face the big screen behind them.

Elnaz had explained that the launch would feature a long trailer, and Nora took a deep breath as the first clip began to run. She and Henrik were in the middle of something that looked like an argument, which made her smile, and in the next clip they were laughing and exchanging an intimate glance. There were a few shots of Henrik walking alone along the quayside and eating in the hotel, then it was back to the two of them baking Lucia buns. And finally a clip of Henrik laughing and looking into the camera with his arms folded. That smile, that laughter made her whole body feel warm.

In the next scene he was sitting opposite her with a cup of coffee, and she was explaining her struggles with the patisserie. It wasn't too bad so far. She came across as calm and likable. Then they went through the list of her cakes and cookies, and—unsurprisingly—she did not look happy.

How will things turn out for our bad-tempered baker? asked the narrator's voice in a dryly humorous tone. Nora didn't feel quite so optimistic now.

Next came a scene where she reacted angrily to Henrik's suggestions, followed by various direct statements for the camera. Nora explained what she disliked about Henrik and his ideas, and her face was flushed throughout, as if she was about to explode any second. A few people were laughing. Then Henrik made fun of all her cookies and how flawed her whole setup was, whereupon Nora said, "Henrik is a stevia-eating idiot from Stockholm who has never baked a decent cinnamon bun." She appeared to be bitter and difficult, and everything she did and said made her seem incompetent and oversensitive to criticism.

The burning sensation in her stomach turned to nausea. The whole thing was unbearable. She didn't dare look out over the assembled journalists; this was sheer humiliation. In the next short scene, Henrik gave her a mild rebuke; she stood there for a moment with tears in her eyes, then stormed out. Hysterical, volatile, and incompetent—that was a fair summary of the Nora Jansson on-screen right now. The clip was only ten minutes long, but it felt like it went on for hours.

Then a clip of Henrik speaking to the camera. "She obviously hasn't managed the business very well, but if you're driven by emotions as Nora is—and you let your feelings determine how your business is run—then that's bound to lead to problems." Her heart was pounding. Though she wasn't surprised by Henrik's words, it nonetheless hurt to hear them.

Then suddenly she saw herself leaning over a table in the café, gasping for air. When she saw it on the screen, she felt as if she were reliving the experience. She looked out at the audience and felt herself struggling to breathe. This couldn't be happening. Her head spun, and she tried to inhale slowly, exhale slowly. She could sense Henrik's eyes on her.

Then there was Henrik on-screen again. "She works too hard because she doesn't understand what's important. Maybe someone with such fragile mental health shouldn't be running a business."

Will Henrik manage to bring the hysterical baker into line? the narrator asked, with a hint of laughter in his voice as the trailer ended.

He promised, she thought. *He promised it wouldn't be included.* He had promised that her panic attack wouldn't appear on the show.

The journalists began to drift over to their tables. Adrian had explained that this was an informal arrangement; they would simply come up to her and ask questions. Nora thought it felt like gladiatorial combat. To her surprise she managed to respond without much emotion; she was operating on some kind of weird autopilot.

Then she heard Hasse Eklund's loud voice drowning out everything else. He must want everyone to hear him.

"I've read in the papers that those two are supposed to be in love, but after watching that, I'm not so sure! It was probably just a PR stunt after all." The words hit home. Of course it was a PR stunt, all of it. "As Henrik said to me last time I saw him, we do what we have to do for the show."

"It wasn't just for the show!" Henrik broke in. He turned to his father and the journalists, but Nora didn't hear the rest of what he said. Hasse's words echoed in her mind. Had Henrik really said that to his father? She shouldn't be surprised—not after seeing those clips. Henrik hadn't kept his word. She had been portrayed as incompetent and volatile. So why should she believe anything else he'd ever said to her about his feelings and what he wanted in the future?

The next journalist looked Nora straight in the eye. "So *is* there a genuine romance between you and Henrik?" She had had enough. She took a deep breath, walked around the table, and headed for the door. She was wrecked. To make things worse, she tripped over the edge of a rug in her high heels. Elnaz caught her. Nora looked at Elnaz in terror, thinking she would try to force her to go back and answer more questions, but Elnaz just took her arm and led her out of the room. Away from it all.

39

Henrik was about to run after Nora, but he stopped and addressed the audience.

"Regardless of what my father just said, and what you saw in those clips, Nora's and my relationship is the real deal." Then he ran. Elnaz was at the top of the stairs, and Nora was racing down them. She grabbed Henrik's arm. "Let her go."

He ignored her and kept on running. "Can we talk?" he shouted.

Nora was already out in the street by the time he caught up with her. She had thrown her winter coat around her shoulders and she was clutching her purse. She was still wearing the high-heeled pumps, and looked frozen. Her cheeks were pink, her eyes full of tears.

"I promise I had no idea—that's not what the production company showed me," he began. "And what my father said just isn't true."

She backed away from him. "I don't know what to believe. I just . . . that was all too much. I need to be alone."

"Nora, please, can't we just talk . . ." He took a step toward her, but she held up her hands as if to defend herself.

"No. I want to be on my own. Don't follow me."

She hailed a cab, jumped in, and drove off, leaving Henrik standing there. She had been on his mind every minute of the last week. He had gone over everything they had said to each other again and again. However hard he'd tried, he couldn't be angry with her, because he understood. Things had happened so fast between them, and just because he was sure of his feelings, that didn't mean it would be as easy for her.

He'd been so happy when she walked into the room earlier. He could see that she'd been thinking, too, that she'd come to terms with her feelings, and when she let him hug her, he was sure. They were going to be together. And now this.

He returned to the conference. Where should he begin? He spotted Ted and went over to him.

"What the fuck was that?" he said, gesturing toward the screen.

Ted held up his hands. "I was following instructions. Don wasn't happy with what we sent in; this was the only version he would agree to."

"And where is Don?"

"He had to leave."

Henrik caught sight of Adrian, who looked slightly panic-stricken as Henrik marched toward him. He probably hadn't had the best day; it's never a good sign when the stars of a press launch run out of the room.

"Why was my father here?"

Adrian's eyes darted from side to side. "I'm so sorry, I had no idea he was going to say something like that."

"But why was he here?"

"He contacted me himself, and we thought that we might as well invite him to join since he was in a couple of the clips . . ." Adrian looked terrified, and Henrik could understand why.

And there he was. Henrik left Adrian, went over to his father, and dragged him into a quiet corner.

"Do you realize what you've done?"

Hasse looked at him in surprise. "What are you talking about?"

"What you said about Nora and me—why did you do that? Why are you so determined to ruin things for me?"

"Oh come on, don't take it so hard—I've been doing this a lot longer than you. It doesn't have to be a bad thing—now everyone will be speculating and wondering. Is the romance genuine or not?" Hasse grinned.

Henrik shook his head. Hasse was obviously determined to destroy his show, and Henrik had had enough. This couldn't go on, and now he had his chance.

"I've been thinking." Henrik looked his father in the eye. "I'm selling my shares in the family firm."

"You're selling your shares?" If his father was annoyed, he didn't show it. He simply raised his eyebrows.

"I don't need the firm anymore. I don't need you," he said in a single breath. He could hardly believe he'd done it, but as soon as the words were out, he felt a physical sense of liberation. And it was a relief. Such a huge relief. He was now free to do whatever he wanted without having to ask for permission, without waiting on anyone else's opinion.

Hasse snorted. Leaned closer. "You need me, Henrik. You need us. We're a family and we support one another."

"Really? Is that why you're trying to start your own show to replace mine? Because you're *supporting* me? Is that why you always try to destroy me and my projects?"

"Is that what this is about? Your bakery? My dear boy, I saved you from a fiasco—you have no business sense. You're just like your grandfather, far too driven by your feelings." He shook his head. "And *Let's Get Baking* is finished—my new show will rescue the brand and our family. No one cares about *Let's Get Baking* anymore, and you pretending to be in love with some small-town baker isn't going to change that. I just helped you out."

"The only thing that's finished is you. You only want to kill off my show because you're afraid of someone being better than you."

Hasse frowned, contempt written all over his face. "I've given you and your siblings everything—everything. You're the heirs to a large, successful business."

Henrik wanted to say that the shares came from his grandfather. Hasse had given him nothing but a life filled with dysfunctional relationships and low self-esteem. But before he could speak, Hasse continued. "I'm the one who made you famous—you have me to thank for everything."

"I'm selling my shares, and then we won't have to have anything to do with each other anymore."

Hasse took a step closer and hissed in his ear. "Fine—just make sure you repay the money you've stolen from the company first."

Henrik looked inquiringly at him.

"We've seen your withdrawals. The head of finance noticed that money had gone missing from one of the accounts. Transferred to Nymans. We could report you to the police. This is serious."

Henrik didn't say anything. He had regarded the transaction as a loan, but he knew that his father was right. It wasn't entirely aboveboard and could definitely be used against him.

He turned and walked out of the conference. It was dark now. Cars were whizzing by, and he could see snowflakes in the red glow of their rear lights. He leaned against a wall, took a few deep breaths. He had so much to sort out, but for the first time in his life he felt free, completely and totally free.

Later that afternoon Henrik stormed into TV24's spacious reception area.

Once he was inside, he slowed down and approached the receptionist with a polite smile.

"Could you please let Don know that Henrik Eklund is here to see him?"

"Of course. Does he know you're here?"

"No—that's why I want you to tell him."

The receptionist tapped on her keyboard and asked Henrik to take a seat. He couldn't possibly sit down, so instead he paced up and down. He tried calling Don while he was waiting, but got no answer.

Ten minutes later, Don appeared. "Hi, Henrik, thanks for an interesting press launch."

"I've called you twenty times."

"I think I know why you're here. Come with me." Henrik followed him toward the door, but the receptionist called after him.

"Wait—you need a visitor's badge." Henrik turned back and took it, fastened it to his jacket.

They went into a conference room and closed the door.

Don sat down at the table while Henrik remained standing, arms folded. "What the fuck was that promo supposed to be? That was nothing like what we agreed to."

"I didn't edit it or produce the content."

"No, but everyone knows it was done on your orders."

"Yes, and we want a show that people will actually watch. TV24 is very pleased with it."

"Nora Jansson was portrayed as hysterical and incompetent. It was farcical and undignified. Like I said—not what we agreed on."

"As I said, we're super happy with the show—this is going to pull in new viewers. And don't worry, we'll include your little romance."

"I don't want the show to go out like this. It's not happening."

"But Henrik, the final episodes are being edited with that angle in mind as we speak—the team's already put in several days' work. We can't change it now. Besides, we don't *want* to change it. The premiere is next week."

Henrik leaned forward. "And I thought you wanted to get away from docusoaps."

Don didn't say anything.

"What was shown at the press launch today is entertainment at the expense of other people's health and dignity—reality in its purest and dirtiest form."

Don still didn't speak, but Henrik could see he had made him think.

"Everything I've produced has been a roaring success," he said eventually. "I know what viewers want."

"If you don't go back to the production company and make them change the angle, I will never work with TV24 again."

Another silence. Henrik was taking a chance; he didn't even know if they wanted his show next year. Maybe his threat wouldn't carry any weight, but he couldn't think of anything else. And he had to fix this; otherwise he risked losing Nora forever.

Don sighed. "Okay, we'll do what you want. But if the ratings are crap—which they will be—you won't have a show anyway."

"Then so be it."

40

1945

Tuula and the children had dinner with Nils that evening. A heavy late-summer shower hammered down on the courtyard outside the kitchen window. When the children were asleep, she and Nils made love on a blanket in the kitchen. They didn't make any decisions about how they would leave the village. Tuula had no plan, while Nils had lots. So why did this feel like the first step in saying goodbye?

The next morning, Nils left early to ride over to the bakery. Aino came over with freshly brewed coffee, and they sat down in the courtyard, which still smelled of last night's rain. The coffee was strong and refreshing. Tuula felt oddly free. She could leave; there was nothing to keep her here. Apart from Nils.

Ritva hadn't gone back to school, and Tuula had allowed Matias to stay home from daycare since she no longer had to go to work.

The two women watched him kicking his ball against the wall.

"Heikki and I talked things over last night, and we've decided to move to Småland," Aino said after a while.

Tuula looked at her friend.

"Heikki's found work at a factory down there. He can start right away, and the friends we visited have found me a job managing a café. I just called my friend from the kiosk down in the village. They've been looking for someone who can bake, and I mentioned you. You should come with us." Aino took a sip of her coffee. "There's work for both of us, and everything is on the up and up now that the war is over. People are starting to eat out, go to cafés, buy cakes. Things are booming—it's only Karl Eklund who wants to get rid of staff." Aino sniffed derisively. "I'm so done with this village. In a bigger town we can be more anonymous, blend in." Aino leaned forward, her gaze sympathetic. "But of course I understand if you want to stay with Nils."

Tuula thought it over. "Nils said he wants to come with me if I decide to leave."

Aino's face lit up. "That's fantastic!"

"I don't know, I . . . He hates his father—at the moment. He's ready to give up the family business—at the moment. But what if . . ." She sighed. "What if he changes his mind, regrets his decision?"

"He's a grown man, Tuula—he can make up his own mind."

"When are you leaving?"

"On Saturday. We've got an apartment lined up, and of course you're welcome to stay with us until you find a place of your own."

Tuula sat in silence, gazing at the rosebush. It had finished flowering, and the petals had dropped, leaving only a tangle of thorny branches. And yet the perfume of roses lingered in the air, presumably from a nearby yard.

"You don't need to make the move now." Aino placed her hand on Tuula's. "You and the children can always join us later, when you feel that you're done here."

"I'm done here now—I don't have a job," Tuula replied tonelessly.

Aino gave her a tentative smile. "You're not done here, Tuula."

◆ ◆ ◆

Tuula didn't mention Aino's plans to Nils; she simply told him that she and Aino were looking for work anywhere in Sweden. He contacted friends and acquaintances to see if she could get a job in one of the neighboring villages. But Tuula knew that her problems would follow her, because she wouldn't be anonymous there either.

Nils came over on Friday evening for dinner. They made a sponge cake together, and he played games with the children. She never tired of looking at him, that kind, handsome, thoughtful, loving man who was prepared to give up everything for her. When the children were asleep, they made love in the kitchen again.

When Nils finally got ready to cycle home, Tuula felt like bursting into tears and telling him what she was planning to do. Instead she kissed him for a long, long time, then let him go without saying a word.

Maybe he sensed something? But he didn't ask questions, and she took it as a sign that she'd made the right decision.

At first light, after a sleepless night, she tipped half of her sourdough starter into a clean jar, covered it with a kitchen towel, and secured it with jute string. When the children woke up, she told them to get dressed, then gave them their breakfast. Their suitcases were already packed; Aino and Heikki would take the children and the luggage to the station, where Tuula would meet them later. She borrowed Heikki's rusty bike and cycled over to Nils's apartment. She crept up the two flights of stairs and left the jar outside his door, with a note:

Forgive me, but I can't make you choose.

I can't let you give up everything.

Yours always,

Tuula

Half an hour later she clambered up the steep steps onto the train. She glanced over her shoulder, as if Nils would instinctively know that she was leaving now. Holding her children by the hand, she left the village just as she had arrived. Her heart, which had been empty and damaged, was now whole again—though battered and bruised.

41

Nora took a few rapid steps, caught the ball, and raced across the pitch. She raised her stick and hit the ball hard. Straight into the goal. Her sixth today. She raised her arms above her head and cheered.

The opposing team, which included Bea and Maryam, swore loudly, while the girls on Nora's team celebrated with her. Tess patted her on the shoulder. They took a break, and Nora took several gulps from her bottle of water.

This was fantastic—a whole hour when she hadn't thought about Henrik and the press launch. But as soon as she stopped playing, her mind went straight back there. She sighed in frustration.

"Have you seen this?" One of the younger girls held up her phone.

Nora looked at the screen.

It was the web page of one of the tabloids. Hasse Eklund Accuses Son of Fraud.

And then a subheading: Henrik Eklund: I Did It Because I Cared.

Bea peered over Nora's shoulder. "What is it?"

She started to read.

"It's about Henrik. Apparently he . . ." She paused, cleared her throat. "He stole money from Eklunds to save my business." She sank down on the nearest bench.

"What? Did you know about this?"

Nora shook her head. "He says he did it because he believed in the patisserie and wanted to support someone who was working hard, someone he believed in."

"And isn't that the person you want Henrik to be? The person you claim he isn't?" Bea put down her water bottle and gave Nora a challenging look. Nora had filled Bea in on what had happened, expecting sympathy from her friend. However, Bea had reacted coldly, said that Henrik had no control over how the show was edited and that what had happened at the launch said nothing about his character or his values. Nora had countered that it was his show, it didn't exist without him, so he had plenty of control over how things played out.

Bea took the phone from Nora and read the article for herself. "But this is exactly what I mean. You say he's not genuine, but if he risked everything—his position in the family firm, even his own liberty—in order to save your business, then he must have faith in you. In what's real."

"Oh my God, don't exaggerate! He wouldn't go to jail for this, surely? Plus he saved his own show too."

"You never know. This kind of financial crime can lead to a severe sentence. I think this definitely shows who he is. He believes in your business and in you, otherwise he would never have done this." Bea sighed. "Why are you being so hard on him? I can tell you want to blame him for everything. I know how easy it is for you to walk away and give him up—just because you're afraid of what the two of you have."

"Thanks, you said all that yesterday." Nora took another gulp of her water, stood up, and got ready to play again.

"But you always get it wrong. You're always desperate to find a reason to break off a relationship. You're scared to commit to someone you really care about."

Nora didn't say anything.

"I've known you for many years, and I know how you work."

"It's so much easier when I only have myself to think about," Nora conceded eventually. "Otherwise it's so painful." The events at the press launch had given her a clear way out; all she had to do was forget about Henrik.

Bea looked at her. She seemed to understand exactly what was going on, better than Nora herself did. "I get it," Bea said. "But why worry so much? Trust him, and try to be happy with what you have. *If* it doesn't work out—which won't happen—and you don't get to grow old together and live happily ever after, then at least you'll have had enough happiness to balance out all the sad stuff. I've never heard of anyone on their deathbed wishing they'd loved a little less."

Nora smiled at her friend and shook her head. Sometimes Bea really was brilliant.

42

1945

When Nils opened the door, ready to set off for the bakery, he saw a small bundle outside. Something wrapped in a white kitchen towel with a red border, which he recognized from Tuula's place. He immediately knew what it was. He untied the string, hoping he was wrong, praying to a higher power—if it existed—that he was wrong.

But there it was, a jar and a note, a recipe with a few lines on the back in neat handwriting.

The words pierced his heart. He went back inside. Stood there for a few seconds before he pulled himself together and put down the jar. He had to get to the train station. If she was going somewhere, then that's where she'd be.

He raced down the stairs. He didn't know what time she was leaving, or where she was heading, but it was his only option. He jumped on his bike and pedaled down the main street as fast as he could, hoping he wasn't too late.

But he still had a chance—it was early, not many trains would have left yet.

When he reached the station, Nils leaped off his bike, dropped it on the ground, and raced out onto the platform. A train was just leaving, and he *knew* she was on it—he could feel it in his heart. The train was bound for Västerås. He ran after it, ran and ran, tried to look in through the windows, but he couldn't see her. Perhaps she was sitting nearer the front? He kept on running, shouted after the train. But it just kept going. And going.

When Nils had reached the end of the platform, he stood there, breathless and empty.

A man came over to him. "Did you miss the train? There's another one at lunchtime."

Nils shook his head, doubling over and gasping for breath. "I didn't miss the train. I missed the love of my life."

He walked slowly back along the platform, looking around. His gut feeling might have been wrong. She might still be here. He scrutinized every face on the way back to the station building. He stopped in the doorway between the waiting room and the platform so that he could see everyone who came and went. There was no sign of the children, or Aino or Heikki.

Something told him she'd already left the village. He knew she'd gone. She'd left him—she'd been on that train.

And yet he stayed where he was—until the last trains of the day had come and gone, and the platform and the station were deserted, and the sky slowly turned bloodred with the setting sun. Only then did he cycle home. Slowly, drained of strength and energy. His lust for life, the thing that had given him his spark, had disappeared.

When he got home, he went straight to the dining table where the sketches for advertising posters were laid out. Tuula's Tasty Bread. It had been meant as a surprise for her. He had employed a professional artist to produce them, but then all that business with his father had gotten in the way. Nils gathered them up, put them in a box, and carried it up to the loft.

He wanted to be mad at her, but he couldn't be. He could never be mad at Tuula.

His beloved Tuula.

Yours always.

43

Henrik scattered flour across the slab. Tipped out the dough he had left to proof overnight. Kneaded it as the cold stone surface slowly warmed up beneath his hands.

As a child he had baked sourdough at least once a month. These days he baked every weekend. His friends loved the bread, Bente had adored it, and they had always eaten far too many slices at weekend breakfasts.

He shaped the dough into loaves and covered them with a kitchen towel. He took down the jar containing the sourdough starter from the cupboard above the refrigerator and stared at it. When Nora had told him the story of her sourdough that night at the hotel, he had thought it too unbelievable to be true and quickly dismissed the idea. But he hadn't been able to let it go completely.

His father wasn't aware that Henrik knew the whole story. He had heard it from Lydia, an elderly lady who had worked at the bakery, then become manager of Eklunds' café in Almtorp.

She had spent many hours there as a pensioner long after the café had been sold to a new owner, sitting happily in a corner with her coffee, newspaper, and a cinnamon bun. Henrik used to hang out there in the summer, and he and Lydia became friends. She told him the story of the sourdough when he was a teenager and said that his paternal grandfather had never forgotten the love of his life. "She simply disappeared—to Småland, people thought, but there wasn't much he could do. He spent a long time searching for her, but he never found her."

When Nora had mentioned the name of her great-grandmother, Henrik had understood how it all fit together.

He left the loaves to proof and went up to the loft and dug out a box containing old documents he had been given after his grandfather's death. He riffled through the photographs, recipes, and sketches for advertising posters, and then he picked out a recipe and a sketch and returned downstairs.

He took a cab to the solicitors' office in Östermalm to sign all the documents. Svärdh & Partners had produced the shareholders' agreement for Eklunds, and two members of the legal team were waiting for him in reception—Charlotta and Johannes. They showed him into a meeting room.

"Thanks for seeing me at such short notice," Henrik said.

"No problem. We've got everything ready." Johannes pushed a pile of papers across the table.

"As I'm sure you know, the agreement states that the other shareholders are entitled to buy your shares," Charlotta explained.

"I understand."

"If you want to take the time to read through everything or consult another legal practice, that's fine, of course," Johannes said. "But it's all very standard. There are no sales guarantees since the buyers are already familiar with the company."

"So there are no obligations on my part once I've signed?"

"None at all," Charlotta confirmed. "There is, however, a deduction here for a claim that the company has on you. It will be taken off the liquidation of your shares." Her expression remained neutral. He didn't know if she'd read about his father's accusations in the press; as far as Henrik was aware, Hasse hadn't reported his son to the police yet. Maybe he realized it wouldn't exactly be good PR. Henrik had made a pretty clear statement, and if he was reported to the police, the facade of the happy family Hasse had built over several decades would be completely shattered.

"Fine." Henrik checked the relevant section; the amount was correct. He picked up the pen, skimmed through the agreement, and signed it.

He strolled from the solicitors' office to the NK department store, where he was meeting Tom for lunch. He took a moment to admire NK's festive window display before he went in. There was an elves' workshop in an elaborate wooden house: elves toiling away, beautifully wrapped presents, gingerbread houses, Christmas stockings. He thought about Nora—she would love this.

Tom was already waiting for him in the restaurant. He greeted his brother with a pat on the shoulder—they didn't really go in for hugs, except when they were being filmed—and sat down. The waiter took their order.

"So you're pulling out?" Tom said, unfolding his napkin.

Henrik nodded. "I've had enough. I'm done with our father." He sighed. "I can't bear to work with him any longer. It's impossible to collaborate with someone who's constantly working against me."

Tom gazed at him. "Dad does seem to have a problem with you at the moment."

"I just can't deal with his whims and moods anymore."

Tom nodded thoughtfully. "I understand. We've always played along, done whatever it took to make him like us. We all wanted to be number one. But what's led you to make this decision now?"

Henrik took a deep breath and looked out the window. "These last few months have been different, somehow. I've gotten to know someone who has no family to lean on, no family to back her up, no financial security at all, and yet she manages to cope all on her own. It's made me realize that I don't need this safety net. Being dependent on something so dysfunctional just makes everything harder."

"Are you talking about that baker?"

Henrik nodded. "I am." Then he smiled.

Tom smiled, too, and took a piece of bread from the basket in front of him.

"How's Ellen?" Henrik asked. "I hardly got the chance to speak to her when we were filming at Dad and Anita's."

"We've separated."

At first Henrik thought he must have misheard. "Separated . . . But . . . Are you serious?" He leaned across the table, clumsily placed a hand on Tom's arm. "How are you feeling?"

His brother shrugged. "Fine. It happened a while ago, back in the summer actually, so I've had time to work through it."

"Back in the summer? But she was there for . . ."

"The filming, yes, I know. I couldn't bring myself to tell Dad—he'll just think I'm even more of a failure."

"Why didn't you tell me?"

Tom simply took a deep breath, and Henrik understood. They didn't talk to each other about that kind of thing. They had always made sure they came across as successful in front of each other; any weakness felt like a failure.

"Things have to change," Henrik said, his expression serious. "You can talk to me whenever you need to."

Tom nodded. "Thank you." He sighed. "I knew that really."

To think that they'd ended up here, unable to share important family news. Henrik thought how sad it was, but he understood Tom. He himself had waited a long time before telling the family that he and Bente had broken up. There was a time when the siblings had meant everything to one another, but somewhere along the way, when they realized what the family firm was worth and what possibilities it could offer, the situation had changed and they had begun to regard each other as rivals rather than friends.

"And the baker? Is it . . . serious?"

Henrik nodded. "It is. But the press launch was a disaster, the trailer they showed was completely out of line, and Dad was there, too, talking a load of crap, and now . . . she doesn't even want to talk to me."

Tom looked pensive. "One of the reasons Ellen and I broke up is that she found the public side of things very difficult—and I wasn't even in the public eye all that much. It must be super tough for . . . Nora, isn't it?"

"That's right."

"It must be tough for Nora to understand it all, with all its twists and turns," Tom added.

"But I had nothing to do with the editing. I've tried to explain it, but she doesn't want anything to do with me."

"Okay, so the editing isn't in your control, but something must have led to those scenes—and yet you're still portrayed as a decent guy. Perfect, as usual." Tom took a sip of water. "What I'm saying is that it can't be easy for her to know what she's supposed to believe. It must look to her as if you've benefited from the fact that she comes across so badly. The clips that were shown at the launch have attracted a lot of interest, haven't they?"

Tom was right. Henrik wasn't much better than their father—who exploited everyone around him in order to succeed. Nora had been depicted as a hysterical woman on the show, and he had contributed to that. He had to admit that he'd known exactly what he was doing while they were filming. Okay, so he had protested over the fake romance direction, but he'd still gone along with it. He'd exploited her. Just like Bente. How could Nora possibly know that he felt differently now? Especially after all she'd gone through . . . She, if anyone, deserved real love.

"Go and see her," Tom said. "Talk to her, show her what's real as far as you're concerned."

44

Henrik arrived in Västervik by train that same evening. It had been snowing, and the place looked like something out of a fairy tale.

He had tried calling Nora to tell her he was on his way, but of course she hadn't answered. He went straight to her apartment from the station. The patisserie had closed for the day much earlier, and the door leading up to her apartment was locked. He tried her number again, but it went straight to voice mail.

He sighed, decided to go for a walk and then give it another shot. When he returned, he saw that the apartment windows were dark. He looked around and decided he had no choice. He bent down, gathered some snow, and shaped it into a big snowball. He took a few steps back and aimed for the window. *Bull's-eye.*

No reaction.

He threw another snowball, then another. Then two more.

Suddenly the light was switched on. She came to the window and looked down at him. Shook her head and disappeared. His phone buzzed with a text message.

I'm sleeping. I don't want to talk right now. Maybe tomorrow.

Those last two words made his heart race. *Maybe tomorrow*—it was almost a promise.

Nora was woken by her alarm. She had slept badly because of Henrik's repeated calls, then his snowball bombardment against her windowpane. Now she had a broken heart, public humiliation, and a disturbed night to thank him for.

But there was something about those snowballs . . . As if the two of them were lead characters in a romantic movie. Romantic movies had a happy ending. And there was something soothing about that realization. It didn't have to be like this. She didn't have to feel angry, hurt, and let down. Maybe Henrik deserved the chance to explain himself.

She got out of bed and got the coffee machine going while she showered and dressed. She poured herself a cup, brushed her teeth, and went down to the bakery.

She switched on the ovens and uncovered the trays of bread that had been proofing overnight. She was *so* tired.

She went into the café, put on another pot of coffee, and began stocking the glass display counters while she waited for it to brew.

It had been tricky for both of them, knowing what was real and what had been a game for the cameras. Could she really blame him for telling his father that he'd do whatever he had to for the show? And now he'd come here, to Västervik. And thrown snowballs at her window. He was obviously prepared to fight for her, and she wanted to hear what he had to say.

When the coffee was ready, she refilled her cup, went over to the window, and gazed out at the deserted street. She took out her phone and wrote a quick message: How about a walk after lunch today? Then we can talk.

Suddenly an acrid odor filled her nostrils. She raced into the bakery and saw smoke coming from the wall above the ovens. A flame appeared, then another. She grabbed the fire extinguisher and sprayed the white foam up at the wall, but the fire had grown too big. She dropped the extinguisher on the floor and ran into the café where she'd left her phone. She called the emergency number and ran out the door into the fresh air.

She quickly gave the address, then stood by the window peering in.

"What's going on?" someone asked behind her.

She turned around to see Ingemar standing in the empty street. "I couldn't sleep, so I came out for my morning walk," he explained.

"There's a fire," she said, unexpectedly calm. "But the fire department is on the way." She could see the smoke billowing from the bakery into the café. "The sourdough," she exclaimed. "The sourdough. Shit, the sourdough!" She had to rescue it. She flung open the door and rushed inside.

◆ ◆ ◆

The winter morning was cold and clear. And pitch dark. Henrik had slept for only an hour or so, then decided to go for a walk.

He received her message while he was out. So she was awake, probably in the café already. He had to talk to her right now, he didn't want to wait until after lunch. When he turned off the main street, he saw a small crowd gathered outside the patisserie and picked up his pace.

"What's going on?"

"There's a fire, the fire trucks are on their way." It was Ingemar, the customer who'd been in the café during the early days of filming. "But she's gone back in to fetch something, the silly girl."

"Fetch something?" The sourdough, of course. Henrik rushed in after her. The smoke hit him like a force field, and he shielded his face with his arm, kept going.

"Nora!"

He ran through the café into the bakery.

"Nora!"

Flames were shooting out from the walls above and around the ovens, but then he spotted a movement on the far side of the room.

"Get out of here, Henrik!" She coughed. "Run! I'll try to get out through the back, but you can't come through here."

Henrik was about to run toward her, but then he realized she was right—she could get out the other way, and he ought to retrace his steps. But he had to be sure she was out first. Then he heard a crash. Part of the ceiling had collapsed, and something landed on top of him.

◆ ◆ ◆

Nora heard the crash behind her. "Henrik?"

No response.

"Henrik?" she shouted, but the smoke had made her throat dry. She turned and ran through the burning passageway. She'd made it—but Henrik?

"Henrik!"

Then she saw a pile of debris where some roof beams and pieces of the ceiling paneling had come down. Her heart was racing, her lungs exploding, and she was gasping for air. She felt the familiar prickling sensation in the palms of her hands, but instead of being paralyzed, all her senses were heightened. Suddenly she could breathe. She was still coughing, but she felt a surge of energy. She ran toward the pile and could just make out Henrik's black quilted jacket, one arm sticking out. She grabbed the beam on top of him, heaved it out of the way, did the same with the next one, and took hold of Henrik's shoulders. He wasn't moving, and his eyes were closed.

"No!" she screamed. She couldn't lose him. *No, no, no.* She couldn't allow this to happen. He couldn't be taken from her. Not him too.

This time she had the opportunity to take control of what was happening, and she was determined to do everything she could to make sure he didn't die.

She tucked her hands under his armpits and began to drag him through the bakery, away from the fire. She could hardly breathe, and she was wheezing as she gasped for oxygen that wasn't there. Nothing was left but smoke and heat, yet it was as if her body didn't understand that. Her lungs kept on battling for air. She held on to Henrik, she could do this. *Had* to do this. She had almost reached the door when her legs gave way and everything went black.

45

Nora opened her eyes to find herself being lifted into an ambulance. She was wearing an oxygen mask, and she looked up in absolute panic at the paramedic standing over her.

"You're going to be fine," the woman said.

And Henrik? Nora wanted to ask, but she couldn't get the words out. Her lungs and throat felt as if they were on fire.

She was admitted to the hospital and put in a private room, where she fell asleep.

When a nurse came in to check on her, Nora woke up. She took a deep breath, removed the mask.

"How is he?" she croaked.

The nurse smiled. "He's going to be okay."

Nora leaned back against the pillow as the tears began to flow. She wanted to believe the nurse, but she couldn't, not until she'd seen him for herself.

"Try to get some rest—we'll let you know when he wakes up."

After a while the nurse came back. "He's awake—you can see him if you like."

Nora needed help to get out of bed, but she managed to make her own way into Henrik's room, which was next door to hers. He was lying there with his eyes open, still wearing an oxygen mask. He had a dressing on his head, and his shoulders were bandaged. She could hardly believe what she was seeing, and she hurried over to him.

"You're okay." She was grinning. "You're okay!"

He laboriously removed the mask and smiled back at her. "I am."

"I thought I'd lost you."

He reached for her and gently pulled her close. She felt the tears pouring down her cheeks as he held her tight. "I'm here."

She shook her head, her voice shaking. "I was afraid it was too late. When I saw you lying there, I was terrified it was too late."

"Nothing is too late." He lifted her chin and looked at her with those eyes that made the whole world tilt on its axis. "And you saved me."

She kissed him gently.

"Why did you go into a burning building?" he asked her. "You went to get the sourdough starter, didn't you?"

She nodded slowly. "Stupid idea."

"And did you get it?"

"I dropped it when I ran to you, so I think it's charcoal now." She gave a weary smile. She hadn't even thought about it until that moment. Her entire focus had been on Henrik, and nothing was more important.

Epilogue

The day before Christmas Eve

Henrik hurried into the living room with a tray of steaming mulled wine, freshly made Christmas butterscotch, and a plate of gingerbread cookies. *Their* gingerbread cookies.

It would soon be time for the last episode of the *Let's Get Baking* Christmas special. The editors had worked day and night to meet Henrik's demands; the premiere had even been pushed back a week so they could finish, and the result was fantastic. The show was a success. Apparently viewers didn't want panic attacks and manipulated emotions. They wanted to see several cups of joyful Christmas baking, a spoonful of small talk, and a pinch of romance. The ratings for the first show were good, and they'd just kept going up.

He put down the tray and looked at Nora. "There's something I want to show you before we watch it."

She smiled. "Sounds exciting."

He disappeared and she glanced out the window. The snow that had fallen had melted away. But the warm glow of the town's Christmas lights and the Advent candle bridges in the windows, plus the fairy lights on her own tree, set the perfect mood.

The apartment hadn't suffered any damage, but the patisserie had been destroyed. The firefighters had managed to extinguish the flames before they spread any farther, but the smoke damage throughout was so severe that everything had to be ripped out and the whole place deep cleaned.

After all her struggles to save it, the destruction of the patisserie felt ironic. But maybe this was exactly what she needed to make it her own. It would be a fresh start, and she could do exactly as she wished. She wanted to keep the same new decor in the café, but the bakery had needed freshening up for years. And now there would be a new ventilation system, even if it was too late.

Henrik had remained in Västervik after the fire and hadn't left.

Tomorrow, on Christmas Eve, they would all go to Bea's sister's house. Bea's grandmother was curious about Henrik, and Nora was sure they would get along famously. She had finally met someone she could take with her—proving that Bea's husband wasn't the only good man around.

On Christmas Day she and Henrik would head up to Stockholm to celebrate with his mother and Vanja. Nora was a little nervous, but she looked forward to meeting them. Henrik hadn't spoken to his father since the press launch, but his brother and sister would stop by at some point during the day.

Henrik reappeared carrying a small box. He put it down on the coffee table and took out a glass jar. It looked like a sourdough starter. He handed her the jar.

"Oh, have you made me a new starter? That's . . . That's very kind of you."

He probably hadn't grasped the significance of her starter; he was looking so expectant that she didn't have the heart to explain that this wasn't the same as the one she had lost.

But then he shook his head. "Let me explain. My paternal grandfather, Nils, fell in love with a widow who came to Bergslagen from Finland with two small children. The boy's name was Matias and the girl's name was Ritva."

Nora inhaled sharply.

"The woman's name was Tuula, and she brought with her a sourdough starter that her mother had given to her in Finland. My grandfather's parents didn't like the fact that he was seeing a Finnish widow, and his father wanted him to marry Birgit, who was my grandmother. Tuula and Nils didn't get to stay together, and the only thing she left behind when she moved away was this sourdough starter."

Nora's eyes filled with tears; could this really be true?

"I took it over when my grandfather died. I knew how much it had meant to him, and I've kept it alive ever since. And baked with it."

Nora opened the jar, breathed in the smell, and with it all the old memories. It smelled exactly like her starter.

"When you told me about your great-grandmother who came here from Rovaniemi in Finland with two small children, it rang a bell. And when you told me her name, I was pretty sure, but I just had to double-check a couple of things to be absolutely certain."

He dug around in the box. "And I wanted to show you this." He produced a white sign with Tuula's Tasty Bread in ornate blue writing.

She took it from him, tears running down her cheeks.

"I've been teasing you about your old recipes, but actually I have one too." He held out a piece of paper, and Nora recognized her great-grandmother's handwriting from the recipe book she had inherited. She laughed, then let out a sob.

"I've got the go-ahead to open the bakery in Stockholm; everything is in place. I've got the paperwork from the landlord, and I thought we could sell the sourdough bread together. We'll share the story of my grandfather and your great-grandmother, and bake the bread using this recipe . . ."

Nora simply nodded; she couldn't speak.

"I know you've been skeptical about whether a long-distance relationship could work," Henrik added.

Nora smiled. "I think maybe that was just an excuse." Her voice was far from steady.

"I don't want to spend time away from you. I *can't* spend time away from you." He sank down beside her on the sofa. His words brought her a huge sense of relief. That was exactly how she had been feeling since he moved in: she didn't want to be away from him, she couldn't be away from him. She had been hoping that he felt the same.

"So my plan is to operate from Västervik. I want to live here—if you'll have me, of course. And we can work together to fix Nymans, get it ready for another reopening. And then we'll run my bakery together. We can hire people to run it, but the ethos and the direction will come from us. I also thought that if it's okay with you, the bakery could be an extension of yours. Nymans Stockholm. You can say no to all of this, of course. I'll understand perfectly if you want to rebuild your business on your own."

Even though she was entirely overwhelmed by the story behind the sourdough—to think that *the two of them* had shared the same starter!—and what he had just suggested, Nora didn't need any time to mull it over. She *wanted* to do this with him. She was done doing everything on her own. Running a bakery with Henrik sounded like a dream.

She gazed at him, and then her face broke into a big smile. "Yes." It was like accepting a proposal of marriage. "Yes, yes, yes, there's nothing I want more."

He leaned forward and gave her a long kiss. She could taste their gingerbread cookies on his tongue. He passed her a mulled wine and picked up the other himself. They clinked glasses in a toast.

She took a sip, then rested her cheek on Henrik's shoulder as the opening credits for *Let's Get Baking* rolled. She breathed slowly in and out, savoring the aroma of the mulled wine and the burning candles.

Her body was suffused with calm. She hadn't felt like this for a very long time. She reached for a piece of butterscotch and enjoyed its smooth flavor, took another sip of wine, admired the tall Christmas tree in the corner, then looked at Henrik. And for the first time in many years, she was being absolutely honest with herself when she thought how much she loved Christmas.

ABOUT THE AUTHOR

Photo © Lina Eidenberg Adamo

Heléne Holmström is the author of *Working Late*, *Office Affair*, *After Hours*, and *Dancing in the Dark*. In addition to writing, Heléne still works part-time as an associate attorney. Another of her main interests is food and wine, and while writing, she simultaneously studied to become a sommelier.

ABOUT THE TRANSLATOR

Marlaine Delargy studied Swedish and German at the University of Wales, Aberystwyth. She has translated novels by many writers, including Viveca Sten and John Ajvide Lindqvist, as well as Johan Theorin and Henning Mankell, two authors with whom she won the Crime Writers' Association International Dagger.